Knight or Knave

THE BOOK

OF THE OAK

Andre Norton &

Sasha Miller

TOR®
fantasy

A TOM DOHERTY ASSOCIATES BOOK
NEW YORK

This is a work of fiction. All the characters and events portrayed in this book are either products of the author's imagination or are used fictitiously.

KNIGHT OR KNAVE

Edited by Jenna A. Felice
Map by Miguel Roces

A Tor Book
Published by Tom Doherty Associates, LLC
175 Fifth Avenue
New York, NY 10010

www.tor.com

Tor® is a registered trademark of Tom Doherty Associates, LLC.

ISBN: 0-812-57758-2
Library of Congress Catalog Card Number: 2001027076

First edition: June 2001
First mass market edition: May 2002

Printed in the United States of America

0 9 8 7 6 5 4 3 2 1

TOR BOOKS BY ANDRE NORTON

TOR BOOKS BY SASHA MILLER

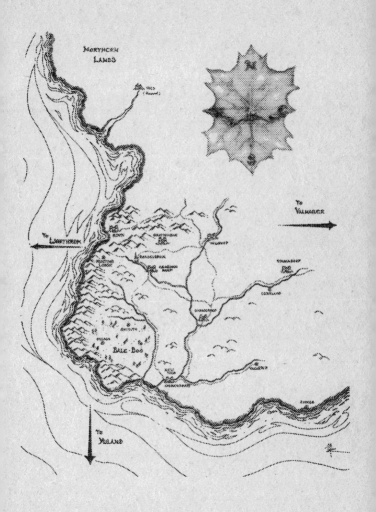

Prologue

*I*n the Cave of the Weavers, the ancient ones toiled over their work, adding first a dusty green strand, then a blue one, then another of brighter green, then gold ones, as their brown old hands twinkled deftly. Each addition sank into the Web Everlasting even before they had let go of it, though the pattern was not yet clear.

The youngest of the Three touched a spot where the dusty green and blue strands crossed. "Is it meet," she asked, "that we blend two mortals in this way, with one doomed?"

"It is meet and altogether meet," replied the Eldest. "For look you here."

She pointed to a design in the Web that was beginning to take shape farther along in the sheet of Time. In form and fashion this design resembled a heavy snowstorm and in it moved fell shapes, each more terrifying than the last. The Youngest recoiled, more a movement of the head than of the body.

"Is that what they will have to face?" she said.

"All in due time, Sister," said the middle one placidly. "We have yet to reach that point, for we have come to a spot where things must change."

"And we do not know yet what that change will be," said the Eldest. "The Web will tell us."

"Then this joining of the ill-omened might ward off the horror that is to come?"

"Perhaps. Perhaps. Be patient. The Web is bound to tell us. It always has, in its own time."

The Youngest returned her attention to the most recent work. "Nothing has blended well in this spot," she said.

"We cannot be concerned with the affairs of mortals," the Eldest said, adding another strand. "It is as it is, and as it will be. Nothing will change that. The Web of Time is all that matters, and if we paused to take pity on those whose lives are interwoven in it, all would become a tangle never to be put straight again. Do not speak of it again."

The Youngest bowed her head in acceptance. But yet, she kept returning ever to the just-added threads, touching them with her brown and wrinkled fingers. Indeed, this was a tangle but even as she looked, it melted and became part of the whole.

One of the life-threads, the dusty green one, frayed and snapped. Carefully, the Youngest clipped it, leaving the fragment that, under her hand, grew and began to change and solidify the pattern the Three had begun. Unexpectedly, as the other two Weavers looked over the Youngest's shoulders, the brighter green thread took up the pattern left off by the dimmer shaded one. It looked strong and durable from that point, with spots left rough to the touch.

"Ah, yes," said the middle Sister. "That was what was needed. Now we can go on."

And as always, the living continued to believe that they were free to make decisions, to act as they believed fit, even as their threads passed through the fingers of the Weavers.

The Youngest glanced back along what had been completed. Yes, there were recorded lives and deaths, Kingdoms' passing. And she knew that the words of the Eldest were true. There could be no mercy, no pity from those who held the threads. It would be folly—and worse, it would ruin the work.

Interested, she watched while the pattern re-formed to accommodate the newly added strands. She recognized what was taking place. A vigorous new strand, not yet the Changer, but close, began to emerge, affecting all it touched. So that was what had been working its way to the surface. All was well. Renewed and refreshed, she reached out and took up the work on the Web Everlasting once more.

One

In the capital city of Rendelsham, a steady drizzle had been falling for days, keeping all inside whose duties did not require that they venture out. Also it was unseasonably cold. Servants kept fireplaces stoked and the damp, green wood they were forced to use—all the seasoned having been used during the winter—sent clouds of smoke over the city. Inside houses where chimneys were not efficient, a similar veil of smoke hung in the air, making people cough and sneeze as they huddled into warm clothing they had thought to put away until winter.

The forced idleness had its uses, however, for there seemed to be no one at court who was not occupied with the problem of what to do with Ashen, daughter of the late King Boroth, newly come to Rendel from the Bale-Bog where she had spent most of her life. This was an illegitimate daughter, to be sure, but one possessing a strong claim to the throne, perhaps enough to topple the new King, Florian, if only the lady herself had been of a mind to undertake such a thing.

Thus, in many residences this topic was the subject of much conjecture, and prominent among them were the households of the Dowager Queen Ysa, who consulted frequently with Lord Royance,

Head of the Council of Regents, and Count Harous, now officially the Lord Marshal of Rendel, who consulted with no one. Rather, he was given to action and it was obvious that the action upon which he was now embarked was the wooing of Lady Ashen herself.

This day Lady Marcala of Valvager—in reality, Marfey, Queen of Spies—had come seeking audience with the Queen, who granted it willingly. "Welcome!" she said when Marcala came into her privy chamber. She turned to her ladies. "Bring heated wine and spice cakes, and then leave us."

Marcala let Lady Ingrid take her rain-dewed cloak to hang near the fire where it might dry. She approached the fireplace gratefully, rubbing her hands. "Even with gloves lined with rabbit fur the cold seeps through and pinches my fingers," she said. "I've forgotten the last time I saw sunlight."

"I welcome your presence, but I know the errand must have been urgent to bring you all the way from Cragden Keep. Come, take a seat by the fire. You'll soon be warm enough."

Lady Ingrid hurried in with the flagon of wine and two goblets, and a plate of cakes on a tray. Marcala poured for both herself and the Dowager and waited until Ingrid had left again before taking up her tale.

"If I could draw upon the heat inside me, I would not need a cloak," the younger woman said, a bitter note in her voice. She drew up the low chair the Dowager indicated and sat down with the air of one on intimate terms with the actual ruler of Rendel. "Instead, I am left to molder in Cragden, while Harous dallies with Ashen here in the city."

"Surely our good Count is not behaving improperly."

"As to that, I do not know. But, to be fair, Ashen lived for many years in the Bog, and defended herself from what threatened from any quarter. Surely she is not so bedazzled that she would yield to Harous's blandishments before marriage for all that he was the one who rescued her and brought her here."

Ysa looked keenly at her noblewoman, her own creation, the supreme spy she had set to be her human eyes and ears in the household of one who might be a threat or a danger to her plans.

She did not miss the reference to marriage, nor did she miss the unmistakable resentment in Marcala's voice. This resentment, Ysa knew, came from jealousy—and this jealousy came from the spell Ysa had herself performed to make sure Marcala's interest focused on Harous. With Marcala enthralled by Harous, Ysa knew she could keep her Queen of Spies under her complete control, first advancing and then retracting her approval regarding Harous. Also, she had seen to it that Harous was in love with Marcala, according to the spell. His ambition, however, was not subject to any such weakness as matters of the heart and therein lay the weakness in this scheme. Ysa thought again about what Marcala had said.

"But you have yielded to the Marshal," the Dowager remarked, trying to keep her tone neutral. She was rewarded by seeing Marcala blush to the roots of her hair.

"He has visited my apartment on occasion. It seemed the appropriate step to take," she said defensively.

"To what effect?"

"He says he loves me. When we are in private he acts like he does. But he is wooing Ashen. And he says he is making good progress."

Ysa kept herself from frowning with an effort. She had enough to worry about concerning King Florian and his latest escapade, without this added. It was all well and good for Harous to pay suit to Ashen, as long as the wench stayed aloof. But if she seemed to be yielding—No, it would not do at all.

"Have you spoken to Lady Ashen?" Ysa said.

"I have not. Though Harous has given me no direct orders, my feeling is that he wants me to stay away from his residence here in the city, where he has installed her. And so I have had no opportunity to visit the lady. Besides, I do not think that she would confide in me." Marcala's lips twisted. "A Princess—so much better than I am. Bog-Princess, that's all she is."

Ysa had to bite her own lips to keep from laughing out loud. Bog-Princess, indeed! And yet, she understood. "It is only natural that you would not be able to summon up much warmth toward her. After all, she is standing in your way."

"If you could but find someone else, another nobleman—"

"Do you know of anyone suitable?" Ysa sipped at her wine, keenly aware that Marcala was not telling everything that was on her mind. It was a delicate problem. Ashen, last known heir of the House of Ash, in ancient times the cradle of Kings, and the late King Boroth's acknowledged bastard daughter at that, had become much more than an annoying Bog-brat or even, in Marcala's amusing phrase, an annoying Bog-Princess. Unmarried, she was the center of a political faction opposed to King Florian, whether she willed it or not, and a temptation to every hedge-knight eager to improve his station in life. Too lofty a marriage and she was a danger to Florian and even to his heir, when he should have one. Too base a marriage, and she was still a danger, because of those who would become angered at the insult and glad to have this matter as an excuse for opposition to the Crown.

She wondered if the rumors about Rannore, the new Rowan heiress since Laherne had died, were true. Well, time would tell if there was going to be another heir to dispute Ashen's claim.

"Perhaps I could think of a suitable candidate," Marcala said. She set the empty goblet on the tray and did not move to refill it. "But my strong feeling is that Ashen will marry no one at all, if she does not want to. She has not been trained to set aside personal feelings, the way she would have had she been brought up properly."

"And what do you suggest?"

"Ask her."

Now the Dowager raised one eyebrow. This was something she had not anticipated having to endure—bringing the bastard child of her late husband into her very home, speaking to her face to face. She had not laid eyes on the girl since that awful day when the King was dying. Royance had brought her into the very death chamber, giving Ysa a chance to throw her support to this sturdy Ash twig rather than the spindly, gawky, unworthy product of her union with Boroth.

And now, this new King, Florian, was creating his own share of personal mischief with Rannore. Her cousin Laherne had died in childbirth, so the story went, only a few months after a visit to Rendelsham. The gossip was that Florian was responsible and also that the aged Erft's passing had been hurried along because of the shame. His younger brother Wittern, a contemporary and friend of Royance, now governed in his place. Ysa had thought to address this matter today, rather than the question of Ashen and a potential marriage. The Dowager sighed. One unpleasantness versus another. Both must be dealt with, but each in its time. Marcala was here present, and Rannore and her guardian, Wittern of Rowan, had not yet arrived at the city.

"Send for Ashen," Ysa said. "Tell a messenger to go and fetch her while you wait with me."

Marcala inclined her head. "Yes, Madame." Then she arose and went to do the Dowager's bidding.

Obern flexed his arm, the one that had been broken in a battle with giant birds atop a cliff at the edge of the Bale-Bog. It was whole and well again, though it ached a little in the damp weather, and this day he wanted nothing more than to go back home. He missed his Sea-Rover companions, missed the freedom of being able to go out in a ship where the sea air blew away the miasma of city life.

That, however, would be as Count Harous pleased. For the moment at least, Count Harous pleased to keep Obern as his "guest" and Obern still did not know why.

Once in a great while, since the doctor had decreed that he no longer needed to keep his arm in a sling, Obern had been allowed to go out on a patrol. As long as it did not involve ranging a great distance from Cragden Keep or actual skirmishing with the Bogmen, who still kept up their campaign of raids on honest Rendelian farmers, he could ride with the soldiers as he pleased. Even that break in the routine was denied to him now, however, since he and Ashen had been removed to Rendelsham and Harous's great house at the foot of the rise where the castle perched.

Still, this part of his sojourn had been interesting. Before now, he had never really learned to handle a horse, and now he was counted more than adequate. He had never been among a group of land nobles, so that he could observe their ways. He had never before attended a royal funeral, or a coronation, when the new King Florian was crowned.

Obern studied Florian appraisingly. So this was the one who had come, as the report had it, to his father, Snolli, with his little private treaty paper in his hand. Obern almost laughed, but that would have interrupted the ceremony. Oh, the King looked good enough stripped to the waist for the anointing but that was merely because he had not yet begun to show the effects of dissipation. He could have had the nicely muscled body of youth, but King Boroth, his father, had gone to fat in his later years and this stripling looked fair to follow. Obern and Ashen, at the insistence of Count Harous, stayed well back in the crowd. Ashen's presence, so Harous said, could be a disruption but it would also have been an unthinkable discourtesy for her not to attend. And as for Obern, well, he was practically highborn himself, so his presence was almost as mandatory as hers.

Obern liked standing next to Ashen in the mass of people filling the nave of the Fane of the Glowing. He liked putting himself between her and the possibility of her being jostled by a rude stranger. Most of all he liked looking at her, at the beauty of her face and form, and her silver-gilt hair falling like pure treasure down her back.

He liked also those rare times when they walked together through the grounds of Rendelsham Castle, and when they passed the high lords going about their business. One he recognized, Lord Royance of Grattenbor, the Head of the Council of Regents, who had questioned him in the Hall at Harous's residence the night the old King died. Others Ashen pointed out to him—Gattor of Bilth; Valk of Mimon; Jakar of Vacaster; Liffen of Lerkland and another, whom Ashen had not met that memorable evening, Wittern of Rowan, lately come to the guardianship of that high House. Of those Obern formed no particular opinion one way or the other except to acknowledge that Lord Royance seemed an able, experienced, and stoutly honest man.

The city of Rendelsham interested Obern because of its strangeness. He was used to the Sea-Rovers' way of life, and a much more casual—one might even say cruder—approach to city building. Here, instead of a cluster of small, sturdy huts, all was whitewashed stone, with carvings and decorations in profusion, and at every corner of the rooftops fabulous creatures rendered so lifelike that they seemed ready to leap down upon the unwary passerby beneath. From the mouths of these creatures the rainwater poured into the streets, away from the walls where it might cause damage. It seemed an ingenious arrangement.

Together he and Ashen made a small pilgrimage to the forecourt of the Great Fane of the Glowing, to view the four great trees that represented the Four Great Houses of Rendel. A courteous priest, passing by, informed them of the history, of how Rowan was rallying and even Ash was making a miraculous revival, with new growth crowding through the dead old twigs. Oak still continued a slow, steady decline, however, and Yew throve, as always. Obern gave the priest a coin, one he had won at gambling, and the grateful fellow then took them inside and showed them the interior wonders, even to the three mysterious windows, hidden away where casual visitors might not notice. One window was shrouded from view by a curtain that, the priest informed them, no one touched on fear of death by Her Majesty's orders. Another showed a Bale-Bog pool, with something just beginning to break the surface. But Ashen gazed longest on the third, a depiction, the priest said, of the Web of Destiny.

"They move," she said, as if to herself. "The hands of the Weavers move."

But Obern could not see it.

These pleasant excursions had been cut short, however, with the arrival of the wet, cold weather. Obern was used to a chilly climate, but this was unnatural, occurring as it did in the middle of the summer. Gratefully he accepted a fur-lined tunic and cloak from the stores of clothing at Harous's residence, and stayed inside as much as his free spirit could bear. He began wearing a cap indoors, the way the Rendelians did, and learned that it, too, contributed to keeping him warm.

Andre Norton & Sasha Miller

Ashen was of a similar mind to him, and fretted when she was kept too long indoors. And so they were drawn together even more than might have been their usual wont, because of the discovery of her high birth and the enormous changes it would be bound to bring to her life. And sometimes they talked about it.

On this day, Lady Marcala had come to Rendelsham from Cragden Keep, visiting the Dowager Ysa. Marcala never entered Harous's town house, but nevertheless Ashen took the opportunity to hide in Obern's quarters while she was in the city.

"I never desired any of this," she told him as they sat close to a fire, sharing a hot drink that Harous's chef had created out of the juice of pressed apples and an assortment of sweet spices. "And if I could, I would let it pass me by. My guardian and Protector, Zazar, predicted that I would have a different road to walk, but I never dreamed it would be so complicated."

"You do look far different from the first time I saw you." Obern smiled. "Though those hide breeches—"

"Lupper skin."

"Yes, lupper-skin breeches—they looked much more practical for the life you were leading then."

"You are somewhat changed, yourself."

He glanced down at the clothing he was wearing—doublet and tunic and a warm cloak over all, with no cross-gaitered hose or fur vest heavy enough to stop a dagger. He straightened the velvet cap on his head. "They took away my old garb. Said it made me stand out as an Outlander."

Ashen laughed at that. "You *are* an Outlander! All who are not of the Bale-Bog are Outlanders, for that matter." She grew sober. "Even I am an Outlander, now. I am not of this world, either. I feel that I have no place."

"You will always have a place, at my side."

She glanced up at him. Her silky eyebrows rose. "What does that mean?"

"I shouldn't have said that." Obern stared at the fire, and then shrugged. In for an egg, in for the clutch. Did he love her, or merely desire her? He thought of her entirely too much and now this day seemed as good as any to decide that it was love that drove him on. "It means that, in other circumstances, I would be bringing you gifts and bargaining with your—your Protector, for the bride-geld I would have to pay for you."

Ashen's face grew pink, and, Obern suspected, not from her nearness to the fireplace. " 'Other circumstances'?"

"I have a wife."

"Oh."

"We were pledged—handfasted—when we were both very young," Obern added hastily. "I never knew her beforehand. She is a good woman, and showed herself to be brave enough on the journey south from our ruined land."

She had pulled back from him a little. "Tell me about your journey."

And so Obern recounted for her the tale of the Sea-Rovers' battles with the invaders from the North, of their flight from their homeland, and the great voyage that had brought them to New Vold. He left out the part about his first encounter with the giant birds or the hideous monster that had tried to climb from the sea onto his ship. No sense in frightening Ashen; let her think that the huge birds were a singular anomaly, and not what he had come to believe they were—harbingers of worse to come as the frozen evil of the North awakened and began to stir.

"Your people must all be very courageous," Ashen said.

Obern shrugged. "Some more than others, like people everywhere."

"What is her name? Your wife."

"Her name is Neave. While we were on the ships on our journey here, I missed her warmth in the night. She was on a different ship from mine, of course, for I could not afford to have her presence be a distraction. Also, if one ship went down the other might be saved. That was the way with all of us who had wives still living after our city was destroyed. And then she became ill shortly after we arrived. I have scarcely been in her company. Since I met you, I have seldom thought of her."

Again, Ashen's cheeks grew pink until she was blushing to the roots of her hair. "I cannot encourage you in this."

"It is not in your power to encourage or discourage. It is as it is," Obern told her. "I love you."

"It is only gratitude speaking. After all, I saved your life when you were so sorely hurt, before we came here."

"I recognize that this might be part of it," Obern said. "But nevertheless, I do love you. Can I be faulted for that? I don't think so."

Ashen arose abruptly. "It is not decent, or honorable, that you speak of such matters. Or that I listen. I like you well, Obern, but please believe that is all—all it can be. When I have the opportunity, I will speak to Count Harous and petition that you be allowed to return home."

"Where I will live on with Neave. But I will think of you in the night."

Then Ashen fled the room, closing the door behind her. Obern knew that, according to Rendelian custom, he must have overstepped his bounds. But Ashen had not been brought up as a Rendelian bred, and neither had he.

Oh, if only—He did not allow himself to complete the thought. It was not Neave's fault that he no longer loved her, if, indeed, he once had. And it was nobody's fault that he loved Ashen or that—he hoped with every fiber of his being—it was only her modesty that made her speak of friendship and not of love in return.

For once, Ysa was mistaken. Wittern of Rowan, the heir to his elder brother Erft, full of years but in much better health, had arrived earlier than expected. Even while she had been consulting with Marcala, Wittern was being admitted to the presence of King Florian. With him was Rannore, her head downcast and her entire bearing radiating shame.

"Oh," said the sovereign lord of Rendel when the two had been brought to where he lounged by a fire, playing a board game with one of his courtiers. A pile of coins lay beside the board, the stakes the players had wagered. "It's you."

"A word with you in private, Your Majesty," Wittern said. "I crave it as a boon."

The King drummed his finger on the board, his hand on the piece he had been prepared to move. Then he set it down and waved his retinue away. "Stay within calling distance," he said.

The group of fawning courtiers bowed and withdrew to a far corner of the room, where they pulled their fur-lined surcoats about them and huddled together for warmth. One of them gestured to a servant, and presently a brazier was brought and lighted so that they could be more comfortable in their exile.

"Yes, well, what do you want?" Florian said. He lounged at his ease, and did not invite the elderly noble or the young woman with him to sit down.

"I think you know, Your Majesty." Wittern took Rannore's hand and made her step forward. "This lady is with child, and it is by you. It is not enough that you debauched Laherne who died in delivery of your child and it with her, but now you would do the same with her cousin. It is not to be borne, sir!"

"And what will you do, to make me marry if I do not choose?"

Wittern's eyes flashed. "I am not my brother, Your Majesty, and Rannore is not her cousin. We are both of sturdier stock than they. I have resources in this land. If you will not of your own accord, then you shall be compelled."

Florian threw back his head and brayed with laughter. "You?" he said at last, wiping tears from his eyes. "You would compel *me*? Oh, I suppose that I must admire your presumption, but hear this, old man. I will do as I please, when I please, where I please, and with whom I please. And you are not man enough to stop me. Now begone."

Tears had begun running down Rannore's cheeks. She spoke up for the first time. "You claimed that you loved me," she said brokenly. "And I know I loved you. I would never have allowed you near me, otherwise. Now I love you not, but honor binds me. I will not bear another kingly bastard. There is talk enough of the one your father sired and the trouble she has brought without willing it."

Florian sat bolt upright in his chair. "You will not speak of that matter," he said. His command was spoiled a little by the break in his voice. "Leave my presence, at once!"

"We will speak of that, and more," Wittern said. "You tell us to begone. And so we obey. But be sure that we will meet again, and soon."

Then the white-haired noble and his granddaughter left the chamber. The courtiers came back and took up their former spots by the fire. Florian completed the move on the board game that he had been contemplating when interrupted.

His opponent, a minor noble named Piaul, grinned. "You lose, Your Majesty," he said as he made the countermove that ended the game. He scooped up the coins as everyone laughed, except King Florian.

❦

Ashen, unsure of herself and wondering why the woman who was her bitterest enemy in Rendel had summoned her to her presence, entered the Dowager Queen's privy chamber. She felt like her heart had lodged somewhere in the vicinity of her stomach and was fluttering like a captive bird. The girl's heart sank even lower when she saw Lady Marcala standing by the Dowager's chair. But Ysa smiled, a little stiffly perhaps, and held out her slender, elegant hands in greeting. The Four Great Rings glinted in the firelight.

"Come closer, Lady Ashen, so we can have a look at you."

Ashen obeyed, hoping that her knees would hold her up, glad that her maid Ayfare had taken pains with her appearance. Also, Ayfare had had the good sense to insist that Ashen not wear the dress in which she had been clad on the occasion of her appearance in the old King's death chamber, but another. This one was made of dark blue velvet, the court color, its warmth welcome in the unseasonable chill of midsummer, and her indoor slippers matched. The wooden pattens every woman wore to protect their fine footwear from mud and mire Ashen had left at the castle's doorway, according to custom.

Of her own accord, Ashen had decided not to wear the necklace

Harous had given her that was a badge of the House of Ash, but another of his gifts, an ornament of silver and lapis beads. Her hair flowed down her back in maidenly simplicity. She curtsied deeply, as Marcala had taught her.

"Thank you, Your Majesty," she said to the stern-faced lady who sat so implacably, waiting. She also wore velvet, but a deep, rich green, and her jewels, except for the Four Great Rings, were of gold and emeralds. Her countenance was beautiful, but her hands verged on the edge of gauntness, though they were still white and elegant. Nevertheless, it was there that she showed her age. "I am honored at being in your presence."

The Dowager nodded slightly. "I have a reason to send for you," she said. "Come and sit, and Lady Marcala also, for your answers concern her as well." She indicated a pair of low chairs that had been set nearby.

Marcala took one with a rustle of skirts and a cloud of the lily-scented perfume she always wore. Ashen, glad that Ayfare was enough of a gossip that she knew of the significance of the perfume made of blue flowers, had chosen one with a citrus tang instead. The Queen, Ayfare said, hated the blue-flower one because it had been the favorite of her great rival, Ashen's mother.

Nobody offered to take Ashen's rain-wetted cloak, so she hung it on a peg beside the fireplace beside another one she recognized as Marcala's. Once seated, Ashen's discomfort did not abate for she felt that something in her life had just come to a crisis point, and she did not know what it was. She wished that Zazar, the great Wysen-wyf of the Bale-Bog who had fostered her, could be at her side. But that was like wishing for the moon. Ashen knew that her own wits would have to be her sole weapons to get her through the coming hour.

Her uneasiness must have communicated itself to the Dowager for she smiled again, frostily. "Be at ease, child," she said. "We aren't going to hurt you. We only want to know what is going on now in your life."

"Surely I am beneath Your Majesty's notice."

"Your modesty becomes you, but it is misplaced. Let me be

Andre Norton & Sasha Miller

open with you. I did not welcome your presence; indeed, for a long time I tried hard to convince myself that you did not even exist. However, here you are, and you cannot be ignored."

"Madame, I apologize for my presence. I know that I am a constant reminder of something unpleasant. But you must realize that I did not request the conditions of my birth. If I could make it otherwise, I would do so, if only to spare you."

The Queen favored Ashen with a frigid smile. "Spoken well. Your breeding shows; also, Zazar brought you up better than I thought. Perhaps there is more to you than I was willing to credit. Now to why you have been sent for. You must know there is talk in many places in Rendelsham of you, of your place here, of whom you will marry."

Ashen looked up, startled. "I have no thought of marriage, Your Majesty!"

"Nevertheless, marry you must. The only question is, who shall it be?"

"I do not wish to marry," Ashen repeated. "When I do, if I do, it will be to somebody whom I love."

"And you do not love Count Harous?" Marcala said.

Ashen glanced at her. She fairly glowed in lavender brocade lined with fur, but a frown puckered her forehead. "No, my lady, I do not," Ashen said. "I admire him enormously, and will be forever grateful that it was he and not another who took me from the Bale-Bog, as my Protector said would happen. For he has always been gentle with me, and his behavior entirely correct. I fear that another would have acted ungraciously."

Marcala sniffed audibly and the Dowager held up a restraining hand. "And yet the rumor is that he would marry you."

Ashen felt her cheeks grow warm. All the talk of marriage this day was making her very uneasy. She wanted nothing more than to escape. But she was required to answer. "He has said that he wished it."

"No!" Marcala said, heedless of Ysa's displeasure. "Are you such an idiot that you cannot see the folly? With you, and what you are heir to, Harous's power would be such that all the other nobles would rise up against him! And that I could not bear!"

"Lady!" the Dowager said sharply. "Marcala! Enough. You forget yourself."

"Yes, Madame," Marcala said. She bowed her head and bit her lip.

The Dowager turned back to Ashen. "The Lady Marcala, for all her impetuous outburst, is correct. A match between you and the Lord Marshal Harous would not be suitable. And so, the question remains, whom shall you marry."

"I know of someone," Marcala said, though Ysa frowned.

"Speak," the Dowager said, a warning clear in her voice.

"Obern. He is the son of the Chieftain of the Sea-Rovers. That makes him almost royalty. He was once hurt, but now is well, still living in Harous's residence here in the city, by his orders. Obern and Ashen are friends."

Ashen drew in her breath sharply. This, coming so closely on Obern's unwanted declaration, was almost more than she could bear at the moment. Nevertheless, there was a possibility for escape. "But he is already wed. He wants very much to return to New Vold— the old Ashenwold."

The Dowager pursed her lips, thinking. "That is unfortunate news, that Obern already has a wife. He would, in many respects, make an ideal match for you. And we need his people as stronger allies than they are now. A certain treaty that was supposed to have been established between us was bungled by—Well, never mind." Ysa clasped her hands, rubbing the Rings. "There have been marriages set aside for dynastic reasons before. Perhaps this one can be as well."

"Your Majesty, no—"

The Dowager stared at Ashen and she subsided immediately. "Do you *dare* refuse me? Do you forget yourself?"

"I crave your pardon, Your Majesty. I only meant that I would not ruin another's happiness for any sake."

"That is not your decision to make. I will tell you this, however. It is very plain that you cannot stay longer in Harous's residence.

You are better kept under my eye. Therefore, you will move at once into the castle. Please see to it. The chamberlain will prepare an apartment for you. Now you may go. I have work to do." With that, the Dowager Queen Ysa dismissed Ashen, who arose at once and started for the door. The other lady made as if to rise as well but the Dowager stopped her. "Marcala, you stay a moment."

But not before she saw a very satisfied look come over Lady Marcala's face. Now, what, Ashen wondered, was that all about? It was as if one of Marcala's schemes had come to fruition, but how could that be?

She set it aside to think about later, glad that she was out of the coils, at least for the moment, of Her Most Gracious Majesty the Queen Dowager Ysa. How she would avoid this formidable lady once she was living under the same roof was another matter. A fresh wave of distaste for the twists and turns of Court life swept over her.

Whomever she married, she hoped he would have similar feelings and they would live in peace and quiet, far away from Rendelsham!

Obern reacted to the news of Ashen's impending move from Harous's town house to Rendelsham Castle with stoic silence. She was, after all, only obeying the Dowager's command and he could not know what had gone on in the private interview to which Ashen had been summoned. He did doubt that Ashen had told Ysa of his declaration of love for her.

This change of residence took her out of Obern's company but also the change removed her from Harous's influence, and that could not be all to the bad. He knew, in the way that a man who loves a woman recognizes when another man wants her as well, that Harous had dark plans somewhere in the back of his sophisticated mind.

Two

*A*fter Ashen had left the Dowager's apartment to begin packing for her move to Rendelsham Castle, Ysa had a few words with Marcala, mostly to soothe her feelings. A servant arrived with the news about Wittern's unexpectedly early arrival. Consulting her daily schedule, she set a time for a meeting with that noble and certain others. Then she dismissed Marcala, to return to Cragden Keep. Ysa had already spent more time on the problems with these women than she could afford.

The servant bowed himself out, to deliver the Dowager's instructions. Then Ysa went to her writing desk to draft a letter. When it was finished to her satisfaction, she wrote out a fair copy. Then she called for a messenger and sent him off posthaste to New Vold Keep, with the polite request that Snolli, Chieftain of the Sea-Rovers, come to Rendelsham so that his beloved son might be restored to him in full health. And also, she added, almost as an afterthought, so that good relations might be cemented between their two peoples. She did not specify what this cementing would consist of. Time enough for that, later, after she had met with the man. He was bound to want something in return.

When that matter had been taken care of, the Queen Dowager,

Lord Royance, and the Lord Marshal Harous all gathered to confront the young King Florian. They sat at the Council table, with Royance at the head. Wittern and Rannore occupied chairs at the back of the room, just outside the light cast by the candles. Rannore leaned her head on her grandfather's shoulder, and he had one of her hands clasped in both of his. Florian entered last, and sat opposite Royance.

"Lord Wittern of Rowan has acquainted us with the problem he and his granddaughter now find themselves facing," Royance said, his snowy eyebrows drawn together sternly. "And furthermore, I find his petition worthy. You, King Florian, are responsible for this lady's condition, and answerable to her guardian. I tell you this: Do not shame her further."

"And I," Harous said. "I would not long remain as Count of Cragden, Rendelsham's Lord Marshal, if the ruler I guard with my own body and might were shown to be unworthy. A fellow who treats highborn women as playthings and abandons them when he is weary of them."

"Both of you men are much too nice. I will speak bluntly. I have learned the art, dealing with the late King," Ysa said. She stood up and leaned forward, her hands flat on the table, and Florian shrank back a little in his chair. "Florian, your father may have debauched a noblewoman, but he was at least careful enough about it that nobody knew except near the last. And you are well aware of the trouble his indiscretion has caused."

"You can't talk to me that way," Florian said, but his tone was weak and Ysa knew that he was merely blustering.

"I can, and I will!" Ysa retorted, her voice like the cracking of a whip. She held up her hands so that the Great Rings, the repository of true power in Rendel, glowed in the light. "*These* show that I can. The Rings still reject you, or they would have gone to you long ago, of their own accord, as they came to me. *Faugh!* You, the King? You grew up pampered and spoiled, for I had too much on my mind to spare the time to devote to your training. Know this, you puppy. I made you King when I declared it in my husband's death-chamber. I can un-make you as well."

Florian went pale. "You wouldn't dare."

"Don't put me to the test. Much as I dislike the thought, my husband's by-blow might prove much more suitable to occupy the throne than you. You would do well to let yourself be guided by me, in this as well as many other matters for, really, you have no other choice."

The Dowager's words hung echoing in the air while Florian fidgeted in his chair, looking from side to side as if seeking an escape. He refused to meet the eyes of anyone sitting at the Council table. Then a change came over him. He lifted his head and smiled at each in turn.

"But of course I will marry Rannore!" he exclaimed. "How could you think I would not? I have merely been having some sport, jesting with all of you. And to think how well I fooled you, that you believed I would abandon the dearest creature in all the world to me." He got up and crossed the room to where Wittern and Rannore waited. They arose in their turn. Wittern bowed to his sovereign, and Rannore dropped in a deep curtsey.

"Now, now, none of that," Florian said. He took Rannore's hands and raised her to her feet. "We shall be equals, you and I. I am your King, but you shall be my Queen, if you agree. Tell me you will. Tell me you will sit by my side, with our son, forever."

"If that is what you desire," Rannore said shakily, "and my grandfather agrees, then that shall content me as well."

"Oh, I so desire. And you, my Lord Wittern? Do you agree to this match?"

As Ysa watched, a number of expressions passed across Wittern's face—disgust, contempt, disbelief at the depth of the young King's cynicism. She knew those emotions well, for she had experienced them frequently toward Florian. Then the nobleman mastered himself and nodded. "I agree, Your Majesty."

"Then we shall hold the wedding as quickly as possible," Florian said with weird gaiety. "We wouldn't want to delay very long, would we? People might talk."

Then, to everyone's dismay and embarrassment, the King tittered.

🦋

Iaobim and Haldin, once proud Sea-Rovers but now confined to land, stood watch while other men, not warriors, worked to erect a kind of shelter over a small field of grain. Because of the unseasonable cold that had blotted out the summer, it was thought that such a shelter might gather what warmth there was to help the faltering plants. Dordan the archer stood watch on the other side of the field. All three of the warriors wore warm cloaks over their chain mail.

The workers had erected pairs of poles at intervals up and down the field, each with a crossbar at the top, and now were stringing lengths of thin cloth along these supports. Iaobim shifted, resettling his sword in its scabbard, more than a little bored with guard duty.

"We should be out on the *GorGull*," his companion muttered, loudly enough for Iaobim to hear. "Not nursemaiding a cornfield."

Iaobim laughed. "You got your orders from the Chieftain, same as me," he said. "D'you think the tales about Bog-men's raids are just for scaring children with?"

Haldin sighed, leaning on his spear. "I haven't seen any evidence. And until I do, I won't believe—"

He was interrupted by a shout from Dordan, from across the field. "Here they come!" he cried. He was already fitting an arrow to bowstring.

Iaobim and Haldin sprinted toward their companion, trying to avoid trampling the tender plants underfoot and also trying to keep from wrecking the shelter their countrymen had been laboring so hard to erect. They reached Dordan's side, and Iaobim shielded his eyes with his hand, trying to see what had alarmed the archer. "You have long eyesight," Iaobim said. "I can see nothing."

"They disappeared in a little dip in the land yonder." Dordan pointed. "But they're coming this way."

At that moment, the Bog-men did appear, topping a small rise. They ran at a steady, distance-consuming trot. There were six—no, eight of them. Iaobim glanced at his companions. "Odds are a little longer than I like," he said.

"I'll see what I can do to even the odds before they get close," Dordan said. He sighted and let fly with an arrow. ·

One of the Bog-men dropped and did not rise. His fellows paused only for a moment, and then kept running. It was clear that their goal was the field, and the workers in it. Dordan fired again, and another Bog-man stopped, clutching his leg. Dordan's arrow protruded from it. He had time for one more shot and then, with a bloodcurdling screech, the Bog-men were upon them.

For an instant Iaobim wished he had chosen a spear this day. Spears were the weapon of choice for the Bog-men—those, and clubs studded with shell spikes—and fighting with a sword let an enemy get too close before he could deal with him. He dodged when one of the Bog-men lunged, and dispatched him with a single blow. Out of the corner of his eye, he could see that his companions were likewise employed. In the space of only a few heartbeats, the attackers were down, dead or dying—all but the one Dordan had wounded. This one managed to slip around the cluster of fighters, obviously intending to take Iaobim from behind, but one of the farmers smashed his head in with the sturdy hoe he had been using to grub up weeds.

"Thanks, Ranse," Iaobim said.

"Pleasure's mine," the farmer replied.

The three fighters quickly dispatched the wounded, and dragged the bodies of the Bog-men to one side, to examine them. "Looks like they're feeling the pinch of the cold weather, too," Haldin commented. "They aren't dressed mainly in mud. What kind of leather is this they're wearing?"

"Skins off those infernal jumping horrors that you find everywhere in the Bog," Dordan said. "And breastplates, too." He indicated a crude form of armor, shell-reinforced, that most of them wore. Then he pulled a couple of empty sacks off one man's belt.

"They came prepared to cart home as much as they could carry."

"Hmmm." Iaobim squatted beside the body he had been going over, thinking. "I wonder what Obern would make of all this."

"No way of asking him. He's probably safe and warm, inside a grand house somewhere in that big city up north. Being catered to by servants of the fine lord who took him." Haldin gestured to a couple of the farmers and they began digging a shallow grave. "Seems he's been gone more than long enough to have gotten loose to come back to us, though."

"Maybe he doesn't much want to escape," Dordan said, grinning. "That lady the city men took out of the Bog when they got Obern—she was a nice-looking wench, for a land woman, even if she was skinny and pale. He might be having a nice tumble with her even now."

Haldin laughed, and even Iaobim had to smile. He had no idea what was going on in the mind of Snolli, their Chieftain, that he would not immediately go and demand the return of his son, but Iaobim knew that Snolli was a far-thinker. He had to have a plan somewhere in that long head of his. But Iaobim, too, wondered what Obern was doing.

"I think we're safe enough from a return visit from these Bog-people, at least for the moment," he said. "Haldin, you go back to the keep and report that the rumors were true. Bog-men have learned to cross the river on this side as well as where it curves to the north, and anytime any of our people are outside our strong walls, they will need to have an armed guard with them. These are fell doings, and perilous times. It is not safe to be abroad in the land these days."

All of Rendelsham was buzzing with the news of King Florian's coming marriage—quickly arranged, even more quickly prepared for. And though it was common knowledge that the bride, Rannore of Rowan, was proving fertile perhaps a little earlier than custom demanded, most were polite enough not to mention it. At least in public.

Naturally, Ashen would be there. She had been established in one of Rendelsham Castle's many guest apartments, located in one of the twin three-story buildings flanking the taller main structure where the royal family lived, and the officials who actually ran the country had their quarters. Under her maid Ayfare's watchful eye, the house steward assigned Ashen's suite on the second floor—close enough to the heart of the castle to provide easy access to all the servants' chatter. Ashen was grateful, for this was near enough for quick access if she was summoned, and still far enough away that she no longer worried about having to encounter the Queen Dowager every time she stepped outside her door. And summoned she was, frequently, for she had, will or nil, become involved in the hasty preparations. She would, she was informed by the Ceremonial Steward who was arranging the elaborate protocols, walk directly ahead of the happy couple in the procession, bearing the marriage rings.

This created a near-panic in Ashen. She turned for help to Ayfare, with whom she had formed a friendship. "I cannot do this!" she said. "I can't show myself to the Court this way. I am here only because the Dowager ordered it, and not through any desire of my own."

"There, there now, sweeting," Ayfare said soothingly. She smoothed Ashen's hair. "You act like you'll be the center of all eyes. Never fear, my poppet. You'll be very much in the shadow of the King and his bride. That's who they'll be looking at." The maid winked conspiratorially. "Besides, everybody'll be whispering behind their hands, counting on their fingers and trying to judge how far along the bride is."

Despite herself, Ashen had to smile. In this matter, she had not had to rely on Ayfare to bring her the gossip. Everyone was talking about it, and about how Wittern, the new Lord of the House of Rowan, had brought King Florian to heel.

"There's rumor that all in the procession will wear white samite and velvet," Ayfare continued. "They say it's to be a very *virginal* wedding."

That comment made Ashen laugh outright. She was very glad that Lady Marcala had given her Ayfare as her personal maid. Younger than the other maids in attendance upon Marcala, and presumably less experienced, her fine features and bearing suggested that she might be a bastard offspring of some noble as well. Once Ayfare had remarked on it, and this circumstance also brought the two girls closer.

There was, Ashen discovered, a place in the festivities for nearly everyone at court. Fitting for his place as the castellan of Cragden Keep, Lord High Marshal, Champion and Defender of Rendelsham, Harous would carry the great sword of state as he had at the coronation. Royance, also duplicating his role in that ceremony, would carry the mace. And so on with other nobles. Each would bear some emblem or symbol or trinket of office and this, Ashen learned, was an honor to be vied for. Even Obern, Ayfare told her, would be included. As there was no actual official station he occupied, he would be given a model of a Sea-Rover ship, in token of the alliance the Dowager and the King hoped to make between the two peoples.

The thought of Obern clad in white samite made Ashen shake her head in rueful wonder. Well, at the very least, all the hustle and bustle served to divert the Dowager's attention—and Harous's and Obern's as well, she hoped—from the matter of her own marriage.

Ayfare's information source about the color chosen for the wedding party proved to be correct, and, sending the castle seamstresses away, she personally set about the task of designing and sewing a dress of white velvet for Ashen. The sitting room of the apartment was soon cluttered with sketches of other ladies' dresses, and with scraps and cuttings of velvet.

Even Ashen, who had come to like the luxury and comfort of Rendelian clothing but who knew little about styles, recognized Ayfare's talent. The skirt was split in a daring fashion, showing an underdress with a front panel of white samite, embroidered lightly in gold thread mixed with touches of blue. More of the embroidered samite would show at neck and sleeves, and the pillow on which Ashen would carry the rings would also be made of the same fabric.

"Oh, you'll look fair and fairer than the bride once I'm finished," the maid said effusively.

"I'll look like a specter," Ashen said. "I am too pale to wear white unadorned."

"Most people are, including the bride. I'm told she's more than a little green around the gills these days."

Ashen had to bite her lips, hard. "Ayfare!"

"Yes, ma'am." The maid obediently subsided, but her eyes were twinkling and Ashen knew it would be only a matter of time before she came out with yet another remark that would prompt Ashen to forget her station and double up with laughter.

It was a welcome respite, here in a place where Ashen knew danger lurked behind every corner, outside the snug haven of her borrowed quarters. Also, it served to bring the two girls closer together.

In New Vold Keep, Snolli Sea-Rover gazed contemplatively at the messenger dressed in the Dowager's livery, who stood before him. "Give your letter to Kasai," he said, indicating a small man who hovered nearby, a drum hanging by a cord from his neck. "He is my trusted adviser. Also, he reads your language better and more easily than I do."

Kasai took the folded note, bowed courteously with it pressed to his forehead, opened it, and began to read. "Usual flowery nothings at first," he said to the Chieftain in their own language. "Ah, here we come to it. Obern, Her Majesty reports, is alive and well, healed from his wounds, and ready to come home." He glanced at Snolli, then at the messenger who was politely pretending not to overhear. "She says she knows we will rejoice at this good news, having thought Obern long dead." He read further. "We're to wait, and come take him off their hands in a fortnight, as there's to be a big wedding."

"The Prince?"

"Oh, no, it seems that the cata . . . the sweet young *man*—is King now. But he's getting married and Obern's to be part of the ceremony. That ought to lighten Obern's disposition if he thinks as much of the new King as the rest of us do. Very highly, of course," he added, for the messenger's benefit.

The messenger nodded without thinking, and Snolli almost laughed aloud. Trust that nest of eels in the capital city to send someone who understood Trader language, which was very similar to the tongue the Sea-Rovers spoke among themselves.

"Queen apologizes if she's offered you an insult by not inviting you, but it's a long journey between here and there, and the omens says the wedding has to be now." Kasai snorted. "Bride must be expecting. Queen says there wouldn't be time to entertain you anyway until after, let alone hammer out a treaty between us. You can bring as big a retinue as you like. There's more, but it's just more flowery nothings."

Snolli nodded, and then turned to address the messenger directly. "Thank the Queen for the good news when you return, and tell her that we are so glad to know that Obern is alive that we cannot take offense at anything even if it had been offered. When she is ready to meet with us, we will be there. Tell her also we'll take Dakin with us when we go," the Chieftain said. "He was left with us in trade for Harvas, one of our people, while we contemplated the terms of a treaty between the Prince, now the King, and the Sea-Rovers. I'm sure both men will be glad to be back with their own once more. And I'm sure also that changing circumstances have made the treaty King Florian proposed very much out of date. We might as well start all over, and being in Rendelsham should make it easier for all."

"Yes, sir," the messenger said. "I will inform my lady, who is properly known now as the Dowager Queen Ysa, of what you have said. And if you don't mind my saying so—"

"Yes?"

"I think you will find my lady more agreeable than the King. He is able but young, whereas she is more—steadfast."

"I'm sure," Kasai said dryly.

"Tell the Dowager also that we know about how the Bog-men have learned to cross the river, for we have run afoul of them ourselves from time to time," Snolli said. "This, and the news of Obern's miraculous escape from death, strengthens what had originally been an uneasy peace at best. And so inform her."

"I will, Lord Snolli." And with that, the messenger bowed himself out of the presence of the Chieftain of the Sea-Rovers.

Snolli drew a long breath. "And what do you think, Kasai?"

The Spirit Drummer spat into the fire, made necessary by the unseasonable cold of this Rendelian midsummer. "I think Obern has earned his reputation for being lucky. By all rights, he should have been bones by now but instead he has been cosseted in the greatest of luxury instead of being thrown into a dungeon to rot, the way anybody else would have. And furthermore, I think the Queen— What's it mean, 'Dowager'?"

"I think it means the widow of a King."

"Well, I think she has something more in mind than just returning Obern to us. She could have done that anytime."

"So she could. And I agree with you. These Rendelians are as slippery as a nest of sea-snakes, and their bite even worse, I'll warrant." Snolli glanced around the room. In the time that Obern had been missing, he had managed to begin furnishing the deserted keep once more, bringing back what the looters in years past had hidden, thinking to retrieve later.

Most of the walls in the Hall were now decorated with an arras depicting Rendelians at work, at play, or engaged in flirtation. Furniture of a better quality than that hammered together hastily by Snolli's craftsmen replaced the crude table and chairs he had once made do with, even though it was carved more ornately than he liked.

Eventually New Vold Keep would reflect the tastes of the Sea-Rovers, and not those of the Rendelians, but Snolli had discovered that much of what he had originally scorned as mere decoration had a purpose. Wall hangings went far to prevent the dankness from castle walls from sinking into one's bones, and glass windows kept out cold winds much better than oiled paper ever did. Also, velvet lined with fur was warmer than mere fur alone, for all the dandified appearance it gave the wearer.

Well, it did no harm. And so thinking, Snolli turned his mind to the more important question of how he was going to feed his people. The extended cold weather in the midst of the growing season had all but ruined the crops they had planted, and Snolli knew he might have to rely on stores of grain the Rendelians had put by, just in case of hard times, for their own supplies were utterly exhausted. The Sea-Rovers in New Vold were already living on what fish they could drag from the sea, and what meat their hunting parties could bring in, and some of their number had died. Therefore it behooved him to step softly around the formidable Dowager Queen Ysa, and look with an easy eye at whatever treaty she chose to lay in front of him.

Later, if the terms proved too harsh, there would be time enough to renegotiate. Or even, Snolli thought with an upsurge of Sea-Rover martial spirit, to go to war.

"I'm not of a mind to wait those two weeks just because the Dowager tells me to," Snolli said. "And I was careful not to promise to wait like a good boy."

"I noticed that," Kasai said. "Wonder if the messenger did. Probably not. He was too busy trying to pretend that he wasn't taking everything in, to report on later."

"We do have that piece of sorry news for Obern," Snolli said with a grimace, and Kasai nodded gravely. "About his wife. And anyway, who knows what we might meet on the way, to delay us? Go notify the men. You know the ones I'll want with me. Let us provision ourselves and start tomorrow, or the following day at the latest. If we arrive early, then we'll get to watch a royal wedding. If not, no harm done either way."

Kasai nodded, and then left to go and do the Chieftain's bidding.

Three

*W*hen *the bustle of* preparations for King Florian's wedding grew too onerous for Ashen to bear, she began to escape into other parts of Rendelsham Castle. Obern's company was now closed to her, because of his unwarranted declaration—a declaration she most heartily hoped the Dowager never learned of—and so she began to venture out on her own.

One of the first places she visited was one where she had been before, the Great Fane of the Glowing. She moved through the door with a group of pilgrims, hoping to catch a glimpse of the kind priest who had showed her and Obern the wondrous, changing windows before, and to her pleasure, she did.

He recognized her. "Lady Ashen," he said, bowing. "How nice to see you again."

"I fear I have come seeking a little peace and quiet from all the to-do in the castle," Ashen said, a little ruefully.

"This is a good place to come to," the priest said.

"Thank you—I don't know your name, or your title."

"Call me Esander. We don't set much store by titles here, where we are in the presence of the Everlasting."

"Then, thank you, Esander."

"You do not have your companion with you."

"No. He is—busy elsewhere with his own part in the preparations."

"You did not quarrel?"

Ashen felt herself blushing. Esander saw far too keenly into a person. Perhaps it was a part of his calling. "No, not exactly. But it is better that we be apart, at least for a while."

"Keep your secret as long as you want to. But remember that part of my duty is to help people with certain personal problems. When you are ready to tell me about it, I will be here. In the meantime, would you like to see more of the Great Fane?"

"Indeed I would!" Ashen exclaimed. "But I thought you showed it all to us—I mean, to me—earlier."

"We barely scratched the surface. For example, did you know that there is a huge library, down in the depths of the mountain on which Rendelsham is built?"

Ashen blinked. A library! Riches untold. Zazar had taught her her letters, of course, but there had never been anything to read just for the sheer joy of it. "No, I had no idea."

"Nor do even the great ones in the castle, I'll warrant. I only discovered it myself recently. The cobwebs were thick across the door. At any rate, it is there, and it is accessible only from a certain chamber here in the Fane, through a secret passage and a steep stairway down."

Ashen was reminded of the tunnels and stairways beneath Galinth, the ruined city in the Bog, where there had also been stored-up tablets containing lore of forgotten times. "Would it be possible for me to see it?"

"If I thought you were not one with whom this secret would be safe, I would not have entrusted it to you." The priest smiled, and a network of wrinkles formed around his kind eyes. "Come with me."

Willingly Ashen followed the holy man through winding passageways until they came to a half-hidden door, which he opened for her. "Later, you will learn the way yourself and not have to rely on me to guide you."

" 'Later'?"

"Yes, Lady Ashen. You will return, and not just to relieve the tedium of your days here in the city, away from the freedom in which you grew up. Sometimes it is given to me to glimpse shadows of what I have no way of knowing, what no one has told me. I see in you that you are someone who needs to read and study and learn. I know also that our Dowager Queen is a student of certain lore, and that some of the books that she was at great pains to acquire, reside below as well. It was through us, indeed, that she got what she has, for we searched other orders to fulfil her desires. Had she been aware of the treasure that you are about to behold, she would have removed it long since. But we hold it safe instead."

"I will try to be worthy of your great trust."

"As well I know you will be." With that, Esander struck fire to a closed lantern and, handing Ashen an additional flagon of oil, touched a spring and opened the secret door. "The lantern will last long enough to get there and allow you an hour of study before it begins to flicker. There is enough oil in the flagon to replenish it enough to show you the way back once more. It is not wise to linger too long in the dark."

"I understand."

Then, with a mingling of fear and anticipation making her pulse pound in her throat, Ashen followed the priest into the blackness beyond the door.

🌿

The next time she visited the Great Fane, Ashen tried, with Esander trailing her, to find the hidden room on her own. She took a couple of wrong turns, but the priest assured her that she surprised him by how easily she picked up the route.

"I was reared in the Bog," she told him. "Sometimes life itself depended on remembering where one had been, and how one got to that place." She did not mention a certain square of spicy-smelling wood, the hearth-guide Zazar had given her. She could have set it for the hidden room, of course, but somehow she felt that this would be much too trivial a use for such a valuable artifact. So she left it where she had put it early in her sojourn in Rendel—the bottom of the little jewel coffer Harous had given her. She tucked it into the lining, hidden under her necklace bearing her family emblem, the mysterious bracelet she had found on a dead man's arm in the catacombs of Galinth, and other less valuable trinkets she had accumulated. "You need not go with me. I assure you, I can find my way both in and out, and your absence will surely be noted sooner or later."

"You will find the lantern, along with flint and steel and the flask of oil, each time you return. This I promise."

"And again, I thank you."

She lighted the lantern and ducked through the doorway. Esander waited until she was out of sight, and then closed the door behind her.

Going surefooted in the near-darkness, Ashen fairly raced down the stairs and along the corridor leading to the door, recently cleared of the cobwebs, behind which waited a glorious store of information. She passed other doors, almost hidden under the dust and veils spun by spiders long since dead, but did not give in to any twinge of curiosity. Those mysteries could wait, possibly forever. She was not willing to let the ones already discovered sit idle while she investigated less important matters.

Esander had found a table in the depths of the forgotten library, and a chair. He dusted them and set them up for her on that first visit. On the table she had left for further scrutiny three volumes of lore that looked interesting, and the oil in the lantern would not last forever. She set the lantern down on the table, adjusted the cover so that it cast a strong ray on the first book, and settled herself to read.

It looked like an earlier, more complete edition of one of the tablets she had begun to decipher back in the ruined city. The characters were clearly limned on the pages—real pages, that could be turned, rather than clay plates. Ashen thought of Weyse, the little furry creature who had been of such help to her in the ruined city, Galinth. She wished she had Weyse, or a creature like Weyse, for companionship. There were echoes in the cavernous chamber, and in the corridors, which she was certain she had not caused. One blessing, though, was that the spiders seemed to have vanished long ago, perhaps because they had eaten all the other insects and subsequently starved. She remembered also the pieces of what looked like bone, which gave off light. Surely, if Galinth had once been a part of Rendel, and if all lore was centered here beneath the Great Fane, there might be something similar—

Ashen arose and took the lantern with her. With a start of recognition, she found identical bones embedded high on the walls, where their glow would illuminate the whole of the vast chamber. But they were dark. How to activate them?

Of course, Ashen told herself. The answer would be in the books, if she were clever enough to find the spell or incantation or trigger, or whatever it took. She returned to the table and began to read once more, eager to know more about this kind of Power. It was, somehow, *refined* and tempered, as contrasted to the earthy magic she had been accustomed to, with Zazar.

She thought she found what she was looking for in the third volume. She checked the oil level in the light. It had not yet begun to flicker so she dared to risk it.

Hoping that she was saying the words correctly, she began to intone them aloud. With suddenness that hurt her eyes, accustomed to the dimness, all the bones burst into light. She shielded her eyes, waiting for them to adjust. When she could see again, to her utter astonishment she found Weyse standing atop the table, staring at her.

"Oh!" she cried. "How wonderful!" She reached out to touch the little creature, hoping to hear an answering soft, loving purr, but to her dismay Weyse scuttled away, out of reach. "Oh, please come back. I have missed you."

Weyse waddled back a few steps, and plopped herself down on the open book, holding her paws over as many as possible of those words that still could be seen around her plump bottom. She glared at Ashen with what could only be described as a baleful air, as if Ashen had committed an unknown transgression.

Ashen stood quite still. She knew that Weyse seldom did anything without a reason. "Did Zazar send you?" she said.

Weyse looked away, and made a soft trilling noise that would have been lost anywhere but in the utter silence of the great Rendelian library.

Ashen thought some more, remembering certain warnings Zazar had given her about exceeding her capabilities. "It is the magic, isn't it?"

Weyse trilled again, but did not leave her station, blocking the words on the book of spells.

"I believe that is your message, sent me by my Protector. I think she wants me to read, and learn, but not do. Not yet. Is that correct?"

For answer, Weyse moved off the book and let Ashen close the cover. Then she allowed Ashen to stroke her soft fur. Even as the girl caressed the strange, intelligent little creature, Weyse began to fade and Ashen's hands went right through her, as if she were no more than a shadow. Then she vanished entirely.

Ashen found that her knees would not hold her and she had to sit down. Fortunately, since she had managed to activate the bone lights, she had time to think and collect her wits before she had to brave the dark passageway back to the outside.

The message had been unmistakable. Read she might, as much as she liked, and study, too—even spells and the making of magic. But putting the knowledge into use was forbidden. This was, in a way, a relief to Ashen, for she had only reluctantly employed a little of what Zazar had taught her or given her while she was growing up.

Very well. There were many other books to be read. One that she had only opened and lightly turned through promised to give

the history of the great families of Rendel, and also the story of the
Great Rings, which were said to be articles of legend.

Were they the same ones as the Dowager wore on her white,
elegant hands? If so, then much study was indeed called for, and,
apparently, as long as she did not try to work any spells she could
learn to her heart's content without being interrupted.

Even so, Weyse's abrupt appearance and then mysterious
method of departure had unsettled the girl. She emptied the little
flask into the lantern, her hands shaking so that she had to be careful
lest she spill the oil, and quickly made her way back to the entrance
to the cavern. There was one last fitting for the dress she would be
wearing for King Florian's wedding, and the wedding itself was a
mere two days hence. Little as she cared for it, the humdrum routine of life outside the secret places of the Fane of the Glowing
might calm her nerves. Also, it might put her in a better, more
receptive frame of mind to learn the next time she ventured down
into the cavern and the hidden library.

The day of Florian's wedding to Rannore dawned cold and clear.
Obern was grateful for what warmth the velvet and samite provided, though he found the dandified cut and ornamentation of the
garments more than a little distasteful. Also, the little gilded boat
he was expected to carry was merely silly.

All the participants in the procession had been given brooches
of gold, the design being the Rowan yellow rose entwined with a
branch of yew. When he saw Lord Royance pinning his on his hat,
Obern did likewise. The women placed theirs according to their
fancy, on shoulder or bosom or on headdress. Pages waited with
baskets of similar ornaments, made of flimsy base metal and painted
gold, ready to throw to the crowds as souvenirs.

The procession gathered in a room just inside the castle doors.
From there, they would walk through the outer ward, out into the
city along a specified route, and back again to the Great Fane of the
Shining. Only a small portion of the city's inhabitants could hope

to fit into this building. The rest would have to wait outside in the cold, relying on word being sent out to them by the luckier ones inside as to what was happening within.

Obern craned his neck, seeking a glimpse of Ashen. Finally he spotted her, standing a little apart from the other ladies. Her hair was covered with a veil; today, only the bride's head would be bare. She saw him and started to smile and wave. Then she ducked her head and busied herself with the small pillow she would be carrying, on which the marriage rings had been tied with white ribbons.

The bride herself, looking wan and pale and more than a little ill, was supported by her grandfather, Wittern, and by Lord Royance. Obern thought the two men seemed to be old friends, by the easy way they had with one another. Royance lifted one hand, a page appeared as if by magic, disappeared just as quickly, and presently returned bearing a tray with a flask and a goblet on it. From the color of the liquid as the servant poured it, Obern thought it must be neat wine. Rannore accepted a swallow, and then another. A little color returned to her cheeks.

Interested, Obern watched the Dowager pull the bridegroom to one side and deliver a short but impassioned lecture in so low a voice that no one save the King could hear it. Florian frowned, looking at his bride-to-be, and then at Ashen, who did not seem to realize that she was the object of a look of pure hatred. That was interesting, and alarming as well. Obern had no idea what was going on between the King and his mother, and even less about how Ashen was involved. Perhaps this was part of the reason for Ashen's being ordered to leave Harous's town house and move into the castle. Then, to his further bewilderment, he found himself the object of a moment of hard and merciless scrutiny from both mother and son.

Obern wanted to know more, but didn't know whom to ask. His speculations were cut off abruptly by the ringing of a bell in the hands of the Ceremonial Steward, who had begun to line up the procession.

"Here, here, and you there," the Steward said. He looked harried and did not shrink from putting hands on those of the high ones who were tardy and directing them to their places. "We start through the door at the stroke of noon."

Fortunately, Obern was stationed well back in the ranks, and in any case his order of precedence was not at all important—at least not to him—and so he continued to dawdle at the sidelines. To his surprise, the Ceremonial Steward beckoned him aside.

"You are Obern of the Sea-Rovers, are you not? Yes, I see by the token you carry. Well, sir, I have news for you. Your father and a company of some dozen men are in the city, and have asked about you. And today, of all days! Well, never mind. Somehow I found room for them, in one of the lesser buildings inside the walls, and you will see them later."

Obern blinked back his surprise. "Thank you, good Steward. This is welcome news, indeed."

The procession had already started and was winding its way out of the great entrance to the castle. Obern checked to make sure his cap was on straight, that his cloak hung properly, and that his hose were unwrinkled. Later, he would find out why Snolli had picked this day, of all days, to come visiting at Rendelsham.

Four

t last the wedding was over, the bride did not faint, the
bridegroom did not ruin the ceremony with some untoward coarse comment, and a great feast had begun in the castle's
main Hall. There were too many people to seat, even in that big
enclosure, so food was set out on long tables, with platters so that
people could help themselves as they chose from the variety laid
out for them. Whole roast pig, haunches of beef, birds without
number prepared in various ways, and a table of sweetmeats, for
the King was known to have a fondness for them—this day nobody
went hungry. Nor did any go thirsty, for kegs of wine and ale had
already been broached. The sounds of celebration filled the air. Musicians played from a gallery over the Hall, and already some of the
revelers had begun to dance.

Obern followed the crowd into the Hall, not intending to stay,
for he was now free to go in search of his father. To his surprise and
amusement he didn't have to go far, because Snolli and his men had
happily invaded the party and were making great dents in the food
that had been provided for the wedding guests.

"Obern!" Snolli bellowed when he caught sight of his son. "It's good to see you, boy! For a while we thought you were dead! Come and have some of this roast pig. It's excellent."

Obern grinned. It was plain to see that Snolli had also been making free with the ale-keg. Those with him—Kasai, Dordan, Iaobim, others he did not see clearly in the press—gathered around, pounding him on shoulders and back, shoving platters of food at him, asking him how he had fared. Somehow he managed to answer through the tumult.

"Well enough. I broke my arm in the fall from the cliff. It's a wonder I didn't break more, but I think I landed on my head. My sword is gone, but it's safely hidden and I know where to find it. And how goes it at New Vold?"

"Well enough, well enough," Snolli said. "We're here to make a treaty with Her Majesty. She told us to wait until after the wedding, but we chose not to."

"What, and miss a good meal?" one of the Sea-Rovers shouted, amid laughter from his companions. "And especially in the company of one who is now known to be the luckiest man alive?"

Obern could not help but notice that the Rendelians were giving the newcomers a wide berth, and he smiled. They did stand out, in their rough garments over chain mail. They had little pretense of elegance among the overly civilized, who did not hesitate to look down their noses at the men from the south or even, when they thought they were being unobserved, to hold perfumed handkerchiefs over their noses. How he had missed the company of his father and friends! He felt a big part of the veneer of fancy manners he had had to put on sliding away and let it go without regret.

"You all look like you could use a meal or two," he said. "Have you discovered that farming is hard work?"

His father sobered. Then he drew Obern aside, to a velvet upholstered seat in a window niche where they could have just a little privacy.

"I wanted to tell you this before we all met with the royal lady," Snolli said, and Obern immediately gave his Chieftain his full attention. "Things are not going well at New Vold. The weather is against us. I've never seen such a cold summer. The local grain is dying, and even the winter-hardy seed we brought with us is struggling. It will grow only if coddled under shelter and given extra warmth. Some of our people also have died."

"Anybody I know?"

"The men may call you lucky, but this luck doesn't reach past your arms' length. Neave is dead. She was sick when you last saw her, and when we thought that you had died, she lost all her will to live. I don't think she lasted a week."

Obern pondered this news in silence. Sorry as he was to hear that Neave had gone on that voyage from which nobody returns, behind his dutiful regret a certain exaltation threatened to burst through. Now there were no obstacles between him and Ashen! To cover this unseemly response, he said, "And my son? How fares the boy?"

Snolli looked a little blank. "Boy? Oh, yes. There was a child. What was his name?"

"Rohan." Sea-Rover warriors were not great lovers of children, not until they were old enough to join the ranks of fighters. Obern was more tolerant of them than most.

"Oh, yes, I remember. The boy is doing fine. Left him in fosterage, of course. With Dagdya. She raises healthy young ones. Come to think of it, she fostered you, didn't she?"

Obern nodded without comment. This was obviously the first time Snolli had even thought about Rohan since the night he was born, some six or seven years ago. Still, if the boy had died, Snolli would have heard about it for he was of Snolli's own blood. Obern dismissed any concern for Rohan, knowing he was safe enough. Time enough to make provisions for him, later.

"Thank you for telling me about Neave, Father," Obern said. "Did she die well?"

"I didn't hear anything to the contrary."

"Then there's an end to it." He looked up. One of the chief

stewards was coming toward them. "I think Her Majesty is going to summon us to a meeting very shortly. Will you require my presence?"

"No, no, it's just dry and boring negotiations between our people and theirs. We hope to get access to the food stores, because I fear we'll need the help. You were just the excuse to bring us here."

"Then I'll take my leave of you. There is something that I want to do."

"Go, go, everything will be well for a lucky man such as you," Snolli said heartily. Both men arose from the window seat. "And change your clothes," he added with a laugh. "You look ridiculous."

Obern laughed also, glancing down at the white samite and velvet he had had to don for the festivities. "No need to tell me twice, Father! I will look for you later."

And with that, he moved off through the crowd, seeking Ashen. He knew of her fondness for both music and dancing, and though he had no great skill in it, he hoped she would favor him nonetheless.

❦

Ashen had not gone into the Great Hall, for her natural preference for avoiding crowds had been tested to its limit by the wedding procession and the wedding itself. She knew that she, if not the center of all eyes, was still on display much more than was comfortable for her. And so she quietly made her way to the building where her apartment was located, intending to ask Ayfare to bring her a platter of food later.

She didn't even reach the outer door. Five men, wearing King Florian's livery, blocked her way. "Stand aside, please," she said, summoning all the command she could put into her voice. "Let me pass."

"We've got orders," one of them, the leader by his manner, told her. "King wants to see you."

"For what?" Ashen said.

"King'll tell you in his own good time. Now come along."

"No—"

But before she could protest further, a heavy cloth was thrown over her, cutting off her muffled scream. She recognized a flash of brocade, something fit for covering a window, before darkness cut off her vision. Pressure through the brocade at arm and knee level told her that she was being trussed securely.

She feared the worst. But none of the men seemed inclined to take liberties with her. Perhaps they were under order—but order from whom? Florian? If so, why? But there was nobody to answer her. She felt herself being picked up and carried away, in what direction she did not know though she felt the bite of cold, even through the heavy cloth. Presently she was thrown, none too gently, into what had to be a wagon, judging by the creak of its wheels, and she began a jouncing journey to a destination equally unknown.

Obern, she thought despairingly. My friend. If only he knew what was happening. He could help me. . . .

In the Council chamber, the Dowager Ysa and Lord Royance met with the Chieftain of the Sea-Rovers, who was accompanied by one of his number, a small man who, inexplicably, carried a drum with him. From the moment she laid eyes on Snolli she knew why her son's feeble efforts at negotiating a pact had come to naught. This was a wily old sea-eagle. He had undoubtedly been greatly amused at Florian's bungling.

"Let us be frank with one another," the Dowager said. She sat at the head of the table, her hands folded in such a way that the Four Great Rings were plainly visible, and Royance occupied the chair opposite. "You could be thought of as invaders of our land, but we choose to welcome you as valued allies instead."

"That's a sound decision," Snolli said. "So far, all we have invaded is an empty keep and some of the land around it."

Ysa had to acknowledge the truth in that. She noted also the lack of title, and put it down to simply his not knowing how to address her. "You are called the Chieftain, are you not?" she said.

"People still call me 'Your Majesty' even though properly, since I am no longer the wife of a King but only his widow, I should be known as 'Your Highness.' "

"Then 'Your Majesty' it is," Snolli said. He grinned. "D'you happen to have something to cut the dust of the road?"

Now Ysa's lips twitched with amusement in spite of herself. She had seen how thoroughly the Chieftain and his companions had sluiced down enough to cut weeks of road-dust just an hour before, at the wedding party. Nevertheless, she gave a signal and presently a page brought a pitcher and goblets.

"That'll do for me," Snolli said, taking the pitcher. "Now, bring some for Her Majesty and our friends."

At this Ysa laughed outright and even Royance made a muffled sound of amusement. "How refreshing! You remind me of how artificial life has become here in Rendelsham Castle!" she exclaimed.

Royance spoke up, though he had been asked to the meeting only as a witness. "Yes, I agree. I think we can bring much to each other, your people and ours." He nodded at the Dowager. "Pray continue, and forgive my interruption."

The small man spoke up. "All that's as may be." He began to stroke the surface of the drum as if unaware of what he was doing. "We need to see what terms you're proposing. And how they fit with the terms we're proposing. My lord. Your Majesty," he added, almost as an afterthought. He accepted the fresh tray the page brought, and poured for both Ysa and Royance before serving himself.

Snolli turned to his companion. "This is Kasai, my Spirit Drummer. He is one of my most trusted advisers for he can see past the veil that separates this world from others."

Doubtful of any such thing, Ysa thought of the little furred flyer, Visp, tucked in its cage in the room high atop the tallest tower in Rendelsham. This creature, summoned through Ysa's successful invoking of a certain spell, served much the same purpose for the Dowager. She nodded, pretending to understand. "It is good to have help of this kind," she said. "For we never know when we will need it most."

"Just so, Your Majesty. Now, let's get down to business. Perhaps it will be better if I tell you what the Sea-Rovers want, and then you tell us what you're willing to give. Then we can start bargaining." Snolli grinned, his strong teeth showing white against his beard. "How say you, lady?"

Vastly amused and diverted as she had not been since the day she had forced a marriage proposal out of Florian for his new bride, Rannore, Ysa inclined her head graciously. "Please," she said. "Begin."

First, ships. Rendel boasted but a handful of ships of war, and those were falling to pieces. But a few merchants' vessels could be commandeered and refitted to add to the Rendelian navy, which the Sea-Rovers proposed to man. Next, full title to the old Ashenkeep, renamed New Vold Keep. This much land, reaching from the southernmost shore to a slight narrowing between the River Rendel and the Barrier River at the spot where the road forked with one branch leading to the city and the other toward the Oakenkeep. Patrol of the road from New Vold Keep to this fork. The eastern stretch of land to extend from the spot where the Rendel joined the Rowenstream and on south to the coast. The western boundary the Barrier River. Southern boundary the sea.

It was roughly the area the House of Ash had called its own, when it was still in its fullness of strength. Ysa glanced at Royance, who nodded. "Agreed," she said.

Reciprocal help, especially along the borders, to quell the increasing number of raids by the Bog-men. "We can take care of our own, Your Majesty," Snolli said. "In fact, we did so just a day or so before we started our journey here. But we aren't horse riders by nature. It goes hard with most of us to patrol the way the lands need looking after, both yours and ours. Our backsides suffer, if you don't mind my saying so." He grinned with perfectly transparent cunning and again Ysa had to stifle a smile. "So if we take sea and land patrols and your people take horse patrol, between us we should be able to drive those raiders right back where they belong, don't you agree?"

"I'm certain that we can work out something along that line," Ysa said. "Royance?"

"I will speak with Count Harous, who is the Lord High Marshal of Rendel, and work out the details as I have heard them discussed. Will this be acceptable?"

"Of course," Snolli said with a dismissive wave of his hand. "There'll be fighting enough to go around, I'll warrant, judging from what we've seen so far."

"Is there anything else?" Ysa said.

The Chieftain turned serious. "Food," he said bluntly. "Your Majesty, if we do not have access to the storehouses here in the city, our people will starve. What we brought with us when we fled the north is gone. We hoped to be able to sustain ourselves, but this unseasonable cold will not allow our crops to thrive, and too much hunting will leave no meat for later. We have already eaten more fish than we like."

"We here in Rendel face the same problems," Ysa said. "We have been prudent in laying food by, but even you must recognize that the supply is not inexhaustible."

"We don't ask for much. Just enough to keep us going until the sun starts warming the fields again or we can figure a way to use the shelters some farmers have invented. They keep the ground and grain warm and let it grow, y'see. We are people who once lived in northern lands, perhaps a little rougher around the edges than the ones who call themselves Nordors, but they are our kindred by birth even as we now seek to become your kindred by adoption."

Ysa suddenly remembered the nobleman who had come years ago, seeking permission for his people to enter Rendel, and the way she had turned him out over a slight involving the wretched manners of the then Prince. Perhaps—no, doubtless—she had acted in too much haste. But he had never returned, and she had had too much occupying her attention to think about it.

Snolli was still speaking. "Your Majesty has to be aware as much as we are, that there is a great danger building in the far North."

A whispering sound filled the chamber and the hairs on the back of the Dowager's head stirred. She knew Power when she encountered it—but where was it coming from? Then she realized that the small man, Kasai, was stroking his drum, and it was from him that the Power emanated. She had not believed Snolli, certain that he was merely boasting. Who would have thought such a rough people could be possessed of access to Power? And yet here it was, in her very presence, so palpable she might have reached out and touched it. She shivered a little, and touched the Four Great Rings, to comfort herself with the knowledge of her own store of Power.

"Aye, danger riding upon danger and no man can know when it will come upon us, but it is sure to do." Kasai half spoke, half sang, in rhythm to his drum. His eyes were closed, his face perfectly devoid of expression. His words might have been the results of drinking too deeply of the wine except that his goblet was untouched. The Power surrounded him, almost visible in its aura. "Perhaps a year, perhaps not until the son of the Chieftain's son is a man full-grown. And yet they will come." Then he seemed to awaken. He glanced at Snolli. "Pardon, Chieftain."

"No pardon necessary," Snolli said. "You speak true as always. As I told you, Kasai is a Spirit Drummer, and he can see what others cannot."

"That is a great gift. Please, tell me more."

Snolli took another pull at his goblet and refilled it. "Cyornas NordornKing is the guardian of the Palace of Fire and Ice. What he guards has begun to stir, and so he will face it first. He cannot prevail alone. Nor can your southern land, not without our help. The Great Foulness, as Cyornas terms it, will come down the coastline, pushing Nordorn refugees before it. The Sea-Rovers have fought minions of this Great Foulness, when we were forced to flee as well. We know how it is done. Help us to live, Your Majesty, and in return my fleet, and the command of whatever fighting ships you possess, are at your service."

Andre Norton & Sasha Miller

Ysa sat back in her chair, impressed in spite of herself. Who would have thought someone so rough and earthy could be capable of such eloquence, let alone have a follower who could tap into the Power simply by stroking his fingers over a drum? She glanced at Royance. He seemed as much taken by Snolli's proposal as she.

He cleared his throat. "Your Majesty, we have heard true words spoken by the Chieftain of the Sea-Rovers and by his companion as well. As both have noted, he has fought what presses down on us daily, and which we will not escape fighting in our turn, however long it takes to arrive in our midst. There is no doubt in my mind that the unseasonable cold that is plaguing us currently is a harbinger of worse to come—like the breeze that signals rain. So if I have advice to give you, it is this. Accept Snolli's proposals in full measure, giving even more than was asked, that both our peoples may survive the coming storm."

"Then I accept," the Dowager said. "Send for a scribe, ink, and seals." She arose. "Tomorrow, the treaty will be ready for our signatures."

"You're a fair woman, and smarter than most. Here, let's clap hands on our bargain."

To her dismay, Snolli spat into his hand and held it out to her to take. She looked at Royance, appalled, but he was just sitting there, head averted and eyes closed, pinching the bridge of his nose and hiding his face as best he could. She thought she could see his shoulders shake.

Snolli was waiting. And so, summoning all the statecraft of which she was capable and remembering that different peoples had different customs, the elegant Queen Dowager of Rendel summoned up a bit of moisture in her own mouth and managed to spit it into the palm of her soft, manicured hand. Snolli grasped it with enough enthusiasm to sway her on her feet.

"You'll never regret it, lady," he said. "Kasai?"

The small man likewise offered a spittle-laced, hard hand for her to take. And then, both insisted on the same ceremony with Lord Royance who had to stand and follow his royal lady's lead.

❧

The instant she could get away, the Dowager Ysa retired to her own chambers. There she scrubbed her hands and then took the secret stairway up to her private tower room, where her little messenger Visp awaited her. She would stir it from its laziness. For too long Visp had lounged idle in its silk-lined basket, dining on dried fruit and nuts, doing nothing as Ysa was consumed by the various details attendant upon a royal wedding.

If Kasai, the Spirit Drummer, was correct, she had some time. If her plans worked out and Obern and Ashen married, any son of theirs would not be a man for many years yet. Still, she could not afford to be complacent. The attack could always come sooner, and without warning.

In addition to wanting to verify Kasai's predictions, she wanted to try a new element of her magical connection with Visp. Heretofore, she had had to wait until Visp returned, to take the information that Visp had gleaned. However, she had discovered a new spell, whereby she might be able to catch a glimpse of what Visp saw, while it was happening.

According to her habit, she removed her cosmetics, dressed in the simple velvet robe, and intoned the spell. Her preparations thus accomplished, she drew the curtain and pushed open the window. Then she took the little winged, furry creature from its comfortable bed and held it up so she could peer into its sleepy eyes. "Go," she told it, "and report all that you learn."

Then she gave it a toss toward the north window of the tower room. Visp flapped uncertainly, still drowsy, and righted itself. Then it began to fly in the direction Ysa desired. Before it had reached the curtains covering the window, it had become invisible.

Ysa took a few moments to touch up her appearance and dress herself once more, and then settled into her red velvet chair to wait. She would see if her new spell was having enough effect to bother with strengthening or making permanent, and then, whatever her decision, she would retire below to await her messenger's arrival back to the tower room. She closed her eyes.

A vision of the countryside began to form. She recognized Rendelsham Castle, even from aloft, as Visp circled it in flight, seeking a direction. Then the little flyer began to head out over the countryside, not due north as Ysa had desired, but more to the north and west. She noted a cart moving along a road, and noted also that Visp seemed to want to fly down closer to this crude vehicle. The Dowager sent a mental command to her furred servant and the little creature—reluctantly, or so it seemed to Ysa—headed once more northward.

The connection began to fade. But she could see the usefulness of it. Later, when there was time, she would reinforce the spell and make it permanent. Now, however, satisfied that she could contact her messenger if the need were great enough, the Dowager then descended the tower stairs. She wanted to write a letter, for it was time and past time to renew negotiations with the people of the North. Now she regretted the poor reception she had given their envoy—what was his name—Count Bjauden. He had never returned after that one unfortunate evening years ago, when Florian had been so rude to him.

In addition, she needed to show herself to those of the wedding guests who were staying on for a few days after. And also she wanted to keep an eye on her son. King Florian had had a very satisfied look on his face when last she glimpsed him at the feast following the ceremony, and she felt sure it had nothing to do with his new status as a bridegroom.

Five

*O*bern couldn't find Ashen anywhere, though he looked in all the public rooms and even dared peek into some of the private ones as well. He made his way outside and along the covered walkway toward the building in which her apartment was located. As if she had been waiting for him, a young woman rushed out, weeping uncontrollably, and caught him by the arm.

"You're Obern, of the Sea-Rovers, aren't you?"

"I am."

"Oh, sir, sir, please help!" the girl cried. "My lady's been taken—"

"Calm yourself," Obern said. He gently disengaged the young woman's fingers from his sleeve. She had it in such a tight grip she seemed fair to tear the samite. "What do you mean, your lady's been taken?"

"Just that, sir!" To her credit, the girl wiped her eyes on her sleeve, obviously trying not to create a scene. "Lady Ashen. She's gone."

"I know she's nowhere to be found, but—"

"Come inside, please do, and I'll tell you what I know. I saw everything."

Willingly, Obern followed the girl into Ashen's living quarters. Once inside, she began to talk even more freely, to the point of babbling.

"Oh, I saw it all—five men in King's livery, and they took her and covered her over with one of the formal tablecloths that was put away for the feast so they wouldn't be spoiled and plain cloth put in their place, and she fought but there was too many of them and I would have cried out only who'd tell what happened if they took me too, and oh, sir, you must help her—"

"Be sure of help," Obern said. His voice sharpened. "But you must take hold of yourself. First, what is your name?"

The girl gulped and wiped her eyes again. "I'm Ayfare, sir, Lady Ashen's maid and her friend, too."

"I can see that. Now, tell me why, if you know, should Lady Ashen be abducted?"

"I don't know about that, sir, but they took her. And the brocade was thick enough so nobody could hear her screaming, or maybe she fainted dead away. Oh, sir, can you help? *Will* you help?"

"My life and honor on it," Obern said grimly. His hand closed on the hilt on the sword at his side—one loaned by the man he had to consider his patron, Harous, and nowhere near as fine as the Rinbell sword his father had given to him as his man's gift. "But first I must know where these men took her."

"As to that, I don't know. I was afraid to show myself, as they went. But if they wore the King's livery, they must have taken her to one of the King's houses. Such has happened before, with a lady of rank."

Obern frowned. "Then the question is, which house?"

"Somebody who knows the King must be found to answer that, sir."

Obern nodded, thinking. Of those he was acquainted with here in the city, the one most likely to be aware of the workings of the King's mind would be Harous, but Obern knew he could not approach the High Marshal of Rendel. Count Harous himself had sporadically wooed Ashen. He would be sure to take whatever Obern told him, give nothing back, and go off in pursuit alone. Obern, cold with the anger of men from the North, was determined that when Ashen was rescued, it would be by his own hand and none other.

Most of the Rendelians Obern had become acquainted with were simple soldiers, not likely to know anything useful. Could he go directly to the Dowager? Obern's lips twisted wryly at the thought. All knew well the animosity that Ysa held for the bastard daughter of her greatest rival. Any concern that might be expressed by the Dowager publicly was, Obern knew, prompted by politics and liable to vanish without much warning. She would be highly unlikely to give him any assistance.

Who, then? Obern scowled, trying to think, and then a name and face swam into his mind.

Royance of Grattenbor, head of the Council. Obern had picked up the information that his family was ally to the House of Oak, and in his youth he had been a close comrade to the old King. Though past his prime, he had been a fighting man by choice and this was clear in his manner and bearing. Obern could see the resemblance between the burhawk that Royance had taken as his personal badge, and the man. If some of the fierce nature of that bird was his, then he would see the kind of injustice that had been perpetrated and would help, if only to the extent of aiming Obern in a likely direction. Making up his mind, he determined to seek a private audience with Royance.

"Stay here," he told Ayfare, "and try to act as if nothing untoward has happened, that your mistress is off enjoying herself at the feasting. I will return as soon as I am able."

"Oh, thank you, sir, thank you." Ayfare made a visible effort at control though she still shivered visibly. "My lady has spoken of you more than once. I think that if anybody can bring her back, it will be you, sir."

Stifling a flash of impulse to discover what else Ashen might have said in his favor, Obern set off to find the head of the Council of Regents.

He discovered Royance easily enough in the main Hall, in serious council with a small gathering of older men, among them the bride's grandfather. Obern knew that he himself could not push, unasked, into that company but a servant well might. He beckoned to a steward and sent him to Royance with the request that he be allowed a few moments' private audience, and to be sure to impress upon him that the matter was urgent.

He watched the steward whisper discreetly in Royance's ear. The white-haired noble glanced up, and Obern nodded vigorously. Then Royance nodded in turn and the steward returned with Royance's message.

"Lord Royance said I should show you to his privy office," the man said, "and he will join you in a few moments."

"Thank you."

Obern followed the servant up a flight of stairs. Beyond several passageways they came to a door which his guide opened, displaying a large, imposing chamber, with a smaller, private one beyond.

"Could I bring you something, sir?"

"Whatever Lord Royance might desire," Obern replied. "For me, nothing." The thought of such indulgence when he must make plain Ashen's danger aroused further the anger burning in him.

The servant bowed. Almost before the door closed behind him, Royance entered. To Obern's relief, he did not look irritated though his manner was brusque.

"What is so important?" Royance said. "We have made the decision with your people—have you some second demand, then?"

Obern had no idea what this meant. His anger had control of his tongue and he blurted it out his errand as bluntly as any Sea-Rover might. "It's Ashen, sir. Lady Ashen. She's been taken, and by what was seen, it's the King's doing!"

Royance's snowy eyebrows rose. He gestured to the chairs by the fireplace. "What kind of a moil is this, boy?" The door opened and the steward re-entered with a tray on which were a flask and two goblets. "Ah, excellent. Warmed wine. The good vintage—not what we're serving below. Drink. This will do you good, I promise." With a wave of his hand, Royance dismissed the servant and poured for both.

Reluctantly, Obern took the goblet the nobleman handed him and sipped. Royance had been right, he discovered. The hot beverage seemed to touch a spot that had been icy ever since Obern had heard the maid's story. He strove to control himself, to push back his anger—and his fear. "Thank you, sir. I apologize for my lack of manners, but you must know that I am relatively new-come to Rendel and—"

"Yes, yes, I know all that. Now, tell me what is important. You say Lady Ashen has been taken? And by the King? What kind of tangled tale is this?"

Obern repeated the maid's story, including the information that the abductors had boldly worn King's livery.

"Are you sure of the truth of this claim?" There was a snap in the old noble's question.

"She seemed very sure, sir. Royal livery is hard to mistake."

And so it was, unless the witness was blind. Deep red the uniforms were, and badged by a bear standing erect, on a background of oak leaves, all circled with the motto, Strength Prevails. Obern shifted in his chair, fighting a desperate desire for immediate action. Useless questions would only delay matters.

"All the Court guards and servants would be clad so," Royance said. He might have been musing to himself. Irritatingly, he was—as far as Obern was concerned—not the least bit alarmed. "Five of them, did you say?"

"So the maidservant said. She was in great fear for her lady."

Royance was silent long enough for Obern to drain his goblet of the heated liquid. Then the older man stirred. "It is good that you came to me, young Obern."

"When I first met you, at Count Harous's keep the night the old King died, I knew you for a man of honor," Obern said. He still seethed to be out doing something. It was hard for a man of action to maintain control among these too-tranquil courtiers.

"Aye, honor binds me, and I fear you have brought me word of less than honorable deeds. The King is here, to be seen with his new bride. However, that does not prevent any issuing of orders so his greatest rival"—Royance put a slight but unmistakable emphasis on the words—"be taken away in secret, that she might be dealt with later."

Obern's hand went again to his sword hilt. He did not dare ask in what manner Ashen would be "dealt with." Instead, he set his goblet on the tray and tried to assume a confidence fast being warped away. "Then we must bring her back," he said. "I mean, I must bring her back. I understand that you, as Head of the Council, could not afford to involve yourself in opening such a coil."

"You have a good head, young Obern. No, I could not because part of my influence rests upon my being impartial to all. I can offer you no open help. But what I can do is make as good as guess as I can, as to where the lady has been taken."

"Only give me a direction, and I will find her." Just let him get started! He was all but in the saddle already.

"It is best to believe that Florian has ordered her taken to a remote hold, well away from any of his other known haunts. Certainly not to the deserted Oakenkeep. Instead, he may well have had her taken to a certain hunting lodge, which, if rumor is to be believed, he has used for similar questionable projects in the past."

Obern swallowed hard, dreading the next question. Still, he must ask it. "Do—do you think she will be harmed?"

"I do not believe her in immediate danger," Royance said. Despite his reassurance, a trace of frown showed between his brows. "If I know our new King—and I *have* known him, from the time he could toddle—any plans for the lady are not yet decided beyond the fact that he wants her out of his sight and that of the Court. He can't be planning what you fear—dishonor. She is, after all, his half-sister. If he intended her death, he would have ordered an assassin—not a company of five men to subdue one slight girl instead. Therefore, if he intends her harm or disgrace ultimately, he also intends to be witness when it happens. No, the Lady Ashen is safe enough. But I would not tarry on the road."

Obern was already on his feet. "I will ride out at once, as soon as I can find a horse."

For the first time, Royance smiled slightly. "I think you might want to change clothes first."

Obern glanced down at the samite-and-velvet wedding garments and his face grew hot. "Yes, sir, I forgot I—I mean, I was in such a—" He stopped in confusion.

Royance's smile widened. "Never mind, young Obern. Believe it or not, I was in love once, too. Now. Can you read a map?"

"Yes, sir. All Sea-Rovers learn the art."

"Good. I will show you a map—I cannot give it to you, as I'm sure you must understand—showing you the location of the King's very private hunting lodge. You will have to memorize it and then convey the information to your companions. Oh, yes"—Royance held up a cautionary hand—"you must take with you a force at least equal to those who abducted Lady Ashen. To do otherwise would be romantic and heroic, to be sure, but also utter folly. This is a matter for planning, and force to meet force."

Obern bit back a hot retort. The old noble was correct. "You are wise in the ways of men," he said. "Indeed, I had pictured myself bursting in and snatching Ashen away—"

"And riding off with her on your saddlebow," Royance finished, a little wryly. "Believe me, young Obern, she will be no less grateful if you do not manage to get yourself killed in the attempt. Listen to me, and learn thereby."

"Yes, sir."

Then Royance arose and took a map of Rendel from a long drawer. He spread it out as Obern came to view it. "Here," he said, pointing to a dot on the map, hidden in a fold of what had to be mountains. "From this spot our late King used to hunt, and even fish in the nearby streams. Later, Florian used it as a hideaway where he and his current light-o'-love could cavort in privacy. At least, such privacy as could be found with a royal guard just outside."

Obern was already thinking of whom he could enlist to accompany him. Dordan, the archer, and Kather and Iaobim. These would be enough, against mere Rendelians. All three of these men had been with him at other times, when there had been trouble brewing, and were to be depended upon. He moved one of the nearby candles closer and studied the map, imprinting each detail upon his memory. Though Florian might not be planning Ashen's dishonor, there was nothing to suggest that his servants might not attempt such. "If the lodge is the place where they have taken Ashen, rest assured that I will find it," he said. "And if she is there, I will bring her back." Without being fully aware of what he was doing, Obern drew his sword a hand's-breadth from the scabbard and drove it back with a sound that echoed in the room.

Half an hour later, before the first hints of a chill and gloomy dusk were beginning to veil the western sky, Obern and his three men were hurrying across the river bridge beyond the city. A little beyond this, the road heading west branched, and Obern turned that way.

"Cart tracks," Iaobim said. He leaned forward in his saddle to view the dusty road. "Theirs, do you think?"

"Wouldn't they have horses?" Kather asked. "A cart would slow them."

"There are horse-tracks, off to the side. They'd use a cart for a prisoner, seems like," Iaobim said. "And especially if the lady was trussed up."

"Any chance of us overtaking them soon?" Obern was watching the sky dubiously.

"Not likely." Iaobim squinted upward as well. "We can make better time than a cart, but they can travel better after dark than we can. They must know the road, and we can't risk laming a horse if he stumbles over something like that." He pointed at one of many big rocks littering the way ahead. "Road's not kept up well. Looks like it's not been used, except for these tracks."

"If we must cut speed, at least take care," Obern said, teeth gritted. He urged his mount forward. "We've still got a few hours of daylight to our aid. Make the most of it."

The men with him nodded grimly. All were dressed warmly in thick wool with fur-lined cloaks drawn over their familiar chain mail, and Obern had another set of similar garments packed in saddlebags for Ashen when she was rescued. The men quickened their pace as much as they dared, but it was rough going. Full night had closed about before they reached a spot where the road became better. If Obern read the signs correctly, the ill-kept road behind them was a ruse to discourage any uninvited visitors when the King was at his pleasures. "We must be getting close." He kept his voice low.

"Aye. Wasn't that a flash of light just between those trees?" Dordan had loosened his bow. "Good thing there's a moon tonight so we can see where we're going."

They dismounted and tethered the horses loosely so the animals could crop grass as they would. Then they began to advance as noiselessly as possible in the direction where Dordan had spotted the telltale light.

Dordan had been correct. Cautiously, they reached the brush wall of a clearing. Beyond, in the open, stood what could only be the lodge. Obern knew at once the expectable layout, from a visit to one such establishment belonging to Count Harous. There would be one good-sized common room on the ground level, and four small bedrooms above. Probably only a single door, but possibly another to the rear, leading to a second small building used as a kitchen. This pattern depended on how much state the King chose to keep when he visited here. By the looks and size of the place, it was meant for the most-limited occupancy. The chimney indicated a large fireplace, where game could be roasted. A lantern candle shone in one window, and in the still air, they could hear men's voices arguing.

"I say we do what we please with the wench," one of them said.

"Not without the King's saying so, we can't. Can't you get it through your thick head this one's special, for him to go to all this trouble?"

"Stupid, she's the King's sister. Half-sister anyway. He sure didn't have her brought here for any games. At least not his personal self, that is."

A fourth voice spoke up, deeper, holding a note of authority. "Wouldn't matter to the King, the way his mind sets these days." Obern's hand went again to his sword hilt and he nearly drew it but stopped just in time. The ring of steel would have given them away immediately. He swallowed hard, to force down bile. "But we keep in mind it's him as calls the tune. We just hold her here until he comes. That's our orders."

There was some general grousing from within, but no real argument. Then, unmistakably, Ashen's voice, hoarse but with no real quaver of fear.

"If you know what's good for you, you'll take me back to the city at once!" she said.

"And who's to make us?" Deep Voice wanted to know. "Nobody even knows you're gone, m'lady."

"Plenty of people *will* miss me," Ashen replied defiantly. "It won't take long for them to discover what's happened."

"Even if they do," Deep Voice said, "they won't know which direction to come looking." He sounded a little amused.

"So? While we are waiting to see just who will come, you might see to a fire. I'm not dressed for this venture. Also, I want some water. I've been eating dust too long, no thanks to you." .

"Saucy wench. Very well. You, Nigal, go get some water. There's a well out yonder. Savros, build a fire. His Majesty wouldn't be pleased if his dear sister got chilblains." Deep Voice laughed at his own wit.

Obern glanced at his companions. They nodded in turn. They didn't need to be warned that as easily as the guardsmen's voices carried in the chill, still air, any noise those outside made would be as audible to enemy ears. Dordan carefully nocked an arrow to his bowstring. The well that Deep Voice had mentioned lay between where the Sea-Rovers lay hidden, and the main door to the lodge. Obern leaned closer to Kather. "See if there's a back door," he breathed.

Kather nodded and immediately began working his way through the shadows, disappearing around the corner of the lodge. He had no sooner gotten out of sight before Nigal came out, pail in hand. He began to work the windlass on the well. It creaked loudly—not good for those in wait. If that noise stopped too suddenly it would alert those within. But it did serve to cover Kather's movements, so he could go about his errand more rapidly than if he had to watch his step and avoid every twig in the path. Dordan bided his time, waiting until Nigal had finished drawing a bucket of water to the lip of the well, and had poured the contents into the pail. A night bird hooted; at that sound, the archer let fly his arrow and the King's man toppled to the ground and did not stir again.

Obern moved forward. In a few economical movements, he had snapped the arrow short, stripped off the man's scarlet livery coat, and pulled it over his own head. With any luck, when he went through the door those inside would hesitate for a fatal moment, thinking it was only their returning comrade. Then he nodded to Dordan and Iaobim. The bowman slung his favored weapon and, with Iaobim, drew sword.

As Obern fumbled with the bucket, making as much racket as he could while returning it to the well, the two men moved forward to take up positions on either side of the door. Then Obern left the pail where it was and returned up the path. He drew his sword, took a deep breath, and sent the door flying open with a well-placed kick. One man knelt at the fireplace, flint and steel already laid aside, feeding kindling to the flames. Two others stood watching. The fourth, probably Deep Voice, hovered near Ashen. For one dangerous moment, Obern allowed himself to look at her. Face pale, deep circles underlining her eyes, her white wedding garments rumpled, soiled and torn, nevertheless she was as beautiful as a fabled Seamaid in that instant.

Obern uttered a war-cry and charged straight for Deep Voice.

Dordan and Iaobim rushed to engage the two idlers and take them down. Savros leapt up and hurled himself between his leader and Obern. Precious moments were wasted before the Sea-Rover had cut him down. But by that time, Deep Voice had his hands on Ashen. One arm pressed her to his muscular body, and with his other hand, he held a dagger to her throat.

"So. Now what do we do, youngling?" Deep Voice said, surprisingly genial. "How did you track us? Never mind, it isn't important. It is all simple enough now. You come a step closer, and this lady dies. Oh, you can kill me then, of course, but what good will it do?"

This kind of man Obern knew well. There were fighting men in plenty, loyal to the man they served, who would be prepared to follow through on such a threat. Outnumbered as he was, still he represented a danger to them all.

"And you there, with the bow. Don't even think about using it. The lady would be dead long before you could let fly." Deep Voice dragged Ashen to her feet and, without shifting the dagger from her throat, moved with her toward the table. "I am Lathrom, sergeant in His Majesty's private guards. And you?"

"Obern, of the Sea-Rovers. With my friends."

"I've heard of you." Lathrom forced Ashen into a chair at the table. "So. Since we now have a situation where neither side can win, what do you say we talk about it?"

"What do you say we don't?" Kather stepped into the room behind him.

Even a hardened veteran like Lathrom could be taken by surprise. Instinctively he looked around, startled by the appearance of yet another enemy from an unexpected quarter. Obern launched himself unhesitatingly at the sergeant. The sheer momentum of his attack carried the both of them clear across the room to slam into the far wall. The sergeant took the brunt of it. Obern rolled over onto Lathrom, pinning him, and by the time his opponent had shaken his head clear, all three of Obern's companions were standing over them, swords drawn and ready.

"On the contrary, Kather," Obern said, panting slightly and allowing himself to grin. "We really should talk about the situation. Don't you agree, Sergeant?"

"I yield," Lathrom said. "Oh, you can take my word on it. I know when I'm overmatched."

Obern cautiously got to his feet and, after a moment, so did Lathrom. With great care, and making no sudden movements, the sergeant unbuckled his sword-belt and dropped it. His dagger was gone already, having been knocked flying when Obern tackled him. "Find the dagger," Obern said.

"I have it." Ashen had scrambled to her feet and retrieved it. The growing firelight shone on the bared blade. Though she did not hold the weapon the way a trained warrior might, still it was clear she knew the dagger's usefulness.

Obern longed to reach for her, to make sure she was unharmed, but this was no girl shaking with fear as he had expected to find. She stood as resolute as any Sea-Rover. "How are you, my lady?"

"Unharmed, but cold and thirsty. Hungry, too. And—" Her voice broke a little. "—so very, very glad to see you."

"And I, you. Kather, please go and get our horses. There is warm clothing for you in one of the saddlebags, my lady, and we brought food as well. We would be foolish to try to retrace our steps before morning, so we must stay here for the night. But we will be on guard." Obern turned to Lathrom. "You will understand, I trust, that we will have to tie you up?"

Lathrom shrugged. "I've given you my word. But go ahead and truss me as you will. It's no more than I would have done if the circumstances had been reversed. You have no cause to trust me overmuch."

"Good. In a way, you might consider it a compliment to you, seeing as how sorely you are overmatched."

Iaobim crossed the man's hands behind him, preparatory to binding him, but Obern stopped him. "Strangely enough, I do think we can take your word. Just tie one arm to the table, and make sure he can't unpick the knots. We wouldn't want you loose during the night, word or no word."

Iaobim grinned; a seafarer knew knotwork, and he was as able as any. In a few moments, he had Lathrom's right arm lashed to one leg of the table in such a way that he couldn't move without dragging it along with him, and the ends of the rope were tied to the opposite leg, out of Lathrom's reach.

Obern inspected Iaobim's handiwork, and nodded approval. "Good. You can still feed yourself. Now, Dordan, go and throw another good length on that fire."

Six

ithin an hour, they were warm and well fed. The bodies of the four dead guards had been dragged outside to be placed in the cart for transportation back to Rendelsham in the morning. The Sea-Rovers all unrolled mats and placed them around the room, guarding the doors even as they slept, having no wish to separate and occupy the rooms upstairs. Now all were snoring, including Lathrom who had no mat, but who seemed not to notice.

Obern sat up quietly. Ashen, her back to him, was sitting close to the fire that was banked for the night, on a rug made of the skin of some huge beast, her legs tucked under her. He arose from his mat and went to kneel beside her. "Are you still afraid?"

She glanced up at him. "No. I just couldn't sleep."

"Well," Obern said, trying to speak lightly, "you are over-stimulated, like a child who has had too many sweets. It isn't every day that one attends a wedding, then gets captured and taken off to the King's hunting lodge."

His attempt at joking was unsuccessful.

"I know," she said. Her body was tense. Her hands were curled into fists. "Why would Florian do this?"

Obern shrugged. "You're a threat to him, Ashen. You may not

understand or listen to rumors, but already there is opposition to the King. And you're the late King's daughter."

"I am who I am. Zazar named me truly—Ashen Deathdaughter. I want nothing except freedom to be what I choose to be!" Ashen's voice was vehement, though she kept her tone low.

"I know you have no part in their plots. If you could be free of this, you would. But it is happening anyway." He wanted so much to take her into his arms and give her comfort. But he knew that trust and need must be hers also, for her to accept it.

There was silence for a while. Ashen picked up a bit of kindling and stirred the ashes. The twig caught fire, and she tossed it into the fireplace. "All I could think of, when they took me, was how I wished you could come and find me. And then you did."

"How could I not?"

"You have always been my friend." She smiled a little. "Even when you were out of your head for a while, seeming to think I would drop you for the underwater ones, back in the Bog."

He smiled in response. "I don't even remember most of what happened, from the time I fell off the cliff until I awoke with you washing the blood off me. I thought I had died and a Seamaid, one of the Sea-ruler's daughters, was tending me."

"Your good sword is still back there, in the ruins of Galinth. And your armor."

"Armor is replaceable," Obern said. "But I admit that I do miss my man-sword. It was Snolli's best, of Rinbell make. It fights for me."

She seemed not to hear. "You tell me that the King is jealous of me. That means I must have a little power. When we return to the city, I will see what I can do to have your sword returned to you."

"Thank you." There was another silence and he moved closer to her. "Ashen, you know that as long as you are alone and unprotected, you are vulnerable to another such incident as just happened. And I might not be there to rescue you again unless—"

"Unless what?"

"Unless you married me."

She sat up straight then, pulling away from him. "I have told you never to speak that way—"

"I know, but there is news. Snolli, my father—he is the Chieftain of the Sea-Rovers—told me how things are at New Vold. Crops are slow in growing, because of the unseasonable cold, and many have sickened and died. Among them was Neave, my wife."

"Oh, Obern. I am so sorry."

"Yes. She was a good woman. But we were handfasted without knowing much of each other. She did her duty." He paused, for the first time wondering what this ordered mating had really meant to Neave. She had ever been a silent girl. "Snolli said that she died well. That is high praise with my people. I hope that they will say that about me."

Ashen sat quietly; her fisted hands slowly loosened. But a flush stained her cheeks. Obern dared to close fingers on one of her hands, and held it. The flesh was icy-cold in his grasp. She raised her head.

"Obern, I know that you must have feelings which must be understood. You must think carefully before you decide what it is you really want."

"I had plenty of time, while we were at Count Harous's keep, and later in the city. My feelings have not changed except to grow stronger. If you had given me the least encouragement, I would have set Neave aside, which is another custom of my people, providing for her for the rest of her life, if only I could have you. That she died does not change my feelings, except to feel sorry for her."

"Obern, you must know that I do not love you the way that you seem to love me. You are the one on whom I know I can rely. My first thought, when they took me, was that I hoped you would find me. But I do not think this is enough."

He had hoped not to bring practical reality into this. But he could see no other way. "This is a union that is good for our peoples,

Ashen. It cements the bond between the Sea-Rovers and Rendel. And, perhaps, someday it might even serve to ease the strain between Rendel and the Bale-Bog."

Ashen blinked, and Obern knew that she had not considered that side of the question. He pressed his advantage.

"I know that you do not love me—not yet, anyway. But do you at least see me as a friend?"

The stain on her cheeks grew deeper. "Yes."

"Then it will be enough. You will see." Gently he drew her to him and kissed her. "Now, sleep. Nothing will disturb you, I swear it. Nothing ever again."

He settled her beside him on the fur rug and covered them both with his cloak. As the warmth of the fire and of his body crept through her she began slowly to relax. Presently she slept.

Never again, he vowed silently. Never will I allow anything to trouble you, Ashen, now that you are mine. My beloved.

Next morning, before they started back to Rendelsham, Obern drew Lathrom aside for a private conversation. The two men spoke in earnest for some time. Then Obern gave orders that Lathrom should not be tied again and, instead, be given his freedom. His companions raised their eyebrows at this, but made no protest.

The return journey was much more sedate, less filled with drama and danger, than had been the one to the King's hunting lodge. Ashen, now mounted on one of the guards' horses, rode with Obern, Dordan close beside. Lathrom drove the cart where the bodies of the dead guards had been laid, and Kather and Iaobim brought up the rear. They could all hear the buzz of speculation from those townspeople who observed them as they entered the city and rode straight to the castle.

"What do you plan to say to the King?" Ashen said.

"I confess, I have no plan. But do not fear. Thanks to you saving my life, I seem to have gotten a reputation for being lucky, and I will rely on that luck to guide me."

Grooms and guards greeted them, taking charge of the wagon and its contents. The driver, Lathrom, accompanied Ashen and the Sea-Rovers at Obern's insistence. "You were fair and just in following your orders," Obern said, "and I will try to save you from being executed for failing to carry out your mission."

"If you do, and I live, I will resign from the King's Guard and become your liege man if you will have me."

"Then all the more reason for me to try."

Obern instructed a steward to go and request an audience with the King, the Dowager, and Lord Royance. In a surprisingly short time, they were escorted into what could only be the Council chamber. Not only Florian and his mother and Lord Royance awaited, but also Count Harous and two other members of the Council—Gattor of Bilth, and Wittern, head of the House of Rowan.

The King, seated at the head of the table, looked up. It was hard to read the expression on his face. He motioned to another steward, who began handing around goblets of warmed wine. Another goblet sat close at Florian's hand, and it was plain to see that he had already made good use of it. "I am told that you have returned our dear sister to us," the King said, "from where she was taken away through no instructions of mine. And here she is. Come, warm yourselves and know that we thank you."

Obern took a step forward and bowed. "Our duty to the King, and to the King's sister," he said. He glanced around the table. "And our duty to you all as well."

"You speak fairly," the Dowager said. She sat at the King's right, her hands clasped in front of her so that the Four Great Rings were plainly visible. "Pray, speak on and tell us the details of this unfortunate incident."

Royance, at his place opposite the King, shifted in his seat. "Yes, please tell us what has happened so that we may reward or punish, as the occasion demands."

"As for punishment, four of the five who took Lady Ashen are dead. And their leader, Sergeant Lathrom, whom I believe to be a true and honorable man, tells me that he was acting under orders he accepted as legitimate, though now he has doubts."

"Legitimate orders. From whom?" Florian scowled.

Obern knew he must tread carefully now, if he hoped to save Lathrom's life. From the moment he had hurled himself at the man and overpowered him, he had formed a liking for Lathrom. That was the way with warriors sometimes, that in vanquishing a worthy enemy one gained a friend. "He tells me that he believed the orders came from you, King Florian. Otherwise, he would not have dared raise a hand against the lady."

There was a stir at the table, and a moment of almost palpable shock.

"But," Obern continued, "later he came to doubt this. Now he believes that the person who instructed him merely pretended that these were your orders, so as to discredit you in the eyes of your enemies."

Florian turned his frowning gaze on Lathrom. "Is this correct, Sergeant?"

Lathrom went down on one knee, his head bowed. "Yes, my King," he said, his deep voice rumbling in his throat. "Obern speaks truly. I do not say this to save my own life, but because this is what I now believe."

"This giver of orders. Does he have a name?"

"I saw no one," Lathrom said. "The orders came in the form of a note that passed through many hands before it came into mine." He took a folded piece of paper out of his doublet and handed it to Obern, who in turn gave it to the King.

Florian merely glanced at it and tossed it onto the table. Gattor, however, picked it up and read it aloud. " 'Take Lady Ashen to hunting lodge at earliest opportunity. King's orders.' " His eyebrows rose though his habitual sleepy expression remained unchanged. "This lends a certain credence to the fellow's story."

Florian laughed, a braying sound that made the Dowager wince. "If I had truly given such an instruction, I can assure you there would have been no evidence later. Therefore, I choose to believe you, Sergeant. Get up, get up. Your life is spared. But I will find out who was at the bottom of this plot, and he won't be so lucky."

Gratefully Lathrom got to his feet, and as he passed by Obern, he murmured, "Your luck seems to rub off." He grinned. "The men were talking."

Obern nodded. Then he bowed again to the King. "Your Majesty is both merciful and just. I think Lord Royance made some mention of a reward."

"Oh, yes, yes, of course. How much do you want? I'll have the coin brought at once."

"The wealth I desire cannot be measured in coin," Obern said. "I petition most humbly for the hand of Lady Ashen in marriage."

At that, the people around the Council table reacted in various ways—the Dowager startled but not disapproving; Lord Gattor looking even more sleepy; Count Harous frowning; Lord Wittern looking surprised; the King saying, "No!" Only Lord Royance hid a smile behind his hand.

"I am of high but not royal birth," Obern said. "Further, I represent a people who can be strong allies to Rendel. What could be more natural than to cement this alliance with a marriage between this lady and myself?"

"What, indeed," said the Dowager. She turned and favored her son with the kind of level stare that, had it been turned on any other, would have reduced the recipient to a bundle of shaken nerves. "And you dare disapprove?"

"I spoke hastily," the King said. "After all, a member of the royal family, and a Sea-Rover—"

"Who, I must remind you, very likely saved your sister's life," Obern said. He had to raise his voice to command attention. "Can you possibly imagine that the enemy who ordered her capture had her ultimate safety in mind?"

"Young Obern speaks truly," Royance said. "But I think we should hear from the lady. After all, she does not strike me as one who would go meekly submitting to her fate, whatever it might be." He bowed to Ashen. "How say you, lady?"

Ashen stepped forward. "I had thought not to marry until I

found one who caught my heart. Now I understand that this is most likely a childish dream. I know that marriage will protect not only me, but also my brother, the King, from another such incident intended to bring dishonor upon him and even upon me. I have learned that marriage with Obern seals many friendships important to the country. Obern is my friend, whom I respect. Therefore, for all these reasons I will marry him if my brother and those members of the Council here present agree."

Though, strictly speaking, the Dowager had no real vote in Council matters, she spoke up first. "It is a solution of which I approve. And so should you all."

Gattor nodded at once, closely followed by Wittern. Royance gave his approval by saying, "Aye" in a firm voice. The Dowager stared at Harous. Reluctantly, as if the movement hurt and after a long silence, he nodded. Then the Dowager turned to her son.

"You see how it stands. We could go ahead without your approval now, but it will go better if you agree."

Florian made an impatient gesture. "Oh, very well. I'll even let the wedding take place here in the castle. Only not too soon after my own."

"Done," Royance said. He turned to Ashen and Obern, who now held her hand tightly. "Four seven-days from now. That will give us all time to prepare. And may I have the honor of being the first to kiss the prospective bride?"

The time flew by for Ashen. She had thought herself busy before, with the King's wedding, and herself only a minor participant. This, though much smaller in scale, occupied almost her every waking moment with this detail and that needing her attention. If she had not been able to slip away for an hour or so each day to the quiet of the hidden library, she felt she surely would have gone mad. Ayfare's delight in having her mistress returned to her unharmed was almost swamped as well, for she found herself in charge of what didn't need Ashen's personal approval.

Ashen thought at first to wear blue, the Ash color, but delicacy forbade that she wear the dress Harous had given her when first he had brought her out of the Bog. She would, however, wear the Ash badge necklace he had also given her. She had been somewhat apprehensive about Harous's reaction to her actually going through with the marriage to Obern, but he seemed to have accepted the inevitable with good-enough grace. Lord Royance's kind explanations helped.

"The Lord Marshal has too much ambition," he told her. "One day it may be his undoing, but not yet, thanks to your Obern. I like that boy. He has initiative. He also had wit enough to turn what could have been a very unpleasant situation into one where the King's dignity was preserved. I can only hope that the King has sense enough to know, and remember, what Obern did for him."

Royance also told her that an apartment was being readied for her in the main building of the castle. "This is yours permanently," he said, "for your use whenever you are in the city. It is on the same floor, though in another wing, as the King's apartments, and the Dowager's."

Ashen nodded, her feelings decidedly mixed. She had enjoyed living apart from Ysa and her son, but Royance assured her that she could not flout protocol by refusing. And there would be Obern to protect her. More and more she recognized that she had made a wise decision in agreeing to marry him. However, more than once, she wished they could just duck into the Great Fane one afternoon and have the priest, Esander, say the words over them and be done with it.

Obern, she discovered, felt much the same way. "But this is what I get for marrying a great lady," he said, laughing. "And I'll put up with anything at all for the sake of that!"

He, also, found his respite from the hustle and bustle of the second royal wedding in one season, by taking some of the Sea-Rovers—along with Lathrom, who had resigned from the King's Guard and was now Obern's closest companion—and going into the Bog. There, following his dim memory and aided by a rough map

Ashen gave him, they located the ruined city of Galinth, and retrieved Obern's Rinbell sword. Expectably, the Bog-men discovered the incursion and attacked. The Sea-Rovers fought them off with only minor injuries to their number, and Ashen discovered later that her heart pounded strangely in her throat at the thought that Obern might have been wounded or even killed.

I must love him at least a little, she thought, to feel this way. And so she turned to the preparations with renewed energy. Feeling in some obscure manner that so doing would honor Obern's bravery, she decided also to wear the opalescent stone bracelet she had found in the depths of the Galinth catacombs, on a man whose body had not been buried there.

To nobody's great surprise, no culprit was ever found for Ashen's abduction, and she put the incident aside, knowing that the mystery would never be solved. From now on, Obern would be there to protect her from anything untoward. Other various comings and goings and news from the outside world passed her by almost unremarked. She noted that the man who would be her father-in-law, Snolli, was remaining in Rendelsham, not caring to make the arduous journey twice in such a short time. When she was introduced to him, he merely looked her up and down at first. "I remember you," he said by way of greeting. "Saw you when they took you out of the Bog. You were thin and pale then, and you still are. But Obern wants you, and that's good enough for me." Then he enfolded her in a hug that nearly cracked her ribs, and went on his way.

The small man, Kasai, was a little more forthcoming. "We were tracking Obern, y'see, and watched while the Boggers attacked them as was taking the two of you away. We had to fight the leavings." He grinned. "D'you want me to look into the future for you? I have that gift."

Ashen considered his offer, knowing that it was one not made lightly. Eventually she shook her head. "I think I would rather not know what lay ahead. If I could change it, I might, and then who knows what else would be disturbed because of that change? And if I could not change it, and it was unpleasant, then I would be even more unhappy than I would have been, innocent of any foreknowledge. But I do thank you for the offer."

"Smart woman. I don't often say that." Then Kasai bowed and followed his Chieftain.

The rough ways of the Sea-Rovers did not offend her, for she had been brought up in the Bog where the crudity of their manners would have been thought of as foppish affectations. In fact, she felt more at home in their company than she did with the Rendelians, even though she had come to like much of this kind of life. However, she did begin to be disturbed because of a certain change in Obern's manner toward her now that he was among his own kind. Sea-Rovers, she surmised, thought it unmanly to display open affection for their women. But, she thought, perhaps that was only for display. Surely, in private, he would be different, warmer and more loving.

Others came and went at Rendelsham Castle, including a new ambassador from the far northern lands. His name was Gaurin and, it was said, he was the son of the other ambassador, Count Bjauden, who had never returned from his mission. Ashen put this information aside, concerning, as it did, things that had happened long before she had arrived in the city. Perhaps she would meet him at the wedding, and perhaps not.

Before she knew what had become of the four seven-days suggested by Royance, she was standing with Obern before a priest of the Great Fane of the Glowing—not Esander, but one far greater than he. She felt numb, a little disconnected from the ceremonies, as she repeated the marriage vows. Beside her, she felt Obern trembling and knew that he was affected likewise. And then it was over, and the marriage procession left the Fane to cross the courtyard and go to the Great Hall of the castle where a feast—considerably smaller in scale than Florian's, but still great enough to honor his sister—awaited the guests. Ashen hoped that at least some of these guests were there to honor her and her new husband, and not in hopes of getting a good meal in a land where food was growing scarce.

At least the weather had abated somewhat. Though not nearly warm enough for late summer, at least the air was not so chill that a fur-lined cloak over her white, blue-trimmed dress was a necessity, if she were quick to get indoors again. Obern's dark green doublet was trimmed with fur at neck and sleeves, and bore silver-and-gold embroidery on it. A memory stirred. Green, like that half-forgotten green cord Zazar had shown her once, long ago, in another life. Obern's Rinbell sword hung at his side. Ashen walked with him hand in hand, and they exchanged glances, smiling.

"You are my husband," she murmured, and he squeezed her fingers.

"Not yet," he said. "Forgive me, but I cannot wait a moment longer. The people celebrating won't miss us."

They entered the castle. When they reached a spot where the corridors branched, he swerved aside abruptly and, half running, led her, to the accompaniment of much good-natured laughter, raillery, and rustic jokes, out of the procession, down the hallway, and to the new apartment that had been set aside to them. Then he locked the door behind them and gathered her into his arms.

An hour later, with Ashen feeling as if her blushes would warm the entire castle even better than the fires roaring in the fireplaces, they joined the party in the Great Hall where the feasters were already at work on the platters of food. The King and his new bride apparently had made their appearances and then left, but the Dowager was present and holding her own kind of court. Harous was there, of course, with Marcala hanging on his arm. He nodded at Ashen briefly, and murmured a perfunctory congratulation. The other woman looked her up and down, smiling knowingly at Ashen's late entrance, and her face grew even hotter. She was afraid Marcala would come up to her and make some untoward remark, but instead the lady clutched Harous's arm more tightly, and turned aside.

Ashen caught sight of Snolli and his retinue, crowded around the kegs of ale, and laughing at some joke known only to them. She hoped it wasn't about the—she had to admit it—somewhat rude introduction to married life that she had just undergone.

Obern's friend Lathrom was with them, his demeanor easy and free. Obviously he had been accepted completely by them all. In the loft, the orchestra struck up a tune. Nobody was on the floor yet for, according to custom, the bridal couple led the first dance.

"One only, and then I'll beg off," Obern said. "But you enjoy yourself. I know how you love it."

He led her out to the middle of the floor, and other couples— led by Harous and Marcala as befitted his rank—immediately lined up behind them. Then they began to tread the stately and sedate measures of a popular dance.

Obern did well enough, but Ashen knew that he had no real talent or love for it, the way she did. And so when the dance had concluded, he bowed over her hand and went to join his father and his companions. Another man immediately presented himself.

"May I have the honor?"

Ashen saw that this one had chosen to dress himself top to toe in spring green. Suddenly, unbidden, the entire memory of that long-ago evening swam before her eyes. Her Protector, Zazar, had brought out a knotted ball of cords, and pulled forth four, seemingly at random. She had always wondered why. Now, with a start, Ashen realized that Zazar had been seeking knowledge of the future.

"Queen," Zazar had said, indicating the brightest of the three gold cords. "King." The dullest. "Prince." That was the thinnest of them all, lacking many knots and none evidently intricate. Then she had picked up the green thread. "Kin unknown."

Ashen remembered the Wysen-wyf's next words so clearly she could almost hear them. "The times swing us along more swiftly. It is not your clan color, but you are green, yes. Untaught in much, yes." She had picked up the green cord and begun running it along between thumb and forefinger. It was slender, hardly thicker than the one she had named Prince, and the knots on it were also few. But of those several were doubled and redoubled.

As Zazar held each of those knots, for an instant, Ashen thought she felt pressure at the nape of her neck as if those strong old fingers had gripped her instead. A tingle of excitement, faint but definite, had spread through her whole body, and she felt a repeat of it now.

The green should have stood for Obern, she thought. But it did not. Why? What cruel joke of fate was this? "Who are you?" she said, half-dazed.

"I am the Nordorn ambassador and my name is Count Gaurin. I already know yours. Please, Lady Ashen, will you dance?"

"Of course," she said through lips even number than they had been during the wedding ceremony. He took her hand and the tingle deepened. As if she were a jointed doll, she went through the movements of the dance. Then she stumbled, for his presence was making her dizzy enough to fear that she might faint.

"Are you ill?"

She glanced at him, blinking. "I—I don't think so. But the crowds, all the commotion—"

"And I daresay you have eaten nothing this day."

"I couldn't."

"Please. Let me find you a place to rest, away from so many people, and I will bring you a plate and something to drink."

She started to refuse him, but looking into his eyes, could not. If anything, he was even more handsome than either Harous, whom she had thought the best-favored of men, or Obern. Her husband. A strong and comely man. She tried to summon up his image, the red-gold hair and eyes the color of the sea, to set in front of the vision of the man she was looking at, but the effort failed.

This one was lean of face, with chiseled, aristocratic features. He had hair the shade of honey, darker than her own, eyes a shade halfway between green and blue, and his skin was the sort that turned brown under the sun. In spite of the unseasonable weather, his face was burnt, most agreeably, darker than his hair. There was a grace to his movements, strangely complimentary to his obvious physical strength. She thought she could never have enough of looking at him, and brought herself back to reality only with an effort.

"Yes, yes, thank you. A slice of cold fowl, and some spiced apple juice, please. I gave orders to the chef, to have some made for me."

He led her to an alcove, half-hidden from the room, and pulled up a couple of chairs and seated her in one. "I will return at once," he said.

Ashen stared through the bubbled and wavery glass of the window, seeing nothing. Scarcely aware of what she was doing, she ran her hand over her body. She could still feel the touch of her new husband's fingers imprinted there, awakened by her gesture. How could she look at this—this stranger, and know that what she felt, seeing him, was only a pale imitation of the ecstasy that awaited her when, if—

She shut off the thought with an effort. No, she told herself. No. This was a delusion, an effect of the strain of the past days on an overheated imagination. Couple that with not having eaten—she remembered now, for nearly two days—and the brusque bedding of an hour previous, and what else could she expect? She willed her breathing to calm, her heartbeat to quit pounding in her throat. She hoped that the Dowager could not see her. Or Lady Marcala.

Then Gaurin was standing beside her, and all her resolution trembled, ready to crumble at a word or even a glance. He sat down and handed her a platter containing a slice of pheasant, and several kinds of fruit. "You must eat lightly, lest you sicken," he told her. "You are very pale."

"And you are very kind," she said. She accepted the goblet of spiced juice and drank it at once. It helped. Then she began to nibble on the fruit. The meat could come later. "Thank you for taking me away before I could make a spectacle of myself."

"How could I not? Lady Ashen, we have but brief acquaintance, but somehow I feel that I have known you all my life. May I speak freely?"

"Of course," she said, both dreading and anticipating his next words.

"They say the Nordors are a cold people, but this is a claim made only by ignorant fools. When I first saw you, I felt a shock of recognition such as I have never known before. I know that is ridiculous, but it is so. And that was even before I saw this." He indicated her bracelet. "Where did you get it?"

She stared at it, at first not remembering that she had chosen to wear it this day of all days. "I found it." She described the circumstances.

"The man was not buried, you say."

"No. He was only a skeleton by the time I got there. I saluted his memory, and in some strange way he seemed to give me this bracelet. It was the finest thing I had ever owned, up to that time. I have kept it carefully, even though I do not wear it often."

He caught her hand and touched the bracelet on her arm. "It belonged to my father."

She gazed at him, not trying to retrieve her hand from his grasp. "Then it is yours, an artifact of your house," she said. She took off the ornament and handed it to him.

"An artifact of a mystery I may solve someday." He held the bauble loosely, not looking at it. "Ashen—"

He leaned closer. Another moment and their lips would meet. *Scandal!* She tore herself away, forced herself to turn aside. "Sir, you presume too much."

"Do I? Or do I only recognize what is so clear that even a child would know? The moment I saw you, I loved you, in the way that songs tell about, when Fate has ordained the meeting. And I do not think my love goes unrequited. Tell me, lady, is this true?"

She could not lie to him, even if she wanted to. Recklessly, she replied. "Yes. But it is folly, it is madness."

"It is what my people call the sunburst at midnight," Gaurin said. "Sometimes it happens to one, sometimes to the other, rarely to both. But, as we know, it does happen. And it is neither folly nor madness, but the coming together of two souls that have loved each other throughout time and have been separated for a while. I have known you, lady. I have known you."

"And I have known you. May every power in this world and any other help me, for this cannot be. I am married—"

"Truly, lady? You do know what I am asking, don't you? If you are not truly his wife, not yet, the marriage can be set aside. It is easily done. As for any objections the King or the Dowager might have, I rank even higher than does Obern of the Sea-Rovers, and an alliance with our people is as important as theirs with the Rendelians, if not more so. And even if that were not the case, I love you and know that you love me—"

"I am truly his wife."

Gaurin's words died on his lips, and with them all the animation that had possessed him before. He just looked at her, his heart in his eyes. "How is this possible?"

Ashen's face flamed hot. She stared down at her platter. The slice of pheasant might as well be putrescent, for all the appetite she had for it. Her body, where the touch of Obern's hands still lingered—

"It is possible," she said, and her voice was harsher than she intended. "That is all you need to know."

Where her face was hot and, she felt sure, very red, Gaurin's turned pale beneath his tan. A muscle worked in his cheek. "Then that is all that can be said—that must be said—about it. Only know this, my Ashen, and you are, somewhere in the depths of your being where only I can touch, mine and mine alone. There will never be another woman for me, not in this life."

Then he did something that, to anybody who had not grown up knowing that some people had use of certain portions of the Power, would have seemed strange. He put the bracelet to his lips, breathed upon it, and returned it to her. It seemed to Ashen that the opalescence flared briefly, and then subsided.

"Let this be a pledge between us," he said gravely. "This has brought us together, and that, too, was foreordained, as if my father had arranged our union. If ever you are in need of anything, put this on, think of me, and I will know, and whatever separates us, even if it is half the world or I face an entire army alone, I will overcome it to be at your side."

She looked into his eyes, feeling that she could lose herself in their depths. "Then never can I dare wear it, for I can never stop thinking of you." Nevertheless, she slipped it on. It felt unaccountably warm, even through her sleeve. "You have opened yourself to me and I can be no less honest. Yes, I am yours and only yours and I know you for my heart's own love—but my body belongs to another. If only we had met earlier—a day, an hour. But such regrets are for children. We are as we are, and I am another man's wife. Yes, I love you, but I love and respect him also and owe him much— my life, in fact, as he owes me his. But I will not forget you." She had to look away. "I—I cannot."

"Ashen." He kissed her fingers.

Her entire body tingled again. "How shall we manage when we meet—"

"We will manage, because we must. You need fear no untoward incident on my behalf, and I know your nobility of heart would not allow you to falter from your vows." And yet he yearned toward her.

With a visible effort he mastered himself. He arose, and helped her to her feet. "Now, come, Lady Ashen, and if your momentary indisposition has passed, allow me to escort you back to that most fortunate of men, your wedded husband, Obern of the Sea-Rovers. If he has the least bit of poetry in his soul, he has missed you sorely."

And with that, he led her toward where Obern was still enjoying himself among his companions, put her hand firmly in his, bowed, and disappeared into the crowd of well-wishers.

Seven

*T*he Dowager Queen *Ysa* sat at her desk, pretending to draft a letter. In reality, her thoughts were very much elsewhere, and only a portion of her attention was given to Lady Marcala, who paced back and forth in front of the fireplace.

The little winged messenger had brought back only a confused impression of what was transpiring to the north; all seemed cloaked in a cold fog the color of dirty snow. Nevertheless, Ysa got an impression of forces gathering, if not yet ready to advance, and another impression, most curious, that these forces thought themselves undetected. She had caught a distinct feeling of someone or something being *startled* when she grasped Visp and drew from it what it had gleaned. Ysa thought it was not coincidence that, from that moment, the unseasonable cold that had gripped Rendel began to loosen.

If only in this, Visp had proven invaluable once again. Of course, with winter the chill would descend once more, but knowing that there was at least a little time when that unseen, unknown force began to move southward, was a comfort. Still, it would be unwise to fritter away what time they all still had. She made a note to reinforce the flyer's loyalty to her and her alone. That little swerve when Visp had flown close to what she now knew was the cart, unlawfully carrying Ashen away in that sorry adventure Florian had arranged—

Something Marcala was saying cut through the Dowager's musings. "And did you see how that Nordorn ambassador was dancing attention on our Bog-Princess? She didn't seem the least bit averse, either, and her married only an hour or so before."

"I did notice," Ysa said. In fact, when Marcala broached the subject, the Dowager's pen had slipped, making an unsightly blot on the drafting paper. "And yet, nothing untoward occurred. Perhaps you are imagining things, Marcala."

"Perhaps you didn't see what I saw," the other woman retorted. "He was holding her hand, and by the looks of them, they weren't talking about what a nice feast it was."

"Ashen was a little overcome with the strain. I understand she had forgotten to eat the past couple of days." Ysa looked at Marcala, wondering what was really behind her complaints. Was she afraid that Ashen and Obern were not truly wed, and that Harous might take up his suit once more? Surely not. The sounds coming from their apartment, when he had all but carried her inside, had reached the corridor and many curious ears.

"That is beside the point. I think that if there had not been that little interlude—" She laughed a little, and even Ysa smiled. "—she would have gone off with him straightaway."

"Gaurin. He holds his father's title, and is of royal blood. In some respects, it might have been better if we had waited when bestowing Ashen's hand, but it is done. And the Nordors, in this case, need us more than we need them. Not so with the Sea-Rovers."

Marcala sniffed. "We? Need Sea-Rovers? Nonsense."

"Rendel has no fighting navy," Ysa said. "We have not had a great need for one heretofore, and our ships have been reserved for trade. But there are things that even you, my Queen of Spies, do not know. There is danger waiting behind the clouds to the North, and if we can delay it by sending the Sea-Rovers against it, so much the better. They have fought it before, and some of them lived thereafter. Snolli told me as much."

Marcala bowed her head. "Forgive me, Madame. I fear that I am so concerned about my lord Harous and where his affections will settle, that I forgot about almost everything else. But you must admit, that episode with Gaurin and Ashen was suspicious."

"Only to those who noticed, and who know about such things," Ysa replied. "I think that you and I are the only ones." Yet, she had to admit that Marcala was right. There had been a tension in the air between those two, and it was not something one would ordinarily sense with a bride and a wedding guest. One might almost think Gaurin a suitor who had come to claim his own and, too late, had found her bestowed upon another.

Ysa sat very still, thinking, and rubbing the Great Rings on her forefingers and thumbs. Marcala had been correct; those two had behaved more like newlyweds than had Ashen with Obern. Therefore, some spark must have ignited between them. But how best to use this knowledge?

For a moment she toyed with the idea of setting aside the marriage between Ashen and Obern, and substituting Gaurin as Ashen's husband instead. Then she discarded the notion. It was as it was, and she had spoken truly; Rendel needed the Sea-Rovers more than they needed the Nordors. At least for the time being. Let nothing presently be disturbed. And who knew what the future might bring?

The Dowager spoke, letting instinct guide her. "Put aside any thought of marrying Count Harous," she said.

Marcala's face reflected her dismay. "Madame. Perhaps you think me unworthy of him. But I assure you, I am of noble blood, on my father's side at least. And I have heard that the *other* lady"— she put an emphasis on the word—"has taken ill and died."

Ysa knew precisely what her Queen of Spies was telling her. She controlled the expression on her face with an effort. So the real Marcala of Valvager was no more and this one need fear no discovery of her pretense. Her Queen of Spies had a long reach, and if she hadn't done it personally, there were plenty of those who would kill if they were paid. Ysa decided to soften her statement. "This putting aside thoughts of marriage is temporary, of course. And anyway, take heart. A mistress always has much more influence than does a mere wife. You should know that."

"I do, Madame, but still—"

"I know. I know. Only be guided by me in this matter. How could I send you hither and yon, bringing me information that only my Queen of Spies could learn, if you were tied to Harous's hearth? No, believe me, your destiny is not marriage. Not yet."

To Ysa's relief, the other did not seem inclined to argue. She lowered her eyes, and curtsied deeply. "I will accept what you tell me, my Queen," she said. "For I know that someday, when the time is right, I *will* be well paid for all my efforts."

"To be sure," Ysa said, repressing a shiver at the scarcely concealed threat. "Well paid indeed."

Obern proposed leaving Rendelsham immediately, to go to New Vold Keep. "That is the home of your ancestors," he told Ashen, "and so you should live there. Not here, in this rat's nest of courtiers and spies and ambassadors and nobles."

Ashen's heart lurched. For a moment, she thought Obern was referring to Gaurin, that somebody had told him of what they had seen between her and the Nordor, at the party following the wedding. But there was not a trace of dissembling in Obern's manner. He had merely been listing aspects of Court life that he had found burdensome. As did she.

"Yes," she said. "I long to be out of this place as well." That she would be trading one stone cage for another was a fact she had to accept. That she would be going where she could not hope to catch a glimpse of Gaurin even at a distance, she must think of as being for the good. Obern was her husband, and it was to him that she owed her faith, her trust, and her loyalty. Yes, far better that she be a great distance from everything and every place where something might remind her of the man with the honey-colored hair, who made her heart pound in her throat with just a glance across the length of Rendelsham Castle's Great Hall. Sternly she told herself that Gaurin must never be a part of her life, and so she must banish him for his good, as much as for hers.

If only she could order her dreams with equal discipline. Nightly she roamed hand in hand with Gaurin through unfamiliar landscapes, the two of them lost in the wonder of each other, speaking of matters she never remembered later. When morning came, and with it reality, she had to smother the impulse to leave her husband's bed and run to the man she truly, and without the shame she should have felt, loved.

"How soon shall we leave?" she asked Obern. "Could it be this week?"

"I see you are as sick of this place as I am," he said. "Yes, this week if you want it so. Set Ayfare to packing our belongings, and I will go and arrange for a wagon to carry them."

Ashen willingly fell to, helping Ayfare with the packing. She would be accompanying them, of course, as would Lathrom and a few of his men who chose to throw their lot with their former sergeant and the Sea-Rovers.

When it came time to take her leave of King Florian, the Dowager Queen, and others of the royal Court, Ashen could not help but notice that neither the King nor his mother seemed particularly distraught at the prospect of her departure. Not that she had expected anything less, of course. Actually, she was grateful that Florian did not throw obstacles in her way just for the perverse pleasure of thwarting her wishes. He was fully capable of such mischief for the sport of doing it.

"Be assured that your quarters here at the royal residence will always be waiting you, should you decide to return for a visit," the Dowager told her. Her face was as expressionless as the façade of a shuttered house, and Ashen could not divine what Ysa was thinking.

Florian was simply indifferent, though his new Queen, Rannore, grasped Ashen's hands warmly. "I wish we could have had time to become friends," she said. "Well, perhaps you will come back often."

"Yes, Your Majesty," Ashen said, curtseying the way she had been taught. "Know that I will ever be your friend, if you want me."

"And so it is settled." Rannore pressed her cheek to Ashen's. "Friends we are, for always."

Both Harous and Marcala wished her a formal farewell, and Harous kissed her hand. "Remember always your ancient motto," he told her, indicating the necklace he had given her and which she now wore openly. " 'Without fire, there is no Ash.' And without Ashen, much of the fire will be gone from the Court."

She dismissed this as just so much meaningless compliment, but it was Lord Royance who presented her with the hardest part of leave-taking.

"I have come to have a great interest in you, Lady Ashen of Ash, and now Lady of the Sea-Rovers," he told her. "You and that daring husband of yours both. May you not be strangers from the Court for too long."

"We will meet again, and as often as I can arrange it," Ashen said. Then, giving in to a daring impulse, she kissed the silver-haired nobleman on his cheek. He smiled at her in return and, remarkably, there was not even a touch of frost in it.

Then she and Obern were off, with an entourage smaller than what her rank might entitle her to, but more than enough to suit her. She tried to ride side by side with Obern except that he had a way of putting himself about half a length ahead of her. Once, she tried to catch up, but he deliberately galloped ahead. Lathrom and his men rode guard. Snolli and his followers had already departed weeks before, and the dust from their horses' hoofprints long since settled. The soldiers drew lots for who got to drive the carriage, for that was where Ayfare rode with the trunks and boxes, and every soldier vied for her attention.

Though Bog-men still occasionally made their raids and forays into lands across the Barrier River, the travelers were not disturbed during the time they were on the road. Perhaps the sight of Lathrom's well-armed soldiers caused any would-be robber or raider to turn aside from anything beyond the thought. The sight of a bridegroom traveling with his new bride caused other people on the road to smile openly, and sometimes to wish them well.

Ashen was interested in the countryside through which they journeyed. The road wound through low hills and when they reached a fork that led from the east, Obern informed her that they were now traveling through what had once been Ash lands.

"We crossed the River Rendel close by Cragden Keep, and we will cross it again close by where it empties into the Sea. When we reach that point, we will be able to see the towers of New Vold, that once was the Ashenkeep."

"Then we will live close to the Sea?"

"Aye, and too close to the Bog for my comfort. When first we came here, the devils stayed behind the Barrier River. Now we're just as likely to meet 'em in the field where we're trying to grow wheat for the winter, as if we'd gone hunting them."

"Perhaps I can get word to the Bog-men, and they will leave off their attacks against you. Against us."

He shrugged. "It is a good thought, but, I fear, impractical. If you ventured into the Bog they would be just as likely to try to steal you as—as someone else was." He laughed. "But for a different reason."

Her heart lurched, and she thought of Gaurin. Then she realized Obern was referring to her half-brother. She smiled at him though he didn't return it. "We are seeing more and more land that is growing a late crop," she said. "The coverings you told of seem to be effective. Perhaps the coming winter will not be as hard on the people as you have feared."

"We were afraid, at first, that the land itself rejected us. But the unseasonable chill has, for the moment, eased a little."

True enough, they were coming upon fields full of crops of new green plants already nearly knee-high even without the shelter of the tentlike coverings, as if the land were trying to make up for lost time. Also, the air was warm enough that Ashen had put aside her fur-lined garments, and wore a light mantle over her riding clothes. "Let us hope it stays so."

Is there, she thought, nothing more between us to talk of than the weather and crops? The things he murmured in her ear in the night, when all were supposedly asleep, were not to be repeated in the light of day, of course. But where had this coolness come from? What had happened to the days when they had been together and never knew the lack of subjects to discuss? Did he behave lovingly toward her only when he was seeking love for himself?

Gaurin—

No! Firmly, she put that thought aside. She must forget him. Gaurin must be as one dead to her. Her life lay ahead, at the end of this road, in New Vold Keep. With Obern. Her husband.

The first days at New Vold Keep were a blur to Ashen. She was given one entire tower for her residence, and there was much fussing and running back and forth and moving her goods in and stowing them to Ayfare's satisfaction. The arrangement of the furniture did not suit the maid and all had to be placed here, and then there, while Ashen fled the disarray until all had been put to rights.

Somewhat to her dismay, Ashen discovered that Obern was not expected to spend each night with her if he chose to be elsewhere. "It is the way of the Sea-Rovers," said one of their women who had been assigned to her. "After all, if they were tied to our beds, how would they go out and bring back treasures for us? But you don't have to worry, lady. It's too late in the year and we still have to prepare for winter. He'll often be there, to warm your bed." She giggled and thrust out her belly. "He has some work to do, to catch up. Most of our brides are full already by the time they're wed. Best way to get a husband."

The rest of the ladies joined in the laughter.

Ashen suspected none of this was a real joke. The window in her bedchamber gave her a fine view of the harbor and, beyond that, a patch of the blue water she remembered from the time she had gone through the caves, fleeing giant birds spawned by the Bog. When she had found Obern, wounded, and needing her care. The window had a strong set of shutters and could be covered with oiled skins as well, but Ashen knew that the pleasant sea breeze of today might turn into storms next week. She was glad that the bed given her was hung with heavy woolen curtains, to keep out the cold, and that each floor in the tower was well supplied with fireplaces.

In the course of settling in and getting her bearings, she was surprised one afternoon the first month she was there, when Obern came in, in the middle of her taking out clothing from one of the chests to shake wrinkles loose, with a handsome boy perhaps ten years of age.

"Here's someone I want you to meet," he told Ashen. "This is Rohan."

"I wish you warmth and brightness of a good day, lady," the boy said. He bowed stiffly and Ashen smiled. He obviously had been coached.

"Good day to you also," she said. "Are you a Sea-Rover?"

"Not yet, lady, but someday." He looked up at Obern. "I want to be just like my father."

Ashen stared at Obern, startled. Only now did she notice the resemblance. The same shape of face, same color of hair. " 'Father'? Do you mean—"

"Yes," Obern said proudly. "This is my son."

A phrase that Ashen had been hearing all too frequently since her arrival in New Vold echoed in her ears whenever she would do something that was the least bit different: "It is not the way of the Sea-Rovers." Sometimes she thought she would pull out her hair if she heard it just one more time. As she had during her days at Cragden Keep, she strove to learn, to fit in. One of the things she had learned was that a man's paying any great attention to his children also was not the way of the Sea-Rovers. And yet, here was Obern. And here was his son.

"I—I didn't know."

"Now you do. Rohan is being fostered by Dagdya."

"Dagdya," Ashen repeated through stiff lips.

"Yes, she is a wonderful foster. When my mother died of a

plague, Dagdya took over completely and I don't think I turned out too badly. I hope that Lathrom will become one of his teachers as well." Obern beamed at his son. "I did want you two to meet, though. I hope you will become good friends."

"Of course," Ashen said faintly. Fostering was, apparently, another part of the way of the Sea-Rovers.

"I hope we will become good friends, too, lady." Then Rohan bowed again, and followed his father out the door once more.

Ashen sat down, her knees suddenly grown weak. Why hadn't Obern told her before now that he had a son? Because, she answered herself, it was not the way of the Sea-Rovers. They did not give their children any great notice—at least the men didn't, any more than they danced attention on their wives. That much she had gleaned, even from her short stay at New Vold.

She put her hand to her belly, wondering if this was going to change, even a little, when her own child was born.

"Obern, I must go to the Bog!" This argument had been going on for several days, and Ashen was finding Obern as stubbornly set against the journey as when she had first broached the subject, over a week earlier.

"There is no need," he said, again. "You are just experiencing what every woman does, with her first child. I'll bring Dagdya to talk to you."

"I've talked to Dagdya, and even she has come to admit that it is something more than that, something beyond her reckoning. I want to go to the Bog. I want to go to Zazar. She is the closest thing to a mother that I've ever had, and at a time like this—" She pressed her lips together firmly. Obern had gotten that closed look on his face that meant nothing further she could say would have any effect on him. The beginning of a plan sprang into her mind. "Very well," she told him. "I'll consult Dagdya again, though I don't think it will do any good."

"Women have been having babies since the world began," Obern said. "This one is no different from any other, even if it is yours."

She noticed he did not say "ours," but chose to overlook it. As much as he loved her—and she was certain that, in his own way, he did—still, he was a Sea-Rover. Now that he was back among them, it was only natural that he thought like one.

Four months had gone by since first she knew she was carrying and there was a *chill* in her belly, where all should be warmth and, by now, the first faint stirring of movement. Instead, all she felt was a dull weight. And she felt ill such as she knew was not normal for a pregnant woman. She had experienced only a little of the morning queasiness that afflicted so many. Nevertheless, she had no appetite and no energy, either. When she picked up a tiny shirt she had once been working on, for the newcomer, she had no heart to stitch on it. She wanted only to lie in bed, thinking nothing, preparing nothing, waiting only to die—

No! To think such a thing was to will it to happen.

At first, Ashen had not welcomed the news that she was with child but she quickly changed her mind. A new life, a baby, would surely bring Obern closer to her, and her to him. Also, it would give her something with which to occupy herself, to keep herself from thinking of the one whom she had sworn to forget.

And she had tried to keep her oath. But still, Gaurin came to her each night in her dreams, though of late his countenance had not been smiling, but rather wore an expression of grave concern. Sometimes he spoke, and his message, though blurred and hard to decipher, was one speaking of her needing help such as even he could not offer.

Could she likewise be haunting his dreams? How else could he know that all was not well with her?

She put that aside. Perhaps later, when she had reached Zazar, and the Wysen-wyf had put all to rights again, she would dare consider it. But for now, she must focus all her thought and what energy remained to her, on the task of leaving New Vold and going, alone, back into the Bog.

She must confide in Ayfare. When she told the maid of her

plans, Ayfare nodded, though her forehead was wrinkled dubiously. "Aye, lady, I see that you would want your foster mother, especially under the circumstances. But to give Lord Obern his due, isn't he right to urge you to talk to Dagdya?"

"By his lights, I suppose so. But Sea-Rover women are a sturdy lot and my guess is that Dagdya has never yet seen a woman in such straits as I feel myself to be in." Ashen shook out a pair of breeches she had filched from Obern's clothespress. "Bog-women are different. Many are ill shaped and have other flaws in their forming. Childbearing comes hard with many of them. More than once I have been in the vicinity of Zazar's hut when she was giving a woman the medicine that dislodges a dead child from her body. She sent me away, always, but yet I knew."

"Lady!" Ayfare's hands went to her mouth. "Don't say it—"

"I must face facts. I feel cold, where there should be warmth. If the child is not dead, then I surely will be, before long, for there is none here to tend me. I must go to Zazar."

"Then go you shall, with my help, though I will worry myself sick, not knowing what is happening. What if some Bog-beast eats you? Or even worse? I have heard stories, and bad ones, too. I will come with you."

Ashen grasped the maid's hands with her own, grateful for her loyalty. "I will be better, just knowing I am on the road to the Wysen-wyf," she said. "I know the Bog and its ways, and you do not. You must stay here. You would just slow me down."

"And you think that I was born in a rose garden? I can take care of myself, and you with me if it comes to that."

Again Ashen demurred, but the maid was stubborn and eventually she gave in. "Very well," she said, "but you must go and get your own breeches. Skirts will just hamper you in case you have to run for your life."

Ayfare grinned. "I'll be ready within the hour, and will get us a little bundle of food to take as well. All you have to do is say the word, and we'll be off."

Secretly, Ashen was gladder for the maid's company than worried about her safety. She dressed herself quickly in Obern's garments. Both breeches and shirt were much too large for her, of course, but she belted in the garments high over the coldness in her belly and laced thongs close together over both arms and legs. When she was finished, she felt they would do, though she wished for the shell leg-armor she had always worn in the Bog. Once she had braided her hair and put a hooded cloak over all, with Ayfare doing likewise, perhaps they would be mistaken for two young men going about an errand, by any watchers on the wall of New Vold Keep.

She knew the paths to follow in the Bog, and could lead them to Zazar's hut without incident. That is, providing they avoided serpents' stings and the Deep Dwellers—the giant luppers such as the one that had very nearly been her doom—were not on the prowl. That day, she had learned that they had a taste for live meat as well as Bog dead. It had surely eaten one of three young Bog-men who had once tracked her with less-than-honorable intentions. She rummaged through her jewel coffer, bringing out the small square of wood polished with age and much handling she had hidden under the lining. She held it to her nose; it still bore a faintly spicy scent. This was a hearth-guide. Unfortunately, though, she had set it on Galinth, the ruined city in the northern part of the Bog, where Zazar had left her to pursue the store of knowledge, and she had no other. She had not had the chance to set it on Zazar's dwelling again before Obern's arrival and her subsequently being taken by Harous and leaving the Bog. She put it back into the box. By the time she was ready, Ayfare had returned, already dressed for the road and bearing a bundle of what smelled like fresh bread.

"Aye, I filched it from where it was cooling on the rack," the maid said cheerfully, "and some cold sliced meat to go with it. Also, I have a flagon of ale as well as water bottles and half a pastry." She held up a wrapped bundle which she then strapped to her back. "Now, with a cloak over all, I look like a hunchback."

"You have done well," Ashen said, smiling. "Nobody would ever recognize you. Bind your legs with thongs as I have done, for there are those that sting and we must do what we can to avoid it. But be quick about it. We need to get started. I want to be in the Bog before night falls."

"I'd rather be at your Wysen-wyf's hut by the time dark sets in," Ayfare said, quickly doing as Ashen directed. To her credit, she showed no sign of shrinking from the adventure before them. "Perhaps, if we put a good foot under us, we can get close."

"If we're lucky we will be there by full dark. And if not, there are plants in the Bog that can make a light for us." Ashen drew the other of the treasures from her former life from the jewel coffer. "And if all else fails, I will try to put you inside the shadow of this."

Ayfare eyed the circular stone, pierced so it hung by a cord, with some doubt. "Is it a weapon? Do you throw it at an enemy?"

Ashen laughed, wondering how to explain the magic. "No. It— it makes a noise when I whirl it overhead. And it puts a shadow over me. It has allowed me to get away from danger more than once."

"Then let us hope it works well enough for us both. Now let us be off!"

Eight

espite the fact that Ashen could almost hear the cry of
alarm being raised from the walls of New Vold Keep, the
two girls managed to make their escape unnoticed. They took the
road across the river and then cut straight west, over open ground,
toward the Barrier River. Once in sight of it, Ashen had little difficulty in finding the waterfall and the cave where she had once
taken refuge from giant birds. Close by, she knew, was a ford and
the girls made their way to the spot. Here, though the river ran
shallow, it ran swiftly and they had to watch their footing as they
waded across. The sun was a little less than halfway down in the
sky.

"My village—I mean, the village where Zazar lives—lies almost
due west of us. If we keep the sun to our faces until it disappears
behind the mountains, even a stranger could find the way. And I
am no stranger. Also, the paths are clear to see."

"Some of them. But others, I daresay, are not."

"There I will guide you. Now, follow me and be careful. You
are, after all, an Outlander." As am I by now, Ashen thought. But
she did not say it aloud. No need to frighten the girl unnecessarily.

They stopped at intervals to rest, and to eat the provisions Ayfare had brought. As the afternoon drew on toward evening, the luppers began to awaken and take up their evening serenade. Mostly it was the cheeps and peeps and croaking Ashen had known from childhood, but every now and then, a deeper bellow could be heard from the depths of the Bog beyond the path, and once in a while a wild cry arose to be as quickly stifled.

Ayfare reached out to take Ashen's hand. "It's only to help you in case you stumble," the maid said. Her voice trembled slightly.

"Have no fear. We have made remarkably good time and, unless I have forgotten all my Bog-lore, the village is just around the next bend, and over a small hill."

Now that they were almost at their destination, the store of energy Ashen had drawn upon for the journey vanished, leaving her faint. She willed herself to go forward, for she knew that Ayfare, good as her intentions were, would not fare well if she tried to go alone into the village where Joal was headman.

Once they had topped the rise, they waited hidden behind such shelter as reeds and mossy branches could provide while Ashen observed the activity in the village. There seemed to be little, which might mean that most of the men were out hunting. Good, she thought. We can most likely get in by the back way.

She led Ayfare, who needed no admonition to move with great care and stealth, along the edge of the clearing where the village was located, toward the back of Zazar's hut. There, a much smaller path had been worn where the Wysen-wyf was accustomed to heading into the Bog, though this quickly disappeared in the sodden ground, for Zazar had seldom gone the same direction twice.

"Now," Ashen said in a low voice.

The two girls hurried across the short stretch of open ground, and around the hut to the door. Without giving the customary identification whistle or the call of "Zazar hearth," Ashen pushed the curtain aside and stumbled over the threshold. Strength entirely spent, she went to her knees and then, with black sparks buzzing and blurring her sight, she collapsed.

She floated in a dream-world, but one in which Gaurin did not visit her. Shadows moved back and forth just out of her range of vision, and once she roused just enough so that Zazar could lift her head so she could drink a potion the Wysen-wyf held for her. It was bitter. Feebly, she tried to wave it away.

"All of it, Ashen," Zazar said sternly. "Drink it quickly and then you won't notice the taste."

Then she did as she was told, after which she remembered little except pain when the muscles of her body contracted. Then something small, sharp, and very cold slipped out. She floated on a quiet lake of relief. How easy it would be to let go entirely, to sink down and down. . . .

Her head snapped abruptly to the side and her cheek stung. She opened her eyes to see Zazar hovering over her, hand raised to strike her again if necessary. "No, you will *not* die, hard as I've worked to bring you back!" The Wysen-wyf's words were like flung stones, each one hitting its mark. "Here, I've got broth for you. No, it isn't like the medicine. Drink it."

Ashen knew that Zazar would drag her back by force if she had to. The girl had to gulp from the cup Zazar held lest the hot liquid spill down her neck and scald her. Ayfare appeared on the other side of her, propping her up with one arm while with the other she took the cup and held it more gently, so Ashen could sip. "Thank you," she said weakly.

"That's better," Zazar said. "I made it from some of the meat you brought, with plenty of salt in it. Now, when you can, kindly tell me why you waited so long. You were nearly dead when you got here."

"My lady complained that she did not feel well. But her husband wouldn't listen to her, and the midwives knew nothing."

Zazar grunted. "So you said earlier. But I want to hear it from Ashen."

"Ayfare speaks truly," Ashen said, and was astonished at how much that short speech cost her. She could feel a little strength returning to her, with the warmth of the broth. "No one wished me any harm. They simply didn't know better."

"Well, they nearly killed you anyway." Zazar sat down on a stool beside the bed—Zazar's own, Ashen realized. "The baby had died inside you, but your body couldn't expel it naturally. Instead, you were being poisoned by it. One more day, and I wouldn't have been able to do anything. As it is, you have a long recovery ahead of you and you must do it elsewhere. It isn't safe for you to stay here, even in my house."

Ashen closed her eyes. Ayfare nudged her with the cup, and she drank a little more broth. "Why?" she said, dreading the answer.

"Joal is not headman any longer. Tusser challenged him and beat him. Then Joal disappeared. I don't think he went to the pool voluntarily."

" 'The pool'?" Ayfare obviously had no idea what Zazar was talking about.

"Where the Bog-people put their dead. For the underwater eaters. The Deep Dwellers."

Ashen felt Ayfare shudder. "It is the custom," she told the maid. "Tusser is Joal's son. I know him, grew up with him, and he hates me for various reasons. Anyway, the dead feel nothing."

"But Joal wasn't dead, not yet," Zazar said. "We had differences, but that fate was a bad one and I would not have wished it on him."

"Then you are right," Ashen said, "and my presence here can only bring you danger. I must go back to New Vold."

"And how?" the old woman demanded. "You're too weak to get out of bed, let alone go where you'll surely die without competent people to help you."

"I'll manage. I must."

Zazar snorted through her nose. "You'll manage nothing, not without my help. Just lie easy. I have an idea."

But Ashen could get nothing further from the Wysen-wyf. All she knew was that, after a brief, whispered conversation with Ayfare, both left the hut after providing her with food and a bottle of water. A few hours later, Zazar returned alone.

"How're you feeling now?" she asked.

"Much stronger," Ashen said. "I got out of bed and walked a few steps, though it tired me."

"You shouldn't have done that, but no harm done, I suppose."

"I wanted to see if I could run if I had to."

Unexpectedly, Zazar smiled. "You'll do," she said. "But you needn't have bothered. All the able-bodied men are out hunting for meat to salt for the winter. Now, we wait until your man and a troop of armed soldiers show up, to take you to Rendelsham. The Nordor, isn't he?"

Ashen started. "I suppose you could call him that, though he is not really a Nordor. He's the son of the Chieftain of the Sea-Rovers. His name is Obern."

It was Zazar's turn to be startled. "But he was not—Never mind. What's done is done, and the Weavers must have a reason for it though we do not know it yet. I gave your maidservant a hearth-guide here, after I left her beside the ford. They'll be here in another day, if your Obern has the least regard for you."

Ashen closed her eyes. "He will," she said. At least that much she could count on. He might blame her for disobeying him and entering the swamp—he might even blame her for losing the child—but he would come for her.

She had been wrong. The first thing Obern did, once he was inside the hut and his men stationed outside, was to blame Zazar. "If it hadn't been for your meddling—" he said, his voice dangerous.

Zazar had never been one to overlook foolishness. "If it hadn't been for my 'meddling' as you put it, your wife would not be alive today," she snapped. Quickly, sparing no grim detail, she outlined the situation for him. "She was more dead than alive when she got here, and that was thanks to *your* keeping her from me."

Obern tempered his anger, if only a little. "And yet, women

have children all the time. What did you do, Ashen, that the baby died?"

"I did nothing," Ashen said. "Nothing. I wanted the baby—our baby." Everything, she thought, depended on his next words.

"And yet it died. And you ran away, into the Bog. Perhaps that is why it died."

Ashen looked away. This rift between them, she thought, would be hard to bridge. Perhaps it never would be. And yet this was her husband, to whom she was bound for life. Worse, it was possible he was unaware even that a rift existed.

She had to make things plain, once and for all, or be lost entirely. "If you believe that I was acting in any way but in an attempt to save the baby, then perhaps we should agree to live apart," she said.

Obern had the good grace to look abashed. "Of course I could never believe anything but good about you," he said.

"Then believe this," she said. Her voice was harsh in her own ears. "Perhaps I spoke true and we should separate. But that would shame you in Sea-Rover eyes. 'A man who cannot keep his wife in her place,' they'd whisper behind your back. Always *you* and no thought for me. No consideration of my welfare. I did not desert you. I was dying, Obern. Zazar said that another day and even she could have done nothing to save me. I only went for help that you couldn't or wouldn't recognize that I needed."

"I know you had your reasons. And yet it was hard to bear, when I found that you would leave me."

She looked away. "Yes. I know." Her words were false in her own ears. It was as if she talked to a log. He still had not grasped her meaning, and perhaps never would. If he had, he would have brought her to the Bog himself, rather than come for her later, and when sent for.

"I am a Sea-Rover, and we treat our women differently from the way the land men do."

"Make your apologies later," Zazar said. "You *are* apologizing to your wife, aren't you?"

Obern nodded, if a little slowly.

"Good. Now, did you bring a litter, as I told you?"

"I did. It can be rigged so horses can carry it, once we get across the Barrier River." He turned to Ashen. "Lathrom is in charge of the men," he told her. "And we'll be taking Ayfare to tend you as well. I still don't understand why it wouldn't be just as well to return to New Vold rather than make the long journey to Rendelsham—"

"You don't have to understand," Zazar said bluntly, clearly out of patience. "Just do it. Obey me!"

"Very well, we will go to Rendelsham," Obern said, with a nod in the Wysen-wyf's direction, "and live once more in that madhouse of a capital. But once you are healed, we return to New Vold. Agreed?"

"Yes, agreed," Ashen said. She had no more wish to be near King Florian and the Dowager than he, but she recognized Zazar's wisdom in sending her where there were skilled physicians to oversee her recuperation.

Then Obern picked her up and, despite her protests that she could walk at least as far as the litter, carried her outside. He held her for a moment, gazing at her, and only then could she see the deep concern in his eyes, a concern that had come out as anger. "I really was beside myself with worry about you," he said. "If anything ever happened to you—"

"I will be safe now that you are here," Ashen said. She put her head against the hollow of his neck. A faint hope flickered that perhaps they could still salvage some of what little they once had between them. Perhaps he would learn other ways of behaving with a woman who was not of the Sea-Rover kin.

"I'll guide you once more to the Barrier River," Zazar said. "And then who knows when I'll see you again."

"Surely not under the same conditions," Obern said. He hugged Ashen tighter before putting her into the litter.

"You're a good man for all your hot temper," Zazar said. "Too bad that—Well, never mind."

"How can I get in touch with you, to keep you informed of Ashen's recovery?"

Unexpectedly, the Wysen-wfy smiled. "I'll find a way to get in touch with you. Now, go." Then she put her hand on Obern's sleeve. "Wait. You have a son, don't you? The child of the wife you once had."

"Yes. His name is Rohan." Obern sounded puzzled, as was Ashen. She had not told Zazar about the boy. Or perhaps she had, while she was temporarily out of her head. If so, perhaps she had told her Protector about Gaurin as well, and how she loved him. That would explain some of Zazar's cryptic remarks.

"Send for him while you are in Rendelsham," the Wysen-wyf instructed Obern. "He will be a comfort to Ashen, being as how she lost the child that would have been her own."

"Yes, I will," Obern promised. Then the little group of travelers started across the open land to where they could pick up the road and make traveling easier for Ashen.

Even with the improved conditions and the way Ayfare had tried to pad the horse-litter to make it as comfortable as possible, Ashen was exhausted to the point of wishing she had died, back in the Bog, when Rendelsham towers finally came into view. They passed by Cragden Keep without stopping, going directly to Rendelsham Castle. There, under Ayfare's direction, stewards rushed from every direction to help her to the apartment that, true to the Dowager Queen's promise, had been kept ready for her when she chose to visit. Others scurried off to find the physicians, while still others went to notify the King and the Dowager of Ashen's arrival.

She fell into a deep slumber the instant she had been put to bed, and woke late the next morning, feeling considerably refreshed. Master Lorgan, the eldest and most experienced of all the physicians employed at Rendelsham Castle, sat at her side.

"You have had a narrow escape," he told her, "if half of what your maid claims is true."

"My guess is that she left half of it out of her story," Ashen said. She yawned. "But I am here, and I am alive, and my instructions were to stay until I was well again."

"Ah yes, the Wysen-wyf." Lorgan smiled. "It was no surprise to me that she sent you. We have had dealings with one another, she and I, over the years. She sent me also this." He showed Ashen a scrap of bark paper with some incomprehensible scribbles on it. "This is the recipe for a particular tonic that I am to brew, and your maidservant is to give you daily. It should have you on your feet before long, unless there is somewhat amiss that Zazar did not detect." He smiled a little wider. "But that is unlikely."

Ayfare appeared at that moment, bearing a tray on which were several covered dishes and a crystal drinking-cup containing something green. Even from a distance Ashen could smell its pungent aroma. "Breakfast, my lady," Ayfare said. "Or dinner, whichever you prefer. But you are to eat all of it and drink the tonic down to the last drop. I prepared it myself."

"I see you are in good hands," Master Lorgan said, as he arose from the chair. "I always like it when my patients have someone to look after them who will bully them into doing the correct thing. And so I give you good day until I see you again tomorrow."

Ashen managed to tell him farewell just before the door closed behind him. Somehow Ayfare had her propped up in bed, a napkin tucked under her chin, and the tray set across her lap before she quite knew what was happening.

"First, the dish of eggs," Ayfare said. "And then some bread, and fruit if you can hold it, and then the tonic." She stepped back and folded her arms, obviously willing to stand over her charge until she had performed satisfactorily.

Knowing better than to argue, Ashen removed the cover from one of the dishes. Inside were three coddled eggs cooked to perfection, on rounds of toasted bread. More bread, untoasted, with butter and a slice of cheese, waited on another plate and yet another bowl held fresh fruit peeled and sliced. "How can I ever eat all this?" she said. "It has been so long—"

"All the more reason to eat now. You are so thin the covers scarcely rumple over you."

Obediently Ashen started in on the eggs, cutting them and the toast to bits with her spoon. The combination tasted surprisingly delicious and before she knew it, she had eaten almost all of it. There was none of that sugary sauce that, to Ashen, spoiled the dish and she smiled her gratitude at Ayfare's remembering her preferences. She put the butter aside, and ate a slice of bread with the cheese, as she nibbled on the fruit. "That was good," she said at last, "but I'm too full to take another bite."

"Not too full to drink the tonic," Ayfare said.

"It smells like—like—"

"Like something from the Bog? I'll grant you that, but it tastes fairer than it smells. I sampled it."

Ashen saw no way out, so she took a sip. Ayfare had been correct. Once past the strong, swampy odor—no doubt some of the herbs and medicinal Bog-plants Zazar knew, the way Master Lorgan knew his elixirs—the concoction was not entirely unpleasant, though it had a bitter undertaste. Ashen drained the cup and then lay back, tired once more.

"Where is Obern?" she asked.

"When he saw that you were in safe hands, he returned to New Vold to bring his son back with him, as that strange old woman told him. Is that the one who reared you?"

"Yes. She is Zazar, the Wysen-wyf, and she's quite famous. It seems that most people in Rendel know of her. I think my mother was trying to reach her before I was born. She died, leaving me orphaned. I am only now becoming aware of how lucky I am that Zazar fostered me."

Ayfare had other news also—the comings and goings of this noble and that, and, most interesting, the information that Count Gaurin was not at Court.

"Has he returned to his homeland?" Ashen inquired cautiously.

"For the time. He's gone to bring more of his people back to

Rendel. From what I hear, things are going poorly up north."

Much as she wanted to see him again, this was an exceptionally poor time for them to renew their acquaintanceship and so she was glad, in a way, that he was gone. "Grant him safe journey." Then she yawned again. "Could I be sleepy again so quickly?"

"Yes. So go back to sleep, and don't worry about anything. I am here to look after you, and soon your husband and your foster son will be here as well."

With a contented sigh, Ashen obeyed.

In another part of the castle, King Florian was pacing the floor, scowling, while his current mistress, Lady Jacyne, wife of a minor court official, lolled on a long chair. She was eating spiced, sugared nuts from a silver dish and was nearly naked, a light robe carelessly belted around her waist. If her intention was to appear seductive, Florian was unmoved by it. "I don't see what all the fuss is about," she said. "Your sister is in no condition to harm you, even if she wanted to."

"That's not the point," Florian said impatiently. "She is *here* and I am much happier when she is someplace else. Almost anyplace else."

"Well, you'd better get used to her presence," Jacyne said with a shrug. "Because she isn't going anywhere until all the poison is out of her system."

Florian stopped in his tracks. "What poison?" he said suspiciously. "Is someone trying to say she's been poisoned?" It can't be, he thought. Someone must be spreading a rumor.

"All perfectly natural, my love," Jacyne said, popping another sugared nut into her mouth. "Sometimes things go wrong. She was pregnant, it died, she couldn't push it out, and you don't want to know the nasty details. But the Bog-witch saved her."

She licked her fingers and Florian stared at her with some distaste. She had been very amusing at first, but her coarse ways were beginning to annoy him. Initially he had thought it an affectation; now he surmised that she really was a common wench who had married far above her station.

"How very unfortunate," he said without inflection.

Then he dismissed the matter as unimportant women's business. He had other things on his mind, and to that end, ordered Jacyne to dress and leave him alone. When she had slipped out the private door, he sent for Rawl, the house servant who had "helped" him some years earlier in the matter of that Nordorn ambassador—What was his name? Oh, yes, Bjauden. Rawl had taken care of the problem neatly and efficiently, with never a hint of anything amiss, and since then, several similar pieces of work as well.

Now that his sister had come back to Rendelsham, after that frustrating business with the Sea-Rover rescuing her and the equally inefficient way Sergeant Lathrom had misinterpreted the orders given him—Florian made a disgusted noise in the back of his throat. Any fool should have understood that Ashen was to be done away with at the earliest opportunity. The instructions in the note—and that was something else that chafed him, that the note had not been destroyed—were just a cover, in case something went wrong. Well, he should be grateful that the note existed after all, though he wasn't. Rawl, however, would not fail him. Florian had to strike quickly, and permanently, before another political faction could start forming around her.

There was a quiet tap on the same private door Jacyne had used, and then it opened a crack and Rawl slipped inside.

"You sent for me, Your Majesty?"

"That I did. I have another, um, *special* assignment for you."

Rawl grinned. "I'm your man, as Your Majesty ought to know by now."

"Hmmm, yes," Florian said, a little sourly. His man had been paid well enough. And would be again, once he learned what Florian had in mind. "There is a certain lady newly returned to the castle. She was taken once, and returned before anything, um, permanent could happen. I want you to remedy that. You've carried others to the Bog both living and dead. I think it would be very fitting to return this lady to that place as well. After all, it was once her home."

"The Princess." Rawl looked very dubious. "Begging your pardon, sir, but are you suggesting she be taken again?"

"The very thing."

"I'd advise against it, sir."

"For what reason?"

"If I may speak plainly, sir."

Florian nodded. "This is no time to hold back."

"Well, though I wasn't a party to it, I know that there was talk all through the castle and out into the city that you was behind the Princess's disappearance. They couldn't lay it at your feet, and that was lucky for you. But if the same thing happens again, now that she's back under your roof—" Rawl shrugged expressively. "You'd be the first one they'd come asking after."

Florian pondered the servant's words, frowning. Curse it, he was right. Ashen must be eliminated, but how to do it?

As if he could read the King's mind, Rawl continued. "We got to find a different way to do it. Servants' talk is the lady is ill."

"Yes. She lost a baby, and had some kind of poisoning with it."

"Well, there you are, then."

Florian blinked, not understanding at first. Then he remembered what Lady Jacyne had said. "All perfectly natural, my love," she had told him. And perfectly convenient. Surely his sister was being given medicine. A dose of poison—more poison—slipped into the brew, and she would slip away quietly with no questions being asked.

Furthermore, he knew who he could get to do this. Poison was not Rawl's style, and furthermore, his duties would not bring him near Ashen's apartment. Jacyne could do it, though, if he could persuade her that she was doing nothing wrong. Also, he could make her think that her station in life would improve significantly. And then—

He smiled as the rest of the plan took shape in his mind. It was beautiful—flawless, even. And best of all, Rawl would still prove useful. After she was dead, let him take his sister's body to the swamp to be reduced to nothing by the hungry predators there. And because there would be a body needed for the elaborate—and carefully sealed—coffin, why, Jacyne would fill that requirement. Once she realized how she had been duped, she must be disposed of. She might be slow of wit, but eventually she would understand what her part had been and she had much too loose a tongue to be allowed to live on.

"You are correct, Rawl. It was a moment's thought only and you have shown me that such an impulse must not be acted upon. Only stand ready, for I will have something else for you to do later."

"Depend on me, Your Majesty." He saluted awkwardly, giving the King a conspirator's grin, and went out the way he had come in.

Florian smiled also, but it was not a pleasant expression as he began contemplating the details of exactly how and when he would arrange for both his sister's and his mistress's imminent demise.

Nine

It was common knowledge that there were people who made their livelihood in brewing poisons both subtle and abrupt. For that reason every noble employed a staff of physicians whose duties included testing for such contaminations, even to articles of clothing. More than one pair of gloves, or elaborately embroidered shirt, presented as gifts, would have proven fatal to the wearer. The wise among them were careful also of the cooks they employed, and paid them well, lest they be tempted by bribery. Still the danger existed. In a world where political enemies would stop at nothing, the wise person took every precaution available.

Florian knew himself to be wise in this regard, and so he sent for Jariad, who had apprenticed to Master Lorgan and learned well his physician's trade. Further, while showing exemplary loyalty to his royal master, Jariad had also shown some talent not only in detecting poisons but also in collecting new and unusual ones. A hobby, he claimed, but a useful one. If there were such a court position as King's Poisoner, Jariad would have filled it to perfection. But instead, he was known merely as one of the staff of physicians maintained at Rendelsham Castle.

Jariad merely raised one eyebrow when Florian told him what

he wanted, without, of course, mentioning for whom this potion was intended.

"I think it should be something slow and lingering, don't you?" Florian said. "Then it would seem like an unfortunate wasting illness. Quite natural."

"I think I know exactly the preparation you need," Jariad said. He bowed himself out, and Florian began to ponder how he could make Jacyne add it to whatever concoction Ashen was being given, thinking she was helping the Kings' sister.

The Dowager Queen Ysa dismissed the last of the petitioners; she had had a full day, taking care of the business that should have been Florian's responsibility. When she was alone, she would find out what was keeping him secluded this time.

She had not performed this particular ritual in perhaps too long. She brought the Ring on the forefinger of her right hand to her mouth and touched it with the tip of her tongue. "Yew," she said.

As usual, her perception altered, and it was as if an invisible part of herself swept through the castle, seeking to know the well-being of the head of the House of Yew, her ancestral House. This leader now was Florian. Ah. There he was.

Of late, swordplay had become almost an obsession with the King. There were actually classes held in the Great Hall, and staged mock combats between students, in which sport Florian engaged eagerly. He was so occupied now. Well, better that than to be dallying with one or another of the string of mistresses he kept, to his new wife's dismay.

As an experiment, she then touched her tongue to the ring on the thumb of her right hand. "Oak." The same tableau presented itself to her eyes. That was interesting. And alarming. She must try to keep from him the fact that, to the Rings at least, he was now in command of two of the Four Great Houses of Rendel. Always they had been allies, but to her knowledge no one person had ever headed both at one time.

Let Florian fritter his time away with swordplay and wenching, and leave the management of the kingdom to her. She was, after all, the one to whom the Four Great Rings had come of their own volition. She was the one with whom the Rings remained. Therefore, she was best suited to her task, as he was to his.

Then, knowing what she would find, she tasted the wood inlay of the Ring encircling the thumb of her left hand. "Ash."

Ah, there she was—the Bog-Princess, in Marcala's amusing phrase—lying asleep and perhaps dreaming of one who was not her husband. She did not look well. The rumors must have been true. Ysa wondered whether she wished Ashen alive, or dead.

Then she touched tongue to the last Ring—Rowan, ever the weakest of the Houses, the one whose traditional ally was Ash, even as Oak and Yew were allied.

Two images, separate and distinct, yet one. Lord Wittern, and also the new Queen, Rannore. This caused Ysa to stop again and think. With Florian as head of both Oak and Yew, and with his wife being at least as important as Wittern in the governing of Rowan, this definitely had the potential of putting too much sheer political power in the hands of one not fit to wield it. Perhaps it was more fortunate than she had thought, that the King was so caught up both in bed-sport and in play with sword.

She tongue-touched the Ring on the thumb of her left hand again, summoning the image of Ashen, daughter of her late husband, and her bitterest rival. The girl stirred in her sleep, as if aware of Ysa's shadowy intrusion. The Dowager withdrew immediately.

Perhaps she should try to overcome her aversion to the girl in truth as well as appearances. Or at least until she had managed to wrest some of Florian's power from him before he discovered the true scope of it and began to use it in inappropriate ways. And, of course, so much depended on whether Rannore's child was a boy, or a girl. Ysa bit her lip, sharply aware that at this juncture she needed allies from any direction she could get them.

Ashen must live.

🌹

"Of course it won't hurt her," Florian said. He pulled Jacyne close and cupped his hand on her cheek, the way he knew she liked to be caressed. "You know how doctors are—all so jealous of each other that if one discovers a cure for some illness the rest won't use it even if their patients are dying."

"Tell me again what you want me to do."

Florian led Jacyne over to a table and sat her down in the chair next to it. He took the chair opposite and placed a small vial on the table. "My sister has been prescribed a daily tonic and Master Lorgan prepares it. You are to volunteer to take it to my sister's apartment. This will be easy, as Master Lorgan is so busy the morning often grows on toward noon before he gets around to taking it himself, and it grows stale. Put six drops, no more and no less, from this vial into the cup, and the lady's health will be much improved in a matter of days. I am assured that this is so."

"It does seem an easy matter—"

"Easy, and inexcusable that Master Lorgan hasn't seen to it himself. But as I said, physicians are a jealous lot."

"You must be very fond of your sister, to be so solicitous of her health."

"I have no other sister—that I know of," Florian said, with a touch of malicious humor. "Of course I care a great deal about what happens to her."

"Very well, I'll do it. I probably would have, even without the title and house that goes with the deed, though I do appreciate the gift. You are a generous King, sir."

"Oh, I can be very generous to someone who pleases me," Florian replied. "As here."

He placed a large purse on the table beside the vial. Jacyne hefted it, and the clink of coins filled the chamber. She peeked inside. "Gold!"

"As I said, I can be very generous to someone who pleases me, and when it pleases me to be so."

She smiled. "Then I must take pains to please you more often. And more completely. Tonight?"

"Of course." He had promised to spend the evening with Rannore, but he knew he could leave early, if he pleaded a headache. And he might as well get what pleasure Jacyne had to offer while she was still able to provide it.

Though she was undoubtedly slow in her wits, she was not completely stupid. Yes, eventually she would realize what part she had played in the death of his dear sister and then Rawl would have another assignment from the king. Almost, now that Jacyne's fate was all but accomplished, he felt a glow of that first attraction for her. He could afford to grant her a few evenings, if that was all it took to keep her quiet. And compliant.

When Obern returned to Rendelsham with Rohan, as instructed by Zazar, he expected to see Ashen looking and feeling much better. To his dismay, her condition seemed to have deteriorated instead, though she welcomed him warmly and bade Rohan sit on the side of her bed and tell him about his journey.

Ayfare drew Obern aside. "I don't know what it is that ails my lady," Ayfare whispered, "but she fades daily, little by little."

"Does the doctor know anything?"

"No. He is as puzzled as the rest of us. I prepare my lady's meals with my own hands, just to her liking, and give her a cup of tonic daily—"

"Tonic?"

"Aye, sir, as written out by that Bog-woman and prepared by Master Lorgan himself. Though lately—"

"What?"

"He hasn't been bringing it to her himself, as he did when we first got here, but one of the court ladies has taken up the duty."

"Which lady?"

"Jacyne, sir." Ayfare wrinkled her nose in a gesture of distaste. "They say she's the King's light-o'-love."

"Thank you, Ayfare. Tell my wife I have an errand. And let Rohan visit her as much as she wants, without tiring her. Perhaps that will cheer her up."

Then, full of apprehension, he went in search of Lady Jacyne. He found her with a group of other ladies, doing whatever it is that ladies did of an afternoon with their needles and thread. She looked up, startled when the steward announced his name, and followed him to a spot where they could speak in relative privacy.

"I've come to thank you for the gracious care you have taken of Lady Ashen," he told her. "I heard that you offered yourself to carry her tonic to her personally."

"It was nothing, sir. I only did what I could to help. And is she better, as our lord King promised? I only leave the cup with the maid, at the door, and have yet to be admitted to see her."

The King! Obern's apprehension deepened. So that silly, dressed-up, crowned nobody Kasai never referred to except to call him a catamite was mixed up in this! That meant no good. Obern knew he could not afford to let his temper flare, not yet, not without knowledge of what the details might be. Deliberately, he decided to lie. "Yes, she is greatly improved. The color is coming back into her cheeks, and the sparkle to her eyes."

"That is good," Lady Jacyne said with a smile. "His Majesty was right, then. Physicians are jealous folk, and Master Lorgan scorned to use the remedy that would cure her."

Obern decided to gamble all on one toss. "Now that I am back," he said to her as winningly as he could, "I am more than willing to take over the duty of adding the potion to my wife's medicine. Surely you can understand how I want to tend her with my own hands."

The lady nodded. "Of course, sir. Wait here, and I will fetch the vial."

He knew he was taking quite a risk, interfering with whatever scheme the King had in mind, and his only hope had been that Jacyne was being used as an unwitting dupe. If so, she would not object. If she knew that what she had been dosing Ashen's tonic with was, in fact, a noxious substance that was making her worse, she would never have allowed him to take over the task. Therefore she was innocent. Vaguely, this knowledge made him feel better.

Jacyne returned quickly. She placed a vial in his hand. Holding it up to the light, he could see that it was still almost full. He opened the vial, sniffed the bitter aroma, and recognized it.

"The dose is six drops, no more and no less," Jacyne told him. "His Majesty was most explicit."

"And how long has she been taking this?"

"Five days only."

That was a relief for it meant the King had not intended to end Ashen's life quickly but rather let her fade away as if naturally. She would undoubtedly recover.

"My thanks, Lady Jacyne. Six drops. I will remember."

Then he bowed, with as much courtier's grace as he could summon, and returned to his apartment. There he hid the vial at the bottom of his clothes chest, first making certain that the stopper was tightly sealed with wax. If it seeped out onto a shirt and then he wore it, he would suffer direly from it.

There were many sea-beings whose weapon was poison, either administered by sting or bite or hidden in succulent, tempting flesh. The Sea-Rovers had long accumulated lore on poisons. Obern knew this one—a concoction derived from certain underwater plants encountered when diving for shellfish. Brush against them once, and one only got stung for one's troubles. But get entangled in them and the hapless victim was apt to die before he could drown. Divers built up tolerance for the poison by eating the leaves and Obern himself had done so. Ingested, it made one ill according to the amount eaten. The stuff in the vial—Yes, it would be serious if it touched the skin, deadly even to him if it were rubbed into a cut. . . .

Blinding rage trembled behind Obern's eyes, and he dared not let it burst out. He sat down, clasping his hands tightly to keep them from rash action. He longed to seek out Royance's advice as he had before, but knew that the stern old man would have to be loyal to his King first, and at best would dismiss him out of hand. At worst, Obern could be imprisoned or even executed for what he longed to shout aloud, for what would be considered a treasonous utterance—that the King was murdering his sister.

What, then, would Royance advise, had this been someone other than the King attempting to poison Ashen?

He could not think. He only knew that if he did not act, and act decisively, Florian would try again, and keep on trying, until Ashen was dead.

"Oh, I do feel much better!" Ashen said, a week later. She had progressed to taking her meals at a table set up in her bedchamber, and now this had become a merry occasion with both Obern and Rohan joining her. "For a while it seemed that the tonic Zazar wanted me to take was making me worse, but it seems to be helping after all. That, and having my family with me once more." She smiled on both of them, particularly Rohan, and the boy beamed in return.

Master Lorgan had not been surprised when Obern had showed up at his door, requesting the potion. "Oh, yes, yes," he had said, "it is very helpful that so many want to take over this task of delivering it to her. And how does your lady?"

"Much improved," Obern had assured him.

"And so shall I observe, when next I visit. I am much pressed at the moment, but in seven-days' time, certainly."

"You will be most welcome." And surely by that time Ashen would have begun to mend in earnest, Obern thought.

He did not want to consider how, later, Ashen's unaccountable recovery could be explained to the King. But a germ of an idea was beginning to form.

Now Ashen took the goblet and drank it down. "Strange, but it doesn't taste nearly as bitter as it once did. Master Lorgan must be grinding fresher leaves."

"Or he has taken to washing the mortar and pestle," Rohan said mischievously. "Back at New Vold, Dagdya would grind up something bitter and then forget before she ground up something sweet, like the sugar she sprinkled on my porridge. The other women were always complaining about it and I did, too."

Ashen chuckled. "No blame to you!" she said. She looked up at Obern. "Do you think we could leave the castle for a while? It's been so long since I've been outside, in the fresh air."

The plan that had been taking form in Obern's mind, once the first flare of anger had subsided, needed only the doing to make it into reality. He had examined it from every angle, and knew it to be sound.

Or, if not, he knew it would have to do. And if he suffered as a result of it, then that was the price he was willing to pay for keeping Ashen safe. Once he was finished with the vicious young King, Florian would never trouble Ashen again. If all went well, he would do it today. In anticipation, he had dressed himself in his best—the dark green he had worn on his wedding day, his doublet covering a frothy white shirt, and he had pinned the brooch in the shape of a ship on his cap.

"Content you to sit in the window this day, my dear lady," he said. "Master Lorgan should be looking in on you today. I sent word to remind him. And then, if he pronounces you fit, we will go out tomorrow. I promise."

"Can I go, too?" Rohan was at his father's elbow, looking up pleadingly.

"That you can, but in the meantime, you may go and search out Lathrom, and tell him that I said you might ride out into the countryside. You should enjoy that, after being cooped up for all this time."

Rohan whooped with joy and dashed for the door, not remembering to take his leave properly. Obern would have called him back, but Ashen stopped him. "He's just a boy," she said, smiling. "Let him be one. Please do not scold him."

Obern grasped her hand and kissed it. "I will only follow to tell him to be sure and take his cloak, in case of rain."

Once he was out of the apartment that had begun to lose the smell of sickness and of medicine, Obern headed straight for the Great Hall. He knew that Lathrom would look after Rohan properly, and he knew also that now that he had set his course of action he would not turn aside. Both Ashen and Rohan were safely out of the way, and the time would never be better.

As he neared the big doors, pulled almost shut, he could hear the clash of steel from inside. Good. The class in swordplay under Sword-master Sedern was still in progress.

He opened the door and went in. The Sword-master had paired his students and now wandered among them, correcting this one's stance, that one's footwork. Florian caught sight of him and lifted one arm in greeting.

"Welcome, brother," he said, and, as usual, the nasal quality of his voice made Obern think of a petulant child. "And how does your lady?"

"Not well, Your Majesty," Obern replied, feigning a sadness he was far from feeling. "She is very like to die soon. I come here to find distraction, if such exists, from my worries about her."

"Distraction is yours. Will you match swords with any here?"

"I might. I am out of practice, though. I could hardly ask any of your fellows to indulge me."

Florian laughed, or rather uttered that bray that passed for laughter with him. Obern might as well not have mentioned the gravity of Ashen's condition. "It's said that Sea-Rovers are born with swords in their hands! Surely you are too modest."

"My skills are nothing beside yours, I am sure. It is said that you are the foremost swordsman in Rendel."

It was an outright lie, but Obern was almost becoming accustomed to dissembling in this place. He held his breath, for all depended on the King's next words. He fingered the hilt of his Rinbell sword; as a close kinsman of the King, he was allowed to wear it in the monarch's presence.

"I am passing good," Florian said. "But I have longed for the opportunity to test my skills against someone who is not at Court every day, and who does not have anything to gain by letting me win. Somebody, in fact, such as yourself. Would you care to play a match with me, my brother? A formal exhibition? First one to give three hits wins?"

Obern could not keep a smile from his lips. "Such would lighten my mood most pleasantly, Your Majesty. But neither of us is prepared for a formal match."

"Oh, come, you have your sword. Remove your coat, take a mask and a padded vest. Find one that suits you, and I will go to my chamber and likewise dress me fit to be seen by the Court. Also, my favorite sword is there, for I won't risk it in everyday practice. Shall we say we begin when I return?"

"Done and done, Your Majesty. Your hand on it?"

"Of course."

Then Obern spat into the palm of his hand and proffered it to the King. After a few moments' hesitation, Florian did likewise.

Then, the bargain being sealed, the King began issuing orders that the mat be set up, that raised platforms be brought for spectators, and that word be sent throughout the castle that Florian of Rendel was matching his skills against those of Obern of the Sea-Rovers, and all who wanted to watch were bid come.

Ten

*F*lorian *rushed to his* apartment, almost exulting. Not only was his bothersome sister on the point of expiring, but also now he had the opportunity of ridding himself of a brother-in-law who could, he felt confident, be expected to become as much a nuisance in his own way once he was a widower.

Quickly he stripped out of his sweat-soaked practice gear and put on a fresh shirt and deep red breeches, Oak's color. Obern had looked quite dashing, in his dark green, and the King would not be outdone. He took a moment to wash his face and hands as well, and to run a comb through his air.

He chose an unstained padded vest he had not yet worn in practice. It was stitched in such a way that he seemed to have rippling muscles across his chest, and Florian thought it so flattering that he had had half a dozen made. The garment offered considerably more protection than this occasion demanded; still, the combatants would be fighting with weapons that had not had the thin edge of lead applied to the blades, to blunt them, and so there was an element of danger. The main purpose was to remind both men where hits were not allowed. He buckled on a long dagger, the secondary weapon for this kind of contest. Then he got down the sword with the jeweled hilt and unsheathed it.

He was probably good enough to take Obern, but he was unwilling to risk the possibility of not administering a killing thrust. Rummaging in a cabinet, he drew out the bottle from which he had filled the vial given to Jacyne and which she had used to such excellent purpose. Carefully, he now touched the edges of the sword with the poison, let it dry a moment, and then re-sheathed the weapon.

There. Now he need not run Obern through—by accident, of course. Just a cut, and the potion would do its work, more swiftly than it had done with Obern's lady wife, Florian's despised sister. He needn't even treat the long dagger. Buckling on his sword and, checking his appearance once more in the mirror, the King of Rendel left his apartment to return to the Great Hall.

On arriving, he discovered that most of the preparations had already been accomplished and some courtiers were beginning to arrive, talking excitedly among themselves. His mother, the Dowager, was not in evidence, and Florian hoped she would not show up, as her presence would surely make him nervous. Nor was his wife present. Probably sick, as usual, in her apartment.

Nevertheless, their two chairs had been placed in the center of the rows of benches being set up on either side of the Hall, down the length of which ran a scarlet carpet mat, the ground on which the combatants would fight. Stewards were setting flambeaus on the walls and lighting them. There was a buzz of anticipatory speculation among the watchers, and when Florian came through the door, some of them spontaneously applauded.

He noted that Obern had likewise been making preparations. The deep green doublet and cap had been discarded now, and, like Florian, he wore a padded vest over his snowy white, embroidered shirt. His long scabbard also had been discarded, and he had replaced it with one that held a dagger like Florian's. Now he was taking practice swings with a sword that Florian immediately decided was inferior to his. It boasted no jewels or ornamentation of any kind that could be seen, though the blade gleamed brightly enough and seemed forged of good steel.

Obern, sighting Florian, advanced toward him, sword in one hand and mask in the other. "Shall we wait a few minutes and let more of those arrive who want to see their King display his skill?" he said.

"Of course," Florian replied. He smiled, feeling magnanimous. He even clapped Obern on the shoulder in a comradely fashion. "We've had too much doom and gloom around here, what with women being sick and all the talk about some threat from the North. The King and his brother shall provide good entertainment!"

"As you wish, sir."

Obern gave Florian a deft swordsman's salute, and Florian raised one eyebrow. The Sea-Rover handled that blade well enough. Perhaps too well. But then there was no cause to worry. Even if he himself lost the match, he would surely score at least one hit. And with that hit, Obern would lose everything.

To Florian's mild surprise, the former sergeant, Lathrom, stepped forward. Behind him was a boy whose resemblance to Obern made it clear that he must be the son Florian had heard about but not seen previously. He was an attractive boy, and Florian disliked him instantly.

"Obern will need a second, my lord King," Lathrom said. "Would you allow me that honor?"

"Yes. And Sword-master Sedern will second for me. With your approval," Florian added, belatedly remembering the courtesies of the sword.

"No better," Obern said. He inclined his head in Sedern's direction, and the Sword-master bowed in return. Then he turned to his son. "Rohan, I had thought you absent. This is something you do not need to watch. But now that you're here, go and sit down and whatever happens, do not interfere. Do you understand?"

"Yes, Father. But I know you'll beat him!"

Obern laughed. "That is not polite, boy. You're speaking of the King."

"I don't care, I—"

Lathrom clapped a hand over Rohan's mouth and turned him toward the rows of chairs. "Mind your father," he said, and the boy obediently, if a bit reluctantly, complied.

"My apologies," Obern said.

Florian shrugged. He chose to be generous, though if the boy had said much more he might have decided otherwise. "Children will be children. I suppose it is good that he is your partisan."

"Even as you championed your own father."

Florian peered at Obern sharply, but the Sea-Rover seemed to have no guile about him. Well, perhaps he didn't know the uneasy relationship that had existed between the Prince and King Boroth when that monarch had been alive. Florian was well aware of the slight esteem in which Boroth had held him, and he had returned the sentiment wholeheartedly, to the point of wishing for the old man to go ahead and die and get out of the way. Of course, all this had happened well before Obern had become a prominent member of the Court upon marriage with the King's sister. His illegitimate sister, but blood nonetheless.

He decided that Obern had not been intending to rattle him with that remark and so dismissed it.

The seconds were already setting up small tables at either end of the mat, bearing flagons of watered wine and cups for the combatants so they could refresh themselves between rounds. Physicians had been assigned to both sides, Master Lorgan for the King, and one of his most talented assistants for Obern. Both Lathrom and Sedern poured from the flagons and drank, to show that the beverage was wholesome. Then they wiped the edges of the cups, and replaced them on the tables.

They returned to the center of the mat and waited for the contestants to approach. By that time, most of the chairs were full and the whispering among the courtiers, particularly the ladies, filled the air like the sound of whirring insect wings.

The Sword-master stepped forward, and the Hall grew silent. "This will be an exhibition match between our Most Gracious Majesty, King Florian, and his esteemed kinsman and brother, Obern of the Sea-Rovers, for the edification and entertainment of all," Sedern proclaimed. "You will fight three rounds, timed thusly." He held up a miniature hourglass. "First round shall be fought with masks and vests, second round with masks removed, and the third, should the bout last that long, without vests, the combatants using sword plus long dagger. The first man to bestow three hits upon his opponent will be judged the winner. If at the end of three rounds there are equal hits between you, the combatants will fight until a winner and a loser is decided. Is this clear?"

Both men nodded.

"Are you ready to begin?"

"I am," Florian said.

"Yes," said Obern.

Then they took their stances on the crimson carpet, blades crossed. Lathrom stepped forward, his own blade drawn. He glanced from one to the other, and then, with a swift upward movement dashed their swords apart.

Immediately Florian pressed to the attack and Obern gave ground. Then they began taking each other's measure with an occasional feint and parry, testing to see where the other man's weakness might lie.

Obern attacked, and it was Florian's turn to give way. They prowled around each other. Behind his mask, Florian's smile vanished, to be replaced with a look of intense concentration. Before he realized that much time had passed, Sedern announced the first round over. The room filled with applause and the sound of excited voices. Somewhere, wagers were being offered and accepted. The next round would surely offer more action, with the vision-blocking masks removed.

Florian and Obern returned to their places at either end of the crimson mat. The King watched while Obern removed his mask and merely wiped his face on a towel, refusing the wine.

"Later," the Sea-Rover said, "when we are finished." He looked at Florian and raised his voice so he was sure to be heard. "Then we will celebrate the winner together!"

"Agreed," Florian said. He lifted his cup in salute, but took only a swallow. Then he, too, wiped his face and scrubbed his hands as well. Unaccountably, his palms were sticky. The Sea-Rover was a better swordsman than he had thought. Florian was accustomed to the mask and Obern was not, and still he had not been able to get through the other man's guard. But this next round should remedy that. Florian resolved that, by fair means or foul, he would inflict a hit upon Obern even if that meant he had to endure one himself.

Once more, the combatants met in the middle. Again, when he was sure that both were equally ready, Lathrom knocked their blades upward and leapt back as both men tried to press forward an attack. Florian began to get the proper sword rhythm. Abruptly he stepped outside of time, and everything slowed for him. Other men had spoken of such a phenomenon, but this was the first time Florian had ever experienced it.

Knowing himself in complete control now, he let himself be pushed almost to the end of the mat, hoping to draw Obern into overextending himself. He dropped his guard for an instant, and, just as he had hoped, Obern lunged and, as if in a dream, scored a hit on Florian's left upper arm, In that same instant, but leisurely, just before Obern's second could declare a temporary halt, Florian gave Obern a similar wound. He could hear the fabric of Obern's shirt tear, thread by thread, as the blade pierced it.

"Hits on both sides!" Sedern cried.

"Agreed," Lathrom said. "But the King's came late."

Their voices echoed distorted and hollow in Florian's ears. "Not too late," he said, with a laugh. "No foul. Shall we rest a moment and let the physicians bind our cuts?"

Slowly, slowly, Obern glanced down at the place where blood was staining the spotless purity of his sleeve. "I've had worse hurts going through underbrush," he said. "I'll rest when you will." It seemed to take him forever to say the words.

"Brother, I like you well," Florian said, and meant it. He was almost sorry that this man of whom he was so fond was going to die. Now he could afford to feel affection for him. "Let us continue, pray."

He floated, weightless, in this strange, timeless world. Without waiting for Lathrom to give the formal signal, he attacked once more, ignoring the spot of royal blood that seeped onto his own shirt. He scarcely felt the hit. It was nothing, and less than nothing, and Florian knew himself to be brave and manly to endure it without flinching.

Full of confidence now, invincible, he pressed forward and, as the watching crowd gasped, inflicted a second hit on slow, awkward Obern, a finger's width from the first.

A woman gasped and another cried aloud, from where they were standing in the doorway, and involuntarily Florian glanced back in that direction. Royance stood there with two women. Impossibly, one of them was Ashen, who should be dying, and with her, Rannore, the heavily pregnant Queen—

Abruptly the bubble of time in which he had been wrapped shattered, and everything snapped back to its proper course.

Obern looked in the direction of the doorway, startled as well. He turned his foot and stumbled on a wrinkle in the mat, his sword still raised. Florian was in the way and the point went through his body.

"No!" Obern cried, his face and voice registering horror at the realization of what he had done. "It was an accident! Forgive me!"

Florian stumbled in turn, with Obern still holding fast to the hilt, and the sword pulled out again.

How strange, Florian thought. Obern's sword pierced my vest as easily as a knife goes through cheese. The blade must be better than I thought. Then his knees gave way and he sagged to the floor.

Eleven

As swiftly as she could, Ashen raced across the polished floor toward the tableau that had transfixed all others in the room. "Obern," she cried breathlessly. "Florian—"

By that time both physicians and the seconds had reached the wounded King. The doctors ignored Obern, to tend to Florian. Florian coughed, and a bloody foam stained his mouth.

"Your Majesty, I fear this is a mortal wound," Master Lorgan said. He sounded profoundly shocked.

Awkwardly, Rannore knelt beside her husband. He sprawled on the mat, writhing in pain. "Ashen came to get me when she learned of the duel," she said. "We wanted to stop it. We never thought—"

"That Obern would be so clumsy he'd trip over his own feet and run me through?" Florian groaned. "Give me something for the pain, Master Lorgan. Quick!"

"If I can, Your Majesty." The physician's hands shook as he fumbled a vial open and shook its contents into the cup that the other physician offered him.

"Neat wine, none of that watery stuff." Florian coughed again.

Andre Norton & Sasha Miller

"Oh, sir, Your Majesty, it truly was an accident—" Ashen was close to fainting. "Please! You must believe it!"

"Believe it?" Florian said, his voice a hoarse croak. "Does it matter?"

"Yes, Your Majesty, it does," Royance said. "I saw it all. He turned his foot and—Pardon Obern or he will surely die for today's misadventure."

Rannore propped Florian's head on her lap, heedless of the blood soaking his shirt and her dress, and began to weep. She took the fresh cup of undiluted wine in which Master Lorgan had mixed the medicine and offered it to the King who drank it down eagerly. Almost at once he seemed easier; it must have been a powerful dose. "It doesn't matter. Obern will die anyway," Florian said. He managed to smile, if a little lopsidedly. "Look you at the hits. If I had given him only one, still he would have died." He glanced over at his shoulder at his sword where it had fallen from his hand.

Obern's eyes grew wide. He dropped the bloodstained Rinbell sword and clutched at his left arm. "I am poisoned!" he said. "I am killed."

"Surely not," Lathrom said. Nevertheless, he went and picked up Florian's sword and examined the blade. "There does seem to be something on it besides blood—"

"Touch it not," Obern said. His face was very pale and a grimace of pain crossed his features. Ashen, still weak from her own illness, nevertheless slipped under his arm to support him. "I know what it is."

Members of the Court had now clustered around and someone slid a chair against Obern's knees. He collapsed into it gratefully and Ashen, strength gone and unable to stand any longer, sank down at his feet. Lathrom began tearing the linen of Obern's shirt so he could look at the wounds.

"What are you saying?" Royance demanded. "Are you accusing the King—"

"Yes, I accuse the King. He spoke truly. I am dying. He has poisoned me with the same mixture he caused to be given Ashen.

Except when it is swallowed, in small doses, it kills more slowly. And with less pain."

Another woman pushed through the crowd. "Sir, sir, Lord Royance, it is true!" She was deathly pale. She stared down at the King, the dawning realization plain on her face.

"And you are—who?" Royance said.

"Lady Jacyne," she said, and a buzz of whispers went through the watching crowd. "Florian—I mean, the King—gave me a potion to add to Lady Ashen's daily medicine. He swore it was to heal her—Oh, forgive me! I didn't know!"

"You were used," Obern said, "as were we all, in our own ways." He bared his teeth in what was intended to be a grin.

Ashen, beside him, only stared, horrified. Events were progressing too rapidly for her, in her weakened condition, to take in all at once. "Husband—" she said.

He pushed himself to his feet and managed to bow to Royance, though the movement brought beads of sweat to his forehead. "I used the King's pride to tempt him into crossing swords with me. I plotted all along to pretend to stumble and thus kill him for what he had tried to do to his sister, my wife. I had thought to do it more cleverly, though. This was truly an accident and my clumsiness was real." He looked around at the shocked courtiers. "I planned beforehand to beg the King's pardon, even as Lord Royance did for me, and I would have accepted it, too."

Ashen struggled to her feet. He turned to look at her.

"I had not reckoned on your being here. I wanted to spare you."

"If only I had come sooner. If only we—"

"I was to blame," Rannore said, her voice faint. "I was ill and had to be persuaded to leave my chamber."

"You are *all* to blame!" Florian said angrily. "And you deserve what you got. Death for Obern, and if not for his meddling, death for Ashen, too—"

"Say it not, Your Majesty!" Royance cried.

"Am I supposed to make a good ending?" Florian coughed again. "At least, thanks to the physician, I am spared a lot of pain—which is more mercy than you will have, Obern. You will die in agony. Lorgan, I command you. Give him none of what you administered to me."

"Give the medicine to him," Royance said. "If he desires it."

Obern straightened, and Ashen recognized the pride she had seen before, when he was hurt and trying not to show it. "I will not need your medicine," he said. "Nor will I have it said that Obern of the Sea-Rovers fell to treachery by anybody, even the King of Rendel." He looked at Ashen, reached out and touched her cheek. "Give the Rinbell sword to Rohan, when he is a man. Tell my father that I died well."

Then, before she could stop him, he drew the dagger that hung at his side and plunged it into his heart. Even as she reached out for him, he crumpled and fell at her feet, dead before he reached the floor.

A wheezing noise made her turn around, even at such a moment. It was Florian, trying to laugh.

"It's all too funny. Don't you see? If I had not had the poison to use, I would have been the one pretending to trip and run Obern through before he got me. But he is dead anyway. I won the contest," he said, twisting his face into a sneer. "I won—"

And then his face relaxed. He took a breath, let it out, and did not take another.

Royance gave orders that both Ashen and Rannore be taken at once to their bedchambers and that Master Lorgan and his assistant give them draughts to make them sleep. "Neither of these unfortunate ladies should have been called upon to witness what we have seen this day," he said. "Now, send for the Dowager—the older Dowager, that is. Do not let her into the Hall until this carnage is cleared away, and the bodies laid out decently. Just tell her what has happened and that it is by my orders and for concern of her that she not come beforetimes."

By the time the Dowager was allowed in, the room had been set to rights and the blood wiped off the floor. Both Florian and Obern had been washed and dressed in fresh garments, and placed on twin biers before the dais on which the throne sat. Their features were composed, and their hands clasped over their chests, holding the swords with which they had slain each other.

"That it should come to this," Ysa murmured, for once shocked to the core of her being. Forewarned, she had changed into black from her accustomed green or dark red. Her necklace, earrings, and bracelets were made of glittering jet.

"Indeed, Madame," Royance said. "It is a dark day for Rendel."

"Rannore. How does she? And the child?"

"Well enough, Master Lorgan tells me. She does not seem in any immediate danger of losing it."

The Dowager nodded. "And Ashen?"

"She, like Rannore, is prostrate with grief. She has taken the guilt for not stopping the contest before it began."

"I doubt that she could have done anything. Not when even I was not aware—" Ysa fixed Royance with a penetrating look. "You know more than you are telling me. Let us go somewhere private, and there you will inform me of what has happened when my attention was elsewhere."

Royance bowed and followed the Dowager to her apartment, where he had conferred with her so often. As they moved through the corridors, past clusters of sympathetic courtiers, he could not help but wonder what would become of a realm with two Dowager Queens and no King. If only Ashen's child had lived. And if only Rannore's would live, and be a boy. . . .

When they were safely behind closed doors, Ysa sent for wine and drank two cups for each one that Royance consumed. Not that he blamed her; it was not every day that one lost a son who was also a King. She did not stop questioning him until she had every scrap of information Royance had to offer.

"You said that Obern had sought your counsel before," she said.

"Why, if he suspected my son of—of what he thought Florian was doing, did he not seek your advice again? Surely you could have turned him from this folly."

"And, indeed, I would have, Madame. But he did not ask."

The Dowager stared at nothing, rubbing the Rings as if unaware of what she was doing.

"Ashen cannot succeed, any more than can Rannore." Ysa's voice was flat. "I have looked at the records. It is against all law and custom. There is no precedent that a woman has ever ruled in her own right and surely not one related by marriage, or by illegitimate connection. There was no need to consider the possibility, until now."

Royance forbore to mention that Ysa herself had as good as ruled for many years, first by will alone, later by virtue of having the Four Great Rings on her hands, and hers was only a connection by marriage. As if she read his thoughts, she held up her hands.

"These," she said, "chose me, as you well know. And so, I have acted as Regent when necessary. But I never claimed sole power. This you know well."

"Indeed, this is so," Royance said.

"Thus, with Florian dead"—Royance could almost swear he heard the unspoken thought *at last* in the Dowager's words—"and his child yet unborn, Rendel will once again be ruled by the Council, as it was during my son's minority. This is the only reasonable course we can take. Do you not agree?"

"Yes, Your Highness," Royance said. "And let us offer prayers that the new Dowager's child be a boy, and that he will be strong, and thrive, and with the help of all of us—you most of all—become a good King in the times to come. With the peril from the North ever threatening us, this is no time for Rendel to show weakness."

"Aye, pray that it be so." The Dowager arose from her chair, cool and calm. "We have a royal funeral to arrange—two of them, I suppose, for we must not offer insult to our allies the Sea-Rovers by slighting Obern, for all that he murdered the King."

"Your Highness—"

"We are alone. We can speak frankly to each other. Obern murdered Florian, and Florian murdered Obern. Let the funeral therefore be equal for them both. We must send messengers to New Vold." She began to pace, clasping and unclasping her hands—not in agitation, but as someone who is thinking rapidly. "Ashen must not return there. She cannot. Her place is—where? I know. I will give her the old Oakenkeep that presently lies nearly vacant with just a token force to keep it from falling into ruin. That should be close enough for me to keep an eye on her, and yet far away enough to content us both."

Royance dared ask a question. "To what end do you give the Oakenkeep to Ashen?"

Ysa stopped, and looked at Royance. She smiled, and Royance knew she had begun to plot and plan once more. In her current mood, and with the wine she had drunk, she might be coaxed into telling him more than she intended. He waited, trying not to show the curiosity he felt.

"Gaurin will be returning soon, with some of his people. You do remember him?"

"Yes. Count Gaurin of the Nordors. I was impressed with him when he was here before."

"Well," the Dowager said, still smiling, "it seems that he was more than impressed with our Bog-Princess, and she with him. And on her wedding day, too!"

"I had heard of no impropriety."

"There was none. And yet there was an attraction that fair made the air crackle around them. At the time, I wondered if I should dissolve that marriage and arrange for another, with a Nordorn bridegroom with more than a little royal blood in his veins."

Royance tried to hide a measure of shocked surprise.

"Oh, don't look so disapproving," Ysa said. She picked up the wine-flask, poured the last measure into her cup, and drank. Then she rang for more. "I just may get tipsy this night."

"Surely Your Highness may do as she pleases."

"And it may please me to marry Ashen to Count Gaurin, to

seal a pact between the Nordors and our people. What d'you think of that?"

"I feel it may be premature, with Ashen such a recent widow, to be considering another marriage."

"Well, I don't. Think, Royance, think. Our alliance with the Sea-Rovers is firm. We *need* the Nordors, perhaps more than they need us. They are the ones who are most likely to know what kind of danger this is that is coming at us from their lands, and even more important, how best to fight it. Even if Ashen and Gaurin had hated each other on sight—which I assure you they did not—I would be working toward this alliance now that Obern is out of the way."

The fresh flask arrived, and Ysa poured a cup for herself, offering some to Royance as well. He declined, and sat staring into the fire. He could not bring himself to admit that the death of the King, Ysa's own son, and that of the son of the Chieftain of the Sea-Rovers had had no more effect on the Dowager than to galvanize her into the middle of another round of schemes and plots. And yet this was the truth that he must face. Suddenly he saw, in place of the black-clad woman in front of him, a glittering spider in the center of a web, plucking now this string and now another, making all around her dance at her will.

"As Your Highness desires," he said. "Now, I beg your leave to go. Surely you will want to mourn in private."

"You mean, to get tipsy in private," Ysa said. "The way my late husband did. And my son." She laughed. She was beginning to slur her words. "Well, go. Go. Nobody is stopping you. Tomorrow we will begin anew."

Royance bowed deeply, and left the Dowager's apartment, closing the door behind him. He beckoned to one of the Dowager's women, Lady Grisella. "You and the other ladies, look to your mistress," he said. "I fear she will be at the wine-flask this night, and she will need your help."

"And who's to blame her?" Grisella said sympathetically. "Surely she's had enough grief and worry to drive a lesser woman mad. Don't worry, sir. We'll take good care of her."

Thus reassured, Royance went to his own quarters. But his heart remained sorely troubled.

✿

Ashen awoke from the drug-induced slumber with her head surprisingly clear. She had to remind herself of the events of the previous day.

"Obern is really dead, isn't he?" she asked Ayfare.

"Aye, lady, that he is, and young Rohan is inconsolable. He was there, you know, and saw it all."

"No, I don't remember. My attention was all on Obern." She pushed the covers back and got out of bed. Though still weak, she knew that she was mending. "When I am dressed, send Rohan to me. I will do what I can to comfort him."

"Aye, lady, I will. Now let me bring you food, and perhaps enlighten you on what has happened while you were asleep."

Ashen sat down at the small table in her room, the one that had been set up for her while she had been so very ill, and began eating the breakfast of fruit and fresh-baked bread Ayfare had brought. She set aside a few pieces of fruit that she knew Rohan liked, hoping to tempt him with it. The maid chattered on, as usual a veritable fount of information.

The Old Dowager, it was said, had taken to the wine bottle. But nobody believed this was a lasting thing; she had had too much experience with what it did to both her husband and her son. It was, instead, the way her grief came out because she had never cared for King Florian. His widow grieved in private, but his latest mistress was indiscreet enough to let her own feelings show to one and all. And other women, who had had liaisons with the King, were now coming forward as if hoping for some largesse in the King's will—

In the midst of this, a thought struck Ashen. "With all this discussion of this lady and that," she said, as neutrally as she could, "do you likewise speak of me when you are with the other maids?"

Ayfare put her hands to her mouth, shocked. "Of course not, lady! But others will talk, and sometimes, if there's no harm in it, I will give them the straight of the story. But to chatter idly of you? I would never betray you. Never."

"Thank you for that. Now help me get dressed, and send Rohan in to see me."

She offered him the dish of fruit when he had been brought in and given a footstool to sit on. "Thank you, lady," he said. Politely, he took a slice of pear and nibbled on it.

They spoke of inconsequential things for a while, and then he asked, "What's to become of me now?"

Ashen thought a moment. The lad was truly an orphan, with neither father nor mother living, his only blood relative the Chieftain of the Sea-Rovers who seemed entirely indifferent to him or any other child. "What would you like?" she said.

"If I could have my way, I would like to live with you," he replied. "But that probably won't happen."

"It will if I say it will," Ashen told him. "With the exception of Zazar, the Wysen-wyf of the Bog, I don't have anybody, either, for my family is long since dead with only a few distant relatives who have never heard of me, or I them."

He thought about that. "So mostly, what we have, is each other. Right?"

"Yes. And that means there isn't anybody to tell us no."

"Then that is settled. Now may I go out? I would like to be alone for a while, or perhaps with Lathrom, if you don't mind. He was my father's friend, and he is sad, too."

"Of course you shall be with Lathrom. You are a good boy to think of others at a time like this."

Rohan walked to the door, his pace unlike his usual energetic bounding, but not before taking another piece of fruit. Ashen watched him go. He would, she thought, be all right. But would she? Suddenly she realized that there were many people depending on her—not only Rohan, but Lathrom as well, and the men he commanded. Ayfare. The future yawned before her, and what it held she could not even begin to imagine.

Perhaps she would return to the Bog. But then, with Rohan now her ward, this would be no place for him, not to mention the others in her care. She did not look forward to going back to New Vold, for the customs and manners of the Sea-Rovers were not to her liking, but the prospect of staying on in Rendelsham, at the castle, was even less inviting to the point of being intolerable. Worst of all was the possibility that she would be bidden to go to stay with Harous. He had only been turned aside from courting her because of the Dowager's orders, and Lady Marcala would not welcome her presence.

Well, she didn't have to face it just yet. There were still the funerals to get through, and she was not entirely healed. But once all that was past her, she must begin considering what she was going to do with her life.

She did not want to think about the fact that her mourning for Obern was little deeper than what one would feel for the loss of a dear friend. Certainly not the abject grief that a loving widow was expected to display. She resolved to go and comfort Rannore. Surely these two women, caught as they had been in marriages that were less than ideal, would find much to say to one another.

Two days later, Rendelsham saw two state funerals, great and elaborate to have been arranged so swiftly. Ashen retrieved the Rinbell sword, Rohan's inheritance, and Obern was buried instead with the weapon Harous had given him. Florian was buried with the jeweled sword which had been decently cleansed of the poison that had once edged the blade. Both coffins were bolted shut, and then put into the royal crypt.

A week after, a message came from the Old Dowager, summoning Ashen. At the hour past noon she was to present herself in the Dowager's sitting room. Ashen left her apartment early, to pay a call on the Young Dowager, as she was already being called. Rannore received her warmly enough, but her eyes were red and it was plain she had been weeping. It quickly became clear to Ashen that she was not weeping solely for Florian.

"Royal widows are the most useless commodity on earth," she told Ashen. "Not like royal wards, such as you. Who is there who is of high-enough station to marry me? Who will be a father to my child?" She put her hand on her belly. "Who will protect me from the warring political factions that are even now forming? Some of Florian's followers—well, let us just say that they are up to no good for anyone but themselves. Once my babe is born—"

"If only I could offer you help," Ashen said. "But I, too, am tossed by the wind and I do not know which direction it will take me."

Rannore caught her hand. "I am sure Ysa has something in mind for you. But I do not know what it is. It may be good, and maybe not, according to her whim. Please, whatever happens, say that you will be my friend."

"Of course I will," Ashen told the other girl. "There are never enough true friends in this world, and I am happy to have you for mine."

Then, the hour past noon rapidly approaching, she had to take her leave.

She found the Dowager alone, for once. Immediately Ashen was on her guard, for Ysa was always in the company of someone— a maid, one or more of her court ladies, Lady Marcala. "I am here, as you commanded, Your Highness," she said.

"Come closer. Sit by me."

Even at that distance, Ashen could tell that Ayfare's gossip had been correct. The scent of wine was heavy on Ysa's breath, but she seemed to be in control of herself even if her manner was considerably more blunt than usual. Ashen took the chair opposite Ysa's, beside the fireplace.

The Dowager leaned forward. "What would you say," she said

in a confidential voice, "if I told you that you were to marry Count Gaurin? That it is my command that you do so."

It had to be a dream. Ashen's heart lurched and soared upward. As if she needed to be forced—

She shocked herself with her eagerness. Propriety demanded that a decent interval elapse between Obern's death and her marrying again. "Surely we should allow a period of mourning," she began. "And Gaurin has not been consulted."

"To the contrary, he has. I sent word to him. He is even now on his way back to Rendel with his followers. He knows that the situation here has changed drastically. I told him you were now free and that I desired to make alliance with his people by a marriage between you. The answer was that he would make all possible speed, and be here within two days to take your hand. He is quite eager, but do not think too highly of yourself; it is not entirely because of you. The fleeing Nordors must have a place of their own, according to the preliminary treaty I have made with them. Therefore I want you married, and Gaurin with his Nordors settled in the Oakenkeep, a fortnight later. All the revenues excepting the Crown's share go to you. Is that clear?"

"Yes, Your Highness." Ashen's lips were numb and she had to force the words out. "Perfectly clear."

Ysa peered at Ashen closely. "Is there something wrong? Do you not desire this marriage? Surely, from what I observed at your last wedding—"

Ashen's face grew hot. "Your Highness, I—"

"Don't try to dissemble with me, girl. I saw you. And I know that you had enough honor to go through with the bargain you had made. But now, when I offer you what your heart must desire, you balk? Why?"

"Your Highness mentioned honor. I cannot honor Obern by marrying another when he is barely in his tomb."

"Very fine of you, I'm sure. If you like, it can be a quiet, very private wedding. But marry Gaurin you will, and there's an end to it." Ysa abruptly turned away, picking up the cup of wine on the table beside her.

"Yes, Your Highness." Plainly, the audience was over.

Ashen arose from her chair, bowed, and returned to her apartment. There she lay down on her bed, stunned. Ayfare, as usual, knew all about it beforehand. Ashen wondered if the maid had some way of finding out everything that went on in the castle before the people involved were fully aware of it. She chattered happily, already planning the wedding.

"Your late husband, Obern, was a good man and no mistake, and he loved you well in his own way, rough though it was at times. But you two were not a good match any more than the Young Dowager and the late King were, more's the pity. And she doesn't even have a lover waiting to marry her, either."

"Ayfare!"

"Oh, yes, lady, I know. There was never anything between you and Count Gaurin. But he was your lover nonetheless."

Ashen let the maid talk on, without hearing her. Gaurin and she, wed. And the Oakenkeep hers as well. Just a few days earlier, she had been worrying how she would take care of all the people who had come to depend on her.

Gaurin arrived at Rendelsham Castle in even less time than promised. He must have pushed his men hard, to cut his journey so short. As commanded, he made his way to the Great Hall where Ysa, Royance, Rannore, and several members of the Council, Harous among them, waited with Ashen. Harous's face was hard to read. If he had hoped to renew his suit for Ashen now that Obern was gone, he was disappointed. However, he showed nothing of what he might have been thinking. Lady Marcala, who usually was as much a part of Harous as the weapon he bore at his side as the Lord High Marshal of Rendel, was conspicuously absent.

The doors opened, and Gaurin, followed by half a dozen of his men, entered, his cloak swirling about him as he strode forward.

Ashen could not help drawing in her breath at the sight of him. Like the rest of the court, he had dressed in mourning, but his face was not sad. Indeed, his features became almost radiant when he caught sight of Ashen.

The Old Dowager gave greetings to the man from the North. "And what news do you bring us?" she said.

"The Great Evil, of which we as yet know little, is preparing to move. It has sent out tendrils seeking knowledge beyond where it has been pent-up for so many years. When it thinks it is strong enough, it will come."

"But not this year?"

"No. And not the next, we can hope. But it will come."

"With your help, we will be prepared for it. Now we shall consider happier matters." Ysa turned to Ashen and beckoned her to come forward. "To cement the ties between your people and ours, will you, Count Gaurin of the Nordors, please state openly before this company that you are willing to marry our late King's half-sister, who is now a widow."

He reached out and clasped her hand. "With all my heart," he said.

"And you, Ashen, royal lady of Rendel," continued the Old Dowager, who, according to Ayfare, had resumed her sober ways, "please state before this company that you are willing to marry Count Gaurin of the Nordors."

She wanted to shout aloud, but refrained. To display the eagerness she felt would honor neither her nor her late husband's memory. "You have commanded me, and so I agree," she said in turn. She knew he could feel her trembling, for he squeezed her fingers and, lifting her hand to his lips, kissed them.

"Because we are still in mourning, it will be no great celebration," Ysa said. "Will this content you, or would you rather wait until the mourning period is ended?"

"I would welcome any condition you might set, as long as Ashen can be mine. Within the hour if possible."

"Then go we all to the Fane of the Glowing, for a priest awaits you there."

Without further ado, they all left the Great Hall and walked the short distance to the Fane. By Ashen's request, Esander, the priest who had befriended her, awaited. As the great ones of Rendel looked on, Esander took Ashen's and Gaurin's hands in his and, in the simplest of ceremonies, married them.

Twelve

*I*t *was not Ashen's* opinion alone that Rohan was an engaging young man, bright and attractive. His fears about his future when his father died proved groundless. Before Obern's body had cooled, Count Harous had petitioned for the boy to go into his household as a page, but both the Lady Marcala and the Old Dowager had firmly disagreed with this plan. Even Royance admitted taking an interest in Rohan and likewise offered his household, but again his offer was discouraged.

Ashen could easily understand why Lady Marcala and the Dowager wanted to keep Rohan from Harous; this would have created a tie between the Count and Ashen, and that, Marcala would not abide. But Royance's offer of favor held many bright prospects for a parentless youngster. Gossip had it that the Old Dowager was unwilling that her Head of the Council have in his household what amounted to a hostage who could be turned to her own advantage, and that she could not abide.

Then, to Ashen's surprise and Rohan's as well, a message came from Snolli Sea-Rover while she was still at Rendelsham, bidding her bring the boy to New Vold.

"What can this mean?" she asked Gaurin.

"It seems that our great Chieftain has belatedly realized that young Rohan is now the heir to the Sea-Rovers," he said. "We must go to New Vold."

"I will not give Rohan up to be reared as a—a near-savage!"

"He has done well enough, being reared as a savage, up until now," Gaurin pointed out. "And Obern as well. I confess, if it hadn't been for his being your husband I would have liked him."

"I grew not to like the Sea-Rovers while I lived among them. Compared to Bog-men, they were civilized. But their ways are not ours."

"Well, we will settle the matter. Return a message to Snolli, telling him that we will be in New Vold as soon as we have established ourselves in the Oakenkeep. That should keep him satisfied for the time being."

They got no answering summons, telling them to come at once, and so Ashen and Gaurin moved from Rendelsham to the Oakenkeep. The castle was situated on a spit of land where the River Rendel and the Rowan joined. A channel had been cut to create an island on which the Oakenkeep floated secure from attack from any but the most determined enemy. The outer walls did not look massive, but within, the keep itself boasted twin gatehouses and ample room to house many Nordors and their families with them. It was dirty and had fallen into some measure of disrepair, and so Gaurin engaged masons and glaziers to repair the walls and to install new windows in place of the ruined shutters. For several weeks, the air smelled of fresh mortar and of the strong soap used to scrub all clean once more.

The Nordors whom Gaurin had brought as refugees from the gathering forces in the North were absorbed easily into the vast living quarters, and also Lathrom and his men. Generously, Gaurin offered Lathrom the captaincy of the guard at the Oakenkeep, and with gratitude Lathrom accepted.

Likewise, Ashen elevated Ayfare to the position of head housekeeper. "I accept, lady," she said, "but only if you take no other personal maid but me. Only I can look after you in a way that suits us both."

"Hire staff as you see fit," Ashen said. "And arrange matters as you will. I know that I cannot manage a place like this without you, having no experience in such things."

Mollified, Ayfare did as she was told, and in an astonishingly short time had assembled the kind of staff that an important castle such as this one required for its proper functioning. Ashen found that her own duties were considerably lightened because of Ayfare's efficiency.

A season later, when Ashen had almost forgotten about the Chieftain's demands, the second message did arrive from Snolli. Ashen knew she could postpone the inevitable no longer. After all, Snolli was Rohan's blood kindred, while she was merely the one with whom Rohan preferred to remain.

Gaurin accompanied her on the journey southward, with a company of mounted and armed men. At first, Ashen had wanted to go alone, not wishing to draw undue attention to the fact that she had married again almost immediately after Obern's death. But Gaurin demurred.

"My presence, and that of our guard, will help them remember to hold their tongues on that subject. At least until after we are gone," he added with a wry smile.

She had been very grateful that he had prevailed when they walked into the Great Hall at New Vold and saw Snolli's glowering face and the grim looks his followers gave them. With cold courtesy—which was to say, a manner that would have been considered unbearable rudeness to anyone not of the Sea-Rovers—he bade them sit.

"Tell me of Obern's ending," he said.

Ashen had thought he would immediately demand that Rohan be turned over to him. Thankful that this was postponed if even for a little while, she began telling of the duel between Florian and Obern.

"A treacherous blackguard as well as a catamite!" muttered the Spirit Drummer, Kasai, when she came to the part about how the late King had poisoned the sword he used in the duel.

"And you say that Obern stabbed himself with his own dagger when he learned that he had been poisoned?" Snolli said.

"Yes. He gave me his sword for Rohan, and bade me tell you that he died well. He deprived the King of his triumph."

"Then all is not in ruin after all." Snolli sat long in contemplation. "Yet you are at fault, and it is truly a grievous one."

The formal tone to his speech warned Ashen that she might stand in peril.

"Under Sea-Rover law, you bear great blame. First you lost Obern's child, which would have been my grandchild, and then, because of you, Obern himself died. I will not mention the disgraceful adventure in the catamite-king's hunting lodge. A proper woman would have died before being taken."

Ashen felt her face grow hot. "Your laws are no longer mine, nor did they ever apply! Do you think I went willingly to the hunting lodge? Sir, I was captured by force! Do you think I willed myself to lose my child? Sir, I almost died! And do you think that I had anything to do with the fight between Obern and Florian, when he kept his plans from me until it was too late? Sir, I lost my husband!"

"And quickly found another," Snolli said sourly. "Too quickly, by my reckoning."

Gaurin arose from his chair and stood before the Chieftain, his hand resting by habit on the hilt of his sword. His graceful bearing dominated the room. "My Lady Ashen has a measure of royal blood," he told Snolli. His tone and manner were not challenging, and yet he commanded everyone's full attention. "Because of that, she would have been a target for any malcontent in the city—indeed, in the kingdom—who wanted to make trouble for whoever came to rule. By marrying me, she could be granted a measure of peace, even as she enjoyed while she had your son to husband.

There are larger matters at stake here, sir, than your own wounded feelings."

An almost palpable silence filled the Hall. Beside Snolli, Kasai began stroking his drum.

"You are in New Vold, the Sea-Rovers' keep, given us by the Dowager Queen," Snolli said. "That makes you subject to the laws of the Sea-Rovers. Under these laws, if I choose, I may execute Ashen for treachery."

Gaurin tightened his grip on his sword hilt, though his tone was as mild as before. "And under my own laws, those of the land in which you live, and probably those of the Sea-Rovers as well, if you try such an outrage, I may hinder you as I can."

Snolli seemed to become aware, as if for the first time, that Gaurin's men surrounded him and that more were stationed outside the room. "You dare threaten me in my own Hall?"

"I do not threaten, sir, and you know it. Indeed, if any threats have been uttered this day, they were from you, against my lady wife. We seem to be at an impasse."

Kasai's drumming grew louder, and as all eyes turned toward him, he began to speak, almost singing the words. "The peril from the North grows stronger as we grow weaker. Let not those who should be allies turn against one another. Mend your differences and drink a cup of friendship. Yes, drink, drink, and know that your quarrel is over before it is truly begun!"

Then he fell silent. He seemed to be sleeping.

Snolli fell silent also, thinking. "I have never known the Spirit Drummer to have a false vision," he said at last. "He spoke of the peril from the North. We gain nothing from being enemies. There may never be true friendship between us, but I will do as Kasai has said. I ask only that Rohan be returned to me, and to his people."

The boy spoke up for the first time. "I want to stay with Ashen," he said, "for she has been kind to me. She was my mother when I had no other."

"You are a young whelp, whose opinion means nothing," Snolli said. "I do not propose to coddle you."

"I don't ask for coddling. But if you try to make me stay here, I will run away."

"That complicates matters." Snolli turned to Kasai, who had awoken from his trance. "What do you say?"

"Let me talk it over with Gaurin. He seems to have the only level head here. Excepting me, of course. You are too angry, and Ashen is only a woman."

Snolli nodded, and Kasai and Gaurin retired to a private room. Lathrom moved up beside Ashen while they waited for the men to return. He was unobtrusive about it, but there was no mistaking his intent to guard his lady. He caught her eye and nodded, and then she knew that he had transferred the loyalty he had felt for Obern to her, and to Gaurin.

In a surprisingly short time the Spirit Drummer and Gaurin came back into the Hall and Kasai told the Sea-Rover Chieftain of their decision. "Rohan will spend the warm seasons of the year with his father's people," he said. "In that time he will learn our ways and even, if you choose, go with us out to sea. He will spend the winter months with Ashen, when there's nothing to do anyway."

Snolli didn't ask whether the arrangement was agreeable to either Ashen or Rohan. "Done," he said. He spat in his hand and gave it to Ashen to shake. Then he dismissed her and she knew that there was no real warmth between them and probably never would be.

She kissed Rohan, assuring him that summers were short these days and would pass quickly. Then, with her companions, she left New Vold, hoping never to have to return.

At first, Ashen had been apprehensive that this arrangement would only confuse the boy and perhaps coarsen him, but Rohan seemed to thrive on it. Some quirk of breeding had given Rohan a more complicated nature than that of the ordinary Sea-Rover, and he seemed to draw sustenance from both her influence and his grandfather's. Perhaps that was one of the secrets of his charm.

As the seasons passed, the Oakenkeep began to return to its former state. Gaurin purchased fine furnishings for the living quarters, and sturdy ones for the barracks. Also, he sent for weavers and embroiderers to create hangings for the walls, not only for the extra warmth they would provide, but also for beauty.

Nor did he neglect the land. As castellan, his duty was to ensure that the people under his care prospered. He gave orders that farmers erect coverings over their fields, as he had heard of the Sea-Rovers doing. This measure met with success, even greater when someone thought of substituting oiled paper for the heavy cloth. Though much more fragile, the paper seemed to gather even more warmth. The resulting crops, though far from bountiful, were adequate with even a little excess to put away for leaner times. Though life could not be said to be easy at the Oakenkeep, under Gaurin's management it became comfortable.

One chilly morning, Ashen awoke, got out of bed, put on a warm robe, and looked outside. The first light snow of the year was beginning to fall. Soon the man-made portion of the "river," sheltered as it was and with little current, would freeze hard enough for children and adults alike to amuse themselves in sliding on the ice. She rushed back and snuggled into the warmth of her bed again, comfortable and content, reluctant to arise, wishing that Gaurin were with her. Then she remembered why she had roused earlier than she intended. This was the day that Rohan was coming back from New Vold and Gaurin would be gone out hunting.

A child wailed from the nursery wing of the residence in the Oakenkeep. Little Hegrin was awake. She would be wanting her breakfast and sometimes she would not let her nursemaid, Beatha, feed her. The baby was long since weaned and eating gruel, but also she was teething again, which made her cranky. It was time for Ashen to get out of bed whether she wanted to or not. The running of a household such as hers was not conductive to laziness on her part, regardless of Ayfare's indispensable presence.

By the time she had dressed and reached the nursery, she discovered Hegrin contentedly hugging a stuffed toy while Beatha spooned gruel into her mouth. The nurse glanced up when Ashen entered.

"I warmed it some, my lady," she said, smiling, "and put a bit of sugar on it. That seems to have made all the difference."

The little girl clutched at the spoon, chewing on it. Ashen could hear the tiny teeth clicking on the metal. She sat down beside Hegrin. "Want a nice crust of bread to chew on, sweeting?" she said, offering the baby the tidbit. Hegrin immediately abandoned the spoon in favor of the tough, chewy bread. She favored her mother with a grin so wide and happy that Ashen's heart turned over. How much she looked like Gaurin, with the same honey-colored hair and blue-green eyes!

"She'll turn heads for fair, when she grows up," Beatha said. "Wouldn't it be nice if one day, she and Peres—"

"We mustn't even think that," Ashen said. She put the baby on her lap and tickled her under the chin, just to hear her laugh. "The new little King's station is so much higher than ours that we might as well be living on different worlds."

"Aye, my lady, but still, with the little King's being born just four months after his father died, and then Hegrin coming along. You and Queen Rannore being such good friends and all, it makes one to wonder."

"Good friends or not, we all know who really rules in Rendel. I am not sure that the Dowager Queen Ysa would be very happy with the daughter of the Bog-Princess, as she calls me behind my back, for her precious grandson."

"My little Hegrin is good enough for any old King, aren't you, sweeting?" Beatha insisted stoutly.

Satisfied that Hegrin was thriving and happy, and well fed, Ashen handed her back to the nursemaid. "I have a busy day ahead of me. Rohan is expected back today, and I want you to make sure that Hegrin is all washed and tidy and dressed in her best. He'll want to see her."

"Wonderful how he treats her like a little sister. Aye, my lady,

I'll have her spotless and chuckling—if she doesn't get into the jampot."

Both women laughed, for Hegrin's appetite for sweets had become legendary, since the time she had emptied an entire pot of jam into her lap and was discovered happily dipping her hands into the mess and sucking her fingers.

The noise of a commotion coming from the inner ward told Ashen that Rohan had arrived. She quickly kissed Hegrin and, checking to make sure that the headdress every proper married woman wore was in place, hurried down the stairs from the residential apartment to greet him. He was just coming into Oakenkeep's Great Hall when she reached the bottom of the stairs.

"Ashen!" he cried. He flung his snow-spangled cloak aside and covered the distance between them in a few great bounds to grab her in a hearty hug.

She returned the embrace and then held him at arm's length while she inspected him with a critical eye. "You've been growing again," she said. "You're taller than I am."

"I'm supposed to be," he said, laughing. "Grandfather said that my birthday in the spring will mark the beginning of my Shield Year, so that means I am nearly a man. Where's Gaurin? And my baby sister?"

"Gaurin should be back at any moment. He has been occupied in hunting meat to preserve for the winter, and wanted to get something particularly fine for your welcome feast this evening. As for Hegrin, she is finishing her breakfast. Then you're apt to find her anywhere at all, since she's walking everywhere. Running, actually. It takes every pair of eyes in the Residence just to keep track of her."

Rohan laughed. Then he waved his hand and a flower appeared in it. It wasn't a real flower—just silk cleverly folded into a bud—but the trick made her smile. "Here, Ashen," he said, handing it to her. "I daresay that I can keep Hegrin amused for a while." He waved his hand again and, even as Ashen held the flower, it bloomed.

"You should be wary of such things," Ashen said, sighing. Behind them, servants were carrying Rohan's baggage up the stairs to the rooms that were always kept ready for him, and a maid was wiping up the puddle left by the melting snow he had tracked in. "I do hope you didn't feel called upon to 'entertain' in Snolli's Hall."

"Of course not. Grandfather has little patience for entertainments these days, let alone silly little magics that I can do. I think he may be getting old."

"Does he still carry a grudge against me for Obern's death?"

By this time, they had climbed a different flight of stairs and reached the solar where a table and three chairs were set and a flask of warmed, spiced cider waited. Rohan poured for both of them, sniffing appreciatively. "Ah, good! I've missed this. To answer your question, yes, he does, even if it's mostly out of habit by now."

Gaurin entered the Hall at that moment, brushing a few flakes of snow off his cloak, and Rohan set his cup aside to run back downstairs and greet the lord of the Oakenkeep. Ashen went to the railing, unwilling to wait to see him until he had come to her.

"Welcome," Gaurin said. He smiled up at Ashen. "My lady has been on pins and needles until you should arrive. Now she will be merry once more."

As they spoke, the two men climbed the stairs to where Ashen waited.

"Was your hunt successful?" Ashen knew the answer beforehand; Gaurin was as skillful in this as he was in any other enterprise he set his hand to accomplish.

"We will have a good feast tonight."

They smiled at each other. Ashen loved to see him smile, to watch the lines at the corners of his mouth meet the ones at his eyes. She touched the opalescent stone bracelet she always wore when he was away from the keep.

"I am thinking of taking Rohan to the Bog to see Zazar, before heavy winter sets in," she said, pouring him a cup of the warmed cider. "Will you come with us?"

Gaurin had visited Zazar's hut several times, and always in

Ashen's company. "Of course, my dear. Is there a purpose to the visit?"

"Rohan has told me that he will be entering his Shield Year next spring. Long ago, Zazar told me that when this time drew nigh, I was to bring him to her. She said that there was something she must do."

"And I would like to see Grandam Zaz again as well." He put his finger beside his nose. "She pretends to hate when I call her that."

"Then go we shall," Gaurin said, "and we should make it soon. The winters have steadily grown worse in this land, and I want us all inside where it is safe and snug before the thundersnows begin in earnest. Perhaps this time, Madame Zazar will agree to return with us, to winter in the apartment you have set aside for her."

Ashen glanced through one of the windows of the Hall. Indeed, she remembered a time when a snowfall like this would have been thought of as heavy, with or without the crashing of thunder and lightning that characterized them these days. It seemed that most of the wan summer had to be spent in gathering firewood for the winter; every wall, it seemed, had wood stacked against it higher than a man could reach. All would be gone before spring came and then the search would begin anew, among the dwindling woods. Already they were having to chop down living trees, instead of gathering dead wood to preserve their sources. Some poor folk had turned to burning blocks of peat, gathered at some risk from the edges of the Bog. Not many more winters and others, including those who dwelt in the Oakenkeep, might have to do likewise. Her thoughts were interrupted by Beatha, bringing baby Hegrin into the solar from the nursery nearby.

"Rohan!" the child shouted happily. It was one of her few words.

She struggled out of her nursemaid's arms and toddled across the polished floor toward him. Quickly he scooped her up in his arms. "And you say that I've gotten bigger?" he said to Ashen. "This child is half-grown already!"

"Greet your father," Ashen told Hegrin.

The little girl refused to let go of Rohan's neck. She merely waved a few fingers in her father's direction as she gazed lovingly at Rohan. "Da," she said.

"If I were a jealous man, I'd say she loves you better than me," Gaurin said, laughing.

"Fortunate for me that you aren't, so you won't be likely to challenge me to a duel once Ashen gives me Father's sword she's got hung up beside yours over the mantle in the Hall. I'm still no good at all with the axe, though I'm passing fair with a throwing-dagger—not that I could get to it with this marmoset clinging to me!" He loosened Hegrin's grip. "There, that's better. At least I can breathe."

Hegrin insisted on staying with her idol all that day, and Rohan amused her with his silk-flower trick and also, that evening, by lighting candles without touching them though Ashen frowned.

"Tomorrow or the next day we'll set off for Zazar's house," she said, "and I don't want you showing off."

"In front of my Grandam? The Wysen-wyf? Not likely. She'd laugh at how little Power I possess. And anyway," he said to Hegrin, who had begun to whimper at the prospect of his leaving again so soon, "the quicker we're gone, the sooner we will come back, my marmoset. And I will bring you a new toy, and maybe even a new trick to show you!"

It had been, Ashen realized, an entire year since she had visited Zazar—indeed, the last time Rohan had returned to the Oakenkeep. "I do not know where the time goes," she told the Wysen-wyf. "I will try to do better in the future."

Zazar sniffed. She seemed little changed with the passing of the years except that she had become sharper of tongue, if such a thing were possible. "You have your own life now, and welcome to it." She nodded at Gaurin. "Now that you finally had the good sense to marry the man the Weavers intended for you."

"Whether the Weavers did it, or some other force, I will always thank you for the great boon of my lady," Gaurin said. He took Zazar's wrinkled old hand and kissed the fingers. She took it back with a shade less impatience than she would have shown to another who dared such a liberty.

"Now, Rohan. Come sit you down by my fire and while Ashen and Gaurin make lovers' eyes at each other, I have something for you." She rummaged in a woven basket and then brought out a tuft of dried herbs and grasses. "Here. This is for you."

Ashen recognized many of the sprigs that made up the tuft. "No," she said, alarmed. "Surely not—"

"Do not meddle! I have had this put away for some time, waiting for Rohan to get close to his Shield Year. Oh, yes, I know all about that. And that before long you'll be getting your father's Rinbell sword that was his father's before him. But here, take this. You are to wear it in your helm instead of the usual bunch of feathers or other useless trash."

"Zazar, some of these herbs are deadly," Ashen said.

"And others are for healing. I don't expect the boy to chew on them, after all. Heed me well. Need drives, and there is a good reason for this."

Then Ashen turned away with a sigh. When Zazar was this insistent, there was no arguing with her. The Wysen-wyf wrapped the bundle of plant sprigs—some of which seemed remarkably fresh for having been put aside so long before—and set it into a basket of other items she would be sending back with Ashen. She knew the basket contained salves and healing-potions, and packets of dried herbs as well.

"Do you still study?" the Wysen-wyf asked.

"I do. The good priest, Esander, has given me several books from the hidden library. He says they are duplicates. Others he has lent me, and those I read and return. Every time there is a traveler who has gone through Rendelsham, it seems that I receive a fresh parcel from him."

"Good. Only, remember—read, but do not presume to practice what you learn."

Ashen smiled. "And risk a return of Weyse, to sit on the pages? Though I would be glad to see her again."

To Ashen's surprise, Zazar actually chuckled. "That was her own idea. I just told her to stop you from being a fool. Anyway, if you and Gaurin will come back during the warm weather, if we ever have a warm spell, that is, I'm of a mind to let you go to Galinth again. I think there is something that may interest him."

Ashen raised her eyebrows, thinking of the skeleton from which she had received the opalescent stone bracelet that Gaurin had recognized as a treasure of his House. "We will return," she promised, "if circumstances allow. In any event, I want him to see Galinth with you as his guide."

"So now go you back to the Oakenkeep and be careful of the ground. Even frozen, some of the places will still suck you down if you are unwary."

"I always remember your teachings. But I wish you would come back with us. At least there it is warm—"

"I do well enough here. You are in the place where you were meant to be, Ashen Deathdaughter, even as I am in mine. And so shall it be, until all changes in this world and we must do as must wills."

Thirteen

$\mathcal{T}$he Dowager Queen Ysa found herself in an awkward position politically. Perhaps it was expectable, but the threat from the North, so long in arriving, had receded in the minds of most of the inhabitants of Rendel. The only overt sign of oncoming trouble was the increasing cold of the climate, with short summers and heavy winters characterized by thundersnows, to which the people had adjusted and accepted. Business for merchants and tailors and dress-makers had never been better—coarse woolen clothing, sometimes mixed with linen, for ordinary people; fine wools and fur-lined silks for the nobles. Many of these fribbets had made of it a game of fashion, seeing who could outdo the next in finery. Tunics were long these days, reaching to the heels, made of the gaudiest colors the dye-masters could devise and dripping with gold-and-silver embroi-dery. To look at these preening peacocks strutting about the Court, one would never dream that disaster loomed just over the horizon.

Ysa, however, knew that this threat was merely delayed. She regularly sent her little servant Visp winging northward where, un-der the cloak of invisibility, it observed and then brought back in-formation for the Dowager to ponder.

She was preparing Visp for another such mission now, taking

the flyer out of its fur-lined home and instructing it on what it must do. "Not to the southeast," she told it, for it was straining in that direction, flapping its wings as if desiring to go contrary to Ysa's command. "Later, you may go and look in on Ashen. Now you must obey me."

Sighing, the Dowager released the flyer and watched as it winged its way northward, winking out when it was still over the housetops of the city. Obedience she could command of Visp, but she had never been able to overcome its inexplicable affection for Ashen.

Well, affection could wait upon necessity. And if it came to a choice, Ysa preferred obedience. Perhaps she should seek another servant, versed in the ways of Power. Instinctively she knew that she must call on help from every direction, marshal her forces, be prepared for whatever might come.

She set out a dish of grain and dried fruit, and some fresh water for when the flyer came back to its nest. She had not lighted the brazier, so, rather than wait in the chilly, drafty tower room for Visp to return, she descended the stairs to the comparative warmth of fireplaces and braziers. There, as acknowledged Regent, she would conduct the business of the realm. She made a note to have woolen curtains made for the windows in the tower, to replace the thin coverings that let too much cold seep through the glass panes of the windows.

The possibility of civil war was brewing, and this, Ysa knew, must be avoided at all costs. She had been pondering how to accomplish this, and believed she had come up with a plan that would work, and even accomplish a dual purpose. Not only could some of the bellicose posturing going on between this noble and that be turned to a positive end, but also some of the young men of Rendel, on whom the brunt of fighting would fall when it came, could receive some sound training. There was no question who should conduct this. Without a second thought, she had determined to put Harous in charge of the project.

Through her agents, she had caused a rumor to be put about

that she was expecting yet another strong Nordorn war party to serve under her personal banner. It was false, of course, for those men who were going to leave the lands to the north had already come to Rendel. From them she learned that Cyornas NordornKing, along with a small contingent of his most-dedicated followers, remained behind. When the menace finally began to move, it would be he who took the brunt of the first attack. He was the guardian of the Palace of Fire and Ice, wherein this Great Foulness, as it was called, had been entombed. However, some years past, the Palace of Fire and Ice had suffered great harm from the impact of a great thunder-star. One wall—the one adjacent to the tomb that held the sleeping body of this Great Foulness—had cracked. Inside the tomb, the Foulness had now awoken and, it was feared, was even now gathering its strength for a new assault upon the land of men.

For Ysa to divulge to the nobles of Rendel what she had learned was unthinkable. Therefore, once again she had had to work in secret—she must take up the burden the Great Rings had placed upon her, scheming and devising a new plan—to accomplish what she knew must be done.

On her table waited the proclamations to be sent throughout Rendel, calling for a show of allegiance in the form of a levy of men, of which some must be at least of the rank of minor nobility, to receive training in the art of war.

Ysa did not even attempt to conceal from herself what must be apparent to all who would receive this proclamation. The nobles among this levy would, if war came, become hostages to assure further assistance.

"That it should come to this," Ysa murmured to herself, "and we must use such means to raise armies for our own defense."

With some bitterness, she considered that the most loyal men in Rendel were those who had fled from the first stirrings of trouble in the North. The Sea-Rovers, now firmly in control of the old Ashenkeep, for example. But in their defense it could be said that when their homes were destroyed they had had little recourse other than to gather the remnants of those who had survived, and move south.

Andre Norton & Sasha Miller

And the Nordors, under the overall command of Count Gaurin, could truly be said to have fled only so that they could fight again, in strength, when the troubles came. She was glad that she had alliance with such stalwart people.

Such, Ysa felt, as she seated herself and began putting signature and seal to the proclamations, could not be claimed for a good percentage of her Rendelian nobles whose names appeared on the summoning papers. Gattor of Bilth, for example. He had never been an open fighter, disdaining the clash of arms as the proper way to settle a quarrel. Gattor looked like exactly what he was—someone who was indolent and slow to act. His very appearance underscored that fact, for he was thick of body and round of face. Even his eyes looked perpetually sleepy. But that was, in its own way, show. Gattor's warring was always conducted in the shadows and seldom could men do more than speculate about his part in the sudden collapse of someone rumored to be encroaching upon his own holdings. Unfortunately, Gattor was not alone. There were many who chose to emulate him, with more or less success.

Such was the overall caliber of the nobility of Rendel. Yes, there was Royance, that old burhawk, loyal to the last drop of blood in his body, and Count Harous, Lord High Marshal and hereditary master of Cragden Keep, the castle that was Rendelsham's primary defense. But men like them were, unfortunately, rare. Though she would not hesitate to put this army of unevenly trained men into his care, Ysa did not fully trust Harous because of his onetime pursuit of Ashen and his present involvement with Marcala. However, lacking no better to replace him, and also to keep him too busy to think of any possible mischief, she now allowed him to assume overall leadership of the muster of Rendelian fighting men, even as Gaurin led the transplanted Nordors.

At least there had never been any doubt of Gaurin's loyalty, nor that of the men he commanded. Though, years ago, Ysa had summarily turned away his father, Count Bjauden, when he had come looking for permission to emigrate with some of the Nordorn peo-

ple, she had since come to regret her hasty action. It had all been
Florian's fault, with his inexpressible rudeness to the Count. Looking back on the incident, she knew that Bjauden had been severely
provoked, and that his offer of mending the Prince's ways was one
that she should have considered more carefully. If she had, perhaps
many things would have turned out differently. To this day she
could remember his exact words.

"Your manners are worse than those of the lowest churl," he
had said, his voice low and pleasant, "and if I had but an hour and
a little privacy I would mend you of them to your mother's rejoic-
ing."

Yes, Florian might still have been alive, and even a decent King,
had she heeded Bjauden's words. Perhaps, if she had but known his
lineage—But she hadn't, and there was no use wasting time with
regrets. Fortunately, Bjauden's son, Gaurin, seemed to have much
of his father about him. When first she saw him, she had thought
he must be Bjauden, with his youth renewed.

Too late, she had learned of the close familial ties between Bjauden and Cyornas NordornKing. He had been, though he had not
claimed the title, a Prince. That made his son Gaurin a Prince in
turn. He would be steadfast when the time came.

Fleetingly she wondered how Ashen was faring, married to such
a splendid man, and then decided that she really didn't care, as long
as the Bog-Princess, that hateful reminder of her late husband's in-
fidelity, was well away from where important matters of state were
being conducted.

She came to the proclamation intended for the Sea-Rovers.
Snolli, of course, was too high in rank to be summoned. Also, he
was probably too old by now for anything but symbolic leadership.
Who, then, would lead them? That son that Obern had, surprisingly,
brought to Court? Now, what was his name—Ysa searched her
memory. Rohan, that was it. He must be of man's estate by now.
There was something about him, as a son of Obern, something that
nagged at her memory, but she could not remember what it was.

As she wrote his name under that of the Chieftain, she hoped that the sorry influence wielded by the Bog-Princess had not ruined him entirely.

Ashen fingered the paper covered with large, decorative writing with Snolli's and Rohan's names and the capital letters picked out in red and gold, looking at the unmistakable signature and the seal at the bottom, in dark green wax over a red-and-gold ribbon. She pulled her fur-lined mantle closer about her, still necessary though the spring was upon them, and gazed up at Rohan. "This is none of Zazar's doing," she said. Rohan had just come from spending nearly a week in the Wysen-wyf's company, being instructed in matters she had not seen fit to divulge to Ashen.

"No. I had it with me. Grandam Zaz found it interesting, and gave me some pretty explicit instructions as to how I was to conduct myself once I was in high company."

"It is definite, then," she said to Rohan. "You must go and take your place in the levy of the Queen's army."

"My men are already with me, and they are finding places to sleep with your own soldiers. Don't be sad, Ashen," Rohan said. His eyes twinkled with suppressed mirth. "You could always come with me and hold my hand, you know, if you think I won't do well in Rendelsham."

Ashen laughed, but not in amusement. "That snake-pit of intrigue? Thank you, but I would much rather stay here, in the Oakenkeep. I can, however, add to Zazar's instructions and tell you what I know of matters at Court, and the pitfalls that you may encounter, though some of my information must be stale by now."

"I would appreciate that," Rohan said, sobering a little. "I came to know a little of what you are referring to, in the short time I was there. When my father—"

"Yes. When your father was killed by the King. But remember always, when Obern died, he took his enemy with him. That, I believe, is important among the Sea-Rovers."

"And not just them," Gaurin said as he entered the room where Ashen and Rohan were deep in conversation. "Greetings, my dear. I understand that you command a company of your people, do you not, young Rohan?"

"I do, though they can't exactly be said to be my followers. Grandfather has seen to it—and I must say that I gave him plenty of help—that the Sea-Rovers in general think of me as being not of much account. I am not nearly serious enough to suit them."

"Let us hope that you do not lose your merry nature anytime soon."

Rohan gave the older man an impish smile. "Not much danger of that, my lord."

Just then Hegrin dashed into the room, a folded paper in her hand. "Father, you forgot this!" she said, and then stopped dead in her tracks. "Rohan!" She ran to him, her silk skirts rustling, and flung her arms around his neck. "I thought you were on your way back to New Vold! Are you going to stay with us a long time?"

"No, I'm afraid not." Rohan pried her loose and held her at arm's length. "Let me have a look at you. Only a week and you're bigger anyway. My, what a young lady you are growing up to be."

"What is that paper?" Ashen said, past Hegrin's happy chatter that filled the room.

Gaurin looked abashed. "It is a companion to the one young Rohan was just showing you, my dear."

"Oh no—"

"Don't fret, Ashen. I don't have to join the levy. At least not yet."

"Only minor nobility," Rohan told her. "Untried youngsters, like me." He smiled again, and then allowed Hegrin to pull him to his feet.

"I don't want to see anybody go," Hegrin declared with some vehemence. "Every time Rohan comes to our house, off he goes again the next day, it seems to me."

"Such are the times we live in, my daughter," Gaurin said.

"I love Rohan," Hegrin said, gazing at him adoringly. "I want to marry him someday."

At that, Rohan burst into laughter. "Oh, no! You are as much my sister as anybody could be!" he exclaimed. "People don't marry their sisters!"

"Oh," Hegrin said. "I didn't think of that. Well then, maybe I could put on armor and ride with you."

"As to that, sweet sis, you are too young."

Hegrin's usual happy expression changed and a frown crossed her brow. Her blue-green eyes clouded. "Too young for this, too old for that, too much a sister for anything else—whatever am I good for, then?"

Rohan laughed again and swept her up in his arms. "When you are just a little older, you will find out, that I promise. Now, come show me what you had in mind, and then I will show you my latest feats of magic. Very small magic, I promise," he said, looking at Ashen who was frowning in her turn. "Just the thing to make pretty ladies smile once more."

Ashen shook her head. "Alas, I fear that your grandfather, much as I hate to admit it, might be right about you. Your nature is very light indeed. Promise me that the warnings I give you about the enemies you might find sitting at your elbow at the Dowager Queen's table don't flit in one ear and out the other."

"Yes, Ashen, I promise, even though there's little chance that I'll be brushing elbows with such high company." He picked Hegrin up and settled her in the crook of one arm. "Now, excuse me, please, but I am informed that there is something that I absolutely must see this very instant. How did you two come to have such a strong-willed child?"

"Yes, of course, by all means, go," Ashen said distractedly. She didn't wait for them to leave before she turned to Gaurin. "If not you, then who will go in the Dowager's Levy?"

"There are several who would serve the purpose. My young cousin Cebastian shows a great deal of promise, and I had been thinking of elevating him to a rank just under Lathrom's if he takes to his training. He should satisfy the levy requirements very well, and also gain more experience so he will be a real asset to Lathrom, and to me as well, when he returns."

Relieved that Gaurin himself would not be called upon to go to Rendelsham, Ashen allowed herself to smile. "Does that mean that you will never be called upon to serve?"

"Alas, no, my dear. When the war comes—and it will come, sooner or later—all must stand ready to do their part, lest the world end, as we know it. But don't make such a long face. Let us be merry while we can. Tonight, we will feast with Rohan and Cebastian, and then send them both off with the Sea-Rovers and our contingent of Nordors to keep our brave young warriors company."

"The trip to Galinth will have to wait," Ashen said.

Outside in the corridor, she could hear Rohan and Hegrin. His step was gay, almost dancing, as he carried the child down the stairs. Hegrin's golden giggle floated back to her parents' hearing, and Ashen feared that despite all her warnings, Rohan was preparing to rush straight into intrigues he was ill suited to deal with.

Fourteen

*R*ohan urged his horse, Red, into a canter, impatient and eager to get to Rendelsham and back at Court. Despite Zazar's stringent warnings and Ashen's gloomy predictions, he actually looked forward to the experience. Rumor had it that Count Harous was going to be molding this ragtag levy from all over Rendel into a functioning army, and Rohan wanted to learn from a man who was considered one of the best at his trade.

Nevertheless, when they came to a tiny village boasting a wayside inn and, even more important, a smithy, Rohan decided to stop there for the night. Red had developed a limp and though he couldn't find anything amiss with the animal's hoof, nevertheless he would lose little by tarrying on the road for a night or two. He sent his Sea-Rovers on with the men from the North, under the leadership of Cebastian, promising to catch up with them as soon as his mount was healthy once more. Perhaps all Red needed was a set of new shoes. One seemed loose, anyway, and if there was one thing he had learned it was never to ignore his horse's well-being.

With Red safely stabled and the promise that the blacksmith would quickly mend what had gone wrong, Rohan paid in advance for a private room at the inn. As he was fishing the coin out of his purse, he recognized the smell of good stew and his appetite was immediately whetted. For a copper bit, the landlord gave him a big bowl of it, heavy with meat and winter vegetables, with newly baked bread as accompaniment. He finished by wiping out his bowl with a crust of bread, ate it, and then sat idly watching a Magician on the other side of the room as he prepared to pay for his own meal and lodgings with a show of Power and trickery. The other patrons had not yet come in to dinner, and except for the innkeeper he and the Magician were the only ones in the room. It was beginning to grow dark, and without thinking, Rohan lighted a candle on the table the Magician was using before he could strike steel to flint. The Magician turned toward him, startled.

"My apologies, sir," Rohan said. "That was rude of me. I should have let you amaze me instead." He laughed, trying to make light of an incident for which both Ashen and Grandam Zazar would certainly have scolded him.

The Magician returned to his preparations. The light from the candle gleamed on his face—as it changed and became that of a beautiful woman! The woman stared at Rohan, and he found himself unable to look away.

No, he told himself, I am but imagining things. This is a man, a mountebank and an entertainer, and what I am seeing is only one more of his tricks. I am not looking at a woman. I am not—

With a wrench he broke the connection, at the same time discovering that several patrons had entered the inn's common room while he had been under the man's spell. From the tenor of their comments, it was plain that none of the newcomers had seen anything out of the ordinary. The innkeeper likewise went about his business as if nothing untoward had happened—if, indeed, anything had.

Rohan ordered a mug of ale and found a place out of the circle of light from several candles the Magician had lighted from the one he had set flame to. From the shadows, he watched the show closely. But the Magician, clearly revealed by the light, seemed no more or no less than what he appeared—a traveling trickster, pro-

Andre Norton & Sasha Miller

ducing flowers from his sleeve, passing a piece of silk over a plate and making a rabbit appear, finding coins in the ears of onlookers.

By the time the show was over and those staying the night had sought their beds, Rohan had almost convinced himself that he had been seeing what did not exist. Nevertheless, he was glad that he had paid extra to have a room and a bed to himself, and that he could lock the door. After tossing and turning for a long time, he fell into a troubled sleep.

In the morning, when he made inquiry, he discovered that the Magician was already gone. With a sense of relief, Rohan went to the smithy to inquire after his horse.

"Nabbut a stone hid under th' poor beastie's shoe, where you couldn't get at it," the man said. "I fixed it up again, right as raindrops."

"Thank you," Rohan said. He gave the man his fee, a penny, and then added another.

The smithy grinned. "Thank'ee. I allus says a man is no better than how he treats his animals, and I judge you a right 'un, sure enough."

"My gratitude," Rohan said. Then he saddled Red, put those articles he had removed for his night's stay back where they belonged, and got on his way once again.

I was reckless, he thought, just the way Ashen has tried so often to tell me that I am. And stupid and foolish to boot. I will *not* do anything like this again.

Red seemed renewed after having the offending pebble removed from his hoof, and as eager to be on his way as Rohan was to put this humiliating incident behind him. By pushing hard, he caught up with the company of Sea-Rovers and Nordors before they had come in sight of the blunt towers of Cragden Keep, Count Harous's stronghold, where, he presumed, they would be lodged.

🌿

Count Harous's barracks were overflowing with young nobles and their soldiers when they arrived. Rohan's head began to swim from all the introductions. He recognized some of the nobles as coming directly from the Four Houses of Rendel, and others as being families allied to these Houses, or related to members of the Council.

Somewhat to Rohan's surprise, he and Cebastian were invited that night to a banquet at Rendelsham Castle.

"Don't give yourself airs about it," Cebastian advised. "Our arrival completes the levy. My guess is that all the minor nobles and lordlings will be there. And furthermore, I think they—that means you and me as well—will find ourselves living in the castle before long. They'll make over us and tell us that we are their honored guests, but we're surety that our own lords will come through with more men, when it should come to that."

"You've been listening to Gaurin too long," Rohan said. He adjusted the new deep green tunic of fine wool that had been one of Ashen's parting gifts, and settled a pendant bearing the device of a ship at sea around his neck. This he had had copied from a brooch that had belonged to his father, and which he now pinned on his cap. "Or Ashen. They are both convinced that we'll be up to our necks in war before another year is out."

"Don't forget, I was born in the North," Cebastian said. His tunic and cap were of a lighter green, and his pendant bore a device of a snarling snowcat, emblem of Gaurin's House. "I was only a child when we left for Rendel and the Oakenkeep, but I remember the talk. Cyornas NordornKing was the guardian of the vault below the Palace of Fire and Ice where the Great Foulness lay. He stayed behind, to delay its escape as he might, but one day it will break free and come upon us. That much I know."

"I will take your word for it, my friend," Rohan told him, "but please forgive me if I cannot be as serious as you are about something I have never seen and possibly never will."

"It is no crime to be merry while one has the chance."

"That's the sort of thing Gaurin would say. Well, I agree—though some might think me a little *too* merry."

Cebastian smiled. "You make hearts glad when you are near. It is a gift, my friend, and one not to be despised."

"Then I will be grateful for it. Now, let us go and see how the Dowager is faring these days."

The young King and his mother were not present; this seemed to be solely the Dowager's enterprise. As far as Rohan could tell, the Dowager had not changed in the years since he had last been in Rendelsham, on the sad occasion of his father's and the King's funerals. Only her hands, adorned with the Four Great Rings which he had heard held the secret of all Power in Rendel, had grown thin and were now marked with pale brown spots. Always interested in Power, he gazed at the Rings, wondering how articles so plain and unprepossessing in appearance could have such a reputation. He almost didn't notice the steward who appeared at his side, murmuring a message.

"Please, I didn't hear you," Rohan said.

"Our gracious lady, Her Highness the Dowager Queen Ysa, to demonstrate her gratitude to the Sea-Rovers and their loyalty, desires to honor you by seating you at the high table. This I am bid say to you, and to bring back your answer straight."

"The honor is mine," Rohan said. He exchanged glances with Cebastian. The other merely raised one eyebrow.

"Also, the Dowager desires to honor the Nordors, and would seat you as well at the high table. What say you, sir?"

"Like my friend, I consider the honor mine," Cebastian said. "Pray, lead on."

The servant showed them to their places. Cebastian's prediction had been correct. All the fledgling nobles gathered thus far were, apparently, dining in the Dowager's company this evening. With the help of some reintroductions and by reading the familial badges the young nobles wore, Rohan marked Gidon of Bilth, sent by Gattor his overlord. With him was Jivon, sent from Rowankeep, and Nikolos, who proudly led Lord Royance of Grattenbor's soldiers. Close behind Rohan recognized Jabez of Mimon, Vinod of Vacaster, and Reges of Lerkland. A few others, whose names neither he nor Cebastian could remember. Rohan noted that of those levies that came from the common people, none of the leaders had been invited to the Dowager's high table, but found their places well below the salt.

Only Steuart, who claimed kinship with the House of Oak, was seated as close to the Dowager Ysa as Rohan was. The Hall was crowded by now, with many young faces among those of older courtiers. With the smoke and the noise, those beyond the table where Rohan sat dissolved into a mass of nameless people. Perhaps later they would become individuals for him.

Ysa took her place, and with that signal, the banquet began.

With the ease of long practice, the Dowager began to engage each of the young nobles in conversation, leaning forward graciously to address each in turn. How did their lords fare, how were conditions at home when they left, were they pleased with their housing?

The back of Rohan's neck prickled a little at that. He exchanged glances with Cebastian, who winked at him. Then he became aware that the Dowager was now speaking to him.

"And how goes life at New Vold? Is all well there?"

"Very well, both at the Oakenkeep and at New Vold," Rohan said. "As Your Highness must know, I live part of the year at one place, and the rest at the other."

"Ah, yes. I had almost forgotten. And your—what should we call her?—your stepmother?"

"Lady Ashen is well, as is Count Gaurin. Both Cebastian and I left them in good health. And their daughter likewise thrives."

"Ah. Their daughter. As token of my goodwill, accept from me this goblet of wine, as is due your exalted rank."

Then the Dowager signaled a steward, who stepped forward and placed a goblet beside Rohan's plate. Smoothly, Ysa shifted the focus of her conversation to Nikolos of Grattenbor.

The back of Rohan's neck was prickling again. By right, if one fledgling noble was to be so honored, then all should be. Both Cebastian and Jivon of Rowan probably outranked him, at least according to Rendel standards, and Nikolos of Grattenbor was certainly his equal. But only he had received the wine.

Cautiously, he brought the goblet close, inhaling the fragrance. Something was wrong. Either the wine had gone sour or—No! Rohan recognized the aroma. It was an herbal potion, similar to one that Zazar used to befuddle the senses of someone when there was painful work to be done, such as setting a bone or helping a woman through a difficult birth. Grandam had warned him of such a potion, saying that under its influence he would be dazed and, for a while, liable to the control of others.

For what reason would the Dowager want him drugged? Rohan could not fathom it, but knowing that there was danger in the goblet that he held, he shifted in his chair so that his elbow seemed accidentally to bump that of Jabez of Mimon, seated next to him. The wine splashed across the tablecloth.

"My apologies, Your Highness!" Rohan exclaimed.

"Entirely my fault, Your Highness," Jabez said. "I fear that my clumsiness has resulted in a stain on your fine linen."

"It is of no importance," the Dowager said, though Rohan thought he detected a frown. A certain coldness came over her manner. She gestured to a steward to come and mop up the worst of the spill. "Later, we will have entertainment, and dancing. May I recommend to you, Rohan, one of my damsels-in-waiting? Her name is Anamara and I fancy that you might have a great deal in common."

"Thank you, Your Highness," Rohan said. He bowed his head courteously. "It would be my honor and my pleasure to partner Lady Anamara, if she would be willing to put up with my own awkwardness."

"Then it is settled."

Again the Dowager turned her attention elsewhere, and again Rohan noted that none of the other young nobles had been singled out as a partner for any particular lady. What, he wondered, was the Dowager scheming now? He began to appreciate Ashen's characterization of the Court as a snake-pit of intrigue.

The sweet arrived, was devoured, and then the center of the Hall was cleared, with tables pushed aside and benches lined up. In the solar above, musicians began playing. A lovely young girl came and stood in front of Rohan, obviously shy. Slim and wispy the way all Ash women were, according to Ashen, she possessed not the light blue eyes one expected with pale blonde hair, but eyes such a deep, brilliant, vibrant sapphire they were almost black. Her face was a perfect heart shape. She curtseyed, and to his amusement, blushed quite charmingly.

"You must be Anamara," he said.

"Yes, my lord. I am bid to come and present myself to you."

"Our gracious lady, Her Highness the Dowager Queen Ysa, has done me great honor. Lady Anamara, will you dance?"

"Yes, my lord." She blushed again as Rohan took her hand to lead her out onto the floor where couples were already lining up for a galliard.

Intrigued, Rohan tried to draw her out in such conversation as could be managed, during the dance, and discovered that she was a distant relative of the Ash family, who had been left an orphan. This, then, was the commonality that Ysa had commented upon. Perhaps the Dowager was not entirely given to scheming after all, for, unless appearances were misleading, Lady Anamara was as fresh and innocent as any girl he had ever known. By the time the galliard had ended, Rohan felt himself quite smitten with her.

The dancing was interrupted, however, by the arrival of the formal entertainment for the evening. To Rohan's astonishment, this proved to be the very Magician whom he had seen, so very mysteriously, at the inn where he had stayed. His caution aroused anew, he conducted Anamara back to the place where she had been sitting, now pushed into the shadows by the clearing of the Hall, and instead of returning to his seat at the high table, sat down beside her.

No sense, he thought, in creating trouble. Who knew what this Magician might take it into his—or her—head to do, in front of the Court? One thing Rohan definitely did not want, was that his small ability with tricks be revealed to all.

But the Magician seemed not to notice Rohan or, if he did, he gave no indication of having seen the young man before. He went through a more elaborate exhibition than he had presented for the common people at the inn, culminating in producing white doves from nowhere, to fly freely into the rafters of the Hall. Then, with a mighty burst of fire and smoke, the Magician himself disappeared as the people applauded and cheered.

Rohan turned to Anamara, hoping to dance with her again before the evening ended, only to discover that sometime when he had been distracted watching the Magician, the girl had slipped away.

Next morning, he went searching for her and finally found her walking in a small garden located outside the castle, close by the walls.

"Ah, here you are!" he exclaimed. "I missed you last night."

"I do not enjoy big entertainments the way the rest of the Court does," Anamara said. "And so I left."

"Is this your special place?"

"You might say so. I come here in the mornings, for exercise, and also I come here when I want to be alone. I used to enjoy the flowers."

"There are still a few left. Hardy ones."

"But all the best have faded. They say it is the unnatural cold that has killed all the others."

"Then I might suggest that you go back inside, lest the unnatural cold blight you as well, for you are the best of all the sweet ladies here at Court and, yea, even in the world."

Anamara blushed crimson. "Sir—"

"I'm sorry. But you are so lovely, I find myself saying things I never thought of before."

She turned away, and to Rohan's astonishment, he knew that she was weeping. "What is wrong, dear lady?"

"Nothing. Please go away."

"Not until you tell me what I have done, that you should shed a tear."

"It isn't you. Well, in a way it is. I feel I can talk to you, as I cannot with others."

"Then pray tell me what troubles you, and I will find a way to mend it. Come and sit, and draw your mantle close around you. I will sit near and warm you with my presence, and you will tell me what is in your heart. Then you will feel better."

"You are kind, but there is nothing you can do," she said wanly. But she allowed him to lead her to a small bench set where what sunlight there was could reach it. There, as he asked a few careful questions, she unburdened herself.

She was but lately come to the Court, and hated it. She longed for her home, but as her father had been killed in a skirmish to the North and her mother had died shortly thereafter from grief, she was in no position to object to the Dowager's summoning her to Rendelsham Castle.

"I suppose some would envy me, supposing I am lucky, but I am not. The Dowager has complete control over me, and I find it hateful. She treats me as if she owns me and so, I suppose, in a way she does. She could, if she wanted to, marry me off to anyone she chose—even someone old and ugly—if she thought it would bring her any advantage."

"I agree that Her Highness enjoys an unrivaled reputation for intrigue and scheming. But it does not seem that she is going to be marrying you off to someone old and ugly today, at least. I am with you. Why not find such enjoyment as you may?"

She blushed again and, valiantly, dried her tears. "It is as you say. I won't be wed at least until noontime."

Both laughed.

"Did you enjoy the performance last night?" she said. Her voice was a little too high-pitched, and Rohan realized that she was trying to change the subject.

"The Magician was quite talented. I have seen him before."

Then he told her about his journey to Rendelsham, and the inn.

"I think I might have liked that better," Anamara said, "a show in a small room, with not so many people."

"There are not many people around now. And so I can show you this." With a flourish, he produced a rose out of thin air. To his surprise, it was not one of the folded silk ones he was accustomed to creating, but a real one, soft, pink, and fragrant.

"Alas, I have bungled it, when I thought to amuse you!" he exclaimed. He turned aside, made the rose wither, and dropped it under the bench. "Please pretend that you did not see me make a fool of myself." Concentrating, he tried again and this time, held out a silk rose to her. "Blue," he said. "The traditional Ash color, though not so glorious as your wonderful eyes."

"You remembered my family connection."

"Yes. As to the color of the great Family, my stepmother, Ashen of Ash, taught me about it. I hope my silly little gift pleases you."

"Very much." Anamara took the blue rose, smiling at him. "I will cherish it always."

"Now, dear lady, though nothing would please me more than to stay here with you all day, playing the fool and covering you with blue silk roses—"

"And saving me from being wed against my will—"

"Yes, that, too. But I cannot stay past the hour. My duties draw me elsewhere. But surely I will see you again."

"Surely," she said, blushing again. Her shyness returned and she lowered her eyelids demurely over her wonderful, remarkable eyes.

"Until then." Rohan remembered Gaurin's graceful gesture when he greeted or took leave of a lady, and brought Anamara's hand to his lips.

"I will count the hours." Her voice was so faint he could scarcely hear her.

Reluctantly he left the garden to go back to where his men and the rest of the Dowager Queen Ysa's Levy waited, to receive his first full day's training under Count Harous, master of Cragden Keep and Lord Marshal of Rendel.

When Rohan had disappeared, Anamara bent and retrieved the withered rose he had dropped beneath the bench and put it with the blue silk one. She kissed the petals and placed both flowers in the bosom of her dress.

Fifteen

or a long time, people had been aware of the fact that the Dowager commanded Power that was not within the province of ordinary folk. It was widespread knowledge that she was accustomed to shutting herself up for extended periods in her own apartment, or in the tower where only she ever visited. Now it was not at all rare for someone to glimpse a tiny flying creature winging its way out of the topmost tower of Rendelsham Castle, and then to watch it wink out of sight. Formerly, this phenomenon had been glimpsed but seldom, and had been easy enough to dismiss as imagination at work. Now it was almost commonplace, and thought little on because it no longer held the kind of mystery it had had at first.

However, speculation now filled the corridors. All the gossip—furtive, and in subdued whispers—centered about the probability of even stranger new Power, either in the grasp of the Dowager or soon to be summoned. Surely this must explain the more frequent sightings of the flyer.

Rohan listened to the tales, sifting out what was patently false from what might be true. Eventually he went to the place and the person upon whom Ashen had long relied—the good priest Esander, in the Great Fane of the Glowing.

"Why, yes, young sir," Esander said in response to Rohan's inquiry. "I know of several good books on the history of Rendel and I will be very happy to see someone interested enough to read them."

"Not just battles and who did what to whom, if you please," Rohan said. "But I have heard a story about a certain King—"

Esander smiled broadly. "I have heard the same stories, and I know the reference. Here, let me search out the volume for you."

Presently Rohan found himself engrossed in a book of archaic lore. In it he learned of a highly talented King, the founder of what later became the Oak Family. He was the one who had first worn the Four Great Rings, and—most interesting of all to Rohan—he was said to have met regularly with unearthly allies. Rohan closed the book and sat thinking, tapping his finger on the jeweled spine. It seemed entirely probable that the present wearer of the Rings also met with creatures not of this world. Whether this was for good or for ill, Rohan did not know.

It was interesting, however. And coincidental. Rohan decided that he did not believe in coincidences. Therefore he must be more careful than ever when dealing with the Dowager Ysa.

He picked up another book that had been on the shelf beside the book of lore, and opened it at random. The words on the page where the book fell open riveted his attention.

> *Though caution and common sense are certainly important, sometimes a risk is called for.*

Intrigued, he read on:

> *If you laugh, you risk appearing a fool.*
> *If you weep, you risk appearing sentimental.*
> *Reaching out for another is risking involvement.*
> *Exposing feelings is risking revealing your true self.*
> *Placing your ideas, your dreams, before a crowd is risking rejection.*

Loving is risking not being loved in return.
Living itself carries with it the risk of dying.
Hoping is risking disappointment.
Trying is risking failure.
Nevertheless, risks must be taken, because the greatest hazard, pitfall, and danger in life is to risk nothing. If a person risks nothing, does nothing, has nothing, that person becomes nothing. He may avoid present suffering and sorrow, but he will not learn, feel, change, grow, love, or live. Chained by his fear, he is a slave who has forfeited his freedom.
Only that person who dares, who risks, is free.

Rohan closed the book, pondering the words he had read. They touched something deep inside him, and he resolved to have this passage copied out so he could refer to it in times to come. Daring, he decided, was good, particularly when compared to trying to live without risk.

Donning his helm, in which he had fastened the bunch of herbs and dried grasses in obedience to Grandam Zazar's instructions, he left the Fane and stepped out into the courtyard, on his way to go to the practice field. There he discovered Anamara, apparently making her way toward the Fane, but being hindered by a group of overdressed popinjays, all clad in the height of fashion and none of them, in Rohan's judgment, worth the cleaning of the steel if they were to be run through.

By the badges they wore—deep red background, with a bear standing erect, on a background of oak leaves, all circled with the motto "Strength Prevails"—Rohan recognized them as members of the late King's faction. It had become a fashion with them, to keep Florian's memory alive despite the presence of the young King, Peres, even though he was still a child. Rohan had run into them before, and for no reason that he could think of, they had been hostile to him from the first moment though it could not be said that they had actually offered trouble. These men were only a little older than he, in their prime for training as warriors, but apparently dedicated to idleness and heavily engaged in as much mischief and troublemaking as possible.

One of them reached out and brushed back Anamara's mantle so he could finger her sleeve. "Fine clothes for a fine lady," he said with just the suggestion of a sneer in his voice. "And where does my fine lady go this day?"

"Please get out of my way, Piaul," Anamara said, her voice trembling.

"But I want to talk to you," Piaul said.

Rohan stepped forward. "The lady is making it plain that she does not want to talk to you."

Piaul looked him up and down insolently. "And who might you be? I do not recognize your badge."

"I am Rohan of the Sea-Rovers, and also connected with the House of Ash."

"And your business in Rendelsham?"

"I lead the levy of my people the Dowager has ordered."

"Oh," Piaul said. The sneer was very evident now. "Now I know who you are. Your father was responsible for the death of our late King, wasn't he?"

"There was an unfortunate accident, and if you will recall, my father died as well. I was there. Perhaps you were, too." Rohan did not see anything to be gained by dredging up the old scandal of the King's poisoned sword.

"In any case, you're just one more soldier among many. A minor noble at best. Next thing to a hostage."

"You were never so high in the late King's favor that he granted you status beyond what your birth entitled you to," Anamara said.

Rohan glanced at her, a little startled at the sharpness of her statement. Her face was pale, and a spot of color tinged each cheek. "Let me deal with this matter, my lady," he said.

"There is no matter," said one of Piaul's companions. "We are just leaving."

"Yes," Piaul said contemptuously. "You aren't even amusing. How fortunate we are that we do not have to associate with the likes of you." He pulled a scented handkerchief out of his sleeve and waved it ostentatiously under his nose. "The smell of fish, I am certain, must be one of your chief weapons of war."

The group of courtiers strolled off, laughing among themselves. Turning a corner, they were quickly out of sight.

"Thank you, Rohan," Anamara said. "Please do not allow their insults to nettle you."

"My only concern is for you."

"Would you escort me to my apartment, then? I do not trust that Piaul. I think he is up to no good where I am concerned."

"I will do so with pleasure, my lady."

He offered her his arm and together they made their way to one of the outlying buildings of Rendelsham Castle. "My step-mother, Ashen, preferred having her quarters outside the castle as well," he said. "She liked living apart, even though, I am told, this very isolation led to her being captured and spirited away."

"She was taken? Why?" Anamara said, startled.

"Nobody knows for certain. But it was very romantic. My father went and rescued her, and they were married shortly thereafter."

"What a nice story. I'm so glad it turned out well—"

"This one won't," said a muffled voice.

A group of men, faces hidden in the folds of heavy cloaks, stepped out from where they had obviously been lying in wait. Two of them grabbed Rohan, pinning his arms, while a third knocked his helmet off and began raining blows on him. A fourth man opened the door and roughly shoved Anamara through it.

"If anybody asks about the Sea-Rover, you are to say that he tried to take undue liberties with you," he said. Then he turned to the ones still pummeling Rohan. "Blindfold him and tie him up. I'll give you your instructions then."

Rohan thought he recognized Piaul's voice. But then someone

gave him a sharp rap on the head. Dazed, he was only dimly aware of his arms and legs being bound and him being shoved into some kind of bag, such as farmers use to bring vegetables to market. He could smell the earthy scents, and also the pungent odor of the sprigs of herbs and grasses in his helm. They must have dropped it into the bag with him.

Leaving no clues behind, he thought dimly. Then he was picked up, to be carried somewhere, and consciousness faded for a while.

He roused a little at the sound of lapping water. That plus the movement of the hard surface under him, told him that he was on a boat of some kind—probably a small one, or perhaps even a raft though the motion was different. Dimly, he could hear voices.

"When we get just a little closer, then's when we knife him, understand?"

"I still don't understand why we have to do him in. Just taking him off to where a Boggins will get him should be enough."

"The lord what's paying us says 'knife him,' so knife him we will. Do it right, and there'll be no hint of who really done it 'cause they'll think it was Bog-men."

The man to whom this one was speaking sniggered. "That'll take Their High and Mightinesses' minds off things, now won't it? Keep 'em right busy. Leave the rest of us alone."

Rohan forced himself to think. These were no gentlemen, though the one who had shoved Anamara through the door and instructed her to say Rohan had tried to take liberties had undoubtedly been Piaul. Therefore Piaul must be the one paying for the current situation in which Rohan found himself. But why?

The *why* of it could wait, he thought wryly, trying to ignore the thumping pain in his head, in favor of the *which*. He had better extricate himself from this, and fast, or he'd surely be taking the Long Boat out on the journey from which no man had ever yet returned.

They had mentioned a "Boggins" and feeding him to it. That

meant they must be headed down the River Rendel toward the Bog. How long had he been unconscious? It felt like a long time, judging from how stiff he was. Well, he found one consolation in his plight. They most likely wouldn't be trying to stab him until they had reached their destination, so that gave him time to concentrate.

Zazar. Grandam Zaz, he mouthed silently. *Come and save your wayward grandson! Or close enough to grandson. I need your help. Please.*

Nothing. He tried again, and yet again, to no avail while the boat journeyed on. He could hear the creak of oars. Then the boat stopped abruptly, going to ground against the mud of a shore—there was no mistaking the syrupy sound of it—and he sensed someone fumbling at the sack in which he was trussed. Any hope that it had all been an elaborate joke faded when the man untied the top and began shucking it off Rohan. The three men facing him had put back the hoods on their mantles, and he could see their faces clearly. Nobody would do that in these circumstances, unless they expected to leave no witnesses.

"Here, turn 'im over," one of the men said. "It has to be done just right. Lucky I have one of their shell knives. Nobody will ever know the difference."

Grandam Zazar! Rohan pleaded silently. *Mighty Wysen-wyf of the Bog! If ever you thought well of me, help me now!*

Something large and terrifying erupted from the river, soaking everyone in the boat and throwing them into confusion.

"It is a Boggins!" one of the men cried. "A Boggins! Push off from shore! Push off from shore!"

Rohan had a jumbled impression of something huge and snaky, with water glistening off its scales, and perhaps vestigial wings as well. It roared, its mighty voice making the leaves of nearby trees shiver. And it bore a human—or nearly human—face.

I have gone mad, Rohan thought. Utterly mad. That is not Grandam Zaz's face. It is not—

The monster bowed its long, serpentlike neck, opened a mouth full of sharp fangs, and plucked Rohan, sack and all, from the boat. It reared even higher while Rohan's captors fumbled with poles and freed their boat from the mud that had held it fast. Then they used the poles as fast as they could to propel the boat and get away from the horror behind them.

"We've done our job!" one of the men shouted. "A Boggins got 'im instead of Bog-men, but it's all the same. Now, pole and row for your lives, boys!"

Rohan discovered that he was curiously calm, considering that he was most likely to be devoured in the next few minutes. But the way the monster was gripping him in fangs that, inexplicably, had not come even close to piercing his flesh, did not inspire in him the same stark, unreasoning fear that it had in his former captors.

"They're out of sight now," said a familiar voice, a little muffled as if the speaker had its mouth full.

To Rohan's surprise, the monster set him down gently on firm ground and then began shrinking, its wings becoming arms, and its tail disappearing entirely. The scaly skin softened and paled. Then Zazar stood before him, looking remarkably annoyed.

"Don't call on me to do that sort of thing again anytime soon," the Wysen-wyf said irritably, as she rearranged her clothing and loosened her limbs. "It's confining in a shape like that, and hard on old bones."

"Grandam Zaz!" Rohan exclaimed. "I owe you my life! Oh, a thousand thanks! I thought—"

"I know what you thought." Zazar stared at him with a critical gaze for a long moment, and then slapped him soundly across the face.

"What was *that* for?" Rohan said, gingerly feeling his stinging cheek.

"For your total stupidity. You are so lacking in wits it should be against the law. My guess is there's a pretty face—and an empty head other than your own—behind this."

"Anamara had nothing to do with it. She wasn't bait, if that's what you're thinking. These men jumped me, and I don't know why."

"Then tell me what went on before."

Obediently Rohan recounted the story of the encounter with Piaul and his toadies, including the passage in the book that had impressed him, and then the way he had been captured. "And I still don't know why they did it."

Zazar snorted derisively. "As I said, you are stupid. Daring and risk without intelligence is worth exactly nothing. Piaul stood high in the late King Florian's favor, didn't he?"

"I suppose so."

"And by killing you, he and his companions might get some small revenge for the late King's death, wouldn't they?"

"But why me? I had nothing to do with it."

"That wouldn't matter, not if there was trouble and dissension to be spread."

Rohan digested this in silence. "But why did the Dowager set me up with the Lady Anamara?"

Zazar stared at him with renewed disgust, and he was afraid she was going to slap him again. "To keep you occupied, is my guess, so she could keep her finger on where you were, and what you were up to, and, as a result, what Ashen was doing."

"But she hates Ashen." Rohan frowned, struggling to follow Zazar's explanation.

"Just so. Don't you know anything?"

"I was just trying—"

"Never mind that. There is work to be done."

"Yes, Grandam." Rohan's meekness was not a sham. He knew that Zazar's irritation with him was justified. "I will follow your direction, I promise. Just tell me what to do."

"Go back to Rendelsham. There is where the real danger lies. But this time use your head, if you can find it."

"I have no idea how to get back. I was in a bag most of the time." He rummaged in the bag, found his helm, and put it on, hoping that Zazar would notice that he had followed her instructions and put the sprigs of herbs and grasses in it.

The Wysen-wyf looked him up and down, her expression sour. "Well, you can't get back across the river unaided. Come with me."

"Where are we going?"

"Back to my village, or close to it."

"Why?"

"To get a boat that will carry your weight."

"A boat? But—but how did you get here?"

Zazar turned and Rohan could swear that she almost smiled. "You don't need to know the details. Just say that I swam."

With Zazar as guide, it took only a little time to get through the Bog to a place, just in sight of the village, where her boat was moored. Then, with both of them poling, they took to the waterways heading due north.

"This isn't the route we came," Rohan said. "We're going against what current there is."

"No. They took you downstream quite a distance. That is why I was late in getting there. I'm taking you back another way, so you can get to the city in a short time. You'll be there almost before the ones who bagged you."

"That ought to surprise a few folks."

"You need all the bolstering-up you can get, after the way you've behaved. Sometimes I swear your head must be solid bone. And you should remember that I will not always be there to save your worthless hide."

"Yes, Grandam," Rohan said. "I promise to do better."

Zazar subsided into muttering under her breath, which, for Rohan, wasn't an enormous improvement as he could well imagine what she was saying.

Nevertheless, the Wysen-wyf was as good as her word. She took the boat into smaller and smaller streams that fed into the River Rendel, stopping when they could go no farther. The low mountains encircling Rendelsham were nearby.

"Go now, and do not dare so much without thinking first," Zazar said.

"Thank you again for my life," Rohan said. He bent and kissed the Wysen-wyf on the forehead. Then he turned and scrambled out of the boat and up onto the shore before she could do worse to him than slap him for his—he had to smile—his *daring*.

Sixteen

Squaring his shoulders, Rohan marched through the gate of Castle Rendelsham. True to Cebastian's prediction, all of the young nobles presumably leading their parts of the Dowager's Levy had had their living quarters moved to the castle. It would be a nuisance, Rohan thought, making dawn muster at Cragden Keep, but it certainly would keep the men under Ysa's close observation.

Almost—the thought came unbidden—like a prison, albeit with better and more luxurious accommodations than most prisons afforded.

Well, this was something he could think about later. Now Rohan wanted nothing more than a change of clothing, a chance to clean and polish what little armor he had been wearing when he had been taken, and a long, steaming bath. A servant, face carefully blank at Rohan's disheveled appearance, indicated the door to the room he had been assigned. It swung open easily when he pushed it and instantly he went alert. The door had not been latched.

A startled exclamation—which was *not* a greeting—stopped him short. Two people looked up, caught going through Rohan's belongings, and, equally startled, Rohan recognized one of them.

The Magician!

Andre Norton & Sasha Miller

The man with him, a castle guard wearing the Dowager's livery, started toward Rohan, drawing his sword. At a gesture from the Magician, the man halted in his tracks. Curious but unfrightened, Rohan approached the guard, studying him as he drew nearer. The guard stood there unblinking, expression blank, poised for another step, but frozen in place. What kind of control was this? Magic? Rohan had not seen any sign of the use of a paralytic gas or a drug. Therefore it must be a spell such as he had never witnessed before. He wondered if he could duplicate such a spell, if he needed to.

With a laugh, the Magician stepped forward. By the time he shrugged off his long cloak the person who faced Rohan had once more transformed into the beautiful woman he had seen at the inn where he had witnessed her—or his—skilled performance.

"Not the least bit surprised, are you, young lord?" she said. Her voice was deep and rich. "That speaks well. I marked you when first I saw you, and that candle trick of yours. That you were able to free yourself from a rather nasty predicament—oh, yes, I know about how the late King's followers set you up for an assassination—speaks well of your talents also." She stared at Rohan in such a way as made him nervous. "Yes, I do believe that you are the partner I have been awaiting. Or at least you shall be, with just a little help. And all that without having to be bribed."

"Your meaning, Madame?" Rohan said. He tried to maintain a cool and unruffled attitude. Best to learn what he could than to make an instant rejection.

With a swirl of her garments, the woman seated herself. She flicked one finger, and a flagon of wine and two goblets appeared on a table near her reach. "Come, sit. Let me explain. But first, I will ask you a question. How would you like to have your small and untrained talents magnified? Shall we say, ten times over."

"Certainly, anyone would say yes," Rohan returned cautiously. He accepted the goblet she filled, but did not drink. "What payment would such a bargain entail, my lady?"

To that she made no answer but continued as if he had not posed a question in return. "I could increase your talents a hundredfold. The only thing you would have to do is to join me."

Now she favored him with a look more than half veiled by thick eyelashes. The skin on the back of Rohan's neck began to tingle—not, he was convinced, because he desired this Sorceress; he had to admit to himself, he did. Rather, he sensed danger in her. He decided to present himself as being just a little stupid and had to stifle a smile at the thought that more than one thought this already.

"I think not, my lady." He replaced the untasted goblet on the table. Not at all astounded, he saw it wink out as the Sorceress's sultry expression became one of sullen disappointment.

"You are making a big mistake, you know," she said.

"Lady, I know nothing of you, not even the name you pass by. Do I now guess, to amuse you? Perhaps you are in league with the Dowager. There are stories—"

"Whom I may be in league with is not your concern, young Rohan."

He changed the subject quickly. "Why did you find it necessary to explore my possessions?"

"That also is none of your concern."

"In that they are my personal belongings, such an action concerns me very much."

The Sorceress's eyes glittered, as bright as gems. "Do not try to match me in talent," she said, "or even to dare question what I might or might not do."

"Oh, I would never dream of such a thing. However, I can call the guard in the hallway and have you and your servant here removed from my quarters." Rohan was proud that he managed to smile. "I'm sure that in his present condition he will make a useful perch for the pigeons."

The Sorceress frowned. "You certainly will not prosper, young sir. Obviously you prefer green fruit to ripe, and folly to wisdom. That little chit you seem enamored of is of no consequence. If only you knew about her. But no matter. It will not be long before you regret your decision, mark me well." She snapped her fingers. The frozen guard came to life abruptly. He took a step, and then another before he realized that the one he had been moving to attack was now in conversation with the Magician—for the one who commanded his service was again a man.

"I believe now we have entered by misdirection the wrong quarters," the Magician said. "I apologize, young sir. Doubtless we shall meet again, under more pleasant circumstances."

Rohan nodded. "Indeed, I look forward to that happy occasion. And so I wish you good day."

The two were quickly gone with formal courtesy. Rohan rang for a servant to bring hot water for his bath. While he luxuriated in the steam and scrubbed the muck of the Bog from his skin, he tried to puzzle out just what had happened—and why. That had been too quick, and the Magician had been "vanquished" too easily. And what about that remark concerning Anamara? Many things he could not understand were left to puzzle him.

Cebastian rapped on his door just as he was dressing for dinner. "Where have you been?" he asked, a little sharply, when Rohan had let him in.

"I have been in the middle of a strange story," Rohan said. As he pulled on his boots, he told his friend of the abduction and his near-murder, and how Grandam Zazar had brought him back by boat close enough that he could easily walk the rest of the way.

"A strange story indeed," Cebastian agreed when Rohan had finished. "You are lucky to be able to call on the Wysen-wyf of the Bog in need."

"I will introduce you, and others of our friends as well. She is inclined to be gruff, but I think she likes having members of younger generations around her now and then."

"Not unlike Her Gracious Highness the Dowager Ysa," Cebastian commented dryly. "Incidentally, she has been inquiring about you most specifically. I told her you were out hunting."

"Thank you. Do you believe she really was some part of a plot, if plot it was?"

"I don't think so, but with that one, you never can be sure. Oh—before I forget. The Dowager has decreed that there is to be an enormous tourney, to be held at the next holiday, about two months from now. All the leaders of the Dowager's Levy are to participate. The talk has been of little else."

"That is very interesting."

"Come now, or we'll be late. And one is never late for the Dowager's table, if one is smart."

They entered the Great Hall together. Cebastian had been correct; everywhere the young nobles were raising voices about the tourney. There was a great deal of discussion concerning the main prize—a suit of exceptionally fine armor.

Rohan took his accustomed place which Her Highness had assigned him, trying not to call attention to himself in any way. At the same time he tried to see any change in her which would suggest astonishment at his appearance. But there was nothing, or very little. Certainly not enough on which to form an opinion on such a weighty matter. He could not be sure at present that he could detect any awareness of anything of the untoward events that had occurred and so he decided that she most likely had had nothing to do with his abduction and near-murder.

"How very thoughtful of you to arrange such a splendid entertainment for us all," he said to Ysa. "The tourney, I mean."

"It used to be a Rendel custom, in times past, to mark holidays with such festivities. I know that training day after day can grow tiresome," she said. "You deserve a respite, a reward. And also, our people deserve to see how the best youth of Rendel comport themselves, even in mock battle."

"Do you think that we are ready for such an exhibition?"

"Count Harous assures me that you are, or will be. And further, he tells me that you show great promise, young Rohan, far more than your heritage as a Sea-Rover might indicate. He says you are fully as able to command on land as, presumably, you are at sea."

"Count Harous is too kind."

Rohan was quickly growing bored with the stilted conversations one indulged in at Court, where words were used to conceal, not reveal. What, he wondered, did the Dowager mean by arranging this tourney? He resolved to do some investigation between now and the date of the event. Also, there was time, if he could get permission from Harous, to make a quick trip back to the Oakenkeep and confer with Gaurin. He would know about this sort of thing.

In the meantime, however, Rohan did nothing but pretend to enjoy himself, as his fellows did, and to engage in flirtation with the Dowager which, he perceived, she enjoyed very much. Later, perhaps, he could dance with Anamara.

The Magician, who seemed now to be a permanent member at Court, entertained them after dinner. Rohan watched closely but not even by so much as a raised eyebrow did the man—or woman, beneath the man's appearance—indicate that he had encountered Rohan earlier that day.

Unfortunately, he could not find Anamara when the entertainment was finished and the music begun. She was not in the Hall, nor did anybody know of her whereabouts. He knew, instinctively, that it would not be wise for him to openly search for her.

Another mystery to add to the growing number Rohan knew he must investigate. He chose another partner for the opening galliard, and, eventually, the Dowager arose. He would never find a better moment to end the boring surface chitchat and excuse himself and so the endless evening drew to a close.

Harous, deeply absorbed by his duties, was unavailable. Having chaffed at waiting for at least a six-day, Rohan started unbidden for the Oakenkeep. He thought about taking Cebastian with him but decided against it, knowing that he could go and make it back faster if he traveled alone.

He was pleased indeed at the time he made. After only a day and a half on the road he arrived at the Oakenkeep and without any hesitation made his way at once to Guarin's private office.

There he faced both his foster father and Ashen, giving his report as carefully and completely as he could.

Gaurin spoke first. "Tell me what the others think about this contest."

"It is causing some rivalry, of course. Some of their sponsors are said to be boasting their choices too warmly, even to the edge of real quarrels. Gattor of Bilth, for example, has disputed heatedly with Lord Royance of Grattenbor. Made a large wager. But the worst, I think, is that company of lickspittles who once formed King Florian's band of intimates. They will not take up arms, but they are everywhere, pushing this one, whispering into that one's ear. They are encouraging factions to form, and they seem to take pleasure in setting one faction against another."

"That cannot bode well for peace in the Kingdom," Ashen commented.

"No, it doesn't. As to the little boy who is King, Peres, he is seen in public more often these days and it is said that a faction is even forming around *him*. It makes being at Court a lot more interesting, but I cannot think that anything good can come of it."

"How does the young King?" Ashen asked. "And Rannore, his mother?"

"Well enough, though he seems a little on the frail side. As to the Young Dowager, she is little more than a living ghost, creeping about when someone lets her out of her apartment, but kept hidden away much of the time."

Ashen frowned, and Rohan changed the subject, knowing of her fondness for Rannore. "Anyway, all this talk about the tourney, and which side will win and who will back whom, was a blessing in one way. It took the attention off me, and my adventures with some would-be assassins—a part of one of the factions, I am convinced."

"Assassins?" Ashen was startled. "You never mentioned that."

"Oh," Rohan said, more than a little abashed. "I thought Grandam Zaz would have told you the story, when next you visited her."

"We have put off a return trip into the Bog," Gaurin said. "Perhaps that wasn't a good idea."

"Grandam Zaz is the one who saved me, you know. Turned herself into a Bog monster the likes of which you couldn't even imagine, and plucked me out of the assassins' hands as neat as you please. Then she slapped me for being a fool."

Both Gaurin and Ashen had to laugh. "She's slapped me for the same reason," Ashen said. "Or, sometimes, even less." She turned to Gaurin. "Would it be possible to go into the Bog?"

"Yes. We've had a break in the weather, and all is quiet at the moment. I think we need Madame Zazar's wisdom to help us decipher what may be going on at Court, and the best way to advise Rohan, when he has to deal with it."

Thoughtfully Ashen turned the heavy stone bracelet around on her wrist, but kept her own counsel.

The next day, with Rohan shouldering a large pack of food and warm clothing as gifts, the three of them made their way to Zazar's hut. Ashen cautiously called on her Bog upbringing to make sure they were not discovered on the way. Down in the village, not as many mud-plastered reed chimneys were smoking as might have been expected, indicating that the men, at least, were out and on the hunt. A spiral of smoke rising from Zazar's chimney signaled that she was at home.

"Good," Ashen observed. "I would not have liked for us to have stayed out here, waiting for her to return from what might be a long errand."

Without any sign of surprise, Zazar met them at the door. "Hot soup's on the fire," she said by way of greeting. "The broth is a little thin by now, because winter is pinching hard. However, it'll warm your bones."

"Here is dried meat and I will arrange to have a haunch of fresh fallowbeeste sent to our usual supply point," Gaurin promised. "Though I think it might freeze before you can retrieve it."

Zazar rummaged in a woven reed box, drew out an amulet, and handed it to him. "Leave it there and I'll be glad to have it. This will keep away predators—or thieves." Then the Wysen-wyf set the newly brought supplies aside and dipped out bowls of soup made more filling by the addition of tart, edible grasses and thick noodles.

"I remember these noodles from my childhood," Ashen said. She sipped from her bowl with obvious pleasure. "I always liked them."

"Well, you didn't come all this way just to compliment my soup," Zazar said. "What did bring you?"

Gaurin and Rohan told her of the oncoming tourney, and the fracturing of the political harmony in Rendelsham, and of the appearance of the mysterious Magician and how the man—or woman—had tried to tempt Rohan. By the time they had finished, Zazar's lips were turned down in an expression of disgust mingled with contempt.

"The Dowager's a fool," she said. "But I knew that from long ago. I know of this Magician. Sorceress, really. Her name is Flavielle. Calls herself Flavian, when she travels in a man's guise, but she's a woman, right enough. She is up to no good, you can safely wager on it. And you say you turned her down on her so-kind offer, Rohan?"

"I did. Something about her put the hair up on the back of my neck."

"Hmph. For once you used your head for something other than to perch your helmet on. Well, with this news I need to do a few things, and that means a trip to Galinth. You three might as well come with me."

"I had been hoping to show Galinth to Gaurin on this trip," Ashen said, "and I want to see Weyse again as well."

"Don't count on much of her company. She'll be helping me. Now, take that pack of food and I'll prepare more, for we'll need it while we're there. No need for shin-armor—all the snakes are in deep sleep—but you can please hand me that new warm cloak you brought." Zazar wrapped the garment around herself, and her dour expression softened. "We don't find a great deal of fur in the Bog, and until lately, haven't needed it much. Thank you."

"I hoped you would like it," Gaurin said. He kissed her hand, and Zazar scowled once more.

"Come along, come along, and don't dally. The sooner we're there and back, the better. Rohan will be missed, if he isn't already, and this absence on top of the other—Well, it won't do his military career much good."

So saying, the Wysen-wyf led them out the back way to where several boats were pulled up out of the water, available. She selected one capable of holding the four of them and, presently, the two men, with Zazar guiding them, were poling their way through the brackish, cold waters of the Bog. More than once they had to break through a thin layer of ice to enter one of the channels leading away from the main waterways.

"At least the Boggins are lying deep," Zazar commented at one point. "They are too sluggish to hunt, when it's this cold."

"Cold of blood, like snakes. I'd like to see one of these monsters for myself," Rohan said. "I have heard enough about them from Ashen. Still, I can't help but be glad for it, that they're all asleep."

"I'll show you a stone one later," Zazar said. "And that should do for you, if you know what's good for you."

⚜

They made good time. Day had not yet drawn on toward evening when they passed a ruined wall of standing stones and entered the drowned gateway and pool leading to the city itself. Ashen uttered a gasp of recognition.

"There's been no change at all," she said. "Somehow, I thought the ruination would have progressed."

"No," said Zazar, "it is as it is, and will remain so until all changes in the world. Here's the landing-stone."

Zazar took the pole from Rohan and jammed it into a crevice between two of the rocks. Then she looped the rope attached to the bow tightly around the pole. The two men climbed out first, and helped the women, though Zazar leapt nimbly off onto the flat stone and was halfway up the slope before Ashen had found her footing.

"So this is Galinth," Gaurin said. "It must have once been a mighty city indeed."

"Rendel's capital, before they built the new city, and that frivolous excuse for a castle."

Ashen turned and stared at Zazar, and Rohan knew that this was a new revelation for her. "What happened?" she said.

"Much," Zazar replied shortly. She raised both her hands palm out and intoned something in a sonorous singsong. The words were unintelligible. Then her chant was answered by a song strange both in rhythm and tune.

"This is as it was before," Ashen whispered. "It is as if Zazar is announcing something of importance, or perhaps asking for refuge."

"Or asking permission to enter," Gaurin returned. "Whom is she asking?"

"I never knew, nor did I dare ask."

"Shush with your whispers," Zazar said, "and follow me."

She led them down the path, up stairs and down, over walls, past ruined buildings, until they came to one that was somewhat less ruined than most of the others. In the courtyard lay a figure, facedown, carved of stone and broken into thirds. Gaurin knelt and touched the pieces wonderingly. But then, at an impatient sound and a gesture from Zazar, he followed her through the open doorway. A curtain hung just inside the doorway, sheltering the interior from the gaze of any interlopers. Inside, they found a fire already lighted and, revealed in the light of the flames, a plump, furred creature that squeaked and trilled when it caught sight of them. It waddled toward them as fast as its girth would allow it to go.

"Weyse!" Ashen cried. She stooped to gather the creature into her arms. "Oh, how I've missed you!"

Weyse began purring loudly enough that the sound filled the chamber where the travelers now found themselves. The little creature grasped Ashen's hand with her slender forepaws and began licking Ashen's fingers.

"Put your things down," Zazar said. "You'll be staying for a while."

"How long?" Rohan asked.

"As long as it takes." Then her features softened a little. "You'll be going back to Rendelsham from here so you won't have to retrace your steps from the Oakenkeep."

"Thank you, Grandam Zaz. But my horse, my gear—"

"I'll arrange to have word sent so it will be waiting for you when you reach the edge of the Bog. Gaurin, I'll need you for that. Otherwise, it might cause alarm in the keep to receive such a message, from a source they know not."

Gaurin smiled, a bit wryly. "I think that Lathrom, who is now my second-in-command, is fairly used to some strange happenings. Still, it is well thought-of by you."

"While we're taking care of this matter, Ashen, you make beds from those mats, like you did before. Rohan, you put away the food and keep Weyse out of the dried grain and berries or she'll have it all eaten before you can blink your eyes. Gaurin, you fetch down a set of clay tablets I'll point out to you. They're on yonder shelf."

They scarcely had time, Rohan thought, to reflect on the strangeness of their surroundings, what with Grandam Zaz putting them all to work so promptly. But then, Ashen had been here before so it wasn't all that new to her. Rohan stowed the packages of meat and dried trail-food out of Weyse's reach. However, he found himself giving in to the pleading eyes of the little furred creature who, in spite of her heft, was giving a good imitation of being on the brink of starvation. He took out a handful of sweet berries to give to her. To his wry amusement, Weyse tugged him to a seated position and then climbed into his lap to enjoy her treat, nibbling the mixture from the palm of his hand. Then she licked her lips, and as plainly as if she had used words, indicated that she would now like a drink of water.

Rohan found a basin set in the floor and, above it, protruding from the wall, a hollow tube of the same rock as the walls, from which trickled a steady stream of water. He wondered that Weyse didn't simply drink from this, but with a philosophical shrug he found a bowl—empty except for a few drops at the bottom—and filled it for her. While the little creature lapped contentedly, Rohan sampled the water himself and found it good and sweet, and not as teeth-cracking cold as he expected.

"We're done," Zazar said. "Now, all of you, leave me alone for a while. Rohan, you go look around outside but mind where you're going so you won't be lost. Not all Bog-creatures are presently in a torpor. Ashen, I think you had something to show to Gaurin. Weyse, you help me."

With a little trilling sound, Weyse waddled obediently over to the Wysen-wyf and stood up, clutching Zazar's skirts with her clever little paws. Zazar picked Weyse up and cuddled her the way a woman would hold a nursing child. "Yes, I'm fond of you, too," she said, in an unaccustomed soft voice. "Now go," she said in her normal, irascible tone to the rest of them. "I'll let you know what I have learned when you return."

With Gaurin's strength to help her, lifting the stone slab set into the floor of the chamber was a trivial matter for Ashen. The two of them, Ashen in the lead, descended the stairway thus revealed and Gaurin pulled the slab down behind them. The light-rods she remembered from years before still burned, but, she also remembered, unless something had changed in this changeless place, the light would fail farther on. She touched the lantern she had brought, reassured by its presence.

"I might wonder how Zazar knew there was something I wanted to show you," Ashen said once they were out of earshot, "but I gave up questioning how she knows what she does a long time ago."

"For myself, I never have questioned Madame Zazar and her wisdom," Gaurin said. "Lead on, my dear."

Just as Ashen remembered, the steps, so even and straight at the top of the pit, soon turned crooked and narrow. When the light-rods failed, Gaurin took the lantern, struck steel to flint, and lighted it. They reached solid flooring and paused to study the small stone-work room in which they found themselves.

"There," Ashen said, pointing. "That is the doorway. It seems even smaller now than it did before."

They both had to crouch to enter.

With the lantern to help them, they hurried quickly through the dank passageway that had taken all of Ashen's resolve to travel those years before, turned left, and discovered the gleam of light she remembered from her earlier journey. Gaurin extinguished the lantern, conserving the oil, as they entered the large chamber at the end of the tunnel.

A few more of the light-rods were dark, but there was still illumination by which they could see.

"It is just as I remember," Ashen said. "The light-rods set at the ends of these stone cases. I remember thinking how the smallest one of them looked longer than I am tall."

Gaurin gazed on the two rows of cases with an aisle between them. He examined the ornamentation on the cases; the sides and lids of each were decorated with a multitude of symbols.

"I never knew what this place was," Ashen said, "but I suspected that I had come upon a place of the resting dead."

"You were correct, my dear," Gaurin said. "This is what is called a catacomb, and these cases are sarcophagi. Tombs. It is plainly a place of honor, such as the common folk do not use."

Ashen touched her wrist and twisted the armband, carved of a single piece of milky, translucent crystal shot through with subtle rainbow hues. "Let me show you where I found this," she said.

She expected to discover nothing left but a pile of dust, but fragments of some of the bones could still be seen, at least pieces of them. To her relief, the man's broken leg, something that must have happened before his death, was hard to distinguish though she could still see the shattered bones in her mind's eye. She would not have liked Gaurin to have seen that. There were but a few shreds of cloth left, and the red color had faded. The air of sadness that had hung over this poor man when first she had stumbled upon him seemed, if anything, intensified with the continuing crumbling of his remains.

Gaurin held out his hand. "Give me the bracelet, please."

She took it off and gave it to him. He placed it on his own wrist, and murmured a few words. Nothing happened for a moment, but then the rainbow colors in the stone intensified and swirled until the glow was almost blinding. It lit up the entire area around them.

To Ashen's amazement, a haze began to form over the sad little heap of dust and bones. An image formed, though it was thin and translucent and the stones on which the remains lay clearly could be seen through it. Nevertheless, with the pricking sensation Ashen had known before when she was in the presence of Power, she realized that this image was that of the dead man as he had once been. Now he wore garments of a deep, rich red, in an outmoded style, but clearly those of a man of consequence. His hair was the color of honey and his features were very like Gaurin's, so much so that they could have been brothers. His eyes were closed, and an expression of deep sorrow lined his face.

Ashen moved closer to her husband and he put his arm around her.

"Yes," Gaurin said, his voice steady, "this was my father. Look upon Count Bjauden of the Nordors."

The man's image did not stir nor did his lips move, and yet a hollow whisper filled the air. "Aye, my son. Count Bjauden was I, who was most foully murdered by an agent of the Prince of Rendel. I must be avenged."

Ashen did some rapid calculations in her head, and realized that in referring to the Prince the spirit was speaking of Florian, before he became King. Gaurin glanced at her, and she knew he had come to the same understanding.

"Time has stood still for him," he whispered to her.

"And yet he recognizes you."

"It is a mystery."

"Speak to him, Gaurin. Ease his soul."

Gaurin thought a moment. "Indeed, murder most foul," he told the pale image. "But well avenged by this lady's husband, who killed the—the Prince in fair duel, but died for his efforts. You have not known, for there was none to tell you. You might have much to say to this man and he to you, on the other side. His name is Obern."

"Obern. He accomplished my vengeance? I will remember."

"Even so. Dear spirit of my father, what else may I do? Shall you be buried in more state than you have now?"

"No. Let me be. I lie with, but not of, the great ones of a bygone land and have waited long for a message such as yours so that I might depart this realm entirely."

"It is thanks to Obern that you may now go in peace, and in honor. When you see him, tell him that his lady is well, for I have her in my care. Assure him that nothing will happen to her while I live."

The whisper was growing more faint. "I will remember."

Then Gaurin knelt and kissed the ghostly forehead of the dead man. The image faded and, as Ashen watched, the few fragments of bone remaining crumbled into dust. Gaurin reached out and for a moment Ashen feared he was trying to bring his father back. But he only picked up an ornate belt buckle that she had not noticed before. It had probably been hidden under the shreds of his clothing, now also vanished entirely, and she had not seen it when first she had come through this passageway. Gaurin got to his feet and gave her back the armband, which had resumed its normal coloration.

"Now we both have a talisman of my House," he said. "I swear that I will never wear another buckle but this." He removed his belt and affixed the heirloom, which was wrought as the image of a snowcat wearing a silver collar.

"Oh, Gaurin." Ashen put her arms around him and leaned her head against him. They stood so, in the warmth of a close embrace, for a long time. When he finally released her, she could sense that the sadness she had felt in the very air of this spot when first she had come upon the remains had, somehow, dissipated. Gaurin's father was resting peacefully at last.

They did not return the route they had come. Ashen took them the long way through the city, as she recalled it, thinking that the open air would help Gaurin, in case he was still troubled by the manner of his father's passing. The daylight had failed by the time they reached the courtyard and the curtained doorway. They did not meet Rohan on the way; rather, they discovered him inside with Weyse settled in his arms.

"And did you learn what you wanted to know?" Zazar said. She tended a pot of stew bubbling over the fire. Ashen realized she had forgotten to eat anything since that early bowl of noodles.

"I learned the answer to a mystery that has troubled me and my kindred for many years, Madame Zazar," Gaurin said. "And, though it was a sad answer, I must thank you for your help."

"Spoken well," Zazar said. "Now come and eat, and I'll tell you what Weyse and I have been up to."

Seventeen

*T*here was, Zazar related, more to the matter than even she had suspected.

The Dowager had indeed engaged the Sorceress—sometime Magician—Flavielle, hoping to obtain another servant of Power, another set of eyes and ears to bring her information. However, Flavielle had plans that Ysa knew nothing of.

Where the Dowager had worked hard and steadily to avoid any sort of conflict among her restive nobles, that very result was Flavielle's purpose. To that end, the Sorceress was the one who had suggested the ill-considered tourney to Ysa, and Ysa, unsuspecting, had acquiesced.

"After all, it would be an occasion for much merriment and much attention lavished on the Dowager, the presenter of the amusement," Zazar commented. "She does love attention."

At the same time, undercurrents of unrest roiled, threatening to break old alliances and forge new ones. This faction was now poised on the brink of war with that one, while others waited to see which might emerge the stronger, before taking sides.

"Civil war brews," Zazar said ominously. "Then, while the Rendelian nobility is busy destroying itself, the Great Menace from the

North will take that moment to attack. Rendel will be doomed."

"Not if I have anything to say about it, if this be the case,"
Rohan declared with some vehemence. He stroked Weyse, who
seemed to have accepted him completely. The little creature purred
softly, snuggling more comfortably into his lap as he fed her another
tidbit from the leftovers of their dinner. "The question is, how best
to go about foiling Flavielle's plans? I can see some danger here. It
was only through Grandam Zaz's intervention that I escaped being
killed and having my fate settled as just another victim of the Bog."

"Go softly, but boldly," Gaurin advised. "Pick your moment and
then reveal all, in as public a manner as possible."

"Listen. Gaurin is right," Zazar said. "However, I'll add this. You
can trust what I have told you. I learned the truth through—Well,
never mind how I did it. Let us just say that Flavielle fell into a
restless sleep."

The Wysen-wyf shuddered slightly, and Rohan imagined her
wandering through the shadows of Flavielle's mind, learning what
the Sorceress knew. He would not have wanted to have undertaken
such a journey and, indeed, knew himself to be incapable of such a
feat. He now suspected that Flavielle had connections to the enemy
in the North, though Grandam Zaz had not mentioned it.
Therefore, he would bide his time and not say anything until he
was more certain than now. He did not dare question her, not after
she had declared that he could trust what she told him.

"Then I'll put a confident face on it," he said. "But I'd feel better
prepared if you, or Ashen, or Gaurin, or even Weyse were with
me."

"Ashen and Gaurin will be in Rendelsham for the tourney.
Know that Weyse and I will be, also, if only in spirit."

"That's all well and good," Rohan said glumly, "but scant comfort if my words aren't believed."

"Here," Zazar said. She handed him an amulet on a silk cord.
"This is a little something I brought back from a source of Power.
Display it at the proper time, and I promise that anybody who
doesn't believe, will change his mind."

"What is the proper time?"

"You'll know. Or if you don't, then there's no hope for you, or for the world as we know it either."

To Rohan's surprise, Ashen chuckled. "Trust Zazar," she said. "She has told me much the same thing on occasion, and it always worked out though I had no idea how it was going to."

"Very well, then, I will," Rohan said.

However, despite the Wysen-wyf's certainty, Rohan could not dispel his basic doubts as he slipped the cord over his neck, tucking the trinket into his shirt for safekeeping and also to hide it from prying—and perhaps unfriendly—eyes. It all seemed much too strange to him. Privately, he thought Zazar must have erred somewhere, that she must have made a mistake, misread what she had discovered while examining the Sorceress's mind in the deepness of an enchanted slumber. Surely nobody would be so wicked as to try to create conflict among the nobles of Rendel, not when there was still the danger threatening from the northern lands! He simply could not believe it.

"Now, everyone sleep," Zazar ordered. "In the morning, I will guide Rohan to the spot where one of the men from the Oakenkeep awaits with his horse and his gear. Ashen, you and Gaurin stay here. Then, when I return, we will go back through the Bog, and you will go to your home."

"How will we know if Rohan is successful?" Ashen said.

The Wysen-wyf exhaled sharply through her nose. "I suppose it is too much to ask you to believe it will be," she said. "You won't have to be told, though. Didn't you hear me say that you'll be making the journey to Rendelsham and witnessing the results for yourself? You'll be expected there, with the rest of Rendel nobility, to attend the tourney."

"I was thinking of other things," Ashen said in protest. She glanced at Gaurin, who smiled at her.

"Heed the words of the Wysen-wyf of the Bog, my dear," he said. "Of course we are bidden to attend, and I will do my best to calm the tempers of those who will listen to me. This is a grave situation, and we all have our parts to play, even you."

"I?" Ashen said.

"Indeed. You can renew your friendship with the Young Dowager Rannore. Her words, though little heeded of late, can still have an effect, particularly if she can make the youthful King aware of what is happening in his country. And it is still his country, however much Ysa flaunts her power."

"I see. Yes, we will all do what we can. And I am grateful that Zazar has the ability to do what she does, and the wisdom to set us all on this needed pathway."

"If I had wine, I'd offer a toast," Rohan said. "But all I have is this." Comically, he held Weyse up, tossed her in the air, and caught her. The little creature, startled, grabbed his hands as if clinging for her life. Gaurin and Ashen erupted in merriment, and even Zazar uttered a snort that could have been mistaken for laughter.

"Cuddle up and sleep with me, Weyse," Rohan coaxed, "and I promise no more toasts for you. Agreed?"

Apparently she did. However, sometime during the night, Rohan roused and discovered her gone, only to find her curled up with Ashen. In the morning, he awoke to see her busy under Zazar's feet as she prepared a quick breakfast before the two of them left on the short journey to the northern edges of the Bog.

"I will say good-bye only for a little while." Ashen's manner was cheerful, but Rohan thought he could detect a measure of anxiety underneath.

"Goodspeed to you, and we will see you in a few weeks, in Rendelsham," Gaurin told him.

The two men clasped hands, and Ashen kissed Rohan. Then he and Zazar left.

❧

When Rohan entered the city again, he discovered to his relief that his absence had not been noted. Indeed, he found himself almost immediately immersed in the preparations for the Grand Tourney, as it was already beginning to be called. Training, under instructors hired by Count Harous, was stepped up so much that not only Rohan but also all of the other young nobles who had been moved to Rendelsham Castle regretted the distance between there and Cragden Keep. Before dawn, they were forced to march rather than ride, and this effort was quickly increased to making them jog rather than walk. This was, Harous told them, to help toughen them up. Rohan massaged his aching muscles at the end of each day, as did the others, and hoped this toughening would be accomplished soon, preferably before it killed them all.

In addition to this part of their training, they put in longer hours at weapons practice and at learning to ride and fight at the same time. Red was not a war-horse, but those young men who lacked their own, as he did, were supplied from Count Harous's stables. The mount assigned to Rohan was a spirited, willful beast, but, his instructors assured him, this was all to the good, as a well-trained war-horse fought as ably as its master. Its name was Ironfoot.

Like all Sea-Rovers, Rohan never developed a real liking for combat from horseback, though he made himself become competent at it because he knew he had to be. Likewise, his axework improved, though he still could not be said to be an expert with the weapon. He was only passable with the lance, though better than some of his peers. However, his sword skills advanced until he occasionally even earned an approving word from Count Harous himself.

"I'm almost too tired to eat," he told Cebastian one evening when they had dragged themselves back to Rendelsham well after dark. "And my backside is full of blisters where it isn't callused. If it weren't for the possibility of catching a glimpse of Anamara, I would forgo dinner entirely." That, he added silently to himself, and the fact that the only way I can determine what Flavielle is up to, is to be in her presence as much as possible.

"The lovely Anamara seems to be avoiding you these days," Cebastian commented. "Mostly what I see is her back as she is leaving the Hall."

"She is shy to begin with, and now I think she is under orders,"

Rohan said. "If you will notice, the Dowager doesn't seem as pleased with me as she once was."

"What have you done to deserve this?"

"I don't know. Perhaps I have avoided her table too many times of late. Well, either I will repair my reputation in the Dowager's eyes, or I won't. I can only do my best."

"As do we all," Cebastian replied.

At least, Rohan thought as they entered the Great Hall together, I think I know now the reason the Dowager was trying to drug me that first night. Insisting that I pay attention to poor, sweet Anamara was definitely a second thought with her. Power, as Grandam Zaz has said, knows other Power when they meet. I think Ysa wanted to have me malleable in her hands so that her Magician-Sorceress could work her way with me, enlist my help with whatever it is that the Dowager has planned this time. The more Power at her disposal, the better.

This also might explain Ysa's coolness toward him, that he had rebuffed Flavielle's advances and the Dowager knew of it. He only hoped that Anamara was not suffering because of Rohan's failure to fall in with the Dowager's scheming.

However, if Rohan's speculations were correct, nothing in either the Dowager's or the Sorceress's attitudes indicated that this was the case. To the casual observer, Queen Ysa had merely turned her attention to another of the young nobles—Vinod of Vacaster—the way a good sovereign would, so that she might not be thought to be playing favorites.

Rohan was not deceived, however. He caught a glance exchanged between the Dowager and Flavielle, and caught also the subtle nod in his direction. The back of his neck prickled in the way he had come to recognize as a sign that he had detected something other folk either could not, or which they chose to ignore. He resolved to be even more on his guard—only wishing he knew what he should be wary of.

❧

Days passed, full of activity, and the young nobles who had mistakenly thought themselves in good physical condition did, indeed, begin to toughen up. Rohan became aware of the presence of the guard who had accompanied Flavielle that evening when he had caught them going through his belongings. His appearance had changed, though. Gone was the Dowager's livery and, in its place, the plain fighting gear of a foot soldier of Rendel, worn by the instructors helping with the training of the men the young nobles had brought with them to Rendelsham. Rohan recognized that there was more to the man than had first appeared; he could be a hired tough, a cut above a street bully, or he could even be a kind of apprentice of the Sorceress. By a few discreet inquiries, he learned that the man's name was Duig and that he was presenting himself as one of Count Harous's soldiers with the rank of sergeant. Rohan noticed as well that Duig frequently had a few moments' quiet conversation with this one and that, and afterward there would be unpleasantness between two of the leaders of the Dowager's Levy. This seemed to happen with more frequency as the date of the Grand Tourney drew closer and, correspondingly, the great nobles of Rendel began to arrive in the city.

Duig never indicated, by word or gesture, that he had ever seen Rohan before, let alone been apprehended in the very act of going through his belongings. And Rohan was careful to maintain the same air of indifference.

It would have been easy to put the whole matter down to a fevered and overactive imagination, but one evening Cebastian, who had been Rohan's closest friend in Rendelsham, tried to pick a quarrel with him.

Rohan was astonished. "And who told you that I was trying to keep you from being knighted, so that your rank would be inferior to mine?" he asked Cebastian.

"One of the people who have been training us."

"It wouldn't have been Duig, would it?"

Cebastian looked startled. "How did you know?"

Then Rohan told Cebastian of his suspicions, leaving out the part about the Sorceress and her offer of—of whatever it was Flavielle was actually trying to tempt him with. Cebastian's anger cooled visibly even as Rohan spoke.

"Thank you, comrade," he said when Rohan had finished. "This casts a clear light on what has lately been a shadowy mystery. Now I understand better what has been going on of late. Jivon barely speaks to Steuart these days, and Jabez has quarreled openly with Reges. And with as little cause as, it turns out, I had to be angry with you."

Rohan remembered what Grandam Zaz had told him—that Flavielle had plans that the Dowager knew nothing of, and that many of these plans centered about the Grand Tourney. "Could it be," he asked Cebastian, "that our good sergeant even encouraged you to report your grievance to the one who put you in charge of the Dowager's Levy? Did he not suggest that you complain to Gaurin when he arrives?"

Cebastian gave him an odd look. "How did you know that?" he said.

"Just call it a guess," Rohan said. "Now we know the basis of quite a bit of tension that is currently going on with those nobles who are already here. Duig is the Sorceress's creature and his assignment is to spread unrest."

"Jakar of Vacaster is not speaking to Lord Royance. Whenever they pass each other, Jakar actually puts his hand to the hilt of his sword. And Lord Royance pointedly ignores him."

Then it must be true, Rohan thought with a sinking feeling in his stomach, though it was beyond all rational belief. Just as Zazar had said, Flavielle was trying to foment a civil war, which was not only against the Dowager's best interests but also against those of Rendel itself! This could even result in Rendel's destruction before the horror to the North had even fully roused itself from its long sleep.

The Grand Tourney was only a fortnight hence, and all the great nobles of Rendel were summoned to be present, even the ones who customarily stayed away from Court. Those living close by were already in residence. He longed for Gaurin and Ashen's arrival at the city. Surely when he could confer with them, he could find a way to foil this dreadful plot. He touched the amulet, still on its cord and hidden under his shirt, but got no measure of reassurance from its presence.

Eighteen

wo days later, to Rohan's immense relief, Gaurin and Ashen did arrive at Rendelsham, a little earlier than expected. Because of their rank, they were given lodgings even closer to the royal apartments than had been the suite of rooms occupied by Ashen and Obern. As soon as Rohan judged they had settled in, he paid a call on them.

Ayfare had already put everything to rights with great competency. Gaurin and Ashen might have been living there for months, for all the traces of upset that a move from the Oakenkeep might be expected to create. Ashen hugged Rohan, and Gaurin clasped his hand warmly in greeting.

"Oh, it is good to see you again!" Ashen said. Then she held him at arm's length. "But you're as hard-muscled as Gaurin is! What have they been doing to you?"

"Training, Ashen," he replied. "Gaurin knows what is required for the making of a warrior."

"Indeed, you look very fit. And what else has been transpiring, since we saw you last?"

Quickly Rohan filled them in on his various discoveries. "I did not believe Grandam Zaz at first," he said. "But now I do. At least in most things. Though the Dowager may think she has the Sorceress to serve her purpose, it is plain to me that she has welcomed a traitor instead. I believe also that the Dowager does not know this, for, apparently, each now goes her own way."

"Worse," Gaurin said, fingering the fanciful hilt of his Court sword. "This Flavielle may even be working for the Great Foulness to the North."

"Such a possibility had occurred to me," Rohan admitted, "but I didn't want to think about it."

"And you say that this sergeant, Duig, has counseled Cebastian to complain to me of you?"

"Yes."

"Then I suggest that you tell him to do so—or, at least, to appear to do so, and also to make certain that Duig knows of his action."

"But sir, our aim is to unmask the Sorceress. How will such a course of action be to our service?"

"All must appear as if this mysterious person's schemes are going as expected. Only then can we hope that she will make an error that we can exploit and thereby expose her for what she is." Gaurin took a deep breath. "Have you had any word from Madame Zazar?"

"No, sir." Rohan touched the amulet he still wore, under his shirt. "Nor has this helped me find a direction. It is in this regard that I have come to question her Powers."

"Let me see what you have there, please."

Rohan slipped the silk cord over his neck and held it out to Gaurin. Made of silver, it was roughly oval in shape, the bottom wider than the top, and bore a design of waves crashing against the edges of the border of the amulet.

Gaurin examined it and then gave it back. "It looks like something fit for a Sea-Rover's badge," he said. "But I feel no touch of magic about it."

"Nevertheless, wear it," Ashen said. "The pierced stone that provided me with a veil of protection at times when I needed it had no feel of magic about it, either, until I said the words that evoked the spell."

"Perhaps Grandam Zaz didn't know the words to this tune," Rohan said with a laugh, putting the bauble back around his neck.

"Don't joke!" Ashen said. "Zazar always knows what she's doing, even if we don't."

"Well, let us hope that she still does," Rohan said, only slightly abashed. "I have a feeling that our time for disclosing the Sorceress's evil plans is growing very, very short. We've got two occasions when we might move to thwart this woman's schemes. A few nights hence there is to be a feast celebrating the congregation of all the nobles of Rendel, and when the tourney is ended, there will be another feast to honor the victors."

"While time remains, hope will also," Gaurin said seriously. "Now go and do as I told you and send Cebastian to me."

With the arrival of Ashen and Gaurin, the seating arrangements at dinner that night were changed. Because of their rank, they would be placed at the high table and two of the young men would be sent down to the second table, with more of them being replaced with the arrival of each contingent of nobles. Joban and Reges were thus demoted, and they sat as far away from each other as possible. Their feud was, obviously, still hot.

Ashen and Gaurin, as was customary, shared a platter and Rohan was placed next to them. She leaned over to address him. "Show me the girl," she ordered. "Point her out to me."

"Girl? What girl?"

Ashen smiled, but her eyes were not warm. "Of course there is a girl," she said. "There always is. Now, show her to me."

"Well, I suppose you must mean Anamara," Rohan said. "There she is."

Ashen raised her eyebrows. "Seated so low?"

"She does not like large gatherings, or so she told me. So she hides in a crowd."

"And yet you like her passing well."

"I admit that I do. If she agrees, I will wear her favor in the tourney."

Ashen shrugged. "And if she does not, then you may wear mine." Then she turned the talk to other matters, but Rohan noticed that she took full note of Anamara, even while the Sorceress was entertaining the assembled company.

By the time the rest of the nobles from all over Rendel arrived for the welcoming feast, the former seating arrangements might as well never have existed. Now the youthful King, Peres, occupied the center of the high table, flanked by his mother and grandmother. The young nobles found themselves seated just below, which suited Rohan well enough but caused a few frowns from those like Vinod who had come to bask in Ysa's attentions. The evening's festivities were truly impressive, as they were meant to be, and every wall and table bore elaborate decorations.

At Rannore's insistence, Ashen sat next to her, with Gaurin beside her. Perhaps it was only because of Gaurin's presence, but Ysa was cordial to Ashen, and to Rohan's relief no coldness on Ysa's part ruined the feast.

Rohan found no opportunity to denounce the Sorceress then, even during the entertainment, nor in the days that followed. Never did he sense anything to indicate that the time was right, as Zazar had promised. His confidence in the Wysen-wyf, despite an occasional spark, was eroding badly. Despair set in and every time he tried to confide in Ashen or Gaurin, all they would do was reassure him to have faith in Zazar. And in her Power.

Gaurin did start a fad among the nobles, however—those who still fancied themselves warriors. The next morning he joined the young soldiers of the Dowager's Levy, and with them trotted in full armor from Rendelsham Castle to Cragden Keep. There, he exercised with them, testing their mettle and their skill. Several of the other newcomers followed suit, though Rohan couldn't help noticing that many of them were red-faced and panting, grasping for jugs of water, while Gaurin scarcely seemed affected. Rohan was proud of the man who had assumed the role of foster father on his marriage to the woman who had assumed the role of foster mother.

"You have come a long way," Gaurin told Rohan at the end of one of these practice bouts. "I might have to work to take you. Had you ever thought about fighting with sword and dagger together?"

"My father used these weapons. But I daresay that he was much, much better than I."

"That's his Rinbell sword, isn't it?"

"Yes, sir." Rohan handed the weapon, edges carefully blunted with strips of soft lead, to Gaurin.

"A very good piece of workmanship," Gaurin agreed, handing it back. "It will never bear the stain of dishonor."

"So the tale goes among the Sea-Rovers. A Rinbell sword will fight only for one it accepts, and if dishonor threatens, will fall from its wielder's hand first, and refuse to fight for him at all. But that is only a legend. Many such are voiced against ancient weapons."

Gaurin smiled. "Of course. Now, guard yourself."

Under Gaurin's instruction, Rohan felt he had learned more in a few days about the subtleties of swordplay than he had in all the set-piece matches instructors like Sergeant Duig insisted upon. More castle-bound nobles, not wishing to be outdone by a Nordorn exile, joined the exercises. Even the Head of the Council, Lord Royance, did not scorn to seek a practice bout with Count Harous. He summoned the spirit of the burhawk that had always been his badge, and through skill if not endurance acquitted himself very well against the younger man.

"We should have been doing this all along," Royance told Gaurin. "We must strive until strength departs and not depend entirely on our youth in the days to come." He smiled, indicating the belt around his middle. "I have taken it in one notch, and in another day or so could gird it up another. Like too many, I have grown slothful and idle."

"Never you, sir," Gaurin said. "You set an example to all of us that is hard to follow."

"I think I will have another event added, specifically for the senior nobility. And I will provide the prize myself."

"May you win it," Gaurin said, with a salute to the older man.

With a laugh, Lord Royance walked off and there was more than a trace of youthful swagger in his gait.

"I think you are the good example," Rohan observed. "Getting these courtiers out of their velvet chairs and into the practice yard has given them something to do besides sit and nurse old grudges. Now we have what amounts to a truce among many who, only a day ago, were at each others' throats. It's better than anything I could have done with or without help." Unconsciously, he touched the amulet Zazar had given him.

"You can rest assured that, with just a little time, this Sorceress would have found a way to turn this temporary truce to her advantage and start even more deadly blood feuds." Gaurin wiped his brow. "What events are you participating in?"

"Only the showy one—the joust. There are those who are much better at it than I, but that doesn't matter. If Ironfoot cooperates, I will get eliminated early. Then I will have that much more time to observe where the trouble spots are erupting, and hope to soothe them."

Sergeant Duig was calling to the young leaders of the Dowager's Levy, so Gaurin slapped Rohan on the shoulder and sent him on his way. "He will be wanting to give you your final instructions for the morrow and your assignments in the lists. Keep your spirits up, and we will meet tonight in the Great Hall."

Nineteen

That evening, Rohan went in search of Anamara, instead of leaving her to the privacy she seemed to desire. He found her sitting at her accustomed table, placed much lower than what her rank as one of the Dowager's ladies entitled her to. She wore a cloak over her dress, with the hood pulled up as if to hide her face.

"I have missed your company, lady," he said. He thought she turned pale. "Could it be that you are forbidden to speak to me?" he asked with a boldness he might not have risked before. But he had taken it for his motto, and so now he spoke his mind.

"No, not exactly," Anamara replied.

"Good. Then I may dare to ask for your favor to wear tomorrow."

"I—I had not thought of such a thing. Would this do?" From the depths of her cloak she pulled out a piece of slightly crumpled blue silk—the rose he had given her, back in the garden on a frosty morning.

He took it from her and held it to his nose. Yes, it smelled of her warm, sweet flesh. "I will wear it proudly, and later I will give you another. Dozens of them, if you like."

She opened her lips as if to speak, and then closed them again.

"Guard yourself," she half whispered a moment later.

He shook his hand a bit and the rose unfolded into a length that might serve as a scarf. "This will make a good token, one that the others will eye with wonder and amazement," he said. "And never fear, I will guard myself well and be your champion always, if you desire it."

She made no answer, only turned away and pulled the hood up closer over her face.

Nonplussed, nevertheless Rohan took her giving of the onetime silk rose as a good sign. Later, he would determine the cause of her shyness and, if he could, dispel it.

The day of the tourney, much anticipated, dawned bright, cold, and clear. People's breath was frosty in the cold air, and the restless warhorses emitted steam from their nostrils. The pawing of their hooves on the frozen ground made a noise like the ring of steel against steel.

A great sheltered stand for spectators had been erected to one side of the tourney field, a flat plain outside the city walls, and the elaborately embroidered cloth of state put in place over the royal box. A set of stairs led from this to a platform only a little higher than the combat field. From this spot, the King himself, young Peres, would award the prizes. This day the Dowager would be in his shadow, and Ashen and Gaurin would be seated with his mother, Rannore.

No, Rohan corrected himself. Only Ashen. Gaurin would be taking part in some of the events hastily planned for the nobles when it became clear that they would not be content merely to watch the striplings and the elders of the realm perform for their amusement. Thus it would be a Grand Tourney indeed. Gaurin had even sent for his favorite war-horse, a great bay stallion named Marigold. Nordors, Rohan had learned, had a habit of calling their fierce steeds by mild, innocuous names—the braver the charger, the sweeter and more innocent the name. Marigold was a very fearsome beast, indeed, and nobody but Gaurin could ride him. When

Knight or Knave

he trotted, he lifted his forefeet high, proudly dancing along his path. When he galloped, he carried all before him from the sheer strength of his charge.

Rohan hoped to catch sight of Gaurin before his own planned downfall. He had to get himself out of the way so that he could spy out what was happening elsewhere. He knew that if he were occupied on the tourney field, any effort he might make was likely to come to naught.

The jousting was scheduled first, the young nobles going through their paces early. This would be followed by assorted exhibitions by senior nobles and set pairs of other, younger men, and then the seasoned warriors would take up the sport with jousts and set-pieces as well before the Grand Melee, open to all who cared to participate.

Rohan had drawn third place in the lists and would run his course against the winner of the first, whoever that might be. His plan was to make Ironfoot swerve at the last moment, so he could fall and be eliminated without glory, but without dishonor. Then he could go and mix with spectators or participants as he chose, rather than be caught up in repeated runs of the course against other young nobles until a champion had been decided.

He entered one of the tents set aside for the use of the junior nobles. These tents stood toward the back, but with flaps open, and it was easy to see what was happening. The stand was filling rapidly, made gay by the bright-colored gowns of the women and the glint of the jewels they wore. Many of the ladies had made bold to throw back the shoulders of the fur-lined cloaks they wore, basking in what sunshine there was, to show off their beauty and elegance.

Both of the Dowagers had already taken their places. Ysa smiled and nodded to the people, but Rannore seemed more thoughtful, even worried, as if King Peres might be in danger. Ashen took her hand and began to speak softly to her.

Cebastian called to Rohan from one of the trestle-tables and Rohan went over to sit with him.

"Take a cup of warmed wine," Cebastian said, offering the

flagon, "and some bread. You shouldn't go out on an empty stomach."

"Thank you for your concern, my friend, but I have no appetite and I want to have a clear head. Perhaps later."

"What's your number?"

"Three."

"Ah. I'm well down on the list, so any light-headedness I feel will have departed long since."

"Good luck to you. May you come out well."

"And to you. Perhaps we'll meet in the lists after all."

Rohan acknowledged his friend's good wishes with a rueful nod of his head. Of course I could come out well in this if I decided to, he thought, but unmasking the Sorceress—or the Magician, the man or woman, whatever the person decided to be that day—was more important. The back of Rohan's neck tingled mercilessly, making him as nervous as if he were staking his entire future on one run with the blunted spears or perhaps facing an enemy of well-proven force and skill.

I have bound myself to boldness and daring, he said to himself. So, bold and daring must I be. To calm his nerves, he concentrated on fastening the blue scarf to his helm. He couldn't get it to stay. The brush of herbs and grasses, given him so long before by Grandam Zaz, seemed too slippery to hold the silk. He needed a piece of string or a thin strip of leather. He took the silver amulet with the design of crashing waves from around his neck. The silk cord it hung from would do extremely well. Quickly he wrapped the cord around the scarf and tied it to the tuft. This time, all snugged into place as if designed for the purpose, though, to his mild surprise, the amulet seemed of its own accord to tuck itself out of view. No matter how he tried to arrange it so the trinket showed, within a matter of moments it was hidden again.

A blare of trumpets announced the arrival of the King and his retinue, and so Rohan gave up the fruitless effort. He must be content that his lady's favor showed. Another blare of trumpets signaled that the Grand Tourney had, officially, begun.

As he nudged Ironfoot into a heavy trot toward the frail fence dividing the course the combatants must run, the amulet rang softly against his helmet, calming him. He accepted one of the blunted spears and hefted it as he moved to one side, awaiting his turn.

The first participants were Gidon of Bilth opposite Nikolos of Grattenbor. An unfortunate pairing, seeing that there was currently bad blood between their overlords, Gattor and Royance. With keen interest, he watched Gidon unseat Nikolos neatly, sending him tumbling onto the frozen ground. Nikolos got up, signaling that he was unhurt, and the crowd cheered. Then he turned to Gidon and said, his words carrying clearly in the frigid air, "We will meet later."

"I look forward to it," Gidon returned. He danced his horse back to the starting place, exchanging his used lance for a fresh one, and Rohan moved into position.

This was good, he thought. Gidon is my friend. Also, he is much better at the lance than I, and I need not even attempt to persuade Ironfoot to swerve out of the course. He saluted Gidon, and the crowd applauded as the other young man returned the salute.

At the signal, both urged their mounts into a heavy gallop. Rohan remembered thinking how good was Gidon's seat and how steady his lance, when the unthinkable occurred.

Instead of his forcing Ironfoot into a false step, it was Gidon's steed that stumbled slightly on a bit of icy clod churned up by the previous run. Under ordinary circumstances, that would not have been enough to affect Gidon's attack and Rohan could still have maneuvered himself into dropping the tip of his lance just enough to miss, but Ironfoot took that moment to put on an extra burst of speed. Rohan's weapon took Gidon squarely in the center of his breastplate and sent him sprawling. The crowd roared its approval.

"Well run, comrade!" Gidon said as he got to his feet. "Good luck for the next course!"

Somewhat chagrined by his unexpected victory, Rohan turned Ironfoot back toward the starting place. A squire took the lance, examined it for signs of weakness, and handed him another. He looked up to discover that this time he was facing Jabez of Mimon, who was, if possible, even worse at this event than he.

Well, he thought, gritting his teeth, if I could unseat Gidon, then certainly another such miracle is possible. Even if I have to do it all myself.

This time he succeeded in pulling Ironfoot's off rein, making him leave the path that was already being beaten on either side of the fence just enough so that his spear missed and Jabez's caught him on the shoulder. Over he went, with a crash that jarred him from top to toe even though he was expecting it and thought himself prepared. He clambered to his feet as the crowd shouted its approval once more. Ironfoot was already trotting off, as if disgusted, and a page caught him to lead him back to the stable and give him a rubdown and a well-deserved bag of grain. There was some laughter from the stands, as if at a joke, and he hoped that his subterfuge had gone undetected by the onlookers.

Whether or not, he never learned. He had scarcely gotten back to the tent when a cry of pleasure went up from the spectator stand. He looked back to discover the Magician, wearing his robes decorated in magical symbols. He had appeared in a cloud of blue smoke and ice crystals that floated down to the ground, like snow. He produced a bouquet of flowers from nowhere and began tossing the blossoms to the ladies above. They squealed with delight as they vied for the flowers. Rohan walked back toward the line of tents set up for the participants, trying to catch a glimpse of Anamara in the crowd, but if she was there, she remained hidden from his sight.

Behind him, Reges of Lerkland prepared to run his course against Jabez. A thunder of hooves, a clash of metal, and the crowd shouted in delight as Jabez in turn became acquainted with the hardness of the tourney ground. Then the tone of the cries changed. Rohan turned, curious, only to discover that Jabez had not gotten to his feet. The tent set aside for the physicians was, he realized, going to see some duty today.

He lingered until Jabez had been carried past, limp and white-faced. To his relief, Jabez's injury seemed to be minor—perhaps only a sprain or a joint out of place—for there was no blood and no further outcry from the viewing stands. Rohan made a note to himself to go and check on Jabez later, when he was allowed to see him.

He made his way back to the tent, hoping to join Cebastian for the warmed wine and bread, but the other young man had already left to prepare for his turn in the lists. By this time, platters of meat and a dish of pears had been added to the fare available so Rohan helped himself. While he ate, he divested himself of the heavy breastplate, unnecessary now that he had been eliminated in the jousting. Carefully, he untied the blue silk scarf—it had brought him almost the luck he had hoped for, he thought wryly—and tucked it into his sleeve. The amulet on its silken cord he slipped back over his neck and under his shirt, where it rested, cold at first and then warming, against his skin.

Reges, who had not unarmed, watched him as he pulled on a warm, fur-lined doublet over his chain mail. "Through already?" he said.

"I decided not to enter the exhibition," Rohan replied. He helped himself to meat, piling it on a round of bread and spoke around a good mouthful. "And you? I take it you were eliminated as well."

"I was, but not before I had put Jovan in the dust." Reges smiled with grim satisfaction. "And Vinod. It took Steuart to unhorse me."

"Steuart is the best of us all with the lance," Rohan said. "It is no disgrace to lose to him. We all knew he would win this prize."

Reges shrugged. "Anything could happen. Jovan said he was looking forward to the exhibition."

Rohan leaned forward. "Look you," he said seriously. "Mend the bad blood between you. It does neither of you any honor to maintain your quarrel, when Rendel lies in the very shadow of danger."

"I see no such shadow," Reges scoffed. "You think that because we are having unseasonably cold weather this means we are all in fear of our lives?"

Rohan understood, all too clearly, how the edge of danger could go off for young men who, unlike himself, had not grown up with the reality of what it meant to flee from the peril of the North. His grandfather, Snolli, had filled him with tales and Gaurin also had his stories to tell, none of them comforting or boding well for the future once the Great Foulness and its minions had fully awakened and begun to march. "The cold is only the smallest part of it," Rohan said. "Why do you think the Dowager summoned her levy of the young nobles of the realm, if not for us to serve as the spear-point of her army?"

Reges shrugged. "I don't know. And I suppose I don't really care, either."

"You should care," Rohan said. "But I daresay you won't."

He got up, suddenly unwilling to continue the conversation. "I'm going to see how Jabez is faring."

"Give him my regards," Reges said, but his tone was indifferent.

Up in the viewing stand, Ashen had caught her breath when Rohan was unhorsed. But, as he leaped up again, obviously unhurt, she let it out in a relieved sigh.

"It is difficult, watching a child—or one who is very like your child—go into danger," said Rannore.

"Indeed it is," Ashen said. "One's husband also."

"I had nearly forgotten. Gaurin will be fighting in the joust, will he not?"

"He is to go against Harous. They are the only ones who could give each other a good match. Later, he will be in the Grand Melee against any and all comers. I know I shouldn't worry, but I do."

The Lady Marcala, wife to Harous in everything but the legal ceremony, occupied the seat next to the Old Dowager, chatting with her, and if she shared any of Ashen's concern, she didn't show it by word or action.

"Gaurin will be all right," Rannore said. "Harous also. The rules of the tourney forbid any serious conflicts, and there will be heralds stationed to enforce it, should tempers rise." The Young Dowager reached out for Ashen's hand, and the two women's fingers interlocked.

"I envy you, Ashen," Rannore said. "There is nothing for me here, though I am doomed to remain at Court unwed and unweddable. You have your husband, your child, a quiet life after the turmoil of your time at Court. If you choose, you can settle down into quiet tranquility."

Ashen turned and stared at her friend. "There is nothing in my life to envy, I assure you. Daily I worry about what awaits us, just over the horizon to the North. When the attack comes—and it surely will come—Gaurin will be in the forefront of the men fighting. It is his nature. And, as far as I know, I will have to stay behind, going mad with worry. I cannot think of a way in which I could help."

Rannore returned Ashen's steady gaze. "And yet, I think there may yet be something for you, if not for me. Your foster mother was the Wysen-wyf of the Bog. She is known to be a very powerful woman. More powerful even—" Rannore leaned closer and her voice dropped so she could not be overheard—"than Ysa herself, though my mother-in-law would never countenance such a thought being expressed aloud."

"Yes," Ashen said. "Zazar possesses much Power. But that is Zazar, and I am not she."

"And yet, I sense in you something that just awaits the time and circumstance. Yes, my dear friend, I believe that you will have your part to play, eventually."

Ysa leaned forward from where she sat on the other side of King Peres, so she could see the two younger women. "Telling secrets?" she said sweetly. Behind her, Marcala laughed behind her hand.

"No, Madame," Rannore said. "Merely speaking of women's matters that other people need not hear."

"Well, look you to mind your manners. We are all on exhibition here. Even the—" Ysa halted and Ashen knew, instinctively, that she had bitten back the words *Bog-Princess*. "Even our dear kins-woman from the Oakenkeep."

"Please, Mother, Grandmother," Peres said. "You are distracting me, and Steuart has but one more course to run before he wins the prize."

The King, Ashen noted, was a reedy youth. The current fashion called for long surcoats, reaching nearly to the ankle, which was a good thing because the King's bony knees made his hose baggy. He seemed a little overwhelmed by the crown he wore, but perhaps that was just the fur lining that kept the cold metal from touching the royal head. She searched his face for resemblance to his late father, or even his grandfather Boroth, who had sired her and whom she had never seen until she had been brought into his death-chamber and he had, unexpectedly, acknowledged her as his own child. She found much more of Rannore in him, which was to his credit, though this meant he was probably not destined to be a great fighting King such as Boroth once had been. His interest lay in watching, and laying wagers on this one or that. Rumor was that he had been nearly sick with impatience, waiting for the tourney to begin.

Ysa patted the King's arm and the Great Rings she wore showed clearly, for she chose not to cover her hands with gloves. "Forgive us," she said soothingly. "We are but women and the fine points of tournament play are beyond us."

Ashen had to turn away to hide the twist of her mouth at the Dowager's words. She knew that Ysa had been following the jousts closely, despite pretending to be gossiping with the woman who had once been her favorite, and that she had marked each one as to his abilities. Just as she would mark the contestants in the events to follow.

They were clearing the field, Steuart having won, as everyone knew he would, in preparation for the set-pieces for the elder no-bles. Absently Ashen took a piece of sweet pastry from the platter that was being passed around in the royal box, and a page handed her a goblet of the hot spiced fruit drink she favored. She began to identify the nobles for Rannore, who was a bit shortsighted. .

"You recognize Wittern, of course. He is matched against—yes, it is Lord Royance. Gattor is going against Jakar, which is a good thing, from all the rumors surrounding both men and their disagreement with Royance."

"It would seem that the nobles are being matched according to rank, rather than ability, then," Rannore said. "My grandfather is certainly no challenge to Lord Royance and never was even when he was in his prime."

"Well, it is only an exhibition, after all. I'm sure Royance will not shame the King's great-grandfather."

Rannore smiled at that. "I suppose we should admire their spirit, which shines as brightly as their white hair."

Ashen smiled in turn. "If the young nobles catch but a trace of the indomitable character that their elders display, our fears about the future of Rendel might be greatly lessened."

"Let them but see the real warriors in action, then, and then they will know what they are expected to live up to," King Peres said. "Ah, there is the trumpet. The contest is about to begin!"

Ashen turned back to view the field of combat. The elder nobles, each seeming determined to show himself hale and hearty, started through their paces, if a little stiffly. She had learned something of swordplay from watching Gaurin at practice, and realized anew that in all of Rendel there was nobody—no, not even Harous—who could equal him. She recognized the moves, the thrusts and parries, the gliding steps and feints. With Gaurin, there was a consummate grace involved as well, a confident bearing that made all who saw him know at once that here was a fighter to be reckoned with.

Here and there on the field, heralds were stationed in addition to personal attendants of the combatants, marking the various areas where the senior nobles were performing for the pleasure of the crowd, and each other. Ashen could almost sense the joy—in some of them, at least—of recapturing some of their earlier prowess as they warmed to their work. Gattor of Bilth, however, she noted

Andre Norton & Sasha Miller

with a wry smile, matched against Jakar, went through his paces laboriously and, she thought, more than a little reluctantly. They fought in a spot close to Royance and Wittern. She wondered absently where a suit of armor had been located to go around Gattor's bulk or, indeed, if one had had to be specially made.

Suddenly the decorum of the event was shattered. Lord Royance, breaking off from his engagement with Wittern, turned on Jakar. "How dare you, sir!" he shouted in a voice that easily carried to the royal box. "You will retract your words immediately, or by all the Powers, you will answer to me here, and now."

Jakar assumed a defensive posture and heralds began to converge on that part of the field. Gattor stepped back, panting visibly, and accepted a goblet from his attendant. He took off his helm, and despite the coolness of the day, began mopping perspiration from his face.

"I will retract nothing, Royance of Grattenbor," Jakar said. "You are as I stated—a blowhard, a bully, and an indifferent fighter even when you were young. You received too many blows on your head when you were not wearing your helm. It is long past time for you to retire from public affairs."

Royance uttered a roar of pure outrage and took a step toward Jakar, obviously intending to defend his honor then and there. Wittern put a restraining hand on Royance's arm, only to have it shaken off.

Ashen got a muddled impression of the Dowager's Magician, still down in front of the spectators' stand, making a series of gestures, and then, to her amazement, Rohan came running out of nowhere.

"Stop!" he cried. "In the name of our lord King and all the Powers, I command all to stop!" In his hand, Rohan held an object whose brightness grew with every word until the dazzling light filled the arena and caused all, even the Magician, to shade their eyes lest they be blinded.

Twenty

lmost at the same moment that Lord Royance turned on his foe, Jakar of Vacaster, the amulet Rohan wore beneath his clothing began to burn against his skin. Also, it vibrated, making his teeth chatter. He had no time for coherent thought—he knew only that he had to get the thing out into the open before it burned through straight to his heart. Maddened by this as well as the intolerable tingling on the back of his neck, he held it up by the silken cord. It was glowing. Dimly he realized that once more Zazar had proven correct.

Now was the time to confront the Magician.

He nearly knocked bystanders to the ground as he shouldered his way through the crowd and raced toward the area in front of the viewing stand, where the Magician still stood. He caught a glimpse of the Magician's hands as he made certain gestures in the direction of Royance and Jakar, and knew that this person was undeniably responsible for the nobles' folly and mischief.

Rohan held the amulet aloft and the brightness grew until all were quite dazzled, shielding their eyes with their hands. Only he seemed to be unaffected, as if he stood in some kind of core at the center of the brilliance.

"Stop!" he cried again. "Even you, Flavielle."

With the pronouncement of her name, the Magician's male disguise fell away and she stood revealed as the Sorceress. The collective gasp of the crowd could not drown out her hiss of rage. "What have you done!" she said, voice trembling. "You dare to interfere with *me*? With—" She glanced up, toward the spot where the Dowager sat, but Yea turned aside and refused to meet the Sorceress's eyes.

"Why, how now, lady," Rohan said. Full of a newfound confidence, he took a step toward Flavielle and was rewarded by seeing her, in turn, step back. "Do you fear the light? Or perhaps it is the truth that you fear instead."

She drew herself up and spread her arms. Snow drifted down from her outstretched hands and tiny sparks of lightning glittered from her fingertips. "You do not frighten me!" she said haughtily. But her voice trembled, just a little.

"No," Rohan agreed, "I don't think I do. But your powers are not enough to extinguish that which I hold."

Abruptly Flavielle abandoned all pretense of being anything but who she was. She crouched where she stood, and the snow began to gather in a drift at her feet. "Where did you get that?"

"Let's just say it was given to me. And so I use it now to conjure you to tell all here present the truth about yourself."

From the stand, a woman uttered a strangled cry. "No—" But then the Sorceress made a gesture and the Dowager was silent.

"You do not want to learn the truth, young sir," Flavielle said. Her voice had lost all its silken quality and now was little better than a hoarse croak. "And I am sure there are certain others for whom the truth is better left unsaid."

"Such as?"

The Sorceress ignored his question, not bothering even trying to hide the contemptuous sneer on her face. "I once told you that it was unwise to set yourself against me. Now, at least, you will have ample time to reflect upon your folly, and what you have brought on those you hold dear."

"Who holds your real loyalty? I conjure you by this, speak now!" Rohan held the glowing amulet higher and advanced a step; again Flavielle retreated, and he realized that in spite of her bold words, she knew a measure of terror.

She cringed away from the light. "Stay back. Yes, as a man, I was in the employ of Her Gracious Highness the Dowager Queen Ysa. As a woman, I am my own creature! As to where my loyalties lie, I leave it to you to puzzle it out, if you can!"

So saying, the Sorceress straightened once more. She made a gesture, murmured a few words, and a cloud gathered around her. Lightning flashed inside the cloud as it swirled, full of snow, and then, with a clap of thunder that reverberated through the arena and echoed from the mountains, she vanished. A stench of brimstone and a minor snowstorm were all that remained. At the same moment, the amulet ceased to glow.

As if released from a spell, the onlookers began to move, asking questions, and rubbing their eyes in astonishment. Lord Royance and Jakar stared at each other, and each lowered his sword.

"My—my lord," Jakar said shakily. "It seems that I have held a grudge against you without cause and also that I have offered you deep insult. Please, forgive me!"

Royance blinked. "No more than I have had hard feelings toward you, who have always been my friend and ally. I crave your forgiveness in turn. And yours as well, Gattor. Let us mend our friendship."

The senior nobles embraced each other, there on the field of combat, and the crowd, as if sensing that a cloud similar to the thundersnow that had enveloped the Sorceress had dissipated, began to cheer. Glancing behind him, Rohan could see that various of his fellows were following suit. Gidon and Nikolos clasped hands, speaking earnestly to each other, as did Jivon and Steuart. Behind them, Cebastian lifted one fist in a salute of victory.

Up in the spectator stand, the Dowager Ysa managed to push herself to her feet and move forward until she stood at the railing that separated the royal enclosure from the rest of the area the privileged occupied. "Good people!" she cried. "Good people, pray, listen to me!"

In a few moments, some measure of order had been restored, and all eyes, especially Rohan's, turned toward the woman whom the Sorceress had identified as her onetime employer.

"I swear to you by these"—she held aloft both hands so that the Four Great Rings of Power were visible to all—"that I am innocent of wrongdoing! I engaged this person, whom I thought to be a man, only in the service of Rendel. Through him, or her, and her Power, I hoped to strengthen this, our realm, against our deadly foe to the north. Alas, I fear I was duped. You have heard our dear nobles, Lord Royance of Grattenbor, Lord Gattor of Bilth, and Lord Jakar of Vacaster beg each other's pardon. Now I must crave your forgiveness as well, knowing that all that I have done has been for the good of you all."

Then she crossed her hands over her breast—again, Rohan noted, so that the Great Rings could not be missed—and bowed her head, eyes closed. He could not help but admire the sheer audacity of the woman, putting everything on one cast of the dice before what she had to know was a fickle crowd.

There was dead silence, and then somebody from the ranks of the commoners down at the fence surrounding the arena, shouted out in approval. All at once, the rest of the people there gathered took up the cry.

"Aye, good Queen Ysa," came the shout. "She's always seen to us and our welfare, right enough. And no harm done, either!"

King Peres stood up and, with courtesy beyond that of most ten-year-old boys, conducted his grandmother back to her chair. Then he returned to the railing, opened the gate, and began descending the stairs until he reached the platform.

"I think that when we have reflected on this day's events, we will find that you have done us good service, Rohan of the Oakenkeep and of the Sea-Rovers," the King said. "Come forward."

Rohan knew that he should be making certain that the Sorceress was really gone from Rendel, but one did not go against the King's orders. Obediently he approached the platform, set only a hand-span or so above the surface of the ground, just high enough so that the King's boots would not get wet from the cold, soggy ground. It put the King almost at equal height with Rohan.

"Kneel," the King said, and once more, Rohan obeyed. Peres drew a Court sword from the scabbard at his side. It was elaborately chased in gold, and bore many jewels on the hilt. He laid the blade on Rohan's shoulder. "For these good services, I herewith dub you Knight of Rendel. Arise, Sir Rohan."

Things were transpiring a bit rapidly for him. He got to his feet, already in imagination feeling the weight of his new title. "A boon, sir," he said.

One corner of the King's mouth quirked upward. "So soon, my good knight? What is it, then?"

"Sir, I crave that you similarly reward my friend Cebastian, and also knight my companions, the leaders of the companies of the Dowager's Levy, for they are not only my companions, but your loyal men both today and in those perilous times to come."

Now the King smiled openly. "Well said, Rohan. You could knight them yourself, but I agree that it would be better, coming from me. Very well, then, approach all who have striven for my entertainment, draw near, and find your reward."

Then, with Rohan standing nearby, King Peres knighted each of them in turn. Cebastian was first, and he and Rohan exchanged nods as Rohan remembered the lie Duig had told about how he was supposedly blocking Cebastian's knighting. It was this incident that had nearly made a rift between them. He looked around, trying to find Duig. He had been among those keeping order on the arena ground, but, like the Sorceress, he had vanished.

"Probably she took him with her," he muttered to himself. "But then, I've always thought he was working for her all along." Why, oh why, couldn't he be off, to make sure? But there was no hope for it. He turned his attention again to the ceremonies taking place. Steuart was next, and to him also went the trophy for the jousting. Then Peres spoke, his boyish voice a little shrill in the cold air.

Andre Norton & Sasha Miller

"The man or woman who was masquerading as the Magician is gone forever. My friends, enjoy yourselves and be merry! Therefore, by my royal command, the tourney will proceed as if nothing untoward has happened. Let the warriors proceed at once to the lists and let us now have more jousting!"

The crowd shouted its approval, but Rohan could scarcely believe his ears. He gritted his teeth, every fiber of his being urging him to go after the Sorceress and make certain that she had truly vanished. He could not shake off the feeling in his bones that she was going to do one last mischief before she left Rendel altogether, but one did not gainsay a royal Command, no matter how foolish or how unfortunate the consequences.

As soon as the Grand Melee was over, and lingering no longer than good manners required after the prizes were awarded, the Dowager Queen Ysa retired from the cold, damp spectator stand into the warmth of her own apartment. She gave orders to make the fire roar, and Lady Ingrid quickly piled on dry wood, which caught at once. Ysa turned to see Marcala, who had accompanied her, standing hesitantly in the doorway.

"Oh, how wonderful to be warm again!" Ysa said. "Come in, Marcala. Ladies, please leave us. And Grisella, shut the door. There's a draft. And send for hot wine."

"Yes, Your Highness." Ysa's lady-in-waiting pulled the door to, leaving the two women alone.

Marcala edged her way into the room with even more evident hesitation. No doubt due to the rift that had opened between them, Ysa thought, even as various quarrels had arisen among the men. And what was it about? Marcala's desire to marry Harous? A trifling matter. And now that her latest covert servant had proven a traitor, she must ensure loyalties where she found them.

"Oh, do come in. Let us be friends again. After all, who else is there in all of Rendel who is a match for either of us?"

Marcala smiled, a little tentatively, Ysa thought. "Madame," she said, with a curtsey. "I have always been your friend."

"Then that is settled. Did you ever see such a spectacle as that—
that charlatan created? All the time, *he* was a woman, and pretending faithfulness when now it is quite obvious he—I mean, she—was
working for the menace to the North."

That startled Marcala out of any diffidence. "Do you really think
so?" She moved forward and held her hands out to the fire, rubbing
some warmth back into them.

"It is the only explanation," Ysa said. She rubbed her own
hands, feeling the Great Rings of Power snugly in place under her
fingers. They gave not the least hint that they were inclined to go
to another, not even the wispy little King, so brave in knighting the
young men that *she* had caused to be in Rendelsham in the first
place! Peres would need her wisdom and counsel for many years to
come, that much was certain.

She only wished that she didn't feel so much contempt for the
lad. He took too much after his mother—though it was a blessing
that his father was not stronger in him. Almost, Ysa wished that
more of Boroth had managed to make it through the bloodlines.
With her, Ysa, to guide him, a young version of her late husband
would have made a King to reckon with!

Well, wishing would not affect reality in this, as in so many
other matters. "Yes, the only explanation," she repeated. "Think you.
'Flavielle,' wasn't that what Rohan called her? That snow she produced at will. Only somebody from the North could do that sort
of trick, or, for that matter, would. Here in Rendel, we have no
great reason to love the snow the year round. Now that I think on
it, I believe that Flavielle was taunting us with it, laughing at us for
being too stupid to know what she was and who she was."

"I think that you are right, Madame," Marcala said. "It seems to
me that the world grew colder the moment she appeared at Court,
but I put it down to my own imagination playing tricks on me."

"Well, she is gone now, and gone for good, I'll warrant. But the
next time I hire anyone to aid me in Rendel's defense, I'll make
sure he—or she—is as reliable and loyal as you."

She smiled at Marcala, and Marcala returned it, visibly relaxing in the warmth of the Dowager's favor, even more welcome than the warmth of her fire.

Perhaps, Ysa thought, she would even reconsider the matter of Marcala's marriage to Count Harous. The Sorceress's appearance in the very center of the Court at Rendelsham must have been a signal that the forces to the North were beginning to think themselves strong enough to march in earnest, rather than send entertainers and charlatans and thundersnows in their stead. Harous had, for all his own peculiarities and investigations into some of the areas of Power that intrigued Ysa, always been loyal to Rendel and to its rulers. If there was to be war, then Harous deserved the opportunity to leave a part of himself behind, in the form of a wife and, perhaps, children.

"I've missed you, Marcala," Ysa said. "Come, sit with me, and let us catch up on what has happened to us both."

One of Rendel's newest knights also had an errand as soon as he could extricate himself from the hubbub surrounding the day's events. When Rohan had made sure that the Sorceress was not in her usual haunts, he searched everywhere for Anamara, wanting to share with her his excitement at being officially ennobled and, perhaps, even to ask her—

Too soon. There were many hurdles to cross, many areas of acceptance still to be gone through, before he could think of winning his fairest lady. First, though, he had to find her.

Not to his surprise, he discovered that most if not all of the late King Florian's followers had vanished, along with Flavielle. Perhaps, he thought, remembering his abduction and near-murder, they had been working hand in glove all along. But more likely they were just followers who were willing to blindly follow their leaders into the unknown. And, obviously, they had picked the Sorceress as a better leader than anybody in Rendel, even the Dowager.

That did not explain his difficulty in locating Anamara, however. Frustrated, he sought out the apartment where Ashen and Gaurin were staying, wanting to talk the matter over with his foster father. He would be back eventually, after he had disarmed and washed following the melee. Surely Gaurin would be able to advise him and, perhaps, even to help him puzzle out where Anamara had gotten herself off to.

Ayfare let him in. "My congratulations, young sir," she said, "if you don't mind my taking the liberty."

"How could I mind?" he replied, laughing. "As many times as you've swatted my bottom when I had gotten into mischief—Well, let's just say, I thank you."

She laughed in return. "Not that you didn't deserve it. But you didn't come here to talk about spankings."

"No, I didn't." He sobered. "I need to speak to Gaurin and, I hope, without Ashen being present. Not just yet, at any rate."

Ayfare's eyebrows shot up. "Well, sir, you must know best. My lady Ashen is with the King's mother, and I don't look for her to be back anytime soon. I can send someone to hurry Lord Gaurin along, if you like."

"Yes, please."

Ayfare summoned one of the retainers they had brought with them from the Oakenkeep, gave him instructions, and presently Gaurin let himself into the room where Rohan waited.

"How now, Sir Rohan!" the warrior exclaimed genially, obviously in a very good humor. He set a large standing cup, heavy with gold and gems, on a table. It was obviously a prize he had won. "I would have thought you would be out carousing with your fellow knights. Or is it a knave you've chosen to be, instead?"

"No, sir, if luck be with me. I've come to seek your help in working through a puzzle."

"If I can help, of course I will."

Rohan quickly related his growing infatuation with Anamara, his feeling that she reciprocated, the way she had given him the favor to wear in the tourney, and his lack of success in locating her. "I wanted to see her, to tell her—Well, to see her," he finished lamely.

"I understand, Rohan. I fell in love with Ashen the first moment I beheld her. And she, I think, with me as well, though honor forbade that she should admit it."

"Really?" It was a story Rohan knew only second- or third-hand. "I would love to hear about it."

"I will tell you about it, sometime later. Now, let us try to decide where it is that your lady has gone."

"I have my fears—"

"Speak. If they are false, then they can be dispelled. If they are true, then we can deal with them."

"Flavielle spoke to me of having ample time to reflect upon what she called my 'folly,' and of what I had brought on those I hold dear. I thought it was a threat against you and Ashen. Now I wonder if it wasn't against Anamara instead."

"It is entirely possible." Gaurin sat thinking deeply for a moment. "I think you should go to the Bog," he said finally. "You owe Madame Zazar a report on what happened when the amulet she gave you issued the signal to unmask the Sorceress. And, despite your confidence in me—for which I thank you—I think she might be better equipped to help you locate your ladylove than anyone else."

"I had considered doing this already, but wanted to talk over the matter with you first. I would be a knave indeed, if something had happened to her and I didn't go to remedy it."

"Provision yourself, and seek out Madame Zazar as soon as possible," Gaurin said. "I have a feeling that the less time you waste, the better."

"Thank you, sir." Rohan bowed to Gaurin, as one noble to another, and, for the first time in his life, knew the pleasure of having the salute returned.

Twenty-one

A namara had never wanted to attend the Grand Tourney at all, and only the fact that Rohan would be participating and wearing the favor she had rashly agreed to give him prompted her to do so. She could not bring herself to occupy the place to which she was entitled, where the gentry took their ease, and thus be on display to all. Instead, she borrowed a plain cloak from a maidservant and took care to hide among the common people who crowded against the fence separating the tourney grounds from the area nearby where vendors and entertainers, tinkers and weapons dealers, had set up their booths, eager to profit from the festival. The smell of hot cider and smoking meats filled the air. Anamara's stomach growled; she had been unable to eat any breakfast that morning. Nor could she eat until she knew Rohan was safe.

Anxiously she craned her neck and stood on tiptoe, trying to see over the people who blocked her view. Then the crowd shifted a little as a group of friends decided that hot food on a cold day was preferable to standing and waiting for something to happen. She gained a vantage point from which she had as good a view as any not seated in the spectator stand.

Gidon and Nikolos were just entering the lists. She watched as

Gidon neatly unhorsed his opponent. Then her heart nearly stopped as she saw Rohan on the horse he had been given, come trotting in to take his turn. There was no mistaking him—the strange tuft of herbs and grasses he wore in his helm would have identified him anywhere even if the blue silk of her favor were not floating in the breeze.

Oh, please, she said silently, let him not be harmed! To think of his wide, sea-green eyes filled with pain or his open and honest features contorted with agony filled her with such dread that she swayed on her feet. She forced herself to stay and watch, hating the spectacle, wishing it were over and done with and that she and Rohan—

She never finished the thought. Almost before the joust began, he had put Gidon in the dust and the crowd was roaring its approval. She gulped, hard, against something bitter that had unaccountably arisen in the back of her throat.

Then Rohan was trotting back to the starting-point and selecting another blunted lance. That meant that he was going to have to fight again, and once more, she would die a thousand times before all was done.

She didn't recognize his new opponent, but the murmurs of the crowd told her it was Jabez of Mimon. She heard bets offered and taken, that Rohan would have Jabez unhorsed even before they properly met. It came as an unpleasant surprise to those betting on Rohan when he was the one who ended up on his backside. Those who had bet against him roared with laughter at their unexpected win.

She lingered only long enough to make certain that he was unhurt. He doffed his helm and waved to the crowd, his red-gold hair shining in the sunlight. Then, knowing that he was safe, she began to make her way up the steep path, back to Rendelsham and the seclusion of her rooms.

She heard voices. Someone was coming down the path she was climbing, and, not wanting to have to offer a possible explanation for her not attending the festivities, Anamara ducked behind a clump of bushes to hide. Presently two people came into view. One was a woman she did not know, and the other a man she had seen a few times before, someone she recognized as the Magician's personal attendant. Duig.

"So today's the day, eh?" he said.

"Yes. Everything begins with the senior nobles' exhibition. That is, if you've done your job properly."

"Oh, never fear, Lady Flavielle. The easiest part was with the young nobles. I've got most of them practically at each other's throats. Many of the warriors are none too pleased with each other, either. But my best work was with the seniors. Old cocks, still thinking they're fit for warfare." The man laughed, an unpleasant sound. "The Florian faction helped, too, more than they knew."

"Then all that is left for me is to give just a small push and the war will begin. Not even the little boy who is King will be able to stop it." The woman laughed as well, and the sound put shivers down Anamara's back. Then she turned more serious. "Now, that one person I was concerned about. . . ."

"Alas, lady, I could do nothing directly. He has countered every effort on my part. Maybe Sea-Rovers are more resistant, somehow, to anything but what they're set on."

They could only be speaking of Rohan. Anamara leaned closer, not wanting to miss hearing a word of what they were saying.

"Perhaps," Flavielle said. "Well, no matter. When the fighting begins he'll be caught in the middle of it like everyone else. Too bad he wouldn't listen to reason. Now he'll die."

"No!" Anamara couldn't bite back the exclamation. Both of the people on the path turned instantly, toward the sound of her voice.

"See who it is," Flavielle said.

Anamara leapt up and made a desperate dash for the path, hoping somehow that she could escape. She got tangled in the bushes and in her own skirts, and the man caught her in an iron grip.

"Leaving so soon?" he said. "The festivities are just getting started."

"Let me go!"

Flavielle waited on the path while the man dragged Anamara back to where she stood. "Who are you, to be spying on me?" she said.

Anamara stood silent, glaring at both of them. Her hands were already growing numb and useless, so tight was Duig gripping her arms.

"I think we've got ourselves a prize," Duig said. "This here's Lady Anamara, one of the Old Dowager's young ladies. A sort of ward, you might say. She and Rohan are sweet on each other, so the rumor goes."

Flavielle smiled grimly. "Yes. I knew her by name only. She was intended for—never mind. Well, then, it is a stroke of good fortune that put her in my care." She reached out, and despite Anamara's flinching away, stroked her on the cheek. Then she gripped the girl's chin so tightly Anamara thought the woman's sharp fingernails were going to pierce her flesh. "She'll come in handy, later—especially if Rohan lives through the next hour. Take her and put her somewhere for safekeeping. I'll deal with her later."

"So I will—sir."

Anamara watched, gape-mouthed, as the woman stepped back, pushing back the cloak that had covered her. She made a gesture, and right before Anamara's eyes transformed into a very familiar figure indeed—the Magician! "But—" Anamara began.

"Silence!" the Magician commanded. "Duig?"

"At once. All will be ready for your command."

Even if she had not been dazed at what she had just seen and heard, Anamara was unequal to the man's sheer strength. He clapped one hand over her mouth to stop any outcry, and began to drag her with him. Despite her struggles, she was forced to accompany him to one of the outbuildings of the city, outside the wall, where he shoved her into a cold, dank room, and locked the door behind her.

She scraped together some of the moldy straw that littered the floor and sat down on it. She had to think, had to work through the implications of what was even now happening—and find some way to escape, so that she could warn Rohan.

And she added to herself, the Dowager and the King and his royal mother and the rest of the Court. But most of all, Rohan.

Now it was clear to her that the man—no, the woman—who, rumor had it, was another of the Dowager's minions, was in fact a traitor whose scheming could very well bring down the nation.

There was no use in battering at the door. It was made of thick wood, strengthened with iron straps. The one window was shuttered, barred from outside, and even if she had something with which to pry up the bar, there was no chink through which to push a tool. She could only wait, helpless and weeping, while worry and terror built up in her.

Even screaming would do no good. There was nobody to hear.

The Bog was, if anything, even more dank and dismal than Rohan remembered from the last time he had been in it, and that had been bad enough. Now a shadow darker and more impenetrable than any he had seen before seemed to lie over it. He could scarcely penetrate the gloom.

Only his knowledge of the ways that Grandam Zaz had taken him, both in and out, kept him from getting hopelessly lost. He found renewed reason to be glad that the cold had sent most of them into permanent winter torpor, and that the human inhabitants were reluctant to be abroad except at need.

He located one of the small boats the Bog-people customarily hid along every waterway, and this made his journey somewhat easier, with his not having to beat his way through sodden underbrush. He put his pack into the boat, picked up the pole, and started poling himself along. To keep up his spirits, he began to whistle softly to himself.

Somewhere in the depths of the Bog, something answered.

Instantly alert, he set the pole into the bottom of the boat and let what sluggish current there was carry him at its own slow pace. As he drifted, he drew his sword and watched cautiously on both sides for any sign of whatever it was that had so responded.

As the minutes passed without a repeat of the signal, if signal it was, he took up the pole again. But he kept his pace slow. He might meet foe or he might meet friend, but whoever it might be, there was no gain in rushing forward headlong, even though he had taken boldness for his byword.

Cautiously, he whistled again.

And again, something answered.

Faint noises from the tourney field reached even to the dismal stone room that imprisoned Anamara. She had long since sobbed herself out but she lifted her head from where she had been resting it on her knees, when the thunder boomed.

A few moments later, there was a noise at the door and Duig opened it. "Get up," he ordered brusquely.

When Anamara didn't move, he grabbed one arm and hauled her to her feet. Behind him, she glimpsed the Magician—no, not he, but the woman Flavielle, still dressed in her robes bearing magical symbols.

"Hurry," Flavielle said. "There's no time to lose!"

"I'll round up the ones we can count on. But can you deal with the girl?"

Flavielle's lips twisted. "She'll give me no trouble. Now go. They're going on with the tourney, if you can believe it. We might have an hour before someone thinks to send after us. We must make the best use of the time we have. Take what followers you can find, and go at once to the seacoast—you know the spot. I'll join you."

"And what about her?" Duig said, indicating Anamara.

Flavielle regarded the girl almost fondly. "Oh, I have some special plans for her. Her lover will regret that he did not renounce her and join me. I'll see to it."

Even Duig looked a little taken aback.

"Well, don't waste time!" Flavielle told him, and her voice had a whip-crack in it. "Go!"

The man turned to obey, leaving Anamara with the woman who, she knew with a sinking feeling, was as dangerous an enemy as any she would ever encounter in her life. Perhaps because she could not hope to live very long—

"Nor do I have time to waste in coddling you," Flavielle said. "Look into my eyes."

Again she grabbed Anamara's chin, and, despite herself, Anamara obeyed. Flavielle's eyes were deep, so deep she could lose herself in them, and something in their depths seemed to be spinning. . . .

The voice became a croon, almost a song. "We will fly away, my little bird, fly to a spot where you will be free. Yes, free and happy, too. Forget all the cares you knew as a lady of the Court, and forget even that you once were a lady. You are no more than a bird who will fly once, and then not again. Come with me, and fly. Fly."

Anamara's cloak flapped in the wind as she soared, hand in hand—or was it wing in wing?—with the other bird. Higher and higher over the land they rose, until the people below were mere dots on a cold landscape.

They crossed a twinkling thread of light and then flew over a darkened land. They began to descend, and the voice spoke in her ear again.

"Here is the place for you, little bird. Men come here but seldom. It is your new home. Your new home, little earthbound bird. Remember this."

Suddenly the air spilled out of her wings, and Anamara tumbled to the ground, her cloak crumpling about her. She looked up to see the woman once more standing before her. She did not know the woman's name, or even her own. She blinked, uncomprehendingly, as the woman spoke to her.

"I cannot make you forget what you have seen and heard," the woman told her, "but I can take away your wits so your knowledge does you no good, nor anybody else. Perhaps there is a hungry big lupper left awake so that you can hope for a quick death here, where death lies waiting around every corner and under every foot-fall. That is what happens to little earthbound birds who blunder into this place. And so I take my leave of you."

The woman raised both arms. With a cloud of smoke and a clap of thunder, she disappeared, leaving the other alone.

I wonder who I am? she thought vaguely. I am not of her kind—the woman who flew. I flew, once. Can I do it again?

She waved her arms, trying to fly, trying to recapture the wonderful way she had soared over the world, but to no avail. The woman had said she could not.

I am a bird-girl, she thought. Earthbound. And this is now my home, though I am sure to die soon in it.

All was silent, with only an occasional sound to mar the stillness of her surroundings. Here there was a plink of water dripping; there, a torporous dweller of this region searched indifferently for food. Everywhere dank moss dangled from trees, and clumps of reeds grew in an underbrush fit to tangle even a light-boned bird-girl for whom this inhospitable place was her deadly home.

Should she stay where she was? Or should she move from spot to spot until she found one perhaps a little dryer than the half-frozen muck where she stood waiting for death? She decided to move.

She discovered another thread such as she had seen while aloft. Some fragment of memory from her old, discarded life told her this was water. A stream, but not like any she had ever seen before. Under the light that glinted on it, this one was dark and murky, and its current slow. But she stooped to drink from it nonetheless and spat out the water at once. It tasted as ill as it looked.

I must find a place with good water, and perhaps food, she thought, while I wait to die, for I am hungry. I wonder what sort of food I eat.

She began to pick her way along what might once have been a

path, avoiding the worse places. Then she heard yet another sound, a different one. It was a kind of music, though thin and a little off-key.

Another piece of memory surfaced. It was a whistle. Birds—tame ones, she knew—responded to whistles. She had seen them, in cages, safe and warm and happy as they preened their feathers. All they had to do all day was sing, and be beautiful to look upon. Though she was only a bird-girl and not in a cage of any sort, it seemed to her to be altogether appropriate that she respond to this whistle as well.

She opened her mouth—her beak—but nothing came out. With some effort, she produced a sound more like a lupper's croak than a birdcall. The music stopped at once.

Disappointed, she started making her way as silently as possible in the general direction of where it had come from. To her pleasure, the whistle sounded again; and again, she croaked an answer. This would not do, she thought vaguely. It was unseemly for a bird-girl to make such an unpleasant noise. It grated on her ears. It seemed to her that she had once been tame, and safe and warm. Even, in a way, happy. Perhaps she could be so again. She must practice her song, and try harder to do it correctly. It was cold here in her new home, and she did not like it. She was hungry. Perhaps if she could sing sweetly enough, she could have her own cage and be safe and warm once more and even have something to eat as she preened her feathers and was beautiful to look upon.

Beautiful to look upon. The repetition of the words pleased her. Beautiful. To look upon.

That second response galvanized Rohan into action. It could be no accident that something—or, perhaps, *someone*—was out there, moving parallel to the stream he floated on. He poled himself toward a bank where he could tie up the boat, clambered out, and took a few steps through the underbrush. He stopped, listening

Andre Norton & Sasha Miller

closely, and was rewarded by the sound of light footsteps and what might have been leaves rustling in the wind, but the air in the Bog was still.

"It's a matter of tracking," he said to himself, so softly that his words did not carry past the spot where he stood. And, he added silently, of being patient. This was a trait which came hard to him, but nonetheless, he must do it.

He began moving as quietly as possible in the direction from which the footsteps seemed to have come. He paused and whistled again, and again a sound came back, a little more clearly each time. It was much closer now.

Still whistling and letting the other one respond, he closed the gap between them. Just one bit of underbrush lay between him and—He stepped out of concealment.

"Anamara!" he exclaimed, so astonished his jaw dropped.

She gave him a quick and nervous smile, fluttering her hands. She did not speak. Instead, throwing her head back, she uttered the trilling, clear cry of a forest bird.

Twenty-two

*R*ohan watched, *his uneasiness* growing, as Zazar bustled around, selecting this ingredient and that out of the pots and jars which had been stashed narrowly on shelves, or under piles of woven mats. Just out of the light of the fire, Anamara sat picking at a dish of the fruit-and-grain mixture that Zazar seemed always to have on hand. He could not help but think that Anamara looked for all the world like a bird perched on a branch, only without the branch. If she could, he felt sure she would have tried to peck out the grain so she could swallow it. Instead, daintily, she picked up morsel after morsel with the fingers of one hand and dropped it into her mouth. Whether she actually chewed or not, Rohan could not tell. Birds, he knew, swallowed their food whole.

"Will she be all right, Grandam?" he said.

"That has to be the twentieth time you've asked me that, and for the twentieth time I'll tell you—I think so but I don't know and won't know for a while yet. Now let me add these seeds into it— Ah. Now I have it."

The Wysen-wyf settled down beside the fire and, taking a smooth rock shaped like a pestle, began to crush the herbs and seeds and other items in a stone bowl that had seen much use. A spring-fresh green smell began to fill the little house.

Rohan could only wait, trying to hide his impatience. Zazar would either succeed, or she would fail to bring Anamara's wits back. Until now, Grandam Zaz had never failed. And yet, there could always be a first time. . . .

"Good," Zazar said after a time, prodding the crushed mixture with her well-trained old fingers, testing it for smooth consistency. "Now, please fetch me that pot of boiling water, if you will."

Rohan hurried to obey. Zazar took the water and poured a little into the dish, and then a little more, stirring carefully. "Too much and it's just soup. Too little, and I can't form it into a pill for your lady. What did you say her name was again?"

"Anamara."

Zazar eyed the bird-girl, thinking, the corners of her mouth turned down. "That fair hair, and the midnight-blue eyes. Some trace of Ash heritage in her background, unless I miss my guess."

"Yes, Grandam. I have heard it said so."

"The Dowager Queen Ysa has no reason to love any of the Ashenkin."

"And yet she had Anamara in her circle of ladies."

"More like she had Anamara in her power," Zazar retorted with a snort. Her work with the herbs seemed to prompt a memory. "Do you still wear that bundle of greenery I gave you for your helm?"

"I do." Hastily he produced the item for Zazar's inspection. "It stays amazingly fresh, most of it. You might want to renew a few of the sprigs that have turned brown, though. In the tourney, I tied my lady's favor over it." He took the length of blue silk out of his doublet and Zazar eyed it, the corners of her mouth downturned even more.

"I suppose that was all right. But favor or not, you must wear it as long as you wear your helm. Give me your oath on that."

"I promise. Do you think this was the Dowager's doing?" Rohan asked, indicating Anamara.

"No. I know of Ysa's activities from the first time she began to dabble in magic, and it isn't her way of doing things. Not her style, you might say." She sighed and scraped a portion of the mixture to one side, and rolled it into a pill. "Well, let's see if we can find out what is in your little birdling's mind." So saying, she held out the pellet to Anamara. "Come on, it's very good. Try it."

Anamara hesitated only a moment. Then she plucked it out of Zazar's fingers and, as she had earlier with those bits of grain and fruit, dropped it into her mouth and swallowed it. Almost instantly, she fell over, eyes closed.

"Grandam!" Rohan said, appalled. "You've killed her!"

"Nonsense, you young fool," Zazar said. "A fool, and a lovesick puppy to boot. No, I haven't killed your little bird. I've just put her to sleep. Now it's my turn."

With that, the Wysen-wyf rolled a second pill from the remaining mixture, and swallowed it. As quickly as Anamara had, Zazar likewise fell over onto the packed-ground floor of her hut, and began snoring a little.

With a sinking heart, Rohan realized anew the danger into which the evil Sorceress had put Anamara. As innocent and trusting as any bird, she would swallow anything that looked like a tasty tidbit, and it might just as well have been poison as a pill made of crushed herbs. The hair on the back of his neck prickled as he felt the old familiar warning that told him of hovering peril.

All Rohan could do was to straighten their limbs as comfortably as he might, and then wait. Not daring to place Anamara on Zazar's bed and leave the Wysen-wyf on the floor, he pulled them both closer to the fire and covered them with mats, for added warmth.

He dipped a cup of the noodle soup—this time thick with boiled meat scraps—with which to console himself while he waited in harsh loneliness.

He discovered that he, too, had drifted off to sleep only when Zazar sat up abruptly, awakening him.

"Well now, that was interesting," she said.

"What was interesting, Grandam Zaz?"

"What I learned, of course. Are you as witless as your ladylove?"

Rohan ignored this, knowing that after working special magic Zazar was always apt to be shorter-tempered than usual. Also, she looked more worn than one might expect, after having awakened from what could have been a refreshing slumber. He dipped a cup of soup for her as well and handed it to her. She drank thirstily, slurping the noodles into her mouth.

"The Dowager didn't do this to Anamara, but you could say she was responsible, in a way," Zazar said, wiping her mouth with the back of her hand. She held the cup out for more, and Rohan quickly refilled it. "The Dowager and Flavielle were in league, as we knew already. What we did not know—and what Flavielle kept hidden from everyone, even from me when I visited her that time— was that this girl, this sprig of the Ashenkin, had been intended as a blood price between the Dowager and the Sorceress."

" 'Blood price'? I do not understand."

"There seems to be precious little that you *do* understand," Zazar said, with a sharp edge in her voice. Nevertheless, she went on between mouthfuls of the nourishing noodles. "When Flavielle had completed her duties for the Dowager, whatever those were, then the Sorceress would have demanded that Anamara be given to her. There was an agreement, though I doubt Ysa was aware of the whole of it. Thus, even if the Dowager tried to extricate herself, Flavielle would have made good her demand."

"For what reason?" Rohan asked. In spite of the nearness of the fire he had fed from time to time, he shivered.

"For whatever use Flavielle decided to make of her," Zazar said. "She would own the girl. She could make of her a body servant— perhaps the kindest fate. She could call upon Anamara's youth and strength for aid in the casting of spells. As for that, I think even the Dowager borrows from others from time to time. With this promise hanging over Anamara, no wonder Ysa discouraged your dalliance with her. And there are other, darker matters."

"Tell me, please." Rohan clenched his jaw. Already he had heard more than he wanted to know, but he knew if he had heard more than he wanted to know, he still had not heard nearly enough.

"Flavielle could keep Anamara to intrigue young men to their doom, as she herself tried with you. Others she could reward with the use of your ladylove's body. Or, she could even take Anamara's life in the casting of some dark spell, and no one would ever be the wiser. All this, and the Dowager, at least in part, knew of it, too, and kept her silence. After all, the girl is only Ashenkin."

"All this you learned during your sleep?"

"I peered into Anamara's head, and beyond. Your lady knew more of how matters stood than she realized. Or perhaps a veil was early thrown over her memory. What I gave her peeled away the layers of fear and helplessness which set her in the Dowager's prison."

"The Dowager—" Rohan muttered darkly.

"She is the rightful ruler of this land," Zazar said, "and will be as long as she wears the Four Rings. Swallow your pride, young lover. You are meddling in matters of which you know little, or nothing. Above all, keep in mind that it is entirely likely that Ysa did not fully realize what fate was likely to fall on this sleeping girl."

Zazar stroked the fair hair back from Anamara's forehead, and Rohan became aware that the Wysen-wyf's gruffness was, at least in part, meant to cover her uneasiness at the girl's intended fate and, perhaps, even her pity.

"She will be all right, won't she, Grandam?" he asked.

"In time. With me to treat her until she is healed. Already I have begun. By morning she will be able to understand you when you speak to her, though she will not as yet reply in language you can understand."

"I think I must go to the Oakenkeep, and there consult with Ashen and Gaurin. He gave me much good counsel in telling me to come to you. If I had not, I would never have found Anamara. If she had truly been left alone, she would have met death long before now." Rohan was staring at that face, so perfect in his eyes, which was so oddly closed to him now.

"Yes," Zazar agreed. "Not all of the great predators of the Bog are in winter sleep." She got to her feet. "Think you that Gaurin and Ashen will be back at the Oakenkeep by now?"

"If not, then I will not be ahead of them by more than a day. The tourney is ended, and neither Ashen nor Gaurin will want to stay for the merrymaking at court."

"She ever did disdain the ways of Rendelsham, though her friend the Young Dowager is there."

"And so, with the dawn, I will be gone."

"Make yourself comfortable by my fire, and later I will escort you to the river's edge. Not all of the villagers are in winter sleep as well. I think that Tusser, our new headman, holds some suspicion regarding the comings and goings of Outlanders to my hut."

"Thank you, Grandam Zaz. How can I ever repay you for all the help you have been to me?"

"You can't," Zazar said shortly. "Now, get to sleep. We must leave before it is full dawn. I will watch the girl for you."

Anamara seemed to have slept through the night, for her position was little changed from the way Rohan had placed her when she had dropped into drugged slumber. During the dark hours, the Wysen-wyf had tucked a warmer cover over the girl. When Zazar roused her, she sat up and opened her mouth, obviously ready for the grain and fruit to be given her. As Rohan filled the bowl, she responded with chirps and whistles.

"Will she be all right here, alone, while you accompany me to the river?" he demanded anxiously.

"As long as she doesn't wander out into the middle of the village," Zazar said. "We could tether her, if you like."

"No," Rohan said. Something in him rebelled at the thought of tying Anamara in her bird-girl state, even for her own safety. "Perhaps if we left another bowl of this grain mixture, she will be busy eating until you get back."

"Perhaps."

The Wysen-wyf put food before Rohan and then busied herself putting her house to rights as she ate her own breakfast. She handed a parcel to Rohan—food and water for the journey, somewhat more than he thought they would need—and turned to Anamara.

"Stay here," she said clearly, indicating the spot where Anamara crouched. "Here. Do you understand?" She placed a bowl of the fruit-and-grain mixture in front of the girl.

Anamara bobbed her head and uttered more chirps and whistles. Despite Zazar's claim that she could now understand human speech, Rohan could not tell whether this signaled either comprehension or agreement.

"Do you think she will do it?"

"I don't know," the Wysen-wyf said. "I can accomplish only so much with her at present. But give me time—Ah, well, we cannot stay the day. Already it grows lighter than I find comfortable."

She got to her feet, pulled on the warm cloak Gaurin had given her, and picked up a staff before plucking aside the hide covering the doorway long enough to have a look outside. "All is clear, at least for the moment. Come along, don't dawdle."

Rohan obediently followed through the opening, to make immediately for the shelter of a line of nearly leafless bushes that marked the edge of the hut clearing. They had not gone a dozen paces, however, before he was aware that someone—or something—was following them.

He turned, half expecting to see some hungry Bog-monster tracking them, only to discover Anamara. She had left her cloak behind and, clad only in her dress and cloth slippers, she shivered a little in the morning cold.

"Go back!" Rohan said, making his whisper as urgent as he could manage. "Back, Anamara. Go to the hut. There's a good girl."

Anamara only gazed at him happily and ran the few steps separating them. She clung to him, looking up at him with adoring eyes, and began to whistle. Hastily he clapped his hand over her mouth. "I thought you said she could understand human speech now."

Zazar had turned back and now stood scowling at the tableau. "She can. That doesn't mean she recognizes the reasons behind your commands. Or that she agrees. Can't you manage the little lackwit any better than that?" she said. "Or should I take a hand?"

Remembering Zazar's quick way with a sound slap across the face, Rohan opened his cloak to shelter Anamara. She crept into the warmth gratefully and put her arms around his waist. "Can we get her back to your hut?" he asked. "This time, I'll take your advice and—and tether her securely."

Zazar moved past him and peered out into the clearing. "Just as I thought. No time," she said. "The village has begun to stir and there are people out on their morning errands. Somebody is sure to spot us and give the alarm. Then both of you would be doomed, and I could do nothing to prevent it. You would be given to feed the Boggins."

"But the pools where you say the Boggins lie—"

"Frozen, yes, and the Deep Dwellers in winter sleep." She stepped closer. "They would kill you, Rohan, and the girl with you. Oh, you would fight bravely, but you would perish. Perhaps they would kill me. Both Tusser and Joal, his father, threatened enough times. And they would stack our bodies until the thaw comes. That is what they would do to us."

Rohan swallowed, hard. "Then we shall have to take her with us," he said.

"I know. And I am not happy about that, though I should have expected it. Well, we can't just stay here talking until the villagers hear and come looking. Follow me."

Using her staff to clear the way and test for unsteady footing on an icy path that was almost invisible to Rohan, Zazar led them out a different way. He was kept busy making certain that Anamara stayed on the path. At unexpected moments she would break free from the sheltering warmth of his cloak and dash away after anything that caught her fancy—a trembling leaf, a glitter of ice, a stray ray of wan sunlight that managed to penetrate the rank growth of the Bog.

"Bind that girl's hands around your middle," Zazar said, exasperated, after Anamara had done this several times. "We can't have her flitting off into the underbrush and getting lost again. Not when you seem to put so much store in her."

"I will keep a closer watch on her," Rohan said. He wrapped Anamara's arms around his waist again and, instead of tying her, held both her hands in one of his. This made for awkward progress, but she no longer could dash away at unexpected moments.

Just when he was certain that even Zazar had lost her way on this unfamiliar path, they emerged from the Bog. Zazar strode over to an overhanging bush and began pulling it away from what it was hiding.

"A—a boat!" Rohan exclaimed. He knew he had said something foolish when the Wysen-wyf glanced up at him with a look of amused contempt.

"Of course, a boat," she responded. "How else did you expect we would get this witless damsel of yours across the river? Did you think she would fly?"

"No, Grandam Zazar," Rohan said, properly chastened. "Again, I must bow to your infinite wisdom."

He helped Anamara into the little vessel, steadying her as she teetered, apparently having forgotten anything she ever knew about boats, and climbed in after her. To his surprise, Zazar took a seat in the stern.

"Does this mean that you are coming with me to the Oakenkeep?" he said hopefully.

"When the little chit came after us I decided that it was high time I visited the place after so many invitations," Zazar replied. "And also, I have decided that I want to be there when you show up with Lady Lackwit and introduce her to Ashen." The Wysen-wyf's lips lifted in a grin that was only partially merry. "I wouldn't miss that little meeting for the world!"

It was a slow journey going on foot. Out in the relative open, Rohan could not keep as close a guard on Anamara as he would have liked, and her sudden asides grew both more frequent and more lengthy as she had freedom to run. Zazar would wait, patiently hunkered down to conserve warmth, while Rohan chased after her. Eventually he learned that if he kept offering her bits of the grain-and-fruit mixture, she was more apt to follow than to flit away.

Because of this, they were much longer on their journey from the river to the Oakenkeep than Rohan would have liked. They spent three nights out in the open with only an occasional stand of winter-blighted trees for shelter, and the only fortunate thing about it was that Ashen and Gaurin were already well in residence by the time they got there.

Rohan led Anamara through the gatehouse and toward the Residence. For once, she did not need bribery to keep her from trying to get away from his restraining hand. Instead, she gaped and gawped as if she had never seen a great edifice of this sort before. She stared upward at the towers topping the surrounding walls, her mouth open.

"This way," he told both Anamara and Zazar, and rapped on the door to the Residence, where they were admitted at once. He led them down a corridor to the Great Hall.

Inside, it was chilly enough that their breath could be seen faintly, and yet it was heavenly warmth itself compared to the bitterness of the outdoors. Rohan found himself blowing on his fingers, only now aware of how very cold he was. "Build up the fire," he said to the steward who had admitted them, "and please notify Count Gaurin and his lady, my foster mother Ashen, that Rohan is here—with visitors." He turned to Zazar with a shrug. "Might as well make it a total surprise."

The Wysen-wyf uttered what might have been a cackle, and then busied herself with coaxing Anamara over to the fireplace where servants were obediently bringing in more wood to add to the carefully banked coals. It was a little green, the best firewood having long since been burnt, and would take a while to catch.

"How now," a woman's voice said. Rohan looked up to see Ashen descending the stairs. "Rohan!"

He rushed toward her and embraced her. "Yes, it is I."

"Nalren said something about visitors—Zazar!"

"And who else did you expect?" The Wysen-wyf strove for her usual gruffness, but she couldn't maintain it. "I am happy to see you well, Ashen, after the strain of the past few days. And how did Gaurin fare?"

"Well enough. He is unharmed. Busy with the accounts. He won a trophy. I heard the commotion and came to see what was causing it." Ashen was staring past Zazar at Anamara where she stood by the fireplace, so close that she was in some danger of having a stray spark from the coals ignite her muddy, stained dress. "And how does this lady come to be in my home?"

"Brought here witless and in a daze, thanks to the Sorceress," Zazar said. "Don't you have anything warm to drink? We really are nearly frozen."

"Upstairs. We do not usually heat the Great Hall these days, except in the evenings. Nalren, put the logs aside until later."

"Yes, lady," he said. "Shall I bring you hot spiced juice?"

"Please. Now, Zazar, Rohan. Bring your—your witless young woman with you. Gaurin awaits above."

Gaurin arose quickly as Ashen ushered Zazar into the small room at the top of the stairs, located where the big chimney in the Great Hall would help warm it at one wall, with another fireplace on the other to make it truly comfortable. "Madame Zazar!" he exclaimed in surprise and pleasure. "You honor my lady's house with your presence." He bowed low over her brown, wrinkled hand, and kissed it. "Ah! Here is Rohan with you. And—Is it really Anamara?"

"What's left of her," Zazar said tartly. "She ran afoul of the Sorceress. There is much to be told."

"Then come and sit, rest yourselves, and take the warmth of the fire. We can wait while you catch your breath before you begin."

Zazar shrugged. "Soonest begun, soonest ended," she said. Then she related, with some prompting and filling-in of details, what had occurred since Rohan had taken his leave of Gaurin in Rendelsham. Both Gaurin and Ashen listened most closely to what the Wysen-wyf had learned in her herb-driven sojourn into the recesses of Anamara's mind.

"Poor lady," Gaurin commented, when she had finished.

Rohan looked at Anamara where she perched contentedly near the fire, dabbling in a cup of the hot spiced juice the steward, Nalren, had brought. She seemed to have forgotten how to drink out of a cup, and so she was dipping her fingers into it and then sucking them.

"Poor lady in truth," Rohan said.

"Poor fool is more like it," Ashen said.

Rohan swiftly turned to her. "You must know that I—I have a great fondness for her, even in her current state. I swear that I will not rest until she is restored to what she once was."

Ashen made a sound of dismissal. "And what was that? A little know-nothing, hiding from everyone, fluttering her lashes at you from underneath the hood of her cloak? At her age I knew enough not to act that green and ignorant, even when I was."

"She was shy with me when first we met, true enough," Rohan said, "but that was before the Dowager promised her to Flavielle. I think from shortly after that moment when the Sorceress arrived at Court, my lady became fearful of her very life, and knew not why, only that she must avoid me. If only she had told me—"

Ashen got up and began to pace back and forth. "And then what? Would you have challenged both of those women and gotten yourself killed for your troubles? It was bad enough that you rejected Flavielle when she approached you—"

"I think that was the only thing that saved young Rohan," Zazar said. "Think, Ashen. Could it not be that Rohan had been the one first picked as the blood price?"

The Wysen-wyf's words put a fresh chill in the air as Rohan pondered the truth in them. "I do believe that Grandam Zaz is correct," he said at length. "The Sorceress had just come to court and it was only after that unfortunate incident in my room that Anamara seemed to grow cool toward me."

At the sound of her name, Anamara looked up at him and whistled softly. She smiled.

"Thoroughly witless," Ashen said. " 'Lady Lackwit' indeed. You named her well, Zazar."

The Wysen-wyf began to laugh, with a sound like a bellows wheezing. "This is all very amusing," she said.

"I do not find anything the least bit funny about it."

"Nor I," Rohan said.

"Well, I do." Zazar settled back in the chair and reached for more of the hot spiced drink. "The boy's fallen in love, that's all. His lady has, at present, the mind of a bird. And his foster mother objects."

"I have much reason to object!" Ashen responded hotly. "Did this Lady Lackwit come from the Court in Rendelsham or did she not? Has anything good ever come from that pit of iniquity?"

"You might say so. Wasn't that where you met Gaurin?" Zazar smiled with a trace of smugness.

The back of Rohan's neck tingled. He knew it was potentially dangerous to come between these two and especially now when they were so close to an open disagreement. He had never thought of Ashen in terms of Power before, but now he realized that she had fully her measure of it, though it lay untrained and unused. He glanced at Gaurin and knew that the older man shared his thoughts.

"Come, Rohan," he said. "This is not a matter for men to meddle in. With your arrival, we have three more mouths to feed. There is still an hour or two of daylight before supper in the Hall. Are you thawed enough that, with some fresh warm clothes and boots, you would be up to seeing if we can find something for tomorrow's dinner?"

"Gladly, Gaurin," he said, getting to his feet. His toes were still like ice, but he would rather freeze entirely than be caught in a small room in the Oakenkeep, between two quarreling women.

"What game is it you are playing at?" Ashen said, when the men had left the room.

"Game? I don't know what you mean." But Zazar's eyes twinkled. Plainly, she was enjoying herself.

"You know full well what I mean." Ashen crossed her arms and frowned at the woman whom she called Protector, who had reared her from infancy. She had never been quite so annoyed at Zazar before, and, if asked, she could not have articulated exactly why. There was something about the girl, Anamara, that set Ashen's teeth on edge. Perhaps she was a spy, sent by Ysa, and this bird-girl act of hers only that—an act. She did not know.

"I believe I will continue to work on restoring Anamara here at the Oakenkeep," Zazar said, unperturbed, her voice and manner as bland as an egg. "It's much warmer here, and safer, too. I won't need anything in the way of herbs and other items that I haven't brought with me. Mostly it's a matter of mind. I think I will ask Weyse to help me. You would like to see Weyse again, wouldn't you?"

Ashen knew that Zazar was secretly laughing at her. "You know I would welcome Weyse at the Oakenkeep if she will agree to visit," she said, trying to keep her own voice neutral.

"Well then, that's settled. Why don't you find a room for me to use? Of course Anamara will be staying with me where I can keep an eye on her, so be kind enough not to shove us out of the way in some stable or other outbuilding."

Ashen took a deep breath to keep herself from a furious outburst. "You know full well there is always an apartment here in the Residence kept ever ready for you," she said, trying to keep the anger out of her voice, "and has been since first we came to live in the Oakenkeep, in hopes that you would come and visit, or even to stay permanently with us. I'll give orders that the fire be lit and the beds freshened."

"Oh, no need," Zazar said airily. "I can brush away a cobweb if need be. Just show me the way."

Grateful for something to do, Ashen briskly led Zazar and Anamara—who would have lagged behind, gaping at the tapestries and furnishings, if Zazar had not held her by the hand—through the upper hallway to the suite that had been set aside for the Wysenwyf. Their breaths were visible in the frosty air. She opened the door, expecting the interior to be as cold and dusty as it had been the last time she had visited, and scolded the maids for not maintaining it better. However, to her surprise, all was warm, clean and tidy, with a fire burning briskly on the hearth. Weyse, curled up on the bed in the far corner, looked up with sleepy eyes. Then she uttered a glad cry of greeting, jumped down out of the trundle bed that was already set up, and waddled toward the people at the opened door.

Involuntarily, Ashen stepped back, astonished, and Weyse altered her course and made for Zazar instead. "Here already, you scamp?" she said, picking Weyse up and cuddling her. "I might have known." She turned to Ashen, who reached out and stroked Weyse's head. "If we could have some hot water, perhaps, so I can give Lady Lackwit a bath, and some food. I still have a little of that grain and fruit that Weyse likes so well, but unfortunately our bird-girl likes it, too. Some warm clothing for her wouldn't go amiss, either. And shoes."

"Of course," Ashen said through stiff lips. "I will send Ayfare to you. She was my personal maid in Rendelsham, and now she is the head housekeeper of Oakenkeep. She will see to it that you have everything you need."

"Good. Now, I'm sure you have better things to do than let the warmth out into that cold hallway." With that, Zazar closed the door practically in Ashen's face.

Ashen resisted an impulse to pound on the door, demand entrance, and have an open row with Zazar then and there. But what would it accomplish? She had a distinct feeling that the Wysen-wyf would ignore such an encounter as easily as she had avoided Ashen's objections earlier.

No, better to leave her to her task. The sooner she could restore Anamara's wits, the sooner the girl could be sent back to the Dowager's Court, where she belonged. Or—Ashen's eyes narrowed.

She was not the ignorant Bog-Princess she had once been, when first she came to Rendelsham. She was very aware of the remnants of Ash holdings that now, by the law of inheritance, were hers. There still existed places where Anamara could be sent and where she would be hidden so completely that Rohan could never find her—particularly if he were commanded to return to the capital city and resume his responsibilities in the Dowager's Levy. Gaurin had told her of his offhand question to Rohan: Would he now be knight, or knave? She knew instinctively that Rohan, now a knight, would not turn knave and desert his duty just to look for a none-too-bright girl who had run afoul of the Dowager's schemings, and suffered for it. Perhaps later, when his responsibilities would allow, he would stay with her as he chose, but not at the present.

Rohan slogged along in Gaurin's wake through the woods to the north and east of the castle. The snow had started again, though not heavily, and he was not at all sure they would be able to start a coney, let alone anything large enough to feed the household at the Oakenkeep. He was grateful for the thick boots and fur-lined garments—clean and dry and, above all, warm—that Gaurin had given him. Both men were armed with bows, in addition to the swords that were always at their sides, and full quivers of arrows were at the ready on their backs. A distance behind them trailed Lathrom and half a dozen soldiers from the keep. No hunters except possibly for the captain, they would be ready to carry home what Gaurin and Rohan tracked.

"Is Ashen often like this?" he asked.

"Like what?" Gaurin paused, searching the ground for tracks

that might show in the new-fallen snow. "Ah. Tracks. Come this way."

"Like she was back at the keep." Rohan moved up to walk beside Gaurin, keeping the line of cloven footprints between them. "I've never seen her so dead set against anyone as she is against Anamara. And for no reason that I can tell."

"Nor I. But I have learned, with Ashen, that she often keeps her own counsel until she is ready to tell me her reasons for this or that. I believe it will be that way now."

"I hope so. After all, Anamara is, in a way, Ashen's kindred. You'd think she would feel more kindly disposed toward her, wouldn't you?"

"I would, but remember that women's ways are not always our ways, my young knight. And what may seem complicated and even devious to us, to them is perfectly natural and straightforward. It is a mystery."

"Yes," Rohan agreed glumly. "And one that I have yet to fathom. Perhaps you will teach me."

Gaurin turned toward him, amused. "I have already imparted to you all the wisdom I possess about the ways of women!" he said. Then his expression became a little more serious. "I love Ashen, from the crown of her head to the soles of her feet. And I know that nothing you or I may say, or even that Madame Zazar might say, would have any effect on her. The one who wins her over to Anamara will have to be Anamara herself."

Rohan bowed his head. "I must accept that," he said, "even though I would have it otherwise." Then he remembered another matter that had been almost overlooked in the tumultuousness of his arrival at the Oakenkeep with Grandam Zaz and his afflicted lady. "Where is Hegrin? I thought to see her long before now."

"We sent Hegrin, with her own household, to Rydale, one of Ashen's holdings. It used to belong to the late King Florian, but nobody wanted it because it lies to the east, near the shore. We found it perfect for Hegrin because it is remote and, thus, likely to be safer than we are here when the attack from the North comes. Also, being close to the sea, it is warmer."

"You must miss her."

"We do, both of us. And that is one more reason I thought Ashen would welcome Anamara as a kind of substitute for the daughter she no longer can see every day. Perhaps, though, she sees her as a rival instead—"

Gaurin broke off abruptly, holding his hand up to signal Rohan to stop.

Rohan obeyed, looking around for signs of whatever it was that had alerted Gaurin. "What is it?" he whispered.

The other man made an impatient signal for silence, and then Rohan heard it—the sound of something large and close ahead, pushing its way through the underbrush. "Fallowbeeste," he said, so softly the sound of the word barely reached Rohan's ears.

Then he gestured again, and Rohan moved off in the opposite direction. He knew at once what Gaurin had in mind. They would try to flank the prey, and then, between them, bring it down. He drew an arrow and nocked it to his bow. Gaurin did likewise. And then the hunt was on in earnest.

Rohan knew that fallowbeeste were sturdy enough to take several arrows and still escape their hunters. He and Gaurin would have to be quick and, above all, accurate if they hoped to provide meat for the castle household. They crept forward carefully, making certain not to step on a warning twig.

Then he spotted it. There it was, beyond the trees in a small clearing! A fine buck, it had paused to search out a bit of grass beneath the covering of snow. The rack of horns adorning its head would make a fine trophy, mounted and hung above a fireplace. Rohan readied his bow, and could see Gaurin, also with arrow nocked. They were too close together for a flanking maneuver. It would have been better also if they could have worked their way around so that they had a clearer shot, from the front, but Rohan knew they dared not risk it. More than one fallowbeeste had fled untouched when an unwary hunter, trying for a more advantageous angle, had stepped on a twig or otherwise sounded an alarm.

He drew back the bowstring and took aim at a point just behind the animal's front leg. With any luck, either he or Gaurin would get the vital spot and the fallowbeeste would die immediately, without pain. The animal froze, lifting its head, and Rohan knew it had sensed the hunters' presence.

Without hesitation, he loosed the arrow, half a heartbeat behind Gaurin's shot. At least one of them hit squarely home, for the fallowbeeste dropped in its tracks without even a grunt.

The men hurried over to make sure it was really dead and not just pretending, so it could scramble to its feet and dash away at the first opportunity.

"The arrows are scarcely a hand-span apart," Gaurin said. "Good shooting, Rohan. I believe you got him."

Rohan knew better; the arrow marked with the spring-green band had struck more truly. He recognized Gaurin's gesture as being that of a good host, and a generous one. "The trophy is yours, though. Or, at least, yours to keep for me. What would I do with this, even if I had it?" He knelt and examined the rack of horns. Sometimes people used them as handles for knives, or sliced them into disks for buttons, but these were much too fine for such a humble use. They deserved to be displayed, as a tribute to the noble beast that had once worn them.

Gaurin took the horn from his belt and blew a clear note. "Lathrom and his men will be here shortly. They will do the skinning and will cut it into sections for the roasting spit. We will finish the stew with fresh bread tonight, and then feast well tomorrow. And we will have some fine leather from this fellow's hide, as well. New slippers for your lady, perhaps, and for mine. A new belt for you, at least, to remember the occasion and I will give you a buckle shaped like the amulet Madame Zazar gave you. We have done a good day's work, Rohan."

"Yes," he agreed, but his satisfaction was dimmed somewhat at the mention of Anamara. New slippers she might have, but what good would they be if her wits could not be restored to her?

During the days and weeks that followed, a peace of sorts descended between the quarreling women. That it was accomplished primarily by Ashen's holding her tongue was immaterial. She could almost feel the relief emanating from both her husband and her stepson. Still, her mind had not changed on the matter. She held against Anamara, and could not articulate a clear reason why.

Zazar always brought Anamara to the table for the evening meal in the Hall, and painstakingly taught her to eat not with her hands but with a spoon, as she could not yet be trusted with handling an eating-dagger. Weyse stayed in Zazar's suite; at least, she never appeared anywhere else in the Oakenkeep. When Ashen wanted to visit the little creature who had befriended her in the lost and ruined city of Galinth, she must perforce go there. She chose times when Zazar was absent.

After dinner, when the Wysen-wyf was in the mood, she proved to have an unexpected talent for the telling of tales from the far-distant time, back before Galinth had fallen into decay and the Bog had formed. But the evening's entertainment never lasted long. The Oakenkeep was too large and firewood becoming too scarce to heat it more than absolutely necessary. People were glad to retire early, to their beds, warmed with heated stones wrapped in wool, where they could pull the woolen curtains shut and thaw cold fingers and toes. Though the custom had always been for people to remove their clothes and sleep bare, it was too cold for that. Men and women alike wore long nightgowns, also made of wool.

Ashen hoped the frigid weather would at least abate enough so that the river thawed. When the meat ran low, people from the castle had to chop holes in the ice before they could hope to catch a mess of fish for their evening meal. At least meat seldom went off these days, as it once did in milder weather. It froze too quickly for that, which was, in a way, a blessing.

Twenty-three

*L*ord Royance strode back and forth in front of the fireplace in the Dowager Queen Ysa's apartment. There was a youthful bounce in his step that had not been seen in a long time. "What a great day for Rendel!" he exclaimed. "Our fighting men must be the best in the world, judging from their performance in the Grand Tourney. Even the youngsters."

"And you as well, my lord?" Ysa said. She sat watching, hoping to appear interested, when in truth the boasting of the Head of the Council bored her nearly into insensibility. Marcala was with her, but the younger woman seemed to be paying genuine attention to Royance's retelling of the tourney's events.

"If I had to, I know now I could take up weapons and fight," he said, obviously greatly pleased with himself. "I would, in fact, welcome the test in real combat! I only wish I had been matched against someone more able than Wittern. Great friend though he is, he is not the man he once was and even in our youth I could have him on his back in a stroke or two."

"You showed yourself very competent. I am only glad that no harm came from it."

Royance stopped his pacing and frowned into the fire. "That

was a very bad situation, with that Magician fellow, or Sorceress, or whoever or whatever he or she was. Most confusing. Even while it was going on, with the fellow working his spells, I knew that I had no real quarrel with Jakar, or even with Gattor, for that matter. And yet it seemed that I could not help myself. Whatever possessed you to put such a person in your hire? What were you thinking of?"

Ysa felt a faint chill down her back, in spite of the heavy green velvet dress she wore. "I did it for the good of the country, my lord Royance," she replied, "as everything that I do is for the good of the country." She held out her hands, with the Four Great Rings on them. "My entire life is devoted to keeping Rendel safe and secure— even while the dangers surrounding us pile one upon the other. Surely you must know that."

"I do," Royance said. "Yes, of course, I know that you have worn yourself thin when it came to the good of the land. But it does seem that you could have checked the fellow's credentials—"

"Do have some more heated wine," Marcala said hastily. "And tell us more about your exploits." She leaned forward to pour, and the scent of her vaux lily perfume wafted out into the air. "We are mere women, you know, and can't be expected to recognize the finer points of arms-play."

"I thought that you would have learned, being so close to Harous as you are, and in a position to watch the youngsters at their training. Pity that I didn't provide two prizes. But Gaurin won the standing-cup fair and square. I hope Harous is not disappointed."

"Of course he would rather have won, but he holds no ill will toward Gaurin. He recognizes and, indeed, admires Gaurin's great skill at arms."

"Harous has a noble heart," Ysa said, "and this brings to mind a matter that I have been thinking on. Let us discuss it, my Lord Royance, now that we are all three here together, for I want your thoughts and sage advice. Then, if you will, you can regale us with more tales of the tourney."

"Why, of course, Your Highness," Royance said. He took the chair that had been set out for him and became once more the Head of the Council rather than the old warrior yearning for one more battle. "What may I offer my advice on?"

"It is the matter of Count Harous's marriage." Beside her, Ysa heard Marcala draw in her breath sharply. "I think it is time and more that he marry, and get heirs. Someday, we might well have a great struggle ahead of us, every indication tells me, and I would not leave his branch of his Family childless."

And also, she thought, I would put Marcala that much more into my debt. This lady has become much too independent of late. She could, if she would, be very helpful regarding a certain matter that Ysa had been thinking on and which needed to be resolved.

"Let us be frank and open with one another," Royance said. The firelight gleamed on his snowy head. "It is not only time for the boy to marry and get heirs, but also it is past time for him to regularize the relationship he and the Lady Marcala have had. The question is, will he be willing to do so?"

"He would be, with you to prompt him," Ysa said.

"And the lady? How say you, Marcala?"

"I have wanted Harous as my husband for a long time. But it was not seemly for me to broach the subject." Marcala's cheeks reddened. To Ysa's astonishment, her Queen of Spies, a woman who had seen more of the world than most people at Court could imagine, was actually blushing!

"I do not know when the attack from the North will come," Royance said, "nor, indeed, if it will come. We have had no sign, only rumors. But there is no purpose to be served in leaving you and Harous unwed, when it is obvious that you are so well suited to each other. There is kinship between you, to be sure, but distant enough that no impropriety could be put to your being man and wife. I cannot think what has been holding him back all this time, other than that maybe, like many a man, the matter has not been put to him in such a way that he recognizes the need." He got to his feet, bowed to Ysa and to Marcala, and took his cloak from the peg. "Yes, I will go to Harous and make the suggestion that now is the time to marry. You may as well start planning the wedding."

With that, he took his leave. Then Ysa had to deal with Marcala, weeping for joy and swearing eternal loyalty, when what she wanted most was to be left in private. With the matter of Harous and Marcala's marriage all but settled, she had something important to do, something that had been left far too long while other matters occupied her attention.

🌹

Once she had seen her highborn guests out of her apartment to go about their business, the Dowager Queen Ysa sought the little secret door. Then she climbed the stairs to her tower room again, where she had ever been wont to go when she needed a quiet place for reflection, or wanted to work some bit of magic.

She entered, locked the door behind her, and stood gazing about. The four great windows looking east, west, north, and south had long since had their transparent coverings removed, to be replaced with heavy woolen draperies. Back in the days when she had been truly young and she had not yet been moved to take up the study of arcane matters, decorative glass panes, capable of opening outward, had been installed even in this high place during a period of remodeling of the castle. Before this unseasonable cold had wrapped Rendel in its icy fingers these windows had mostly stood open and here was the best place to come and catch an evening breeze. Now, however, Ysa was glad that drafts had been reduced to a minimum.

The great chair, carved from blood-colored wood of such density that it required very sharp tools and great strength to work it, still stood in the center of the round chamber, and also the table fashioned of the same wood, close beside it. Her book of magic awaited her there.

She struck spark to the brazier kept ready for her, and moved to the smaller table and chair, much less ornate, where she sat to take off her coif and remove the light layer of cosmetics that was all she needed since she had renewed her youthful beauty. Successful magic required that she come to it in as unadorned a state as possible. As was her habit, she lighted a candle and set it beside the mirror, admiring herself as she worked. Her hair now bore no trace or strand of white, and shone with a crisp ruddiness to rival the hue of the wood of the great chair. It tumbled down her back when she took the pins out, a glorious riot of color. For a moment, she felt that all the light and color in the world had been concentrated in this one lofty chamber, high above the city of Rendelsham, centered on herself.

She tried not to think about Flavielle, once Flavian, whom she had hired, and of the treachery the woman had attempted and nearly succeeded with. Ysa had told him—her—everything, even to the miscarriage of Ashen's and Obern's child. Now she knew she had just been used as a conduit of information, whether important or not. If it had not been for that oaf Rohan and his timely confrontation with the woman, who knew what kind of mischief she would have wreaked? Ysa supposed she should be grateful to Rohan, but could not summon up the feeling. Once more, as frequently happened when thinking of him, she was reminded of something that nagged at the back of her mind. But she could not remember it.

Well, Flavielle was gone now, and Ysa knew she had to repair her hold on the Kingdom, and on her own Power, lest more of her plans come to naught. The Four Rings gleamed in the candlelight. She told herself that the movement she had felt on her fingers at the moment the Sorceress stood revealed and the young King Peres had chosen to assert his authority, had been nothing but a nervous twitching of her own. Secure they were on her hands, and there they would remain. She would see to that.

She reached for the simple hooded robe of red velvet, grateful for the warmth of the garment. The brazier had not yet taken the chill off the air. She pulled the hood up over her head and fastened it in place with a plain hairpin in place of the jeweled ones she ordinarily used. She went to a box covered in silk, roused the drowsy flyer that slept there, and picked it up. Then she moved to the great chair and settled the flyer in her lap. She picked up the book, opened it to a previously selected page. Before, she had merely tested out the spell, not bothering to make the full preparation, and so it had been but a temporary one. She began the ritual.

With the ease of practice, she intoned the words. The Power of them reverberated from the stone walls, and created a nexus of energy that hung in the air before her. Like a cloud, its outline shifted and altered. Then, before the flyer she held could even try to break away from her grip, the nebula swooped down upon and *into* it through its open mouth. It gave a great, startled leap, and then was still.

"Now," she said with some satisfaction, "with this spell we shall find out if I can see what you see, as you experience it, and not wait until later." The flyer seemed to be holding its breath, and she stroked it until it got over the shock of the cloud's invasion, much stronger than it had been the previous time. Eventually the creature stopped trembling, and gripped the fabric of her robe with its tiny paws.

She picked it up by the nape of the neck. It struggled in her hands, panting, kicking, and flapping its leathery wings, but as she had done when first she summoned it, she held it up on a level with her eyes, imposing her will upon it, dominating it. "You are not hurt," she told it. "Be still. This is all to the good."

The creature's mouth opened again and, for a moment, Ysa thought it was going to try to bite her with its sharp teeth. Its tongue was purplish red, and curved up at the end. It chittered and then uttered a thin, high shriek of protest so shrill it hurt Ysa's ears. Nevertheless, she continued to hold it until it had regained a measure of calm. She carried it to one of the windows, pulled back the curtain, and opened the casement a crack.

"Go out over the land, and seek," she said, pleased enough to be generous. "You may even fly to the Oakenkeep, but do not linger." Then she let it go, into the air. Its wings spread and beat and, as always, as it went its outlines grew more and more hazy until it vanished entirely. She watched for a moment, and then closed the window again and pulled the curtain to. If her spell had worked correctly, she would see what it saw when it suited her, and wherever she might be at the time. Also, she would know when the flyer had returned, seeking to be admitted again. It would need to have a window opened so that it could get in. She checked to see that a dish of grain and another of water was ready.

As clearly as if it had been within the hour, Ysa could visualize in her mind's eye the amulet Harous had once shown her, years before. Whether made of wood or of stone, she did not know; it had a gray sheen as though well rubbed, and was fashioned into the shape of a winged creature. Despite the polish, an observer could see that the creature was represented as furred rather than feathered. Its tiny eyes glittered with gems. And his claim—

"Zazar, Your Majesty." His voice had risen hardly above a whisper as if there might be listeners in the room. "This came from Zazar."

She had accepted it at the time, but now did not believe it. Could not believe it. Would not. In fact, the whole claim was quite preposterous. This was not the kind of work Zazar engaged in. But she had let the matter go at the time, being too absorbed in the problems presented by Boroth's last illness, and the possibility that an heir would emerge to claim the throne she had determined would go to her son. An illegitimate heir and an unworthy son, to be sure, but the demands of dynasties could not be concerned with such niceties.

Also, she had been assured of Harous's complete loyalty then, despite his delving into matters arcane and, perhaps, dangerous. Not that she was any less certain regarding him now, but prudence demanded that she make her own investigations.

For once, Ysa felt security such as she had not known in years concerning what might or might not be stirring in the North. Surely, with the defeat of the Sorceress, that threat had subsided, possibly forever. Instead, she had now decided to learn whether or not Count Harous really did have a flyer such as hers, and if so, what use he was making of it. Further, if he did, and the use was not to her liking, she now had the means, through Marcala, to acquire the amulet and, with it, a second flyer.

Marcala's admission that he came to her apartment, rather than admitting her to his quarters, was the key. Boroth had never bothered with such niceties; he had been fully capable of entertaining his women in his and Ysa's marriage bed. Harous, however, kept to the dubious proprieties of an irregular liaison. He visited his lady in her apartment, only when the lady indicated that such was welcome. His own quarters remained private. Therefore, when Marcala married Harous, she would be allowed access to all rooms in Cragden Keep, and thus able to locate the amulet, wherever Harous had it hidden.

Perhaps Visp, her flyer, would even encounter Harous's flyer, if indeed he possessed one, in its journey northward. Yes, there was much to learn and, now that the Grand Tourney was past and the Sorceress sent packing, she had the leisure at last.

Ysa found herself reluctant to descend the stairs and become enmeshed, even peripherally, in the beginning of the hubbub that always surrounded an important wedding. There was time to verify that the spell was working correctly before she had to leave the tower. She returned to the great chair, seated herself, and closed her eyes, concentrating. At the same time, the vision of the flyer opened behind her eyelids.

Up, up she flew, above the cover of clouds that ever covered the land in these days. The cold sun sparkled on the tops of these clouds and the air burned in her lungs. Still she flew on, ever farther, confident in her invisibility that she could avoid whatever hazards she encountered on the way.

Once before, she had done this by way of a temporary spell—seen through the flyer's eyes directly. Now, however, this ability was under her command. And she proposed to make the best use of it.

🌺

Even Ashen could tell, grudgingly, that Anamara was beginning to improve. Whether it was Zazar's work or Weyse's influence, the girl gradually ceased her nervous, birdlike gestures, and instead began behaving as one very young, who is being introduced into the company of adults for the first time.

"Indeed," Zazar said when Ashen asked her about it, "the effects of the Sorceress's spelling have erased most of Anamara's memory of herself. Oh, now that I've worked with her for a while she knows her name and those of her late parents, but she is like a little child. And, like a child, she will have to be again taught almost everything else that she once knew. I am convinced that my work here is almost accomplished. After I leave, it will be up to you to tutor her."

"I!" exclaimed Ashen. She stared at Anamara where she sat on a footstool close beside the Wysen-wyf, gazing at the two of them in turn. "I bear no responsibility for this girl nor obligation to assume her welfare. Further, I have no intention of doing any such thing!"

"And yet, it must be your responsibility. I grow old, and I am not up to the task."

Ashen turned to the Wysen-wyf. She looked unchanged from when she had been the closest thing to a mother to Ashen, and her energy seemed undimmed. Zazar glanced back at Ashen, and Ashen caught the tiniest gleam of amusement in her eye.

"Old!" she exclaimed. "I think not. You must find another excuse."

"I must get back to my hut, and my business in the Bog."

Ashen allowed herself to laugh, but only a little. "And only now does it occur to you to worry about what the villagers may be doing to your house, to your belongings? I think not. No one there would dare touch any of your things or sample any of the mixtures you keep in pots on the shelf, for fear of being poisoned—or worse. I know how carefully you have taught them to be wary of you. No, Zazar, I do not believe you."

The Wysen-wyf shrugged. "Well then, do it because the girl is your distant kin, and if you still cannot summon up enough charity, then you will do it for Rohan's sake."

Andre Norton & Sasha Miller

To that, Ashen could find no ready objection to give voice. She set her lips firmly, and looked away.

"Most of all"—Zazar's voice cut through the cold air like a whip and Ashen involuntarily met her eyes again—"you will do it because I instruct you to."

"I—I am surely beyond your having to instruct and discipline me," Ashen said, and knew her words to sound feeble, even in her own ears.

"You will never achieve that lofty status. You have entertained me mightily, Ashen Deathdaughter, and I suspect you know it. But I will be open with you now. I have done as much as I can do with the girl. She is like a very young child. Now, think. Would you rather leave her to her fate, having suffered much at the hands of the minion of a woman you have no reason to like or even to trust? Or would you prefer to take this child into your care, as a member of your family, to rear to be a suitable consort for young Rohan? That is what it amounts to."

Abashed, Ashen felt her cheeks grow warm. She had not considered the problem from this point of view, being so taken with her personal animosity toward the girl that there was no room for any other thought.

"Very well," she said grudgingly. "I will take her into my care because you have ordered me to do so, though I do not want the burden she is sure to be."

"Did you hear, child?" Zazar said to Anamara. "She has agreed to look after you."

Anamara gazed at Ashen and smiled happily. She opened her mouth and spoke the first word she had uttered, to anyone's knowledge, since the Sorceress had taken away her wits and made her think she was a bird. "Mama," she said.

In Rendelsham, all attention both at Court and in the city was on the approaching nuptials of the valiant Count Harous of Cragden, Lord Marshal, the Champion and Defender of Rendelsham, and the brilliantly beautiful Lady Marcala of Valvager. Not since the coronation of the infant King Peres had there been such an excuse for a celebration. The cooks and bakers were busy preparing an enormous feast, using as much of the stored wheat to grind for cakes and pastries as they dared. Huntsmen scoured the hills nearby for pigs and fallowbeeste, which they preferred to bring back alive to slaughter and cook at the last minute. When they could not, they butchered and dressed the meat and laid it outside to freeze, where it would keep without spoiling.

Harous himself went about these days with a bemused expression on his face, accepting congratulations and the occasional dig in the ribs and confidences that he was, indeed, a man much envied in his selection of a bride. That he was not exactly the one who had done the selecting was a secret kept among Lord Royance, Marcala, and the Dowager Queen Ysa.

Because she was not expected to oversee every detail of the approaching festivities, Ysa found time frequently to visit her tower and send out her flyer. Now that she had harnessed the ability to see directly what Visp observed, she flew with it all over Rendel, assessing their readiness for meeting the danger that waited, just over the horizon to the North.

For the most part, what she saw pleased her. Of course, the people stayed indoors as much as possible, conserving all the warmth they could muster, but also they were beginning to become accustomed to this new way of life that had come to them.

Everywhere in Rendel, people, building more of the shelters the Sea-Rovers had invented to erect over their tender plants, kept their food crops alive and yielding. There was not the bounty there had been in warmer years, of course, but the people would not starve. Cows stayed in barns, not being let out into pastures to graze, and so escaped being frozen. Sheep and goats grew astonishingly thick coats, and the wool, come spring, if there was a spring, was bound to be of prime quality. Here and there a few hardy souls ventured outside and discovered that they could find ways of going about their business without freezing.

Ysa marveled at the adaptive ways of her people. Even as she observed them through Visp's eyes, she stroked the Great Rings on fingers and thumbs and was glad that Rendel had been given into her able care.

🍂

"No, Anamara," Ashen said firmly, "I am *not* your mama. I have said that I will take you into my care, and so that I will do, but you are not to address me as your mother, or even to think of me that way." She glanced up at Zazar. "I intend to send this girl to Rydale, as soon as I may, to be tutored by those who have my own daughter Hegrin in their charge. I can think of nothing better to do for her. Or with her."

"I suppose that will be enough," Zazar said with a shrug.

"What about Weyse?" Ashen asked. "Can't she help you?"

"Look around. Weyse has already gone back to Galinth, but if need is urgent, I will call on her."

"Home?" Anamara said hopefully.

"Rydale is your home, not Galinth," Ashen said. "Yes, I will send you home."

"Home," the girl repeated, and said it yet again. "Home. Mama, home."

"Go to bed," Ashen told her. "You will leave in a few days. Zazar, I must have time to get her ready. She doesn't even have any clothing of her own—just those few rags she was wearing when she came here. Everything she is wearing is borrowed!"

"I suppose those of the nobility put great store by such things." Zazar took the girl by the shoulders and turned her toward the bed that lay waiting for her, though she looked back at Ashen with growing hope.

"Home? Mama?" she repeated.

"She will be a part of my household. She must be treated decently, even if I have no great regard or affection for her. And try to teach her a few more words by morning, if you please," Ashen told Zazar. "Before your own departure. You have the knack for it, and I don't."

At dawn the next morning, Ashen and Gaurin presided over a hearty, warm breakfast of thick gruel and broiled slabs of meat, served with diluted heated wine. The two travelers—for Rohan was also leaving, to return to Rendelsham—needed as much internal fuel as possible before they braved the chill outdoors. Also, Ashen had given orders that parcels of food be prepared, one for Rohan and one for the Wysen-wyf, to see them on their journeys. Those in the Great Hall sat at a small table screened away from the rest of the room, close by the hearth. A small fire, very different from the one that roared in the evenings, warmed the enclosure.

Rohan helped Anamara with her food, correcting the way she held her spoon and cutting her meat for her. "Must you send her away?" he asked.

"I have told you repeatedly, Rydale is the best place for her right now, with the tutors to teach her and help bring her back to herself," Ashen said. "With Hegrin there already, it will only amount to their having two children in their care instead of one. Also, I promise, I will require frequent reports as to her progress, even as they keep me informed about Hegrin. As there is still some traffic between here and Rendelsham, it will be easy to send the information on to you."

"Would that I could go with her," Rohan said, taking the spoon away from Anamara and putting it back into her hand the right way, so that food would not spill out before she could get it to her mouth.

"You must return to the city," Gaurin said. "Know that, even as Ashen has given orders that she know of Hegrin and Anamara—so must I know how you fare, and Cebastian with you. I have a feeling that the war we have anticipated for so many years is not far away now."

"Do not say it!" Ashen exclaimed. She almost knocked over her flagon of wine, but righted it before it could spill and stain the cloth. "With everything else that has happened of late, I could not bear it if you were called away. Worse it would be if both of you had to ride out to battle."

Gaurin kissed her fingertips. "You will bear it, when it happens, for it most certainly will. On that day, you must take counsel of Madame Zazar, and she with you." He glanced at Zazar for confirmation, and the Wysen-wyf nodded. "I will feel better if you and she are together then, so that you can look after each other."

"Count on me," Zazar said around a mouthful of gruel. She helped herself to another cut of meat. "I have no real desire to stay alone, with war at our doorsteps. In all of Rendel there will be no place safe, but here at the Oakenkeep is as secure as any other."

Gaurin lifted her brown old hand in turn and kissed it. "Thank you, Madame Zazar. I will owe you a debt I can never repay."

"We're almost even. After all, you have had to put up with Ashen all these years," Zazar said tartly. "Not to mention Rohan."

Gaurin laughed, the sound echoing from the rafters of the nearly deserted Hall. "You did better with Ashen than you think," he said, smiling. "I don't think you wanted to rear a foster daughter who was entirely without spirit."

To Ashen's surprise the Wysen-wyf grinned in return, and she knew her husband and her protector shared a level of understanding and even humor that she would never, in all likelihood, achieve.

🌸

Delay matters as they would, the hour for departure arrived. Ashen climbed to the top of the westernmost tower, where she could observe the travelers and could determine what they were doing, even at a distance. The day had dawned bright and clear, though the freshening breeze was colder than she expected and she was glad to have her fur-lined cloak to wrap around her. She stood in what shelter there was to be had, gazing out over the snow-covered countryside.

Zazar, Rohan, and Gaurin all left the keep together, along with a company of soldiers, for it was not safe these days to go unescorted in Rendel. Despite the improvement in growing and maintaining food supplies, the country had more than its share of desperate, hungry people who would not scorn to waylay a lone traveler in hopes of improving their own meager lot.

The party split into different directions almost immediately. Zazar, on foot as usual, having scorned the offer of a horse to ride, turned west. A few soldiers turned from the main body, obviously intended as a guard for Zazar. Ashen could hear their voices, as the sound carried in the still morning air though she couldn't make out the words. However, from what she could hear in the sharp tone of Zazar's voice, it was equally obvious that this escort was scorned by her and was being sent on their way. They rode back to join their companions more eagerly than they had departed. Zazar, unafraid of any ruffians who might waylay her for the food she carried, cut across country, and Ashen knew her objective was the ford across the Barrier River. Thence she could reach the Bog easily enough. Ashen was grateful that she had, at least, dressed warmly.

Gaurin rode north with Rohan as far as the spot where the road forked. Then the two men waved and Gaurin turned back, to the Oakenkeep. Most of the soldiers turned back with him, but half a dozen traveled on with the young knight.

Ashen tasted bitterness in the back of her throat. Someday, she knew, Gaurin would ride north again, with an even larger company of men at his back, and he would not return to her, to safety. Struggling to hold back her tears, she returned to the warmth of their apartment, to await her husband's return. For a while, as they could, she would see to it that they found what comfort they might in each other's arms.

Twenty-four

*T*o *Ashen's surprise and* annoyance, a summons came almost on the heels of Rohan's departure, that they must present themselves at Court, for the marriage of Harous and Marcala and the attendant feast.

"We could have ridden with Rohan, and kept him company," she said with a tinge of bitterness in her voice.

"Or kept him safe?" Gaurin said, amused. "These things happen as they will, my dear. They have bidden us be there, and so go we shall, tomorrow, or the next day at the latest. I daresay it will be less wearing an occasion than that of the Grand Tourney."

"I had planned on sending Anamara to Rydale, once we were not preoccupied with Rohan's departure. My women are not nearly finished with the sewing, and need another week at least. Also, I wanted to make sure Zazar returned safely to the Bog."

"Who in all of Rendel would dare cross Madame Zazar?" Gaurin said, the corners of his eyes crinkling with amusement. "Don't worry, my dear. This is a minor annoyance at most. You can leave detailed orders about Lady Anamara's relocation, and even though Ayfare won't be here to carry them out, she has people trained by now. All will be accomplished while we are away. You do not have to stay and bid her good-bye."

And so, Ashen swallowed her complaints and prepared for the journey. Actually, she did have business there, returning a parcel of books to Esander, the kind and generous priest at the Great Fane of the Shining. She had taken these away after the tourney, and hoped to find more with which to occupy herself once she and Gaurin returned home—where, she hoped vehemently, they could stay put for a good long while. As a wedding gift, she selected a silver-gilt box in which to keep face powder and two matching bottles for scent, the sort of useless ornaments Marcala might like.

In Rendelsham, all was brightness and gaiety. It was as if there were no blight of winter on the land, only an unexpectedly long cold season. This came as a surprise to Ashen, and she remarked on it.

"People must have their occasional amusements," Gaurin told her, "or they will turn to brooding and mischief. It is good to see happiness for a change, and no sign of nobles at odds with each other."

Indeed, the city seemed well off as Ashen could scarcely remember it, back in the days when she had first come to Cragden Keep, and thence to Rendelsham Castle. The townspeople as a group were, perhaps, not as plump as she remembered, but they were clean and well dressed in warm clothing, and their spirits seemed high. Also, there were vendors on every corner selling food and drink, and mementos of the approaching occasion. They lined the approach to the castle and Ashen and Gaurin had to pass through a veritable gauntlet of them just to get to the entrance.

"Thought the Marshal would never get around to it," one such told Ashen when she stopped to examine a tray of gaudy trinkets. "Marrying his pretty lady, I mean. My guess is it's just the first wedding of many, what with talk of war in the air and young men being what they are, and that's good for business!"

Andre Norton & Sasha Miller

Indulgently, Gaurin bought her a brooch in the shape of a vaux lily, set with paste stones, paying far more than the bauble was worth. "It's a fitting symbol, don't you think?" he said.

Ashen bit her lips to keep from smiling. "She's been after him for as long as I can remember." She regarded the lily brooch. "I'll keep this in my jewel box because you gave it to me, but if you don't mind, I won't wear it very often."

At that, Gaurin threw his head back and laughed aloud. "May I suggest that you do not wear that Ash necklace at the wedding," he said, when the fit of merriment had passed. "Better the false brooch than a reminder of something the Marshal gave to you back when he was courting the Ash heiress. It might dim the spirits of the bride, if she caught sight of it."

Ashen touched the necklace she was wearing around her neck. The center was a gold circle, set with a gleaming blue stone like the ones in her earrings, also a gift from Harous, she remembered. On either side of the circle, a gold chain, set with smaller stones, was attached so it would hang straight. "Never mind about Marcala," she said. "Does it bother *you* that I wear these things? That they came from Harous?"

"It did at first," he said genially. "But then I realized that this was the only heirloom of your house that you could hope to possess. Now I find it very thoughtful—even touching—that Harous thought to have that broken brooch made into a necklace so that you could wear it as often as you liked. I wonder where he found it."

"He never told me." A faint recollection of something she had once glimpsed, as if through a fog, trembled on the edge of her mind—fleeing for her life in the Bog, a shadowy figure bending over the lifeless body of Kazi, a flash of something bright. Then, with the blare of trumpets from Rendelsham Castle, the memory was gone before she could grasp it.

"We must hurry, in case something important is happening," Gaurin said. "In any case, I have a gift for you myself."

As it turned out, trumpets blared these days in Rendelsham Castle for any reason and, sometimes, for no reason at all. When they had been established in their apartment and Ayfare was, as was her usual custom, setting everything to rights, Gaurin went to pay his respects and also report their official arrival. Ashen left for the Fane of the Glowing, a carefully wrapped bundle of books under her arm.

"Thank you once again, kind Esander," she said, handing him the parcel. "I would have returned these to you more promptly, but there has been little opportunity. Travel has been difficult, and the roads, where they are not frozen, are nearly impassable, even by horseback."

"Pray, do not concern yourself, my dear Lady Ashen," the priest said. "Nobody cares about these books anyway, as I have told you, except the Queen, and she does not come here often. But see what I have for you! I stumbled upon it as I was looking for something else, not even in the hidden library. Most curious, it was hidden in a secret panel in the wall of a very obscure room in the Fane, a place where people seldom go. And yet, when I but touched a spot in the molding above a small fireplace, the recess opened at once. It was as if I had been destined to find it, at just that moment."

Ashen accepted the volume with hands that shook despite her efforts to control them. The book was obviously very old and, just as obviously, extremely valuable not only for what it contained but also in and of itself. It was bound in blue velvet—a little faded and the worse for having been used, but still in remarkably good condition, probably because of its having lain hidden for so many years—and the hinges and locks were of gold set with precious gems. The large title, worked in such ornate letters that she couldn't make it out at first, was a single word, *Powyr*, and it was embroidered in pure gold thread into which many beads of gemstones had been included. Under this were more embroideries, and she realized that these were the words of the subtitle. *Ye Boke of Ye Fayne*, it read. With great care, she opened the book at random. The writing inside was as beautiful as the cover and all the capitals were picked out in red and gold, with lavish illustrations on the title pages of each section. The thick, creamy paper, or whatever had been used in its making, looked as fresh as it must have been the day it was bound, with no yellowing or crumbling from age.

"I couldn't possibly accept this," she said, wishing with all her heart that she could. She held it out to the priest.

"No, it is yours," Esander told her, folding her fingers around the book. "After all these years, and given the interest you have in the subject and the great respect with which you approach it, not like the—Never mind. I have a feeling about you, Lady Ashen, and have had since the first time I met you, in the company of your unfortunate late husband, Obern. This feeling prompted me then to give you what I can, and continues to this day. Since this book is not a part of either the library to which all have access, or that beneath the Fane where only you and I go, then it is mine to do with as I will. And I will to give it to you."

"Thank you," she said, humbled. "I will guard it, and will use it—if I use it—as well as I may."

The priest wrapped the precious object in the covering Ashen had used for the books she had returned, and handed it to her. "Go in peace," he said.

That evening, at the wedding-eve dinner in the Great Hall, Ashen wore her best blue velvet gown, and the new necklace Gaurin had given her—strands of alternating pearls and sapphire beads, from which depended a modern rendering of her Ash badge in gold. With it, she wore matching earrings and bracelets. It was a gift that would have impressed even a Queen, and when she opened the wrappings it took Ashen's breath away at the very sight of it.

"I commissioned this made when we were in the city for the Grand Tourney," he told her as he fastened the ornament around her slender neck.

"You are so generous. A mere 'thank you' seems so inadequate for such a beautiful gift."

"You are the loveliest woman in the room," he whispered in her ear as they entered the Hall.

Inside, all was warmth and light, and the sounds of celebration filled the air. The smell of good food wafted from the doorway through which the pages were just beginning to bring the dishes, and Ashen's stomach reacted in anticipation. Obviously, no expense was being spared. This was just the feast prior to the real celebration, for the wedding would be on the morrow. A woman clad in deep red came toward them.

"Your Gracious Highness the Queen Dowager Ysa!" Gaurin exclaimed, cordiality in his voice. "We bring greetings from the Oakenkeep." He bowed and Ashen dipped a deep curtsey.

Ysa acknowledged the gestures with a nod of her head. "It has been but a short while since last we had the pleasure of having you and Lady Ashen in our company," she said. "I trust that all has been well in the meantime?"

"We scarcely had time to miss being in Rendelsham before this happy event summoned us to return," Gaurin said. He seemed to be perfectly at ease, and even enjoying himself.

The Dowager was clad in satin and velvet this evening, with many strings of garnets and pearls around her neck, and the Oak badge prominent on her headdress. Ashen noted that Ysa's jewels were certainly no finer than her own though the other woman's pearls were larger. "Is the Dowager Rannore dining in the Hall tonight?" she said.

"She is, and the King as well," replied Ysa. "Yes, we and our Court are truly gay now that so much—discordance has been removed from our midst."

"We have Rohan to thank for that," Gaurin said.

"Oh, yes, Rohan."

"He has indeed come to a man's estate. His father Obern would be proud of him."

To Ashen's astonishment, Ysa started, and turned deathly pale beneath the rouge on her face. "A—a man's estate," she repeated. She swayed, seeming to be almost on the verge of swooning. Gaurin reached out a hand to steady her, but she waved him away. "It is nothing. A momentary dizziness. Yes, yes, Rohan is a very special young man." Another blast of trumpets sounded, giving her a chance to recover her composure fully. "Ah," the Dowager said, turning toward the door. "That would be the King."

She moved away, and Ashen, relieved that this interview was over, began to search for their places at the high table. As before, she and Gaurin would be seated beside Rannore. The King occupied the center of the table, with Ysa to his right, and the bridal couple was placed on her other side, to honor them. Ashen observed Gaurin's easy manner with Harous as they greeted each other. Though the men were peers, still Harous held the title of Lord High Marshal and, as a result, could be thought of as Gaurin's commanding officer.

Harous bent over Ashen's hand. "Greetings, my happy Ashen," he said. "Will you congratulate me in my own happiness?"

"With all my heart," she said, "and your bride as well."

"Thank you," Marcala said, and the two touched cheeks, as women will who are not fond of each other, but who are determined to be cordial.

Marcala's neck and ears glittered with amethysts that matched the gown she wore, and her scent of vaux lilies hung in the air. Ashen thought about the days when her sole ornament had been that pierced stone amulet with the strange power of concealment. How far she had progressed on her path to civilization.

Ashen and Rannore embraced with much greater warmth. "Oh, how glad I am that you are back so soon," Rannore said. "I find that I missed you, even though we have not been separated long. Perhaps someday I can come to the Oakenkeep for a visit."

"That would be wonderful!" Ashen exclaimed. "Nothing would please me more. But would it be permitted?"

"The King scarcely sees me these days. He is no longer a child, though not yet a man, and his grandmother and the Council have more influence over him than I ever will."

"You know you are greatly welcome," Ashen said. "In fact, why don't you come with us when we return?"

Rannore looked at her intently, and Ashen realized that Rannore's suggestion, hardly more than a wish when she uttered it, was becoming a reality in her friend's mind. Also, by the time they returned, Anamara would no longer be there and, Ashen realized, she would miss even that unwelcome visitor's company. It had given her something with which to occupy herself other than worrying about Gaurin.

Rannore nodded. "I accept," she said firmly. "I will go with you to the Oakenkeep."

"Good. Just be aware that we are country folk and the keep is no Rendelsham Castle. We lead a much more simple life there than here."

"It sounds wonderful."

Some of Gaurin's retainers had been bidden to the Hall as well, and had been given places at the trestles below the dais. Ashen caught sight of Rohan, seated with Lathrom, and both men saluted her with some pleasure. Then Lathrom saluted Rannore, who nodded in acknowledgment.

"Who is that man?" she asked. "I think I have seen him somewhere before."

"He is our Captain of the Guard. He was once a sergeant in the late King's company, and was, in fact, in charge of the men who—who spirited me away when Obern came to my rescue. Later, he repented of this action and swore fealty to Obern and then, when he died, to me and my household. He is a good man, both loyal and very able."

"And very attractive. Yes, I remember him now."

Then Rannore turned the talk to lighter matters, more suitable to dinner conversation, leaving Ashen to glance curiously at Lathrom and then at her friend, wondering if some spark had, perchance, passed between them.

And what, she wondered, as the feast progressed, had caused Ysa to be so disconcerted when Gaurin but remarked on Rohan's now being a man full-grown?

🍂

Ysa fled the wedding eve feast as quickly as decency would allow. All through the meal, the words of Kasai, the Spirit Drummer who had accompanied Snolli of the Sea-Rovers to Rendelsham on the occasion of King Florian's wedding, so many years before, had rolled through her head like ominous thunder. "Perhaps a year, perhaps not until the son of the Chieftain's son is a man full-grown. And yet they will come."

How could Ysa have overlooked that it was Rohan, Obern's firstborn, whom Kasai had been speaking of, as the Spirit Drum whispered through the Council chamber, and not that child of Obern's that Ashen had miscarried!

Coldness not born of the chill weather seeped through her bones as she climbed the stairs to her tower so swiftly that she had to sit and rest, nursing a stitch in her side. It had to have been the Sorceress's baleful influence, and it was still working against her! Ysa had never been so careless as to forget such a vital piece of information concerning the danger that, she now knew, had never abated, even once. Gaurin's words had acted like a veil lifting over her memory, erasing the shadow the Sorceress had put there. To think that when Ashen had miscarried, she had even entertained the thought that the danger from the North had abated, perhaps vanished entirely!

What a fool she had been—complacent, unheeding. Now she had to work swiftly, if she had any hopes of avoiding the effects of this unthinkable folly. She took the flyer out of its nest and carried it to the window. "Go and seek," she told it, "but this time go northward and do not return until you find out what is afoot."

Once she had ascertained that it was flying straight and true toward the north, she returned to the carved red-wood chair, where she sat, straining forward, as if to hurry the little creature on its way. Without noticing what she was doing, she clasped her hands together, rubbing the Great Rings over and over, as if for solace and comfort.

❦

The Young Dowager Queen Rannore looked about the apartment she had been given at the Oakenkeep, nodding appreciatively. "I thought you said this was a kind of rough frontier castle," she said to Ashen. "If once it was, you have made of it a real home, and a remarkably comfortable one at that. I was expecting something little better than cold stone walls!"

Ashen smiled, knowing that she was blushing. "What we have to offer, we do so with a full heart," she told her friend.

"I didn't realize how unhappy I truly was in Rendelsham," Rannore said. "Not until I had left the city well behind did it seem that I could take a deep, clean breath."

"It has not been easy for you, these last few years."

Ayfare entered the room with a tray bearing two cups and a flagon of the hot spiced juice that was Ashen's preferred beverage. She set it on a table close by the fireplace. "Is there anything else you will be needing, Madame?" she said to Rannore. "I couldn't help but notice that you came alone, with naught but the guard around you. I have a young woman, Dayna, working here and she is not badly trained. I will be glad to assign her to you during your stay. And if you require my personal services, you have but to ring." She indicated a bellpull by the door.

"Thank you—Ayfare, isn't it?" Rannore smiled again. "I will gladly accept Dayna as my maid while I am in residence here, and I will surely call, if there is anything I need."

Then Ayfare curtseyed and left, closing the door behind her, and both ladies sat down to enjoy the hot drink. Rannore sighed deeply. "I couldn't tell her or, for that matter, anyone but you, that I don't trust any of my staff of women. They were all in Ysa's hire once, and might still be, for all I know. I want to enjoy myself without fear that my least word or deed will be reported to that one!"

"We must give the Dowager Queen Ysa our dutiful love and regard," Ashen said carefully.

At that, Rannore chucked. "No one that I know of in Rendelsham feels anything close to 'dutiful love' for her."

"Rannore!" Ashen said, trying to put reproof in her voice, but she couldn't maintain it. Between them, and in private, they could be open about their lack of respect toward Rendel's true ruler. Both ladies dissolved into laughter, and it seemed that a great weight had lifted off each.

"What do you want to do while you are here?" Ashen asked, when their decorum had been restored once more. "Shall we arrange for a hunt? How shall we entertain you? There is often music and dancing, but our ways must seem simple beside what you are accustomed to."

"Most of all, I want peace and quiet, and rest. I am content to be alone with friends, with perhaps some embroidery or other sewing for a pastime," Rannore replied. "And free, unbridled talk. You have no idea—well, perhaps you do—how tedious it is at Court to always have to be watching what you say, lest it be reported and misinterpreted."

"If companionship is what you seek, it is here for you. If you require solitude, then you have come to the right place for it. As for sewing, my mending basket is never empty. However, this evening, I propose to show off my highborn guest for all to admire, at dinner in the Hall. Our chef has been worrying about his cooking ever since I sent word that you were returning with us, and he is exceptionally nervous that you will think we are only one cut above Bog savages when it comes to how we live, and how well we eat."

"I'm sure everything will be wonderful," Rannore said. "Do you think that Lathrom will be among the ones at table?"

"As Captain of the Guard, it is his duty to attend when he is not out on patrol or otherwise occupied," Ashen said. "And even if it weren't, I'm sure he would not miss the chance to be in your company. I saw the looks that passed between you, in Rendelsham."

This time it was Rannore's turn to blush. "Do you think me wicked, Ashen?" she asked. "Wicked to think about him the way a woman thinks about a man?"

Ashen leaned forward and clasped her friend's hand. "No, I don't think you are wicked. Remember, I knew your late husband, my half-brother, the King. I had no love for him, and I think that you must have married him out of a sense of duty. I can think of no other reason for you to have done so."

Rannore stared into the fire. "When you are carrying a man's child, it is easy to convince yourself that you love him—or, at least, can honor him enough to make a life together." She seemed to be talking primarily to herself.

Ashen nodded, remembering her feelings toward Obern, which, uncertain though they were, must still have been stronger and more durable than anything Rannore and Florian had ever had between them. "And especially when that man is the King, and you carry the heir," Ashen said.

"Especially then. Well, I paid for my folly in allowing him to take liberties. I should have thought about my poor cousin, Laherne, and how badly she fared at his hands. But when he threatened to have my grandfather—" Rannore clamped her lips together firmly.

She didn't need to elaborate. With those words the entire sorry tale unfolded for Ashen, and she had to keep herself from recoiling at the perfidy shown by someone to whom she was—had been—so closely allied by blood. "It is over and done with," she told Rannore, "and you can thank the Powers that you lived. Yes, you have paid for whatever folly you committed—paid in full, and overflowing—and that debt is now canceled. The young King, Peres, is still a stripling, but he seems fair to be a good-enough ruler when his time truly comes. And if he can pry the Kingdom out of Ysa's hands. My guess is that Ysa has been the one reminding you of your 'indiscretion,' whenever she thought you needed putting in your place."

"That was the very word she used. Among others." Rannore swallowed the rest of her spiced juice.

"It is difficult to go against that woman in the best of circumstances," Ashen said, "and yours were far from good."

"Tell me how you managed to come out against her as well as you did," Rannore said.

And so, obligingly, Ashen began relating the story of how she had come to the Court, and Harous's role in training her to be a lady instead of a Bog-brat. She told of how Marcala had been assigned to this task, and how Ysa had reacted when she learned that her husband's illegitimate daughter was alive and possibly representing a threat to her iron rule of Rendel.

The two ladies were still in conversation when Ayfare returned to the guest chamber, to let them know that dinner was ready, and their presence requested in the Hall by Count Gaurin, and by Captain Lathrom as well. Hand in hand, they descended the stairs. Ashen thought she had never seen Rannore's cheeks so pink, nor her eyes so bright as when Lathrom offered her his arm, so he could escort her to her place at the high table.

Anamara awoke while the stars were still bright. Ever since they had left the big stone place, she had kept on all her clothes even when she went to bed, hoping that this chance would come. Last night, she had willed the men to sleep, all of them, and willed herself to wake up when they were all deep in slumber. Stealthily she slipped out of the makeshift tent the soldiers had erected for her, and made for the place where the large animals—they were called "horses"—were tethered. She selected the one she had ridden the previous day and led it away from the camp as quietly as possible, pausing from time to time to listen for any sounds indicating that she was being followed. But she heard nothing and, by the time she was far enough away that the light from the campfire could no longer be seen, she judged that she had successfully escaped.

Then, and only then, she clambered onto the horse's back and dug her heels into its sides, urging it to retrace their steps toward the north and west, back along the way they had come. Only this time, she would avoid the big stone place where the rivers met.

The nice lady with the pale hair who was sometimes cross, back there, had said Anamara was going to be sent *home*. But Anamara, still with many of the instincts of a bird, knew that they were going in the opposite direction of *home*. The other lady, the stern one who flew and who had held her face in her strong fingers and told her who she was, had told her also where *home* was. Therefore, if she had to return *home*, it must be to that place, damp and dismal and unfriendly, but *home* nonetheless.

Perhaps she would see Rohan there again. Or, if not him, then the old woman who had tended her in a little house, and later, after they had all arrived at the big stone place. She wondered if the furry one, Weyse, would also be there. She had liked Weyse. Weyse crooned to her and purred when she stroked her, and patted Anamara's face with clever little paws and coaxed her to share her food. Yes, Weyse was probably already *home*, and Anamara could scarcely abide the time it took to get there so she could go and find Weyse.

There would be a river—not the one where the big stone place crouched guarding the waters. She remembered that, and the boat. It was different from the streams she had had to cross to get there. They had ridden in a boat. Now, the horse would carry her across. When she got to the river, she would be nearly *home*.

When she judged she was close to the big stone place she left the road and traveled cross-country, in more of a straight line, and so arrived at the river in only a couple of days' journeying. Though he had broken through crusts of ice and forded the streams easily enough, the horse refused to go near this river. She had to leave him and search for a place where the ice was thick enough that she could cross, or where she could wade. Eventually, downstream, she came to such a spot, where the water babbled over a stony crossing that must have been made by men. Here the stream was swift enough that ice did not form. Without taking off her shoes or giving any thought to the chill of the waters, she walked straight into the stream and across the shadowy borders of the Bog.

The message came to the Oakenkeep while the residents were still at dinner, welcoming their royal guest. One of the soldiers entered, still in traveling clothes and not having paused long enough to wash the road-grime off. Bending low, he whispered in Gaurin's ear. He glanced at Ashen, then at Lathrom. "Come with me so we can talk in private," he said. "It cannot wait."

"I will make our excuses," she said.

Leaving Rannore a little puzzled but graciously taking up the duty as temporary hostess to the feast, Ashen, Gaurin, Lathrom, and the soldier left the Hall for the small upstairs room Gaurin used as a study. There, mincing no words, the soldier related the news that Anamara was missing and all their efforts had not been sufficient to locate her.

"How can that be!" Lathrom exclaimed. "Didn't you set a guard? Do you have no trackers, that you can't pick up the trail of a single girl who is a little addled in her wits?" He glanced at Ashen. "No offense, my lady."

"None taken. Her mind is, truly, befogged. Is there any indication of where she might have gone?"

"None, Lady Ashen," the soldier said, obviously grateful to be addressing her rather than enduring the wrath of his commanding officer. "All we know is, she stole a horse, and by the few tracks we found, we determined that she was headed north and west."

"Then she was traveling toward the Bog," Gaurin said. "And, somehow, knowing enough to avoid passing near the Oakenkeep."

"And how long has it been since you noticed she was missing?" Lathrom said, with heavy irony.

"Five days, sir. We searched hard, truly. The lady might as well have flown away, for all the traces of her that we could see. We did find the horse, though."

"Five days. And in this cold. With rivers to cross, and probably no food except what might happen to be in a saddlebag." Gaurin sighed. He turned to Ashen. "I am sorry, my dear. I fear that, under the circumstances, even if she managed to reach the Bog, she must have perished by now."

"She was in my care," Ashen said numbly. "Zazar put her into my care."

"No, my lady," Lathrom said. "I am to blame. I should have gone myself, to ensure her arrival safely at Rydale. If there is punishment to be dealt out, it must fall on me."

"We will speak of punishment later, if at all," Gaurin told him. "You were bidden to Rendelsham, even as we were." Then he turned to Ashen. "We must notify Madame Zazar, and we must also inform Rohan."

"Yes," she said.

"Not that either of them can do anything, but they should know."

"Yes," she repeated. She could scarcely believe the news the man had brought. How could they have been so careless? Or, perhaps, this was a remnant of whatever spell the wretched girl had been put under, that she had been able to elude the men set to watch over her.

She dreaded Zazar's wrath. Anamara was dead, and Ashen was sorry for it—sorry for Rohan, actually—but her passing would solve many problems Rohan did not need to deal with just now.

She hoped that, one day, Rohan would be able to forgive them all for the loss of his addle-pated lady.

When he learned of Anamara's disappearance, Rohan left Cragden Keep and went directly to Zazar's hut, following a trail that had by now become familiar. "Have you heard? Have you seen her?" he demanded.

"I have heard, and no, I have not."

"She must have been coming here."

"Perhaps," Zazar said. "The Bog is a big place. Remember, you found her wandering somewhere to the north of here."

"Grandam, I don't know what I'll do if I have lost her—" Tears welled up in Rohan's eyes. A moment later, they spilled down his cheeks as Zazar slapped him, hard, across the face.

"Stop that!" the Wysen-wyf said fiercely. "Stop it, I say!" She slapped him again, even harder, on the other cheek.

Rohan, shocked out of his grief over Anamara, could only stare at her. Then he noted a gleam of moisture in the old eyes that glared so sternly into his and knew that, in striking him, Zazar had somehow been striking out at herself as well, sharing the responsibility for the girl's disappearance.

"Nobody is to blame," Rohan said. "Or we all are."

"Did you see anything as you came through the Bog?"

"I eluded a couple of hunting parties on the way."

"Then you must assume that your lady is dead," Zazar said flatly. She led him to a seat beside the fire. "If she survived to cross the land beyond the Oakenkeep and here, she had to cross more than one river. She could have fallen through the ice and drowned. If she fell and did not drown, she must have fallen ill from the cold and crawled away to die. Or, supposing that she made it to the Bog, without knowledge of the place and how to elude those she did not want to encounter, the hunting parties must have caught her and she is dead at their hands. But know this, young Rohan. She is surely dead, and the sooner you understand this, the better off you will be."

"I will never understand it," Rohan said, and heard the words thin and hollow in his own ears.

"I will keep you here tonight, and in the morning you must return to Rendelsham. Be very careful. You were foolish to risk coming here. Those hunting parties you saw are out in the Bog from every village, even this one, for hunger drives. Even if you wore a badge of my own devising, it would not save you if you were taken. You were foolish to come here."

"Yes, Grandam," he said, bowing his head. "Only, I thought you might help, or might know of something, anything I could do."

"There is nothing," Zazar said, her voice once more flat and without intonation. "Only that you must now survive." She reached out and touched the tuft of herbs and grasses in Rohan's helm. "Survive, and do as Fate decides."

In the high tower atop Rendelsham Castle, the Dowager Queen Ysa sat as one paralyzed in her chair, watching what her flyer was seeing, shocked beyond disbelief.

Everywhere, the forces in the northern lands were stirring, and some already begun on their long march southward. She had been idle and lulled into a false sense of security, beguiled by the Sorceress into thinking the land was safe because Obern's heir by Ashen had perished. But while she slept and her eternal vigilance flagged, the Great Foulness had been busy marshaling its minions against the time when it would break free at last from the Palace of Fire and Ice, guarded so long and so well by Cyornas NordornKing. As if from a great distance, she heard the words of Snolli, at that council when they had worked out the treaty between Rendel and the Sea-Rovers. "He will face it first. He cannot prevail alone."

Even as she watched in horror, great pale beasts, breathing crystals of ice and ridden by white-clad horrors, stumped forward awkwardly. Bellowing and trumpeting, they assaulted the walls and methodically smashed them, stone by stone. An old warrior, snowy hair blowing in the wind, challenged them fiercely, only to be cut down with his nobles and stretched cold upon the ground.

Ysa's hands were clasped, hard, against her mouth. The Great Rings cut into her lips. Cyornas NordornKing was no more. His had been a valiant, useless defense, and the time he had bought would—Ysa knew as a certainty that froze her heart—be inadequate. The great beasts reared high and their riders shrilled cries of triumph and of challenge.

Then they began to lead the armies on their march southward.

The great beasts walked with a ponderous tread that shook the very ground beneath them. Always, over all, the air reverberated

Andre Norton & Sasha Miller

with their bellowing and the ice-crystals of their breath formed cold clouds around them. One of the riders threw back her hood and, with a chill beyond what had taken her before, Ysa recognized the Sorceress. She gazed around, alerted by something, and Ysa knew that her flyer's presence had been recognized.

Flee for your life! Return at once! She sent out the message with all the urgency she could muster, and the flyer immediately turned and began winging its swift way back toward the south, frightened not only by Ysa's command but also by what was happening around it that it had been forced to observe.

Flavielle was perched on the beast's neck, just behind the horrible head. She nudged it with her heels. It stretched white leather wings and lifted itself into the air, seeking the invisible flyer. Snow fell from under the wings as it flew. In that moment of pure, unreasoning panic, Ysa recognized what sort of creature Flavielle rode, and those still-hooded horrors with her. Could they even be men? Their mounts were the most fell creatures ever dreamed of in the nightmares of men, that until now had been relegated to tales and legends.

Ice Dragons. And they were marching on Rendel.